Praise for Tom Connolly

'An epic love letter to New York City, *Men Like Air*
is bold, absorbing and very funny. Tom Connolly
has a quiet brilliance.'
Evie Wyld

'I loved *The Spider Truces* by Tom Connolly, a debut
about a boy whose father tries to shield him from grief
after his mother dies, and so prevents him experiencing
life itself... A lovely, beautiful book.'
Rosie Blau, Man Booker Prize judge

'A very fine, funny and moving read.'
David Baddiel

'A magical coming-of-age novel... [A] fierce,
humane and hazily poetic work.'
Guardian

'Lyrical, warm and moving, this impressive debut
is reminiscent of Laurie Lee.'
Meera Syal

'Beautiful debut about a son trying to
break free from his father.'
Financial Times Best Books of the Year 2010

'A funny, moving and quirky coming-of-age
story. Hugely enjoyable.'
Deborah Moggach

Also by Tom Connolly

The Spider Truces

MEN LIKE AIR

TOM CONNOLLY

First published in 2016 by

Myriad Editions
www.myriadeditions.com

First printing
1 3 5 7 9 10 8 6 4 2

A CIP catalogue record for this book is available
from the British Library

ISBN (pbk): 978-1-908434-88-3
ISBN (ebk): 978-1-908434-89-0

Designed and typeset in Stempel Garamond
by WatchWord Editorial Services, London

Printed by CPI Group (UK) Ltd, Croydon CR0 4YY

For Ruth and Joe

1

'The rain woke me,' Dilly said.

She turned a little in half-sleep and pulled him to her, so she could rest her head.

'Don't think so,' Finn whispered.

'Yes, I could hear the rain against the windows,' she insisted, with soft sleepy affection. 'It was definitely raining. It woke me. It was nice. Felt dreamy.'

He let it go. He was beginning to get the hang of the way she saw things, and to know not to try to talk her out of any of it. Her eyes were closed. She made a low purr, at his thick-veined, boxer's hands stroking the soft skin of her forearm. An elderly man across the aisle smiled at the two of them, as they repaired his skewed, lazy, ungenerous notion of youth. He was too old to notice the chasm of an age gap between a raw nineteen-year-old boy and his flamboyant twenty-four-year-old girlfriend. They all looked like kids to him, everyone on board.

Dilly slept again and Finn sat at an uncomfortable angle, so as not to wake her. She had not heard the rain. There was no rain up here. If she had looked out of the window and craned her elegant neck downwards, she would have seen the clouds, thirty thousand feet below. Finn watched the softness that fell upon her face on the rare occasions it was not tied up in speech, and he felt pretty sure that he loved her. When she turned away from him in her dreaming it freed him and he massaged the stiffness out of the slim, bindweed muscles that roped down his neck.

The roar of the engines, which in its relentlessness had become silent, returned to him and reminded him where he was headed, provoking the shiver of excitement that had been denied his childhood. In four hours, he'd be in New York City. It still seemed impossible.

When Dilly woke, she found Finn filling out a visa waiver form.

'Why have you ticked the "have criminal record" box?'

'I've got one.'

'And you've put Glenn's address on the form.'

'We're staying at Glenn's.'

'He's in prison. You can't mention his name. What the hell, Finn!'

He scratched out Glenn's address and scrawled in microscopic handwriting above it that of Dilly's parents on Long Island, which she dictated. He changed his answer to the criminal record question, wedged the form into his pocket and kissed her on the lips. She pulled the blanket across them both and beneath it she unzipped him and rested her hand inside. Later, over Newfoundland and Nova Scotia, he watched her as she studied her Lonely Planet. Occasionally her eyes flared and she scribbled a note into the margins or drew an exuberant circle around the name of a bar or a shop that promised her the fulfilment of some uncertain desire.

'I wanna *own* the Lower East Side,' she said, and her eyes did the dance that dared him not to agree. 'I want to fuck it and come. And you call it the LES, by the way. Everything's abbreviated.'

He had read the book for himself, perhaps the only person to read a Lonely Planet guide from cover to cover, like a novel.

'LES? You sure?' he muttered.

2

'Are you American or am I American? Me, I am. Am I a country peasant who left school aged twelve or is that you? It's you.'

'Sixteen,' he murmured.

'Yeah, and more fool you.'

More fool you. He thought about it. More fool you. Morefullyou.

A couple of months ago he would have wondered what it meant, but now he knew not to look for meaning. What she said rarely signified anything. Conversation was for her all about ebb and flow, about musicality and muscularity, about humour and pace and a smattering of facts. Facts could come either with or without foundation. What made something factual was the force with which it was said.

He didn't like conversations to drag on. He simply wanted to be her boyfriend, to keep getting away with it. He was proud of the age gap, beyond happy at the state of his sex life. He was convinced now that he was in love with her. He might tell her so after they first made love in New York City. He had intended to tell her at the top of the Empire State Building, until she'd mentioned, when he was going down on her the previous week, that she didn't believe in the Empire State Building and that the Chrysler Building was the thinking person's ESB.

She liked to read during the early stages of cunnilingus. It was when she put a book down, folding back the corner to mark her page, that he knew he was doing alright. The previous week, she had placed the Lonely Planet on the bed and combed her fingers through the mop of his hair between her thighs. 'I wouldn't be seen dead going up the Empire State Building with a load of Japanese tourists,' she had said, and shut her eyes.

Maybe he wouldn't say he loved her. He didn't want to make a fool of himself. Only, it felt as though he ought to say he loved her, considering what she was doing to him most nights and allowing him to do to her, both of which were, presumably, love.

She delved into her bag, with undue urgency. 'I have to brush my teeth or I'll go insane,' she said, rummaging furiously. Facially, she made searching for a toothbrush look like a non-pilot landing a 747 in a storm, mid-colonoscopy.

Above Boston, she snuggled up to him and kissed him tenderly, with minty breath. Her kisses were brief and soft and dared him to believe he had found peace. He lay across her, his head in her lap and his feet pressed against the cabin window, his long legs, clad in cheap, skinny, market-stall jeans, concertinaed across the seat. She stroked his hair, which he loved. He clasped the sleeve ends of his sweater and turned his head into her body. He flirted with sleep, aware of the dried blood in his nostrils and the bruising to his ribs that were the legacy of a farewell fight with his uncle and for which the silent, pushed-away part of him knew he would have to pay.

Finn was a quiet man, but when he smiled his face illuminated as if against his wishes. It was the smile that made people think they could take advantage, or take him under their wing. Neither was true. Beneath his stillness lay the capacity to be excitable, or dreamy, or incisive. He was more intelligent than he would ever admit. There were rooted explanations for his reticence, but it was also, simply, that he suspected that most thoughts which occurred to him had been voiced by others and he saw no point in repeating what had already been said.

Dilly had contrived their first meeting, when all she'd known was that he was the lad who had blown up the garden shed of a man caught punching his wife's dog to death. She had noted his boyish looks, his flushed cheeks, and the mop of jet-black hair, parted to the side to let her in on one half of his soft, youthful face. He was pretty now and in a short time he'd be handsome, no doubt in her mind. Welded to that face

4

was a stern, unforgiving diffidence that could have seemed ugly if he weren't so fucking beautiful to her, if his pale green eyes weren't so insanely intense and his smooth, high cheekbones so incredibly fucking fine. She used expletives to describe his beauty to her sister Phoebe in San Diego. Phoebe tried to copy Dilly but could no more swear than she could undress with the light on. Dilly told Phoebe that when she and Finn were out together passing dogs came up to him and stood patiently for him to pet them, which he did with an easy, firm love that made her wonder if he should be living wild. Sometimes this made her admire him; other times it made her envy him, and panic about all the things she would never be.

She opened her brand new journal and wrote across the top of the first page, 'April 10th 2006'. She stared at the blank paper, determined not to be obvious or banal, but nothing emerged immediately in the place of cliché and soon she saw failure in the empty page. The man sitting in front of them was not suffering the same lack of words. His voice had been irritating Dilly for some time and now she watched the back of his head lean fractionally towards the woman beside him as he showed her a photograph of his daughter.

'That's my little girl. Isn't she beautiful?'

The woman sighed but no words followed, only a sound that indicated she was precisely as stupefied by the exquisiteness of the man's spawn as etiquette demanded.

'Doesn't she just have the happiest face?' the man continued.

'What is she meant to say to that...?' Dilly hissed, under her breath. Under her breath lay Finn, who opened his eyes and saw Dilly muttering to herself. 'Is she going to say the child's got a hideous face?'

'Eh?' Finn asked.

The woman in front lobbed the ball back. 'Absolutely, she's beautiful. Oh, yeah.'

The man continued at an easy, knock-up pace. 'I know. She has the loveliest temperament – nothing fazes her or stresses her out.'

Finn felt Dilly's substantial abdominal muscles tauten beneath his head as she sat forward, wedging Finn against the seat-back of the row in front.

'Just what do you imagine your daughter's got to be stressed about?' Dilly asked the back of the man's head. 'She's, what, two years old? For Christ's sake!'

Finn sat up and put his hands over his eyes, in the hope it would make him invisible. The man and woman in front turned in disbelief but Dilly had already returned to her Lonely Planet. Finn smiled apologetically.

'It's true, though,' Dilly whispered, to a glossy photo of Times Square she felt embarrassed to have stumbled upon. 'Why do people talk about children as if they're adults? Let them be children. I wish I could be.'

Her eyes were full of questions she knew no one would answer for her. She had once cried as she lay next to Finn. 'I feel like an alien,' she had said. 'No one sees things like I do. No one gets me.' And he had been unnerved at seeing her both naked and tearful, as if the combination made him in some way brutish. 'I'm an alien,' she had snivelled.

'No, you're not.' And he had wrapped the bedsheets around her.

Finn watched her now as she wrote notes in the guidebook. If he told her to apologise to the people in front, she would refuse and freeze him out and they would endure a silence that was as natural as breathing to him and a huge act of will for her. They possessed only one method of making up and they couldn't resort to it on a plane, despite legends to the contrary. He would say nothing. He didn't want to upset her right now. Or to lose her. He'd never meet another girl like her. And, after all, sometimes she was sweet. And after she reached orgasm she was soft and helpless and affectionate, almost humorous. Those were his favourite moments, better even than the sex or her long, rambling, obscure stories about places she might have been to in the hazy chronological inconsistency that was her adult life thus far. And often she cooked exotic meals and put chillies or spices in her mouth while preparing the food and sucked him while the food cooked and then told him to fuck her while his manhood was burning rock-hard with fire. And it made her feel great and it made him feel like a stud, though he could feel little else. None of this did he wish to lose.

He clambered over her and stood in the aisle, did a few stretches, and took a look around. He wondered if all the people on board had sex lives similar to theirs. Why not? What did he know? Maybe the modest, embarrassed, fumbling sex with Sharon Mitcham, the girl who had asked him out on a date soon after his dad checked out... maybe that sort of sex was rare and most men regularly had their penises marinated as foreplay. Sharon Mitcham was Finn's only other lover, and she used to hug him after they made love. He was pretty sure, as he recalled it now, that on the four occasions they slept together, despite his poor showing, she'd hugged him for hours afterwards. He missed that suddenly. Sharon didn't talk much. He liked her. It occurred to him now, in mid-air above the Eastern Seaboard, just how much he had liked her. He hadn't thought about it when he was sent to the detention centre for blowing up the shed. There was too much else to think about. He went to the Mitchams' house to explain to Sharon why he had to go and they sat together on the sofa holding hands while Mr and Mrs Mitcham sympathised with Finn for all he was going through, and hid their relief. He couldn't remember feeling anything that day, for her or about her, or about leaving. But, he was feeling it now. All of a sudden, two years later. Out of the blue, at thirty-eight thousand feet. He was missing Sharon Mitcham, and all the hugging.

Dilly looked up at him. 'Germaine Greer said, *You're only young once, but you can be immature forever.*' She nodded in the direction of the row in front. 'That's the point I was trying to make to that guy before he chose to get offended.'

Dilly often quoted women to back herself up. Finn, who, the Lonely Planet guide to New York City aside, had read one book in the past three years (*Sleepers*, stolen from the reception of his lawyer's office), found her quotes impressive. But the name Germaine Greer meant nothing to him and he didn't want to ask who she was and get dragged out of his own thoughts right now, and especially not into Dilly's. He smiled politely and retreated to the back of the plane, which banked left and began the earliest stages of its descent. His stomach fluttered and, beneath the anticipation, he felt a stab of nausea at what he had come to New York City to do. He had come to tell his brother what had gone on, and to punish him for it. The trip had other purposes and dreams, of course. To accompany Dilly to her parents in Long Beach was a purpose; to see the Rangers at Madison Square Garden a dream – and to stand at the top of the Empire State Building (alone, it would seem), eat a hot dog on a street corner, find the museum where they shot the last scene of *The Squid and the Whale*. And he had convinced himself he'd bump into those guys who made *Eternal Sunshine of the Spotless Mind* (they just had to be the sort of people who lived in NYC) and thank them for it. Fifth Avenue, Central Park, cheap jeans, riding the subway as if he knew where he was going – all of these things awaited him, as did the ambition to meet Glenn out of prison in five months' time and give him some of the cash he had earned, in lieu of rent. But primarily, Finn was here to deliver a deft, powerful left jab to the brother he had not seen for eighteen months (his right hook was way too dangerous), in return for the humiliation and pain his brother's leaving for New York City had visited upon Finn's life.

8

Stooping to look out of a window, he jettisoned these thoughts and those of Sharon Mitcham into the firmament and replaced them with the anticipation of what awaited him: New York City. It was a prospect like no other. These people around him now would scatter across the city, into buses, taxis, cars, into the arms of people or the grip of solitude, into a city of a billion fragments that made perfect sense for some but remained shards of confusion for others, standing at angles that did not piece together and among which Finn would hope to define the shape of his brother, Jack.

2

Having had no choice but to watch his mum drink herself to death and, four years later, cradle his father's body as it bled empty on to a B-road, Jack had decided to return order to his world. These past three years, he'd been making a pretty neat job of it.

If there was one thing he was loving this morning (and there wasn't one, there were many) it was the new Brookstone coin organiser that had arrived in the post, with which he could round up his loose change and know where he stood. Jack was also loving that his punctuality had left him time to take the coin organiser back up to the apartment, unpack it and leave it ready to be filled with coins on his return from work. He loved the brand of green tea he was using these days and the Thermos of it he'd taken with him this morning as he strode out down Third Avenue. He believed the tea had perked him up after feeling under the weather these last two days, and that was a huge relief. He was happy that he had only thirty-nine pages of his outstanding Robert Lipsyte book left to read, as that was exactly the sort of page count he read in bed at night, which meant he'd be starting Harvey Frommer's history of New York City baseball on the subway tomorrow.

A standout employee in AIG's mortgage-backed securities division, Jack was gradually learning to convince himself that the financial logic on which the monolith he worked for seemed to be based was viable. He loved the new Excel templates on the upgrade, the smell of his girlfriend's sweaters, the spin class at NYSC and that the Prince Deli was stocking coconut water. He was happy also that in the post this morning had been the agnès b. eye-mask he had ordered for his girlfriend, Holly. He felt sad that Holly wore an eye-mask in bed but he respected that she needed to and believed it was the ultimate gift, to give the woman you loved something that positively upset you because she needed it and wanted it, that this was what giving meant, and that if she absolutely had to wear them then he was going to get her the softest, prettiest eye-mask out there. All in all, Jack loved his life, and that was the aim.

Right now, however, he was having an unproductive working day, and that was tough for a man who disliked inefficiency as much as chaos. His distraction was a fear that he had flunked the most recent phone call from his little brother, the one last month when Finn had announced he was coming to New York City. Phone calls from Finn were rare, and Jack worried he'd not seemed genuine in inviting him and his girlfriend (whose name escaped him) to stay. He had made the offer genuinely, but mindful of the logistical complexities. Finn would have the sofabed, obviously, but in terms of Jack and Holly moving round the apartment and all four of them using the bathroom, well, it would mean disruption. Jack would have to do his crunches in the bedroom instead of the living room and he wasn't sure he'd be able to get his feet under the bed, as it was a divan, but obviously he'd find a way – that in itself wasn't a deal-breaker. One thing was for sure: if Jack's concern about the arrangement had been present in his voice then Finn would have picked up on it. Finn required little persuasion to take offence.

Jack unfolded two brown napkins on his desk and placed his dressed crab sandwich on them. The reassuring electrical burr of the office re-entered his head. He took a look around. Even the least evolved of his male colleagues seemed to have their heads down in work, a situation that was pleasing to him and had no hope of being sustained. A hard core of them were incapable of remaining at their seats for more than twenty minutes at a time. They were the ones who would approach each other's desks with the vacant, amused, goofy expression which betrayed that they had not yet decided what nugget of humour to unleash. They would ad-lib some jewel, designed to conjure up the spirit of their frat or the locker room, or of the other night in the sports bar when they had waaaaaaay too much to drink and had an awesome time. In contrast, Jack believed in working when he was at work and in talking in the office only if he had something to say about work. He was old-fashioned, and a bit freakish, in that respect. Athletic, nice-looking, impossibly polite and with that thick shock of neatly cut jet-black hair, Jack was liked by women in the firm. His male colleagues, who did not deny his superior professionalism, had a line on him they considered hilarious: 'We thought Jack was gay, but turns out he's British'.

Sandwich eaten, he went to the restrooms and washed his face. His reflection bore a warning of rare ill health: a slight reddening in his eyes and at the pinch of his nose. He patted his face dry and threw the paper towel into an overspilling bin. Halfway out of the restroom, he hesitated, then doubled back and pressed the paper towels down with his foot so that they did not spill over and cause the cleaners unnecessary work.

As he straightened up, he felt dizzy and knew he had a cold coming on.

'Damn...' he said to his mirror self, wanting to be in perfect shape for his baby brother's arrival, even though Finn had snubbed his offer to stay in favour of some apartment downtown.

He returned to his desk with a roll of toilet paper under his arm and found Kit waiting for him.

'There were some great jokes flying around at Scottie's bachelor party last night, it was a blast. You can imagine. It was a riot...' Kit said, with an approach to anecdotal storytelling that left Jack to fill in the gaps when it came to characterisation, setting and, well, anecdote.

Jack's inbuilt bullshit-detector told him that a sizeable minority of the guys working around him, earning six figures and chasing the Christmas bounties, lied through their teeth when talking about the quality of the parties they attended and the quantity of their sexual activity (they exaggerated upwards, to be clear) and Kit was the embodiment of the AIG buck who had more chance of conquering Everest without oxygen than playing out the sort of sexual conquests and extreme sport weekends he and his like would boast about in vague, suggestive terms. And vague was vital, unless you had an excellent head for keeping consistent your fictional detail (lies, if you will). Jack struggled to relax with these men who seemed so terrified of women, so clueless about them, that they had adopted the most bereft of vocabularies to deal with their terror.

Kit, as was his habit, picked up a couple of items on Jack's desk and put them down moments later not quite where he'd found them. Apart from struggling to spell the word 'derivatives', Kit's role in the office seemed to be to ruffle Jack's equilibrium.

'You don't get many fat gay guys, do you?' Kit ventured.

'Go away.'

'Or, maybe there's millions of fat gays but it's just too much to admit to two humiliations. They are clearly, undeniably fat, so they keep the gay thing under wraps.'

'Because being gay is a humiliation?'

'I think so. If we're being honest. Deep down. Don't you, Jack?'

13

'You're an idiot.'

'Are you saying you're gay, Jack?'

'How old are you?'

'I'll have to take that as a yes?'

'You're a disgrace to your company and this city,' Jack muttered, in a mild, uncensorious tone, designed to end conversation.

Kit laughed under his breath, but it was less a manifestation of amusement and more a sign of his curiosity over the workings of a mind like Jack's. 'You actually believe that it's possible in this day and age to be a disgrace to something, don't you, Jack?'

Yes. Jack believed that implicitly. He thought men like Kit were a letdown to the company that paid them, particularly if that company was of the stature and credibility of AIG and situated in a city as extraordinary as this. Jack felt privileged and overwhelmed (still, three years in) to call New York City his home and he expected others to feel the same. He needed a strong opinion on this because, without one, his decision to leave England when he had might appear suspect.

He blew his nose and coughed into his tissue and warned himself there was no way he could get ill with Finn due in town. He set about getting back down to work but found himself recalling the woman walking ahead of him on Third Avenue earlier that morning. She was tall and thin and leggy and wearing fine, tight jeans (Italian jeans, he presumed, for no reason). When she flicked the long dark hair off her shoulder, he glimpsed her face and saw that she was deeply tanned. He watched the movement of her buttocks, in as much as she possessed any, for two or three blocks (he wanted to think of it as her *ass* but felt that he couldn't pull off a word like that even in the privacy of his own thoughts) and imagined himself and the woman together. Aware that he needed to stop staring, he diverted west on 88th Street, stopped for a moment for a slug of green tea, and spent the rest of the 80s on Lexington, reminding himself that the thoughts he had had about that woman were not right. He blamed his brother, as if Finn's imminence was encouraging him to think about things he normally wouldn't think about (namely, removing that woman's knickers with his teeth) because these were the sorts of things he presumed Finn was doing regularly back in England. In Jack's head, Finn had that way about him and Jack didn't.

An email from Kit appeared: HEH BIG MAN! WAS JUST BLOWING A LITTLE AIR AND TAKING A QUICK BRAIN-BREAK. NO OFFENCE INTENDED JACKY-BOY. KIT.

Jack sent back immediately: NONE TAKEN. ALL GOOD. CHEERS, JACK.

He glimpsed Kit lean forward to read his screen and wave in Jack's direction. Jack raised his hand in return, without looking up from his desk, and felt satisfied with the balance of power in the exchange. He returned to work. Today was going down the plughole. He had achieved next to nothing by his standards. (It was a day of spectacular productivity by Kit's.)

He ran through the checklist that acted as his pacifier on the occasions he experienced this kind of self-doubt or distraction. It went something like: this city suited him perfectly; his girlfriend was great and he was lucky to have her – even though she wore an eye-mask to bed and never slept naked, not even after sex, which he hated but didn't mention; he had money; he liked his apartment, or at least he presumed he did; his brother was safe and hadn't blown anything up for some while. Jack was content and life was gratifyingly tidy. He decided that what he needed to do was schedule his head-cold away so that one, there were no chinks in the armour when his brother showed up, and two, he could get down to some work, and three, there were absolutely, categorically no chinks in the armour.

He took a blank sheet of paper and composed a thirty-six-hour timetable. It consisted of six vitamin- and energy-rich meals, this evening's spin class, a brisk fifty-block walk to work tomorrow morning instead of taking the subway (a walk during which he would studiously avoid gazing at women's buttocks and remain faithful in thought as well as deed to Holly), a sauna tomorrow lunchtime at NYSC and an hour on the elliptical and treadmill tomorrow evening. Plenty of sleep, and no alcohol (he could take it or leave it; it had made an orphan of him, after all). He felt optimistic about this plan. Good. Excellent.

He wrote four work emails and saved them to his drafts folder. He would send them at three in the morning. He did this from time to time: set his alarm for the middle of the night to fire off some pre-prepared correspondence, as the image of the employee who worked into the night sat well with his bosses.

He went home and made himself honey and lemon in hot water and turned in early. He set his alarm for three and lay in bed reading the last pages of *Why A Curveball Curves: The Incredible Science of Sports* with a tray heaped in loose coins on his lap, which he fed one by one into the coin organiser. This was Jack's mother-ship moment: learning from a book and tidying up his world, simultaneously. Life was sweet.

3

The walkway to the terminal was all carpet, no oxygen. Dilly
bundled Finn into the first restroom on offer, locked the
cubicle door and pulled at his leather belt. 'You're beautiful,'
she told him, going down on to her haunches and unzipping
him. He watched her passport rise gradually out of the back
pocket of her jeans in time with the rhythmic bobbing of her
buttocks as she sucked him. He arched over her back and
took hold of the passport before it landed on the pimpled
floor. Despite the immediate circumstances, human nature
obliged him to take a look at her passport photo. In doing
so he discovered that Dilys Parker's surname was Vela, not
Parker, a development that preyed on his mind without
disabling him.

When she had zipped him up, she rose to her feet and
he handed her passport back. 'Why is the name in your
passport Vela, not Parker?' he asked.

She licked her lips. 'That was yummy. I was married. No
biggie.'

He tilted his neck so that a mop of hair fell and drew a
curtain over half of his face. 'I didn't know.'

'Obviously. No one knows anything until they are told.
By definition. I'm telling you now, so that's no longer the
case. YOU – NOW – DO – KNOW. I got married at eighteen.
I'm not married any more. Well, not in practice.'

'What happened? Why didn't it work?' he stuttered.

'It did work. It just didn't last. That's it. No mystery. No skeletons. No sweat.'

'Is he out there?' He meant America.

She shrugged. 'He's gotta be somewhere. Europe probably.'

The notion of a physically perfect, mature (meaning anything over twenty-one), olive-skinned Mediterranean male drew up a seat in the frontal lobe of Finn's brain, without assuming a precise physical appearance.

She whispered in his ear. 'I can't wait for you to fuck me in Manhattan.'

He smiled bravely. Given the events and revelation of the last few minutes, the possibility of delivering on that front seemed remote.

'Don't worry about the past,' she said, taking hold of his hand as they rode the travelator. 'You're the present.'

On the immigration concourse, overhead signs directed them to different queues. They let go in slow motion, holding hands for as long as possible and dragging their fingertips across each other's palms. From the back of the queue for passport control he watched her breeze through the US Nationals line, and as she descended towards the baggage carousels she did not turn to look back at him.

Finn had not shaken off his childhood habit of picking out happy families in crowds, watching them until the longing and jealousy warped his day out of shape or he was caught staring. There were plenty of them here, in the lengthy queue that snaked towards a line of mostly unstaffed passport booths. It was a bad habit, one that achieved no catharsis, one he needed to drop, but in this instance it was a more tolerable train of thought than dwelling on that prototype-in-perfection who was Dilly's ex-husband. He nudged his backpack forward with his foot. Up ahead, he saw a red-haired security guard patrolling the headland between the front of the queue and the booths. The guard was big-armed and fire-armed, and reminded Finn of someone: he had the same hair, freckled face, pallid complexion and brick-wall physique as the man who had threatened Finn on his first date with Dilly, the man who had materialised from a crowd of drinkers in the pub and fixed Finn with lifeless eyes that brimmed with the capacity for easy violence, and said, 'You called me a cunt.'

In the minutes prior to the man's intervention, Dilly and Finn had sat in silence, their conversation run dry. He'd known she was not right for him – too terrifying, too old, too everything – and the fact that he fancied her had to be weighed against the fact that he fancied everyone. As for Dilly, she was bored by his lack of words, his refusal to talk about blowing up the shed, and by his failure to 'get' most of her cultural references. Her mind had been wandering since fifteen minutes in and she was ready to quit the evening.

'You called me a cunt.'

Finn felt the life drain out of him. He understood the deal for young men of his physique: that for any drunk man who needed to prove himself he was worth attacking.

'No, I didn't,' Finn said.

'You called me a cunt.'

The man glared, the way large, drunk men did. He swayed a little, yet seemed impossibly strong, his feet rooted to the spot, his hands clenched. His lips were moist, his mouth lazy and sunken, weighed down by great reserves of vitriol. There were no negotiating points here. He wanted to fight. He wanted Finn to make the mistake of standing up or being cocky, providing the trip-wire for violence.

'Please leave us alone.' Finn's voice was thin. He looked apologetically across to Dilly. She was shaking with fear but it was the sadness in her eyes that struck him, their betrayal that she understood that she was not in danger here, that she knew Finn was the sole focus of abuse. The glance Dilly cast him, its offering of a beautiful solidarity, instantly changed his feelings for her from lust and disinterest, to lust.

'No one calls me a cunt.'

'No one did.'

'You did.'

Finn's insides were hot but the fear had already been replaced by disappointment. He had been asked out by this dazzling older woman and he had presumed the whole world would share in his happiness – that it would wish him well in this adventure, do anything it could to help, slap him on the back as he entered the pub with her, wink knowingly and a little enviously (if he were being honest with himself) as they left.

But, instead, yet another man of violence stood before him, demanding to be navigated. 'Outside, now, you cunt.' The veins and tendons in the man's neck stood proud on his clammy skin.

Finn knew he could rip this man apart and that if he did he'd be condemned as a repeat offender. He hated the way the world seemed to work. 'I'll meet you outside in one minute. Let me say goodnight to my date first.'

The man thought about this, the effort of which made him list to one side. 'You're a fucking cunt,' he hissed, betraying a slur. For the first time, drinkers nearby turned and looked across. Finn looked at them, making sure to catch their eye, and waited for the rescue boats to launch. But none came. They averted their eyes. They looked at their drinks, at each other, at the middle distance. They looked anywhere at all but at Finn.

The man left the pub and took up position outside. He leaned his forehead against the window and glared in at Finn. Finn put on his coat. His legs threatened to buckle at what seemed like another conspiracy against his chances of happiness. Men walk to the electric chair with more poise, he scolded himself.

'Stay here. Don't come outside,' he said, in a lifeless, commanding way that rekindled Dilly's interest in him.

'Where is he?' she said.

They looked outside. The man had gone. Finn went to the door and stepped out on to the pavement. He felt the dislocation of air behind him as the door to the pub swung shut. The street was quiet. The cold air stood shoulder-to-shoulder with him. The man had not left. He was face-down on the pavement, mouth open, legs splayed, one arm flat against the tiled wall beneath the windows. To Dilly, who appeared now at Finn's side, he looked like a melted Dali timepiece. To Finn, he looked merely drunk, and Finn had seen drunk many times. He looked over his shoulder at the men inside the pub. Gutless wankers, he wanted to say, but as usual he kept his counsel.

She took him to a bedsit above a shop and left him in a room of objects from London markets that implied a lifetime of travel. She reappeared wearing a silk scarf from Gujarat wrapped around her waist, and nothing else. She threw the cushions from the sofa and made up the sofabed with sheets stored in a chest in the corner of the room beneath copies of *Aperture* magazine. In the early hours of the morning she watched him sleep and whispered aloud that she would turn this boy into something better than he was now. A better lover. A more cultured man. A more stylish man. A man. She would give him all this and seek nothing in return other than his beauty and to be left alone without having to be by herself. He heard her whisper all this to herself, like an instruction from that part of her that knew best to the bit of her that never learned. None of it made sense to him, and most of what he had heard so far in his life he had tried to forget.

Now, in the hushed atmosphere of Newark's arrivals hall, Finn shifted uneasily at recalling that it was the threat of violence that had brought him and Dilly together. The security guard, who had never in his life picked a fight or called anyone a cunt, cast an eye over the aliens entering his homeland and beckoned Finn forward to a booth. The immigration officer took a look at Finn's passport and visa form and immediately said, 'The address on this document is unreadable.'

Finn stooped forward to take a look, but was parried by the officer's open palm. 'Return yourself to behind the white line, please.'

Looking down, Finn saw the line on the floor, a foot or so from the kiosk. He took a step backwards.

'This is not read-worthy. What was the reason for striking out the first address?'

Finn's mind went blank, leaving his mouth open and his face contorted in thought.

For immigration officials like Elmore Baker of Trenton, New Jersey, getting young bucks like this English guy to either hit the verbal diarrhoea button or clam up was one of the sports of his profession. 'Who lives at the address you removed from the form?'

'My friend.'

'What's the name of your friend?'

'His name.'

This was not a question on Finn's part, merely two expressionless words fulfilling no purpose.

Elmore exhaled a slow, deep, losing-the-will-to-live breath. 'Yes, his name.'

'But we're not staying there now so it doesn't matter.'

'It matters to me.'

'Glenn Walker.'

The official turned to his computer and began typing.

'If...' Finn started, then retreated.

The official stopped and looked at Finn. 'If...?'

Finn pointed to the man's computer. 'If you're looking him up, it might say prison, but that's not a fair reflection.'

'Jail…' the official said, and returned to his computer. 'I'm not looking him up.'

'Oh. Sweet.'

'I'm looking you up.'

Finn laughed nervously, just when he meant not to.

Elmore created his own silence, held it longer than was natural, then broke it. 'You need to fill out a new form.' He struck a thick line through Dilly's parents' address on the form. 'Is the purpose of your visit business or pleasure?'

'Pleasure,' Finn replied, watching the thick black pen line cover up the Long Beach address. 'American pleasure, if that helps,' he added, opening his wallet to a picture of Dilly.

Elmore took a look at the striking young woman. 'Why am I looking at this?'

'Just 'cos, I dunno, she's American,' Finn faltered. 'She'll tell you, you know, to let me in. She's got the address we're staying at.'

'Why don't you know?'

''Cos you just put a line through it.'

'You don't know where you're going?'

'She does. She's American.'

Elmore took another look at Dilly. The photo was a head-and-shoulders shot taken from above when Dilly was wearing a strapless dress which she claimed to have got from a Blue Cross shop for a fiver but which had in fact been gifted to her by Zara in return for a donation of seventy-five pounds. The crop of the photo was such that Elmore Baker needed to have been there to know Dilly was not butt-naked. Finn reached for his wallet and Elmore held it out of reach, and looked closer still at Dilly.

'Nood?' Elmore asked.

'What?' Finn hadn't understood Elmore, but instead of making that clear he went with the flow, just to move things along. 'Oh, yeah, a bit, she can be. Can I have it back?'

Only then did Finn get what the man had said: nude. Nood. And, in the silence that followed, he sensed the tumbleweed roll across Elmore's sense of the absurd and it struck him that Dilly really did look extremely fucking naked in the photograph, that the camera angle most definitely led the eye to Dilly's seemingly uncovered breasts, that the backdrop was clearly a bed, and that no one should be expected to work out for themselves the entirely truthful back story that he and Dilly had been sharing a tub of Ben & Jerry's vanilla when a modest mini-food-fight had ensued, leaving ice cream smeared around Dilly's lips at the precise moment Finn took this snap, and that none of this looked good, apart from looking absolutely tremendous.

'Are you showing me a sample of pornographic material?'

'What? No! Shit. Fuck off! No.'

'Did you say *fuck off* to me?'

Finn shook his head. His mouth had clamped itself shut. (Stable doors, horses.) He felt sick now, a sensation stirred by the malignant anxiety which US immigration officials would expertly propagate, along with an impression that one's experience of the United States might never get further than a terminal building.

It was the undeniably curious cocktail of innocence and strength etched and chiselled (respectively) on Finn's face that was at that very moment persuading Elmore to let this one off the hook. That, and the proximity to the end of his shift and the start of tonight's episode of *24*, inspired him to send the infuriatingly attractive young Brit to the back of the hour-long line to fill out a fresh form.

Dilly sat on their luggage, combating the irritation of waiting for her man by deleting old text messages. Nearby, she heard French being spoken and was jabbed by the self-loathing of not being able to speak a second language. This was a seasonal self-disgust she inflicted on herself whenever she heard French, Italian or Spanish around her.

The revulsion was duly followed by the time-honoured resolution to learn French and one day have an apartment in Paris. She dismissed herself as a fake, and became forlorn. She wondered about Finn again, torn between concern and annoyance, not wanting to commit to the wrong one of those two emotions and miss out on the other. She was surprised by the relief she felt when he appeared. It reminded her of the liberation to be had in forgiving. (There were two epiphanies she resolved to learn from every time she had them, only to forget about them until the next time. These were, that to forgive someone rather than convince herself she had been horribly let down always, but always felt good; and that every time she saw someone in a wheelchair she remembered how lucky she was to be fit and healthy and would never complain about anything again, ever.)

They kissed and groped until they were moved on.

'I spoke to this woman in baggage reclaim, she was wearing an Alexander McQueen coat which I asked her about and turns out she's a film producer and I'm really sorry to tell you this but she said the part of New York City where *Royal Tenenbaums* was set doesn't exist in real life. It's completely fictional so your pilgrimage there... well, you know, can't be done. Are you upset?'

Finn shrugged. 'No. If it doesn't exist then I'm not missing anything.'

She held his face. 'You're great. I wish I could handle disappointment like you.'

'Well... it's not really very important.'

'Everything is important,' she said, 'otherwise nothing might be, and I can't face that.'

They went in search of the bus that Finn insisted they catch so as to stay on budget, the bus that came to a standstill in thick, crooked traffic on the approach to the Holland Tunnel, where the fact of queuing seemed to hit Dilly like a stray bullet, leaving her slumped and lifeless in her seat.

'If we'd taken a taxi we'd be there by now,' she moaned. 'Because taxis fly?'

She stared accusingly at the insides of the tunnel, then started to giggle, aware of what she could be like. She knew that he was looking at her, waiting for her to look at him. This made her laugh some more, and squirm in her seat. She morphed her laughter into another groan, achieving a perfect mixture of both.

It struck Finn, the proximity to his brother. He was now on the same slab of the planet as Jack. Jack's face, Jack's body, Jack's self-contained smile, his busy schedule and impeccable appearance, his regularly monitored body mass index and resting heart rate, the squash shoes to which he probably still applied whitener, the girlfriend who stole him, the money he seemed to mistake for love... it was all suddenly close by, and that felt momentous to Finn and dazed him in equal measure to the low Manhattan sun. He fell into a light sleep, rocked by the occasional forward movements of the bus, and woke when the towering buildings that had stolen into the landscape while he slept pressed their shadows against his eyes. He felt his heart rate quicken. He recited to himself the names that Jack had told him in a history lesson dressed up as an email, and which Finn had memorised with an ease he would never admit to; Mana-hatta, New Amsterdam, Gotham, the Empire City, New York City, the Big Apple, the City that Never Sleeps. He was here, on a journey that had once seemed as likely as going to Mars. He squeezed Dilly's hand and turned to tell her that he loved her, but she was engrossed in her phone and didn't look up.

4

In the corridor between the elevator and their apartment, Jack ran into his girlfriend, Holly. 'Don't kiss, I'm coming down with something,' he said.

'Poor you. I won't, though, you're right.' She ran on the spot prior to a game of squash and doing a stack of laundry before her late flight to Atlanta to start a three-week business trip. He offered to do her laundry and they asked each other how their day had been (both had been fine) while remaining at a germ-free distance of eight feet a little too expertly for lovers so young (he twenty-five, she twenty-six). To anyone watching, they would have looked like neighbours.

She blew him a kiss across the divide. Her smile was pretty and her eyes beautiful. She was generous and kind. He watched her go and a familiar twinge of regret that they didn't have sex more than once or twice a fortnight pinched him. He smiled neatly, to disperse the twinge, and kept the smile pinned on so that when she turned at the elevator it was waiting for her.

Their apartment was seven hundred and fifty square feet of almost sophisticated but ultimately characterless comfort. They weren't there enough for it to matter. From the fifteenth floor their views were of the sky above Harlem. Jack decided to go across to the Kinsale Tavern, which he used as his living room, reading the papers on his laptop and his history books there. He took a seat at the bar and ordered a glass of water, a nest of nachos with melted cheese and a chicken sandwich. Feed a cold, starve a fever. You could count on the fingers of one hand the things of value his mother had taught him.

Jack had never been drunk in his life. He had wanted to be, after the second funeral, but the thought of burying an alcoholic father and turning to drink himself had been too wretched. And, anyway, it had been a time of stepping up to the plate, of being organised (not a problem for Jack), of keeping himself in check emotionally (ditto), of looking after Holly, who was new on the scene and in her first year in England, and of trying to figure out what the heck his kid brother thought of it all.

'Pretty selfish of Dad. At least Mum just killed herself, no one else,' was all Finn had said on the subject, then and since.

Before Jack and Finn's father died, Holly had already been pining for New York, where she had gone in '96 from home in Seattle to study at NYU. She had waited four months after the funeral before raising the subject (she had intended to wait a respectful six, but couldn't go the distance) and discovered that Jack couldn't wait to get away.

'You look awful,' she said to him, kindly, on her return to the apartment from the laundry room. She knew he'd be frustrated at getting ill when his brother was due.

Jack put the kettle on the gas and broke a Karvol capsule into a bowl. She told him he should take a day off. He looked at her as if she was insane. 'I can run this cold off tomorrow morning. I see guys letting it slip all around me, hearts giving out on them, high cholesterol, all that kind of thing. I don't wanna die in my fifties like Mum and Dad.'

Holly placed her backpack by the door and checked her tickets. She filled her water bottle from the filter jug. She stood behind Jack and placed a hand on his shoulder and flinched as the menthol steam rose to her eyes. She held her breath and kissed the back of his neck. 'You're a fit twenty-five-year-old, Jack. And you know what? Neither of your parents actually died.'

'We didn't cremate them alive.'

'Jack, that's an awful thing to say.'

He apologised. He had thought it was mildly amusing, his dream of how understated ripples of repartee between lovers could be.

'My point is that they were both killed, effectively,' she said. 'They didn't die naturally of heart attacks and stuff... so you shouldn't worry about dying. I mean, worry about getting killed, sure, but not about just dying. Not yet.'

From two hundred feet above, Jack watched Holly step on to the sidewalk and flag a cab. The sky above the Upper East Side was crystal-clear, the darkest blue. Jack picked out the planes from the satellites and pictured his baby brother, out there, somewhere, choosing not to come to him.

Beneath the same cold sky, Finn craned his neck upwards and his mouth fell open. Around and above him, it seemed, stood every skyscraper he had ever glided over in the opening credits to every New York movie he had seen. He recognised it all, and was shocked to find it better in real life than in his imagination or in the cinema. Nothing had ever failed to let him down until arrival in this town.

'London is a man, Paris is a woman, and New York a transsexual.' Dilly stood on the sidewalk, with her arms spread out wide and a grin on her face. 'Angela Carter.' She looked happy. Impossibly happy.

'Who's Angela Carter?'

'She is... who she is, my lover.' She picked up her bag and walked, and Finn followed her. Although there was little that was compatible between them, they shared a dislike for the Port Authority and an instinct to get away from the crusted streets around it. For a few blocks they remained nervous and tight-lipped on the sidewalk, then relaxed and began to look around openly, and pretty soon she told him to stop gawping. 'Looks ridiculous,' she muttered.

'Don't care,' he muttered back. 'I'm in New York.'

'New York City, not New York; they're different things.'

But, miraculously, he thought to himself, you knew where I meant.

She stopped abruptly and screamed. 'OH MY GOD!'

It hurt his ears. 'What?'

'LOOK! The New Yorker Hotel! I'm sure that's famous. That's the sort of place you check into if you decide to write a Pulitzer-winning novel.'

He ignored the question of what constituted gawping and admired the hotel's red neon. He was always willing to admire whatever impressed her, out of politeness and a desire not to seem ignorant. He saw on her face that expression of hers which he mistook for deep-in-thought but was in fact the deep self-doubt of a familiar enemy flashing across her line of sight, an image that visited her often, of a train passing slowly in the night, its lit carriage windows the accusing eyes of millions of lines of literature and history and philosophy she had never read and would never read, but which she felt compelled to imply she knew.

She faltered. 'Maybe I'm thinking of the *New Yorker* magazine... not the hotel.' The energy drained from her and turned down the volume on her voice. 'The hotel might not be famous at all. The *New Yorker* magazine – that's what I meant. That's very famous.' She put down her bag and watched the faces gliding past her on Seventh Avenue. 'Why are we walking?' she asked, as if to wrest back control of the evening. 'What in Christ's name is going on?'

'It's only five inches on the map,' Finn said. 'We could walk.'

'Walk, to the other side of Manhattan? Did you think that was going to happen?' She hailed a cab. It took them downtown and Dilly saw the names of Lower East Side haunts she had circled in the guidebook and her excitement returned. Finn watched her as they continued on to a corner of the neighbourhood the book had not mentioned. She put two thousand pounds' worth of Nikon back into her bag and folded her arms across it as the cab pulled over. 'Don't tell me this is it... Don't tell me this is it...' she muttered, pleading to the same gods she turned to for turbulence-free flights and a career in fashion or the arts.

'This is it...' the driver said. 'Jackson and Grand.'

Finn unfolded Glenn's scrap of paper and double-checked the instructions. The words were in caps, SAM'S HARDWARE STORE. He looked out of the window at the grisly row of five-storey buildings among which the store was crouched on its haunches, two storeys high. The whole street was peeling paint in sodium light.

He looked at the reflection of the driver in the rear-view mirror. 'Can we come home with you instead?'

The driver's big face crumpled and his chest heaved a couple of times, suggesting an ability to laugh, if pushed. 'Fourteen-fifty,' he said, and looked straight ahead at the dust-coated neon reflections on the hood. He was the sort of solid, decent sixty-year-old man Finn could imagine wanting to hold on to.

They stood where the cab left them.

'He lives above his shop; we have to call him,' Finn said.

'So, call him.'

'Use your phone?'

'What's wrong with yours?'

'I didn't bring it.'

'You didn't bring it what? To America?'

'Yeah. It's pay-as-you-go. It doesn't work abroad.'

'But...' She was incredulous. 'How are we going to stay in contact?'

Finn looked confused. 'By being next to each other?'

'Really? You've got no phone?' She found it freakish how little he used his phone. 'You're serious?'

Finn shrugged. 'Can we just call this guy?'

They called and the lights came on inside the hardware store. An elderly man wearing expressionless grey skin opened the door to them and said nothing as they followed him in and he disappeared into a store room out back. Dilly looked outwards, for a hint of her dreams beyond this crease in the city.

'Perhaps,' she said, 'it will all look different in the daylight. Tomorrow is another day.'

That was what Finn's father would say, each night as he climbed the stairs. It was a ritual Finn would listen to from his bed. 'Goodnight, sleep tight, tomorrow's another day...' and from downstairs Finn would hear his mother call, 'Yet another fucking day.'

The storekeeper returned, holding a small brown pay-packet envelope with Glenn's name on it. Back out on the street corner, Finn took Glenn's key from the envelope, checked the instructions and studied the map.

'Less than an inch from here.' He tried to sound bright.

'And that's a good thing?' she replied.

Between the high-rise blocks of the Housing Corp, Finn glimpsed the shimmer of the East River and felt the cool breeze of the draughts beneath the Williamsburg Bridge. He hadn't envisaged these housing estates, big, ugly sprawls like the one he was born into, except brown here instead of pale grey. And it somehow felt better to him, to be beginning on the margins of his image of New York City rather than at its centre, to have inadvertently landed in the underbelly. (This idea, like so many, he did not share with Dilly.)

Where 10th Street met Avenue D they found the Gully, as Glenn called it in his instructions. It was a stubby, dead-end street of a dozen buildings on each side, at the end of which a high brick wall separated the street from the Housing Corp.

Industrial chimneys somewhere out on Queens perched in miniature on top of the barrier wall, belching ivory-coloured smoke into the night.

The street was a miscarriage, a row of old townhouses out on a limb, carved up into apartments and industrial units, and left to fend for itself in the shadows of a vast haunted self-storage facility and the Con Ed plant. Halfway along the Gully was a mechanic's shop that Glenn had offered up as a landmark. It had died some time ago and was now decomposing. A security shutter was pulled unevenly down across the shop front and the bottom corner of it had been crowbarred open like a torn envelope. Next to it, at the top of six steps, was a reinforced metal door. The ground-floor windows had been painted with tar, directly on to the glass. On the sidewalk was a pile of rubbish that had been there long enough to have weathered and attained personality.

'Yeah... he said it sort of doesn't have a number,' Finn said.

'This isn't happening,' Dilly muttered. 'We're going to your brother's.'

He ignored her, climbed the steps and unlocked the two security locks, then opened the numberless door with the Yale. He looked back at her. 'It'll be fine,' he said.

'It won't, and anyway, I don't want fine.'

He led her up a lightless stairwell which reeked of engine oil. Inside the apartment, Dilly could not speak. It was less messy than she had feared, but it was cold and dark and bare and the despondency of it jabbed her in the stomach. Finn dropped his bag and went to the large cast-iron radiator and turned the knob. She resented the trace of enthusiasm in his movement as he explored the apartment (and it was a studio, not a fucking apartment) and turned on another radiator that hissed and spluttered into life, and the way he seemed to think it was a bonus that the light switch worked.

From the only window, she looked down at the aluminium roofs of a row of workshops. She shuddered at what looked like a dead snake but might have been an inner-tube.

'It's a shithole, but it's not a whores-and-heroin shithole,' Finn said.

Dilly drew a short half-breath and soured her lips, causing Finn, uncharacteristically, to chatter nervously.

'It's a Shane Meadows location but not, you know, *City of God*.'

'This is not the dream,' she said, icily.

'I thought the dream was us being together in New York City.' They swapped positions, circling each other, and he looked out across the backyards to the East River. Behind his back, she flung herself on to the bed and lay on her stomach with her face buried in her arms. 'No one's gonna hurt us,' he whispered, 'it's just a place.'

She leapt up off the bed, clutching a pillow to her stomach. 'I'M NOT FUCKING SCARED OF ANYONE HURTING ME, YOU LITTLE PRICK!' And then she screamed from the middle of the room, until spit was clinging to the roof of her mouth and she was bent double, her legs bowing under the weight of her rage. Screamed as if she were giving birth to the building, as if possessed. Screamed the way an infant would scream. Finn watched, frozen to the spot. His head rang: Jesus fucking Christ! Look at her! Jesus fucking Christ!

She stared accusingly at him and spoke, the words deformed by her mouth dredging for oxygen. 'You must have known what this place was gonna be like – he must have described it to you.'

'It's a free apartment from a twenty-one-year-old guy in jail for the second time already. What were you expecting? And anyway, blokes don't describe apartments to each other.'

'Yes, and it's women who pay the price for that, throughout their lives.'

As usual, he had no idea what she meant, and no intention of asking.

Softly, he continued, while trying to acclimatise to the insanity of her outburst and to somehow play it down. 'I hardly know Glenn. I met him last summer, you know that. We hung out for a bit, he kept saying I should come out here, then he emailed and said the apartment was ours while he was inside if we wanted it... that's it... that's all I know.'

'I forbid you to call this an apartment. It's a hovel.'

It was only now that Finn noticed a scrunched-up envelope in Dilly's fist.

'What's that?' he said.

'Note for you.'

'Where was it?'

'Please acknowledge that this is not an apartment. Tell me it's a hovel.'

'Can I have that note, please?'

'Say it out loud, that you understand this place is a hovel. Because if you think this is an apartment you and I are on different planets.'

He stared at her, mouth open, shrugged, shook his head. 'It's... a hovel.'

She handed him the note and he took it to the window.

Monotone, through her hands, she said. 'Does the note say, *This is a practical joke, you guys, this isn't really where I live, I live on Mercer Street above a designer shoe shop, the Manhattan equivalent of Emma Hope, here are the keys. Ha ha.* Does it say that?'

'Who's Emma Hope?'

'Christ.' She sighed and let her shoulders sag. 'I'm allowing into my body the penis of a man who hasn't heard of Emma Hope shoes.'

'Glenn has a part-time job loading dishes at Chelsea Piers... says I can go and see if they'll give me his job until he gets back. Sweet.' He looked at her brightly. 'We're on our way.'

She undid the top two buttons of her dress. 'Work... boring.' She removed her underwear from beneath her dress and sat on the bed. 'Didn't your parents leave you money?'

He turned his back and looked out at the view. Two yards away, a semi-naked man sifted through a pile of scrap metal by a work-light. He had a white Nano strapped to his greasy upper arm, and earplugs in his ears. 'I have to earn money. You said you were the same.'

'I say a lot of things.' She laughed at herself. 'That's such a line, but it actually applies to me: I do say a lot of things. What about your brother? He must be loaded.'

'We're not having that conversation again. Thanks to me we've got a place in Manhattan.'

'Yes, our *place in Manhattan*... here we are...' She sat up and hugged herself, rocked a little back and forth and stared at the floor. 'I'm an asshole. What did I expect? This is me we're talking about... the freak idiot... why do I raise my hopes? I'm such a loser.'

Finn kept reading. 'He's given us his parents' number in New Jersey... says they'd love to have us to stay. He's put in brackets, *I wouldn't bother. My folks are pretty depressing and it's not that nice a place.'*

Dilly stared at him, mean and sexy. 'The guy who lives here describes somewhere else as *not that nice*?'

She finished undressing and slipped beneath the bedclothes. He joined her. They hugged, pressing their naked bodies together for warmth, entangling their legs.

'Don't be mad at me, just listen,' she whispered. 'Please don't let's stay here. I hate it.'

'We can't afford hotels and we're not having the conversation about my brother again.'

She snuggled up to him. 'I understand...' she said.

For a few moments after his eyes had closed Finn listened to the hum of the city and the muffled rattle of the Williamsburg Bridge, and, although he was imagining it, the chug of boats on the river. He felt a veil of tiredness cover him and, with pleasure, he stepped off the ledge into sleep. She parted her legs a little and allowed his hand to settle between her thighs, where he liked it to rest. He woke after forty-five minutes, and was all slow motion, anchorless with slumber. He detected the subtle cinnamon aroma of Dilly's massage oil. He opened his eyes and saw the bottle nearby him on a bedside table made of wicker. A trickle of oil slid down the side of the bottle and Finn was aware that his penis was hard and beautifully sensitive. He placed one hand beneath his head and smiled at her. She was kneeling between his legs, massaging his oily erection. She was wearing his best shirt, the only one with a collar, the one he intended to wear when they went out to Long Beach to meet Dilly's parents. It was white and plain, and unbuttoned. She wore it as she rode him expertly and afterwards she lay star-shaped across his body, both of them a sheen of oil and sweat.

She took his right hand and placed it back between her thighs and whispered to him, 'Please don't make us go straight to my parents. That will play right into their hands.'

'Don't worry...' he whispered.

'There's a world of difference between asking your brother for money and using his spare room. Please take care of me.'

'Okay, baby...' he muttered, and fell asleep again.

5

This place was not what Finn considered a café. The presence of chorizo in the scrambled eggs made it a restaurant.

Dilly watched him load his fork, watched him chew exuberantly, felt the vibration of his tapping feet, watched his eyes suck in the kinetic energy on the streets outside. He looked so pure and pretty and fuckable to her. She loved what he amounted to, and loathed the inevitability that she would spoil, in some small way, how he saw the world, without meaning to at all.

She washed the eggs down with black coffee and felt the caffeine flirt with the nervous energy that underpinned her every waking hour, like inseparable friends who were no good for each other. She took the camera from her bag and aimed, as if attempting to take something captive. She wasn't certain what it was, but she'd know it when she saw it. She twisted in her seat, looking for images out of the windows, and her heart quickened at the thought of a career as a photographer of interiors for *Wallpaper** magazine.

'Has another Beatle died?' she asked.

'What?'

'This is the third Beatles song they've played in half an hour. Which one would you think?'

'What?'

'Which one would you think would die next?'

'How would I know which Beatle will die next? Neither of them, hopefully.'

'I didn't know you were such a fan.'

'I'm in that space between being a fan and wanting them dead.'

She waved for more coffee.

'But,' he added, 'everyone would keep Ringo and let Paul go, given the choice.'

She smiled at his nonsense. It was a new thing to her. In her not inconsiderable experience, relationships were for serious stuff, and intense stuff, for fights and sex, whereas nonsense was for between girlfriends, and she was in another one of those phases of her life when she didn't really have any girlfriends.

She put the camera back in her bag with a roughness that made Finn uneasy, and yanked out two street maps, spilling a beaten-up old paperback of Hemingway short stories on to the floor. Seeing the book, Finn felt faint, and momentarily deaf, as if he'd hit the surface of water at speed. He was barely able to speak.

'Why... have you got that?'

She gathered the book up and held it at arm's length, looking at it dispassionately. 'What?'

'I don't want you to have that.'

'You don't want me to read Ernest Hemingway?'

'Can I have it back, please?'

'Don't be weird. I haven't read it.'

'I'm not being weird.'

'Looking like death because I have borrowed a book from you is weird.'

She was right in theory, but in practice this particular book was not one he kept out on the shelf. 'Where did you get it?'

'Can't remember.'

'I keep that in a drawer.'

'I haven't even opened it. What's the big deal?' She handed it to him, leaning back in her chair so that he had to strain forward to reach it. 'Seriously, what's the biggie?'

He decided that her asking probably meant she hadn't read it, but still he felt sick at the sight of the book here in New York City.

'Okayyyy…' she said, sitting upright and clapping her hands together. 'One map for you…' she handed him one of the two identical *Streetwise* maps of Manhattan '… and one for me. Don't unfold them in public. It's tacky.'

'Why would one couple want two identical maps?' Finn asked.

'I thought, if we split and then met up this evening… It's fun to explore alone and then compare notes.'

He smiled the false smile, and wanted to swallow but knew that swallowing would appear weak. 'Whole point of having a girlfriend is doing stuff together.'

'Sure, I'm agreeing, but we don't want to be together twenty-four hours a day.'

'Isn't it a bit early to have a break from each other? It's day one.'

'So I've wasted my money on two maps?'

She was content to ride out the silence that followed and the many other moments identical to it, when a boyfriend took offence at something she'd done or said. He looked away. The Lower East Side remained exotic to him, and he urged himself not to lose faith in the great adventure, nor to be demoralised by the suspicion that he spent his life being let down by those closest to him.

He stared at the Hemingway book. It chilled him that it had spent time in her possession. It was hard to believe she hadn't looked inside, difficult to imagine she hadn't been working her way through the lines and lines of his own scribbled notes in the margins, but he managed to believe it because he wanted to.

She was done with this particular silence. 'This is what I am going to do today. It's up to you if you come with me or do your own thing. Unlike you, I won't take offence. After visiting Ground Zero – which I know you refuse to do, we've had that convo, yadda yadda – I am going to go to the Bloomingdale's on Broadway and treat myself. I like the idea of the juxtaposition of the two elements in one day. Tragic and celebratory. Spiritual and material. Also, it's what this city needs: for us to shop and act normal.'

So, act normal, he didn't say.

'I just need today to be fascinating on many levels.'

Finn dwelt on the implication that, for Dilly's day to be fascinating on many levels, she needed to spend it without him. It took his mind off the Hemingway.

'But,' she went on, 'I guess I could move day two to day one and vice versa.'

'What's day two?'

'The Park and the Dakota. Or, P and P, I'm calling it.'

'P and P? Or, P and D?'

'P and P. Park and Pilgrimage.'

He didn't ask.

Day two became day one so that they could be together, and began at the MoMA design store, where she bought a set of glass tea-light holders and pinched the bridge of her nose at the onset of a possible migraine when Finn asked if she wanted to go inside MoMA itself. 'No, thank you, my gorgeous man. Just the shop. I'm twenty-four and already feel like I've been through every art gallery in the world, twice over.'

On arrival outside the Dakota, she went down to her knees, positioning the glass tea-light holders on the sidewalk in the shape of a heart.

'What are you doing?'

She held one of them up. 'They're made by a Norwegian designer called Lotti. She's totally amazing, and incredibly young, the cunt.'

She took a book of matches from her pocket and cupped her hands around the candles as she lit them. Finn took a look at the box. Lotti's ten tea-light holders had cost one hundred and eighty-nine dollars, a month's food in Finn's money.

'Crap!' Dilly hissed, as the breeze extinguished the pathetic flames. She raised her head a little and waited, as if reading the proximity of the next lull. Finn watched her. The breeze dropped and Dilly nodded to herself, as if she'd played some part in it, and had all the candles alight to greet the security guard, who said, 'You can't have those there.'

Dilly ignored him and set about re-lighting the candles as they sputtered out again.

'Lady? You cannot have those here.'

'Let's go,' Finn said, with a voice that barely reached her.

She looked up at the guard. Her eyes burned pretty and fierce, and she used the quiet, calm voice that unnerved lovers and family members alike. 'Do you understand the meaning of vigil?' She turned her back before he could reply.

Finn bent down to gather up the candles. She pointed at them without looking at him. 'Don't touch them, lover.' Turning to the guard, she said, 'I feel sorry for you, I really do.'

He could live with that. He said to Finn, 'Take your candles to the park, like everyone else.'

Finn picked up the candles. When he turned, he found Dilly sitting, crumpled, in the middle of the sidewalk, crying into her bag. He crouched beside her and said gently, 'Hey, what's wrong?'

The tears flooded out of her. She wailed. 'Broken it! I'm an idiot.' In her hand, still inside the bag, was her camera. The lens was cracked. She sat upright, rigid, with her eyes closed, thrust her chin up to the sky, gritted her teeth and breathed heavily. Finn watched her. She was trying so hard to usher this anger through her, not allow it to engulf her.

He was unaware that he was pulling the same faces he made when watching *Jackass*, appalled by how tormented she could be.

'JEEEESUS, DILLY...' She squeezed the words out through her clamped jaw. 'I COULD KILL YOU! DILLY IS A LOSER.'

Finn found the third person thing pretty weird too. She often did it, and never in a positive way.

'I have an underwater disposable. You can use that.'

'No,' she said, in a dead tone. 'Thank you.' She was fighting herself. 'That's why I invested in a digital SLR. I was gonna do a little book of all the things in the park that resonated with me, a Wolfgang Tilmanns-stroke-Nan Goldin type thing.'

'We'll get it fixed.'

'Will *we*? With *our* money?'

He hated her for that.

'The park is ruined for me. The whole point for me of the park was this book idea I dreamt up on the plane over. Some of it was Turner Prize stuff – okay, I'm not British – but not on a throwaway fucking camera. The whole book would be photos done all in one day and it'd just get me noticed, without me having to invest months and months of time on it. That's how these things happen: they just hit a vein. Pow, and you're in. Everyone's talking about you.'

He had no idea what she was talking about, and looked for something familiar. The Yoshino cherry trees were in bud. He pictured the sap rising through them. He understood them as fully as he didn't understand Dilly. Trees made sense to him, a knowledge he had absorbed while working near to them, with people who knew about them, delivering them, handling them, watching and listening, the first time that he had enjoyed learning, allowed knowledge to smuggle itself in without the smell of the classroom.

'Mind if we do the park another day?' She spoke with the life gone out of her. It made her sweeter.

Finn took hold of her hand and led her gently away. She took a few deep breaths and talked herself down from the window ledge of being Dilys Annalese Parker or Vela. They passed a young Chinese guy with a massive Afro that bounced and wobbled like a jelly. It gave Dilly pleasure and she revived. 'So cool...' she marvelled. 'Very, VERY knowing. I get his references. Let's go to SoHo now.'

In the taxi, she waited until they were down on East Houston before mentioning that she had called his brother.

'How?' Finn asked, confused. 'Why?'

'How? I got his number from your Hemingway book. Why? To ask him if we could stay.'

'So you did read it,' he muttered.

'No,' she said, 'not at all, but I glanced inside and saw Jack's 917 number in your handwriting on the inside cover. No biggie.'

It scared Finn sometimes, to think that he could feel so angry towards someone he made love with. It confused him, and he presumed it made him bad.

'Anyway,' she said, sweetly, 'I like your book, I think it's cool.'

The taxi was stopped in traffic by a pool hall on the corner of Bleecker Street. Finn yanked open the door and marched away.

She called it *his book* as if he were writing a novel. Pages yellowed by time, the red band across the book's cover faded to the hue of a Remembrance poppy, it was the volume of Hemingway stories which Finn had taken from a shelf in the living room on the evening Jack had found their dad dying on the lane and packed Finn off to his uncle and aunt's house eighty miles away.

With his father not four hours dead, Finn had read 'Indian Camp' in the heavy traffic that his uncle blamed him for, accusing Finn of being too slow to pack a bag, too ungrateful of the round trip being made on his behalf. Long after he had finished reading the story, he stared at the pages and watched the rhythmic sodium shadows pace out the distance of his rehoming across the page. And, as his uncle cursed the journey and cursed Finn, Finn's big brother sat beside their father's corpse, offering the man a forgiveness on his and Finn's behalf for which Finn would not have given his permission.

Finn had been writing in the margins of the Hemingway book for the three years since that night. It began with a message to Jack, asking him to fetch him back and not leave him with his aunt and uncle for the ten days until the funeral, the transcript of a text message he never sent for fear he was being selfish. He wrote it instead, and other pleas to Jack, between the printed lines of Hemingway's stories. He buried his desperation there and they buried his father on Finn's sixteenth birthday. The book peered out from his suit pocket and he wrote cries for help into it during the eulogy he refused to listen to for its mockery of the truth. Uncle Trevor had leaned across and slapped the book to the floor, the dead weight of his torso pressing against Finn's ribs. Finn was slight and skeletal then, and, every time he felt his uncle's breath on him, he resolved to make himself strong.

The stain of Finn's blood on the open-leaf spine of the book had settled into the paper like ink on a blotting pad, spread its blurred arteries across the margins of the middle page towards the printed words, before running dry. Jack and Holly had been on the plane to New York City when Uncle Trevor grabbed the book out of Finn's hands and wedged it into the base of Finn's nose as he screamed at him to 'take your thick head out of the sodding book' and to 'buck up your ideas and show some bloody gratitude for being offered a home'. He had rammed the open palm of his hand against the book, jabbing it into Finn's face, causing a sac of blood to burst from his nose on to the paper. The blood had acquired a certain painterly beauty in fading, and endowed the open spine with a lipstick kiss.

After that, every rage, every screamed word, every filthy, angry torrent that had spewed out of his uncle's mouth, Finn had transcribed in minute handwriting, simply worded but relentless in its graphic detail, haphazardly covering every space in the margins and between the lines. Dilly marvelled at the idea that Hemingway's stories had not been complete until her lover added to them. It made her feel like a part of something.

Finn needed only to hear his uncle's voice in the house to taste the snot and salt that clogged the back of his throat when he was pushed and shoved and hit, when the back of his neck and the tops of his shoulders were gripped agonisingly tight by angry hands that yearned to get away with greater violence the same way other hearts yearned for love.

When Finn discovered the boxing club, his scribbled words evolved from descriptions of what his uncle did to him to ones about what he was going to do to his uncle, and much later, after he had blown up the shed of the man who killed the dog, he wrote in his room at the detention centre descriptions of hitting his brother so that his brother knew how it felt to be here, and of landing one blow that drew blood and forced Jack to crawl on his knees to a corner far away enough to buy enough time to get to his feet without being hit again, as Finn had had to do on three occasions, each one his birthday.

The book was full. Every moment of harm had been described and dated. To Dilly, it was a work of art, a beautiful object, and it had not registered with her that it represented a bodily experience, that it was real. She could not see beyond the perfection of Finn's minuscule handwriting, how pleasing it was to the eye, and the poetry of his simple language alongside Hemingway's. To Finn, who had many times imagined handing the book to Jack and leaving him alone with it, perhaps to observe Jack as he read it, the book was an unwelcome fellow traveller which he wanted to throw from the Brooklyn Bridge and send to the tides.

She caught him up halfway along Mott Street and walked beside him, saying nothing (she wasn't stupid) but looking at him all the while so that, when he looked at her, she'd be ready for him. But, he didn't look at her and she grew tired of waiting and became distracted by the boutiques, which brought out a religious streak in her.

'Oh my fucking God!'

'Jesus Christ almighty!'

'Mary mother of oh my God!'

She stamped her feet at what she called the *effortless cool* of Café Gitane and squeezed Finn's hand excitedly as she led him into a vintage clothing boutique. Inside, among faded denim shirts and worn out cowboy boots and corduroy jackets with leather elbow-patches, Dilly became overexcited, holding shirt upon sweatshirt up to Finn's body, his face indifferent to garments that cost more than the Air India flight over. 'You'd look so great in this.'

'Two hundred dollars on a shirt?'

'Say "bucks" not "dollars"… this belt is incredible. This is perfect for you.'

'For eighty dollars, I expect my belt to be attached to two pairs of jeans.'

The store assistants wore taut, pained expressions as Dilly rifled through the stock. And Finn could recognise the look on Dilly's face, or part of it at least, for somewhere amidst the frenzied eyes and open mouth that had taken over her features as she thrashed in a sea of vintage, he saw the breathless hunger in her that he liked. It was sex. This was how she looked during copulation. This was an animal experience for her. It was full of desire, it was about touch and smell, and it brought profound, temporary fulfilment that covered over the unreachable desires.

'I wish you wore stuff like this. Don't you have a credit card?'

She reminded him of a riderless horse at the races, the one that could not be stopped and was left to exhaust itself while onlookers prayed it didn't cause too much damage to itself and others.

'You know I don't.'

She stamped her feet and giggled and gave him a hug. 'I'm sorry! It would just be so great for you and me to be seen out in stuff like this. It's harmless. I'm not saying it matters, it doesn't, but it'd also be so awesome. So perfect! It would mean a lot to me, actually.'

Later, she came to an abrupt halt outside the Café Colonial, gasped with pleasure at the look of it, and marched inside. Cradling a cup of coffee in both hands, she continued to scan the décor adoringly. It was all so tasteful and classy. The pale green woodwork against cream-painted brick, the tiled black and white mosaic floor, the huge map of Brazil, which looked old (deliberately tea-stained, she suspected, which is fine, but don't think you can fool me), advertising posters that by dint of being old appeared innocent and not cynical, a framed Miró poster, the massive ceiling fan. Finn watched her drink it in. It made her look so happy.

She smiled. 'Isn't this music awesome?'

He hadn't really been listening. He did so now. A punky female Irish voice, against a strange biblical piano accompaniment, sang 'Holy Holy Holy'.

'I thought you hated religion.'

'I said I like the song, not believe in it. I hate religion but I quote St Augustine. Everything is a matter of context. That's true of the whole of life, by the way.'

She reached across and held his hand, looked him in the eye and shivered. 'The sex is great. I'm sure that when I was nineteen and sleeping with all those nineteen-year-olds they weren't as good at it as you are.'

He looked down, which she misread as embarrassment. 'Modest Finn...' she whispered. She released his hand and returned to her coffee. As she drank it, she looked out across East Houston and the moisture rose in her eyes. She thought about how she had just been in the store. She often revisited past scenes in her life. She played them back as if they'd been taped. It never made for happy viewing. She looked Finn in the eye. 'There's a home video of my fourth birthday and I am handed this great big birthday card but there are all these presents around me so I'm not interested in the card and I barely glance at it and hand it to my dad, really dismissive, without looking at him, and grab the presents. My parents love that tape but I hate seeing it, how spoiled I look, how ungrateful I was.'

'You were four.'

'So, I make resolutions... about myself. About my behaviour. I hate the word *behaviour*. I make a list of things I won't do next time I'm with people. I promise myself I won't talk again without thinking. But the next time I remember the resolution is the next time I have broken it, and I'm watching myself on rewind, making all the same old mistakes.'

She looked across to a reclaim yard, at the pedestrians caught in a wall of hot sun on Bleecker Street, and began to cry.

'I wish I could burn the tape. You're lovely, I'm very lucky,' she said, to the window-pane. 'Let's get our stuff from that shithole and go to your brother's place. Please.'

6

Jack stood motionless, his body overtaken by flu, his forehead resting against the door as he listened out for their footsteps in the corridor. When the wait became longer than he had calculated, he wondered if Finn and his girlfriend were having sex in the elevator, à la Joan Collins in *The Bitch*. He had this habit of bestowing upon his brother's life that which he considered unattainably exotic in his own because, handsome, athletic and solvent though Jack was, he had not yet been consummately seduced.

Hearing them approach, he began to rock back and forth so that when he opened the door he would appear casual, and busy. He found Finn's Cheshire Cat smile waiting for him, the one that obscured everything else. He still had no idea what lay beneath it. The smile was familiar but Finn had new eyes. They looked out at Jack mechanically, reflective surfaces that unnerved him, although he didn't realise it and put the queasy feeling down to his ill health.

If there did exist a way to let go of the adoring baby brother and welcome in the tall, powerful, still young man in his doorway, Jack either didn't know of it or couldn't bring himself to do it. As he hesitated, Dilly stepped in between the boys and thanked Jack for inviting them, too profusely. With the arm that he had raised in the embryonic stages of a pat on his brother's back, Jack found himself waving to Finn across Dilly's body.

'Don't get close to me, I've got something.'

Jack had imagined a variety of greetings for his baby brother. Being Jack, he'd even rehearsed a few. But, as ever, the unseen, uncontrollable force seemed to take over when he attempted to communicate with Finn, and put words like 'don't get too close' into his mouth, eighteen months since he had visited him last and gotten nothing out of him.

'Right,' Finn said.

Dilly scanned the apartment and, seeing just the one bedroom, downsized her maths on Jack's earnings. Jack saw the disdain written on her face and stood as if he had no right to be there. 'I'll be right back,' he said, and went to the bathroom.

'When are you going to hit him?' Dilly whispered.

Finn slumped. Some inner part of him recoiled, the mimosa leaves of his bruised nineteen-year-old heart. She had read the book.

He stared past her to the skyscrapers made pale and paper-thin by the waning sun.

She had read the book.

He stood, cut adrift again from love or anger. And he felt stupid and wondered if he'd have to go through with hitting Jack just to keep her.

'You read it?'

'No! How dare you accuse me of that? No way am I that sort of person. I literally opened it up and saw something about hitting him and I went no further. Apologise for accusing me.'

He shook his head, not at her request but at the madness he was on the brink of indulging yet further. 'I'm sorry.'

Dilly took a shower and the brothers sat side by side on the sofa in a silence moulded by Jack's fear of saying the wrong thing and appearing inhospitable, the effect of which was a remoteness that made Finn feel like driftwood. After three years alone in the unpoliced province of his uncle's

51

hospitality, Finn found himself clear, at last, about one thing: the man next to him was merely an older brother, no guardian angel, no protector, no hero. Jack already looked different to him and Finn knew well enough that this was him, the beholder, altered and that Jack was probably unchanged and unchangeable. It left his anger unsure of its target.

'Nice flat,' he said.

'Thanks...'

Finn concentrated on the view of the darkening sky through the window.

'Apartment...' Jack added. 'Dilly seems nice.'

'Thanks.'

'A bit older than you?'

'Clearly. Thanks for having us.'

'Course. How's everyone back home?' Jack asked.

'I am everyone back home,' Finn said.

After that, they sat in silence. And after that, Jack turned in for the evening, on account of his cold.

In bed, Dilly was subdued and did not want to make love, citing Jack's germs and sleeping in the living room as the reason. Finn sat up against the cushions. He looked at the back of the *Shaun of the Dead* T-shirt Dilly was wearing. It was his *Shaun of the Dead* T-shirt. He loved her to wear it. It seemed an intimate, softly amusing thing of her to do. He rested his hand on her back. Her skin was warm and a little clammy beneath Simon Pegg's face. She reached out behind her and squeezed Finn's finger. He felt that he could detect the building move, a dreamy movement. He pictured all the buildings in Manhattan swaying at night, to rock the adults to sleep. None of his ideas of New York City had children in them. He had no clear sense of what childhood was, anywhere, let alone here.

He felt aware of his brother in the next room, of their bodies in close proximity. He was confused about what he thought of Jack. He had expected it to be simpler, black and white, but they had come from the same parents once upon a time, a short way back in the unfathomable past, and today that seemed to mean something. It surprised him that he cared even a little bit. They lay a few feet from each other now, held in mid-air where the sounds rose from the street to a muted, drifting song of opportunity, and where, hanging on the wall that separated them, was a slightly out-of-focus aerial photograph of the ugly chalet bungalow Finn and Jack's parents had moved them to against their will. From five hundred feet in the air, Finn and Jack's home was as inconspicuous as their parents had been at ground level. Finn stared at the wall between them and it grew thicker as it absorbed the hurt and sourness that bewildered him so.

When he woke, Dilly had gone, and taken her bag and Finn's stuff too. There was a scribbled note on the pillow.

Meet me at noon on the northwest corner of Canal and West Broadway and 'try to keep an open mind'.

This last bit alluded to a line from *Badlands*, which they referred to often as it was the only film their tastes had so far found in common.

Jack appeared in a bathrobe looking rough and moved around the walls of the apartment straightening his numerous framed historical maps of New York City, even though they were not askew.

'What time is it?' Finn asked.

'Ten.'

'Oh, man, I really slept. Why aren't you at work?'

'Not feeling too hot. Your girlfriend was up at six, making some weird shapes.'

'You mean Dilly?'

'Of course I mean her.'

'That's Dilly-yoga. It's a bit weird. She's made it up herself, I think.'

'Looked artistic.'

'She could make a fortune with it here, Americans love that bullshit.'

Jack sat across from Finn, too pissed off at him to share the couch. You wanna move into a hotel, he thought, you move to a bloody hotel. 'I had a phase reading lots of novels when I moved out here, 'cos I didn't really know anyone and I was alone most of the time.'

'What about Holly?'

'Well, yeah, when she was out doing her stuff, I mean. And I liked Doris Lessing.' Jack wanted to ask Finn if he knew who Doris Lessing was but didn't want to sound patronising. Finn didn't ask because he knew how his brother hated to be interrupted. 'She wrote this book called *The Grass Is Singing*, and in the intro to it she's talking about racism and apartheid and she says that racism is the atrophy of the imagination.'

There was silence. When Finn was sure that his brother had stopped talking, he asked, 'What does that mean?'

'It means a failure of the imagination – that, if people could truly imagine what it is to be the other person, they wouldn't mistreat them. Prejudice, it's a failure of our imagination.'

Finn nodded and sipped his tea. What with his brother's tendency to read and Dilly's to talk, he felt sandwiched between a lot of words.

'My point is,' Jack said, 'shed your stereotypes at the front door to this city. Forget the "seventy per cent of Americans don't have passports" stuff, get over the apparent meaninglessness of "have a nice day" and the obscenity of "super-size me". This city is full of extraordinary people. It's the most amazing place with a fantastic history.'

Finn laughed beneath his breath, impressed by his brother's knowledge and earnestness. If Jack was going to fuck off to America and abandon him, at least he seemed to be making the most of it. The laughter made Jack feel small. It humiliated his serious nature by a further increment, as had Dilly's revelation to him earlier, during a modified downward dog, that Finn was insisting they check into a hotel today.

Abruptly, Finn stood up. It was not a Finn-like movement; he was the least jagged of men. But this was not how he'd imagined it: Jack being ready for them, having a bed made up, talking at him in that knowledgeable way Finn had always felt quietly warmed by. Jack had lost the right to do that sort of thing, and Finn couldn't hear himself think for the noise of his blood pumping.

Jack watched the prowl in his baby brother's movements. Christ, he had filled out! The breadth of his shoulders, the veins in his arms; this was his kid brother in a man's body, with an animal movement about him that left Jack unsure what was happening. Then, calmly and without a word, Finn left the apartment and Jack had the most outlandish sensation that Finn had been on the brink of destroying the place.

With Dilly's note to guide him, Finn emerged from the subway into the blinding cold sunshine of Canal Street and, as his eyes adjusted, he heard Dilly shout 'Yo!' from across the street. It was not a Dilly thing to shout, and it reeked of a guilty conscience. She led him into the SoHo Grand. In the elevator, she blindfolded him with a silk scarf. 'Trust me…' she whispered. He could hear the moisture in her mouth and gave her the benefit of the doubt. Perhaps they were about to have quickie sex, something they had had a lot of in their four months together, but not in places as pleasantly scented as this. She led him into a room, shoved him so that he fell backwards on to a bed, which he allowed himself to bounce and settle on, and his cheek came to rest on the softest sheets that had ever touched him. He felt the mattress sink a little as she knelt over him, positioning herself one small movement from how his uncle would pin Finn's shoulders to the floor with his knees.

Dilly removed the blindfold. He looked at her as the silk slid off his face, welcoming the suggestion of sex to the same degree that he resented the allusion to violence. His peripheral vision took in the compact extravagance of the room, in the corner of which was their luggage. This was a declaration of war against the values of their trip, where being together and being on a budget in New York City amounted to more than any young lovers could possibly want.

He smiled at her and said, as kindly as he could, 'We're staying with my brother. Now that you've dragged me there, we're not leaving.'

Her mouth fell open. Lost for words, she instead pressed her bottom down against his groin, opened her thighs.

'It was – ' she emitted a quick burst of dismissive laughter, as if offended by the need to explain ' – your brother's suggestion?' She ended the sentence with the upturned questioning tone that implied that Finn was stupid for not knowing this, and that she had hoped not to need spell it out to him.

Finn's head dropped to one side again. He stared at an iPod dock on a chest of drawers. 'Oh.'

'Yes. I was doing my practice when he had a quiet word with me. He said that... because he's feeling so sick, and he's got a lot on and really needs his own space, it'd just be better if we were back in our place. I don't blame him and I hope you don't either. He's not to know how bad that shithole was. Anyway, I've taken care of it. Leave everything to Dilly.'

'How much?' he whispered.

'Less than four hundred bucks a night.' She had decided when she checked in to be brazenly honest in reply to this dull, inevitable question.

'Can you get off me please?' He squirmed beneath her agitatedly. She considered for a moment pinning him down but could already feel the strength of will in him. He walked to the bathroom and slammed the door shut. It made her jump. A less expensive door would have splintered.

After ten minutes of silence she spoke through the door. 'We have to try and do things in style. I'm sorry. Not my rules, Manhattan's rules.' She tiptoed in and sat beside him on the tiled floor. He didn't look at her. He stared instead at the tray of complimentary soaps and oils. Finn had grown up with very little and been content. His parents' dalliance with a middle-class life had damaged them all irrevocably. Nothing enraged him like material wealth, especially in a hotel his own fucking brother had banished him to.

She waited, patiently at first because she was happy, very happy, to be here and it was hard for her to look any further than that. He reached out and took a bar of soap to look at, rather than pay her any attention.

'The soap smells of marzipan.' He was disgusted. He was outraged: the money on this hotel room could keep them alive, or be a gift to Glenn, someone who would need all the help he could get. 'Now my hands smell of fucking marzipan!'

She laughed and her laughter grew hysterical but her eyes were as kind as he had ever seen them. 'It's the first thing that's ever made you angry,' she cried. 'This makes you angry and not all those other things! Oh, Finn!'

He didn't know if he loathed or loved her, but experience told him what would disguise the pain of Jack's not wanting him to stay. One thing was for sure, he decided, as he reached across and held her hand: he was going to stop making the mistake of wanting anything from Jack. She gripped his hand tight, causing the blood-rush in him, and they kissed deep through her laughing mouth, and it felt dirty to him and welcome, being laughed at by her when she wanted him to fuck her. It was the best of ways to forget. He knelt at her, with her legs spread high and his ribcage pressed against the back of her thighs, a towel under his knees to cushion them against the bathroom floor. She moved up on to her elbows to stare at him. Eye contact like this always drove him crazy to please her. At her prompting they swapped positions. She wedged the towels beneath her knees and he a robe beneath his head. As she came, her head thrashed from side to side and her eyes drank in how fucking cool this bathroom was, and she called out breathlessly:

'Herr God, Herr Lucifer,
Beware
Beware.
Out of the ash
I rise with my red hair...'

She gasped and folded in two and smothered his face with her hair. His body was locked and somewhere in her oration he had come, but had not felt it and was aware only of being spent. They talked in whispers about a shared New York City, the one they could both agree on. It was short on detail, necessarily, but it was the two of them, soft and affectionate, equally in love with everything around them. This temporary harmony was the true miracle of sex.

'Your hair's not red,' he whispered.

She laid her hand on his stomach and played with the line of wispy hair between his belly button and his pubic hair. 'I don't think hers was either.'

'Whose?'

'Sylvia Plath's.'

'Who is that?'

'Someone inspirational to me.'

'Yeah, but who?'

She wiggled into a softer position and sighed as if to sleep. 'She's a French singer and poet, the little sparrow I think they called her except she's dead now. *Je ne regrette rien*. I think she's dead. Not sure. She might have killed herself or her husband killed her, he was a poet I don't know, I'm not sure, who cares. I'm going to keep your juices inside me all day.'

He kissed her gratefully.

'Which reminds me – when we go out to my folks, don't mention my marriage.'

'Okay,' he said, blankly.

'They don't know I was married.'

Finn was torn between asking why her parents didn't know and why her keeping his juices inside her had reminded her of her marriage. And, then, to his surprise, he discovered that he didn't give a fuck. And that this was probably the only way to be Dilly's lover: to allow the madness to wash over him.

She lifted herself off him and crawled out of the bathroom on her hands and knees. 'Legs like jelly,' she laughed.

He stared at the bathroom ceiling. Sometimes, he felt like saying to her, *Thank you for being my lover, for this period of time. It's been very kind of you but you don't have to keep doing it. You'd be much happier with one of your own kind. I'll miss you but it's gonna happen sooner or later and you've sacrificed enough time on me already. I had a great time and I learned a lot. So thank you, I am going to put you out of your misery. You must go back to your people now.*

In the bedroom, Dilly put down her *Oxford Concise Dictionary of Quotations* and tested herself on the two she was committing to heart today. Two a day, every day. In time, even if only half of them stuck, that'd be a lot of knowing. She stretched across the sheets and placed the book back in the zip-up compartment at the back of her suitcase. She watched the change of light on the ivory walls, plumped two pillows beneath her head and draped herself among the bedclothes like an artist's model. He found her like this, gazed at her pale, lean, naked back for signs of movement, and was overwhelmed by affection for the speechless version of her. The muted rumble of SoHo seeped through the walls as if he had strayed the wrong side of a movie screen. They slept, and when they woke it was late afternoon and they were met by the consuming hunger that came after sex and before old age.

'You choose where we go,' she said in accordance with an earlier resolution not to dominate. 'What's on your list?'

'*Sleepers*. I wanna go where *Sleepers* was set. I looked it up.'

On the streets she was snoggy and loving and she draped herself across him. He felt like a million dollars. Eight blocks later, her dislike of walking bubbled to the surface and she hailed a cab to take them to Hell's Kitchen where nothing of the landscape of the book or movie was to be found but where Finn seemed content simply to know it had all happened once upon a time. He picked out a diner on Ninth Avenue called the Red Flame.

'You totally sure?' she asked.

She chose the window seat and feigned pleasure at the place but already her mind was wandering, searching for something better, becoming disappointed by the day, returning her to that corner of herself from which she found it impossible to love.

On the next table, a couple laughed, collapsing into each other as if to share the burden of their happiness. Dilly presumed they were laughing at her but they were not, they were laughing at themselves and the way they still took a look at the menu here before ordering what they always ordered. The woman took hold of her husband's hands across the table and joined him on the bench seat. Finn watched them with a quiet, mouth-open wonder, as the woman snuggled against the man and kissed him on the lips. 'William...' she purred, and then she placed her mouth against his ear and whispered in it and the man, who was short and rather formal-looking, kissed his wife on the lips and stroked the river of walnut hair that had turned a thousand heads in the neighbourhood.

Dilly glared at Finn, blushing with embarrassment. 'You are so staring...' she whispered.

Finn didn't hear her. This couple were a miracle to him, to be so old and so in love.

William leaned away from his wife, to admire her, as if unable, still, to believe his good fortune. She had filled out handsomely in her fifties, but had not yet aged. She had a powerful, sensuous frame to support her trademark mane, and her eyes and mouth burned with a desire to express happiness. Kathleen Turner in *Prizzi's Honor*, thought Finn as he gazed at her. It was one of his favourite old movies.

'Are you married to each other?' Finn asked. He couldn't help himself.

Dilly muttered 'Christ almighty...' and hid behind her menu.

The woman looked Finn up and down. 'Twenty-seven years,' she said.

'Sorry about him,' Dilly said, and tugged at Finn.

'Don't we look it?' William said.

'No, you look like you just met, like you're having an affair.'

'Twenty-seven years...' the woman repeated, amused by Finn.

'That's good. Sorry to butt in.'

'No problem,' William said, kindly.

A waitress brought zucchini fritters to the couple and called the woman by name; she was Joy. Around them, the Red Flame hummed with conversation and laughter and the scraping of cutlery on crockery and the calling out of orders. William and Joy talked and ate and all the while they put three hundred fliers for their church recycling scheme into

61

three hundred recycled envelopes. Joy ate with a passion, breathing deep with appreciation and sighing her approval between mouthfuls, so that Finn, who had had sex on the brain since meeting Dilly, could have believed Joy had another lover positioned beneath the table. In truth, the only man she had ever made love to was sitting right next to her.

'You're still staring,' Dilly hissed, and kicked Finn under the table. He turned back to her, smiled sheepishly. She grabbed his hand and kissed it, in an impersonation of the couple, who made her want to vomit, and she heard that voice that said she had no right to be with Finn and it made her feel sad in the same way that seeing ranting homeless women with knee-length socks made her fear for her future and obese people eating junk food made her want to weep. She knew that if she looked into Finn's eyes right now she would burst into tears and by the end of the evening there would be enough truth in the room for them to have split up.

A waiter brought a large jug of water and two tumblers which he left stacked one on top of the other, a touch that Dilly liked for being informal, intelligent and stylish, and which enabled her to regain her lack of composure. There were slices of cucumber in the water and Finn bobbed one with his finger. 'Soup's a bit thin,' he said.

'Don't do small talk, Finn. It's not you. Your inability to talk shit or force humour is going to get you laid all your life, so don't mess with it, please.'

Beside them, William tuned in to Finn and Dilly's conversation and thought to himself how much nicer the boy would look in a collared shirt, maybe even a suit. He had the ideal build for a suit. He'd feel better about himself too, no doubt about it. William scanned the restaurant proprietorially. He loved the ebb and flow of the Red Flame. He liked the season being reflected by the coat rail, empty in summer, three deep in winter. He liked the clock set into the back of an old colander hanging on the wall above the cash register. He liked Sandra, the waitress whose wristwatch William once mended as he ate breakfast, alone, one Saturday morning when Joy was at work at the health store. He liked Sandra's laugh, and the draw of breath within it that sounded like a plea to be rescued from having too much fun.

Dilly had noticed the colander clock and wasn't sure if she loved it or detested it. Anything in between was not an option. The line of bullet holes on the wall beneath the clock she presumed, wrongly, was art-directed. On the opposite side of the avenue, a boarded-up shopfront had 'Store for Rent' in big red letters on the chipboard. She watched a dog-walker use it as a stop-off point for his pooch to take a shit by the chained entrance doors. A man in overalls painted the words HAPPY EASTER in freehand on to the outside window of the Red Flame. He had already drawn bunnies, eggs, baskets of chocolates with ribbons and, incongruously, a pizza.

Dilly pulled a face at the food when it arrived and was visited by the familiar, shudder-inducing fear that she was missing out on a better party just around the corner.

'I wanna see places…' she muttered.

'What do you want to see?' Finn asked. 'We can do whatever you like.'

'Something like that bar called 182 or 872 or whatever. That bar where the doors to the restroom cubicles are made of see-through glass and everyone in the bar can see you going in but when you lock the door from the inside the glass frosts up. I showed it to you in the magazine. I was so happy. I want to be in places like that and watch people and kiss you in front of those sorts of people. You would look amazing in places like that. We would.'

'We'll go. Now. No problem. Let's go.'

'No…' she whined. 'It was in Tokyo. I sometimes feel you're deliberately missing the point. Places *like* that!' She sighed. 'What do I have to do to be understood?'

Finn looked at his hands, glanced at the next table. William smiled back at him. Finn didn't know what the hell Dilly was talking about and the smiling man seemed to understand that. Both men turned, instinctively, towards the sunlight and watched the owner of the Red Flame step out on to the sidewalk and hand the window-painter a cup of coffee and stand back to look at the display. He jammed his hands on to his hips and a big, jowly smile spread across his face.

Finn and Dilly ate quietly. She sometimes resented Finn's enormous capacity for long silences, as it diluted the impact of her own deliberate, point-making ones. As they left the café, Finn stopped and admired the windowpainter's work.

'You're really good,' he said.

'Thanks.'

Dilly rolled her eyes at the painted pizza and walked away.

'You should paint professionally,' Finn said, 'I mean, real actual paintings, for people to buy.'

'I do paint real actual paintings for people to buy.'

'Why are you doing this, then?'

'Because people don't really, actually buy them.'

'Idiots.'

'Thanks. Where you from?'

'England.'

'Pretty cool.'

'Yeah.'

'You paint?'

'No. I'm a gardener, sort of.'

'That's very cool.'

'Not really.'

Dilly was a block ahead of Finn, watching him say goodbye to the nobody painting the café window. She turned and walked on. Finn saw her, knew he'd need to jog to catch her up and for the first time he couldn't be bothered.

He recalled the sensation of getting home from school to an empty house, of heading straight out again to walk in increasingly wide orbits of the neighbourhood in the hope of seeing his brother around the next corner, and praying that, if it were his mum he met, she would not shake, or behave as if she was out of focus.

He allowed Dilly to disappear out of sight. Feeling lonely on the streets of Manhattan felt better than all the other places he'd ever felt lonely – exotic in its way – and he received another sympathetic smile from the man called William as he and his beautiful wife left the café.

While Finn meandered south, William took Joy's hand and walked home with her through that area they refused to call Clinton. They could have lived someplace nicer than the stretch of West 36th Street dissected by the Lincoln Tunnel approach, but they liked the nest they had made there and they liked the view and not having debts and the pact they had made to get out of bed each morning glad to be alive, to prefer laughter to sadness, to take pleasure in the detail of their day-to-day existence in Hell's Kitchen and not to look beyond it.

'We don't want eyes too big for our bellies,' William had said, a quarter of a century ago, summoning the presence of his maternal grandmother.

'Let's not push our luck…' he had heard Joy say whenever they had contemplated change, and on that tearful day when they gave up on having a child.

William opened the door to this life they had mastered and watched Joy go straight to the bedroom, where she switched on a lamp and turned back the sheet. Their bedroom was small, only marginally bigger than the bed, but had a dressing room the size of a wardrobe off it. It was separated from the lounge by a bead curtain. The lounge doglegged into a kitchenette and a glazed door led straight from the kitchenette to the bathroom, which was small and filled by a huge tub that had been here in 1981 when they moved in. The apartment was bright, with large windows held together inside by thick layers of gloss paint which William and Joy liked to apply every other spring without any preparation and wearing smocks like children in an art class. The shelves were filled with CDs and cassettes stacked in messy rows. There were a few books lost amongst the music, none of them fiction.

William took the mail to a small desk tucked into the corner of the living room, dropping it on to a pile of paperwork beside the outmoded PC that dominated the desk. Mail depressed him, reminded him of a world knocking relentlessly on the door of their life, trying to get in. He sat back and looked at the shelves above him, one filled with back copies of the *Chelsea Clinton News* and Municipal Arts Society magazines. Post-it notes stuck out from these journals like archaeological signposts in the bedding planes of a marriage driven by good causes. Another shelf had box files of church paperwork and another was crammed with correspondence and articles relating to organised opposition to the West Side redevelopment. Three identical and never-perused copies of *The Earth from the Air* (Christmas presents every one of them) served as book-ends, a brass Buddha (William had just liked the look of it) serving as a fourth. The shelves bowed beneath the weight of it all and William contemplated a clearout.

He took a light beer from the fridge and shared it with Joy. The bottle floated back and forth across the apartment, a baton passed between them as they walked and talked and tied up the trash and opened the post and shared it and shredded it and looked for the TV remote. They undressed, he wrapping a towel around his waist, she putting on her robe. They drifted happily on autopilot, swigging the beer, sharing a belly laugh here and there and talking about chores they needed to do as members of the Stewardship of God's

Creation Recycling Scheme, which William still prayed would be renamed simply the Recycling Scheme. He and Joy referred to their church as 'the Club' because 'the Church of the Disciples of Christ' was a mouthful, even for people of faith.

William ran a bath and sat on the laundry box watching it fill. She hovered at the door, asked him to scratch an itch in the small of her back; when he had done so, he watched her leave the bathrobe where it had slipped to the floor and wander naked into the lounge. He heard her mute the TV and put on a Lead Belly tape. He leaned over the bath and threw water on his face, felt her rest a hand on his back as he patted his face dry. He kissed each of her breasts on his way to sitting down again. She tested the water and inhaled the scent of the bath foam. She said, 'Mmm... nice...' and Lead Belly sang, 'My girl, my girl, where will you go? I'm going where the cold wind blows.' He put his arms around her waist and rested his head against her tummy. He felt her run the fingers of her left hand through his hair. She held a sheet of paper in the other.

'You'll like this,' she said.

'Tell me...' he replied, climbing into the bath and letting out a long sigh as he submerged himself in hot water.

She sat on the side of the tub and read from a flier. '*This Saturday is the Hanging of the Greens. Join us as we decorate our sanctuary in the creative company of friends. Don't forget to bring the kids. The fun starts at 1pm after coffee 'n' cookie hour.*'

'How many people do that?' William said, lowering his mouth into the water and blowing bubbles. 'Forget to bring their kids?'

She giggled, and it told him that they would have sex later.

'Shredder,' he said.

She put the papers aside and climbed into the bath, groaned with contentment. The steam rose from the water.

Every few minutes, she lifted herself up an inch and allowed the hot water to course between their bodies and prevent their skin from sticking. His hands rested on her belly, hers on his knees. They went to bed and made love and afterwards she reached for the remote control on the bedside table and played the CD where she had queued it up to her favourite post-lovemaking song, 'Kisses Sweeter than Wine' by the Weavers. He lay on top of her and offered gentle kisses to her shoulders and breasts because she loved them so much and because they drowned out the words of the song he disliked, and he felt himself diminish inside her.

7

'Are you going to celebrate?'

The final conversation Jack had with the probate lawyer in London left him wondering if they had become friends. It also left him lying in bed with a fan of loose papers on his lap and the phone in his wavering hand as he tried to imagine who he would have celebrated this with, had he felt well enough.

He pulled away the covers and sent tumbling the papers that he no longer needed to keep in order. He was not the sort of person to burn them as a gesture, but he could at last put them away and close the box (after getting them back into order). In a kitchen cupboard was a shapeless collection of alcoholic options for the non-existent guest: a few beers, an unopened bottle of gin, Holly's slimline tonic, and a bottle of corner-store cava. He put the cava in the fridge and this act of preparation for a hypothetical gathering succeeded in marking the moment without threatening him with the actual act of celebration. Michael Hollins, Jack's monotone, chosen-at-random-and-at-distance lawyer, was right.

'You should mark this moment, Jack. It's been a long old haul and it's taken a bit out of you. Although we've never met, I get the impression you've had a few sleepless nights. It's done. Celebrate.'

Jack did not in fact allow such things to keep him awake at night. The result of exhausting oneself with exercise was good sleep. There was also, he believed, something about living close to the East River air. He went often to the waterside and stood pressed against the railing, watching the traffic roll over the Triborough Bridge, or the cranes building Long Island City, and felt the river's ether preparing him for sleep. A stillness pervaded even when there was noise. Today, he would have liked to go to the river wrapped in his duvet and throw the papers into the water. They would tell a tale to the rod-and-liners downstream. They would wash up at Stuyvesant Cove in any old order and tell a disjointed story from this era where a husband and wife could set sail in a paper boat with their sons on board, be lent every line of credit going, enough to stop working then immediately forget how to, then forget how to live, and die with a parting gift to their first-born son of a sinking, mouldy financial chaos that required plastic gloves and a peg on the nose.

Who to celebrate with, hypothetically? Holly was absent, naturally. Finn was in the dark, thanks to Jack's masterful withholding from him of all knowledge of the crap their parents had left behind. He was already down to people he preferred less than solitude.

He feared that life was living him rather than him living it. People endured moment after moment after moment. They survived and survived again (until, of course, finally, they did not) but, on a day when the familiar voice of stranger and friend Michael Hollins LLB had given him permission to celebrate, mere endurance seemed meagre. What he could do with was some sound advice. He could do with someone appearing at his bedroom door, tucking him in, plumping the pillow, telling him it was all going to be alright, and, trickiest of all, him believing them. Someone to sob against and complain to about the hours and hours of his life taken up in mopping up the mess, with the help of Michael Hollins at three hundred pounds an hour. It was perverse, he knew, that if his mother were alive she'd be the one to soothe him, oblivious to the scorched earth of her ways. It would be she of all people who would offer a philosophical view. His dad was all about silence but his mother had had a taste for deep thinking when drunk. Jack wondered if one day he would be offered free, sober advice, or had he missed out on that now? By your mid-twenties were you expected to get on with it, with no further nuggets of wisdom, and to somehow live off the ones that reeked of gin? He wondered if some men received guidance from their wives. He liked the idea of it, it aroused a certain aching in him, but somehow the prospect of laying himself bare to the woman he made love to seemed an impossible one.

The shadows of early spring were cast long, throwing a tree, still bare-limbed, on to the grey-slabbed side of the buildings opposite the apartment and the elongated shapes of pedestrians marching after themselves with outsized limbs. Jack watched from the corner window of his bedroom, wrapped in his dressing gown. Late afternoon and not dressed – unheard of. A man in a trilby and a raincoat, collar up on his neck, crossed the avenue, his sideburns and muscularity old-fashioned. For a split second it could have been the seventies or eighties. So many angles in this town allowed for time-travel, placing Jack inside the TV version of New York City seen in the corner of the living room in the 1980s, watching a long-since-dead middle-aged man go about his unreconstructed business, possibly enjoying his heyday. And, inevitably, Jack wondered if his own dad ever had a prime, and he knew enough about his parents to be sure that before Finn was born they had enjoyed a certain exuberance and happiness and expectation, without ever harbouring ambition or the vein of curiosity. And perhaps way before that his dad enjoyed a golden age, of earning a first wage, of women and the idea that anything was possible.

A man of Jack's age stood against the smoked windows of the Kinsale Tavern. The windows muted the reflections of the traffic on Third Avenue and a slow-moving line of ghostly yellow cabs passed through the standing man's body without him flinching. From his elevated position, how could Jack be sure that the man existed at all, with the traffic driving through him and no way of calling out to him? The inverse thought also offered itself up, that the man was down there on the street but that Jack, high up at his bedroom window examining a detached world, existed to no one but himself. This was why he disliked being off work: the space for thought it created, and the feeling of invisibility. Staying busy took care of most things.

The elevator security guy at his office had asked Jack, 'What's your Harlem Beach?'

Jack hadn't known what that meant, and guessed that he was being invited to ask.

'It means, a place you can turn your back and be at peace. I'm Louis. I'm from Maui.'

'Hi, Louis. Jack.'

'English?'

'Yes.'

'London?'

'Yes.' (What was he going to do, describe his home town to a guy from Maui?)

'Welcome to New York City.'

'Thank you.'

'Harlem Beach is where I go to fish. Not often enough but you got to know it's there, even if you don't get to it as much as you'd wanna. Someplace to get away from all this crazy, beautiful stuff. Someplace to just… whatever.'

Within six months, Jack knew that his own Harlem Beach was the reading room of the public library. And among the very first things he read about in that hallowed place was Harlem Beach and the East River, because Jack would look up any subject that helped him understand another person better, Louis from Maui included. It was a shame that no one had written a book on Finn, to offer his big brother a clue. He could easily understand Louis from Maui's pact with the river, and with many human beings Jack felt a chime that would never be expressed by him or heard by them. A silent sound was his connection to people. He thought there was something noble about good deeds that went unknown, and was not wise to the tissue damage of resentment they left on him. He liked the idea of the small actions that accounted for only a few precious hours here and there but suggested a life lived on its own terms. *I fish the Hudson at Harlem Beach every Sunday morning* was a preferable thing to have known about someone than *I live a mere act of survival, in turmoil at the things I cannot cope with.*

Jack experienced a palpable, innate excitement on entering the reading room, a threat to his composure, an offering of childhood made to him a decade late. It was the place he could recall the ecstasy of learning. To study had been life in freefall pleasure for Jack. Work was satisfying, but learning was on another level, and he worried that his continuing self-education was already confined to moments stolen from adult life. Jack still clung to the memory, in Pizza Express the night before he left for New York, of overhearing Finn tell Holly that his brother should be a time-traveller, not a businessman (to Finn, like many teenagers, any man in a suit was a businessman; there were no delineations between the professions) because for his mute, impenetrable sixteen-year-old brother to understand that history was Jack's true love was the greatest and least expected of offerings. The next day, he flew three thousand miles from it.

Jack returned to his bed, lay on his back in the tight cocoon of his duvet and sent a text to his baby brother on Dilly's number. The laziness of the day, the lifting of the burden of probate, the solid wall of flu-fuzz behind his eyes, all loosened him up and he texted without the usual detailed analysis of how to word himself with Finn, nor the accompanying self-doubt. *Finn, it's Jack. Hope you're having fun. Call me, was thinking about you.* By Jack's standards, this was a love letter. He was throwing himself at Finn.

Dilly didn't pass the message on because she and Finn were naked and in a sweet moment after the excellent moment, and Finn always went quiet upon mention of his brother. She didn't want Jack bulldozing their evening.

'You're so lovely,' she said to Finn.

'We've got to stop falling out,' he replied.

She looked puzzled. 'I don't think we do,' she said, softly. 'Not really.'

He thought she was joking. He glanced down at their glistening bodies and felt pleased with himself. She was such a robust lover that in their four months together his penis had become tougher and a little desensitised, all to the benefit of his staying power. And he was learning that oral sex, the conferring of, was a miracle of largesse that garnered undue appreciation. Dilly had taught him, from the get-go, to regard sex as a continuous stream to be dipped in and out of, to think of it as a wedding banquet, to indulge, pause, then indulge again. She had also weaned him off saying 'thank you' after intercourse. He had taken a few weeks to get out of the habit, but it was a huge improvement for her when he did.

Her breathing wavered now above the liquid surface of sleep. Cradled in the sugary opulence of sex and fine bedding, she enjoyed a few moments of peace before the tides dragged her back towards her own self-loathing. Her parents had brought her up to believe she could do anything with her life, but had neglected to suggest something in particular or to mention that endeavour was requisite. She stared at the ceiling and saw a vague, gloomy premonition of how her life might not turn out to be.

'Let's get drunk,' she said, knowing Finn so little.

An hour later, she exited the cab on Ludlow Street as if on to a red carpet. The Gay Hussar restaurant (page 78 of the guidebook, double-circled by Dilly) was almost full, a wall of noise. The owner was a tall, raven-haired woman wearing bright red lipstick and a polka-dot tea dress that hinted at a passion for swing dance. She led them to the table for four by the window that Dilly insisted on and warned them they'd have to share it when the place was full.

'This is the best table in the place,' Dilly whispered, implying previous visits that did not exist.

An old-time jukebox perched on the wall played the Squirrel Nut Zippers. Books torn and scuffed by love filled shelves too high to reach. Dilly pulled a Moleskine notepad from her clutch bag and ended its virginity by writing the words 'effortlessly shabby'. She stuck out her arm to block the owner, almost punching her in the womb. 'Can we get a pitcher of mojito?' she asked, impatiently. The owner narrowed her eyes, withered Dilly, and walked away.

'Not into cocktails,' Finn said.

'No, no, you have to, please, that's how I imagined it.' She sat upright, breathed in and smiled deliriously as she checked out the restaurant's contents, material and human.

The restaurant was filled with good noise, through which a waitress came to them, hidden behind the jug of mojito she carried with both hands. She was tiny, Japanese-looking and spoke with a pale, smoothly arched New York accent. She was polite and pretty, her hair held back by a single silver clip that sat at an angle. She wore a grey sleeveless dress that had the simplicity of a uniform.

'I LOVE her look...' Dilly said, as she watched the waitress go. She grinned at Finn, poured the drinks and patted the seat next to her. 'I'm so happy,' she sighed. He sat beside her and they kissed with the taste of the rum on their tongues and soon, in the blood-rush of snatched alcohol, they were groping beneath their menus, and she moaned in his ear her dreamy plans for their future.

'You're gonna have to sit opposite each other, we need the table.' The owner stood over them. Beside her stood a man who was exactly the kind of chic urban horse-whisperer Dilly pictured when she masturbated.

'They can have those two seats, I want my man next to me,' Dilly said, pointing to the seats opposite and already slurring a little.

'That doesn't work,' the woman said.

'It works, sure it works, two seats is all we're using.'

'You gotta sit on one table, two other people don't want to sit looking at two strangers.'

Finn disentangled himself and returned to his seat. The horse-whisperer took a seat next to Dilly and pitched a brief smile diagonally across the table in between Finn and Dilly. He was a little older than Dilly, maybe twenty-six or twenty-seven, and extremely good-looking, rugged, stylish. The Japanese waitress appeared and inflamed Dilly by kissing the man on both cheeks.

'Siouxsie coming?' the waitress asked.

'Yeah, I'm early,' the man said.

'Get you a beer?'

'Thanks, Amy.' He took a palm pilot from his breast pocket, Marlboro style, and slouched back on his chair to use it.

'I'm so getting one of those,' Dilly told the man, leaning across to him. The man smiled but kept it brief.

Finn went to the jukebox. On the graffiti-strewn wall, someone had written *The stars are my Chandelier*. He held the sides of the jukebox, kicked off with 'London Calling' and sang, perfectly in tune, word for word with Joe Strummer, beneath the volume of sound already in the place. His voice brought the Japanese waitress to a standstill as she passed close behind him. She watched him singing into the jukebox, her face at his chest height. Finn closed his eyes and pictured Steve Bachelor, the landlord of the Robinson Crusoe pub on the estate back home, who played Finn and his friends bands from the ancient past, the Clash and the Fall and the Ramones, when they were twelve years old, from a set of speakers aimed out of the windows of his flat above the pub on to the concrete yard where Finn and the other boys rode their bikes and made ghettos out of Steve Bachelor's doomed car restoration projects.

'Great voice…' The waitress's words yanked Finn back into the room. 'Where you from?' she asked.

'England,' he said. She was so tiny he felt the urge to crouch down. 'Where *you* from?'

'Queens.'

'I meant…' He stopped himself and felt like an unworldly fool.

She helped him out. 'My dad's Japanese.' She smiled and her skin smoothed across her cheekbones like pools of moonshine beneath the jet-black pupils of her eyes.

'What should I eat?' he said, to keep her a second longer.

She sized him up. 'The burger is pretty magnificent. You could handle it. Alternatively, you never regret a lamb shank polenta.'

Dilly poured the last of the mojito equally into her tumbler and Finn's, and placed the glasses side by side to check they were level. She pressed the empty pitcher against her forehead and looked through the glass at a distorted view of the women in the restaurant – their bodies, hair, clothes, accessories, their mannerisms – lustfully dissecting them and instinctively fashioning the edited highlights into one great evening, which would, ideally, be shared with a guy like the one on their table; good-looking, older than her, a match for her, interesting and effortlessly cool, working in graphic design. She was twenty-four years old for Christ's sake; she was ready now for the sort of life a man like him would bring to her, although she doubted if he would ever want her the way Finn did, and that was a lot to give up.

As Finn returned, Dilly squeezed out between the tables, gripping the handsome guy's shoulders and grazing her pubic bone against his broad, muscular back. 'Need more booze,' she said, 'gotta keep this show on the road.' She squeezed the man's biceps. 'Look at you!' she said, 'I mean, you can be, like, a graphic designer or something and have muscles like this. It's the only thing I miss about this fucked-up country.' She pointed at Finn. 'He's got the muscles but that's it.'

Finn bowed his head. The handsome guy watched Dilly being ignored at the bar, a detail that told him all was right in the world. 'I guess I have no idea why she thinks I'm a graphic designer.'

'She lives in hope that everybody is,' Finn said.

Dilly returned, throttling a bottle of wine by the neck. She poured three glasses and slid one of them in front of the guy, who pushed the glass an inch back in her direction before taking a swig of his beer. The man's girlfriend arrived and Dilly became sullen. Finn watched the third glass of wine sit in the no man's land between the two couples. It made him uneasy. He stretched out his leg and tapped Dilly's ankle with his foot, in the hope of encouraging her to angle her body back towards him. Dilly ignored him and looked expectantly at the couple and Finn realised, with dread, that she was drunk, and waiting to be introduced by a man who didn't know her to a woman who knew her less.

'You remember Angela?' the girlfriend said to her man, as she took her seat.

'Sure,' he said.

'I just bumped into her. She quit documentaries and she's a rap artist now and we can go see her tomorrow night at Lambs to the Slaughter.'

Dilly leaned towards Finn and whispered loudly, 'That's what I want! Isn't that great? One minute you're a film-maker, the next you're a rapper? I want that.'

The girlfriend angled her chair away, so that every sinew and nuance of her body told Dilly to fuck off. Finn needed no instruction on how to ignore people whose drinking left him fearful of their next move. He turned his attention to the view outside of a gap on Ludlow Street where a building had been demolished. The site hoarding was covered in fliers and in front of them the sidewalk smokers were lit by blue neon light spilling from the bar and grill alongside.

The Japanese waitress came over. She and the girlfriend hugged and rocked.

'You look so sexy tonight, Soooze!'

'Thank you, Aimz!'

Dilly mimed being sick. She filled her glass. Finn looked down at the waitress's tiny feet, at the small tendons outlined beneath her pale grey canvas plimsolls, at the way she balanced on one leg, tapping her calf muscle with the non-standing foot, and he logged her name. Amy.

'Cozy,' Amy said, addressing the object of Dilly's thinly hidden lust, 'if you're ever looking for a singer, this guy has an awesome voice.' She pointed at Finn.

'That right?' Cozy said.

'Not really...' Finn said, with the diffidence that had no traction in this city.

'You play?' the girlfriend asked. Finn shook his head and she slugged her beer and turned away, finding Finn's modesty irksome.

Dilly raised her head. It seemed unstable on her neck, a couple of kilos heavier than it had been pre-mojito. 'Cozy!' she exclaimed. 'That's an interesting name for a... for a name.'

The girlfriend tested her. 'After the drummer....'

Dilly shrugged and pulled a face. The name meant nothing.

79

'What drummer?' Finn asked.

'Cozy Powell,' Cozy said. 'He was a drummer in the seventies and eighties. My dad was a roadie for him. Worshipped him.'

'It's a great name,' Finn said.

'It is,' Cozy's girlfriend said.

Dilly shrugged. 'The past doesn't cut much ice with me.'

'He can play "Dance with the Devil" out of his nostrils and it sounds like a full drum kit,' the girlfriend said, to annoy Dilly, and because it was true.

'But I'm not gonna.' Cozy smiled.

Dilly snorted. 'Men are so repressed. You won't drum; he won't ever sing for me even if I milk him dry.'

Finn bowed his head. The table fell silent. Dilly slumped for a moment, then scraped her chair back and marched outside. She made her way along a line of smokers on the sidewalk and bummed a cigarette. Finn had never seen her smoke before.

'How old are you?' Cozy asked Finn.

'Nineteen.'

'How is being nineteen in 2006?'

'Better than eighteen in 2005. When were you last nineteen?'

'Ten years ago.'

Finn filled a tumbler with water and slid it into Dilly's place to await her return. He glanced at Cozy, who was watching him.

'Sorry about...' Finn motioned towards Dilly's empty chair.

'No need,' Cozy said.

'You and her...' the girlfriend, Siouxsie, said, 'it's kind of like watching Buzz Lightyear dating Cruella de Vil. How come you met?'

Finn thought about this a while, then shrugged. 'Just lucky, I guess.'

Cozy smiled, then laughed.

'You're alright,' Siouxsie said, tossing her hair back, and nodding her approval.

Dilly returned to her seat, re-energised. 'I'm sorry, I was crass. I apologise. Hey, I am going to sit in this place and write a novel. I love it here.'

'I thought you were going to rap,' Siouxsie said.

'Maybe so. Maybe so. I'll write the whole thing here, and it'll be like an unhindered, brilliant stream of consciousness, not held back by normal narrative rules, just a flow. It'll be very quick to do and it'll be non-edited, not even the typos. I'm not wasting my time on all that crap when I'm writing for the cellphone generation. Like a Lars von Trier approach to the Great American Novel. I'll do book signings here, where I wrote it, put this place on the map.'

It wasn't clear who she was talking to. It was only clear that she was talking.

The check was a reminder to Finn that he was poor. Dilly watched a bead of sweat form on his forehead as he read the numbers and she, as if her greatest gift was to never cease to amaze, sobered up and held her purse beneath the table and discreetly took out a sheaf of twenties and slipped the notes into Finn's hand. She got up and headed unsteadily for the restroom, stopping to whisper in his ear, 'You take care of it.' And, save for the detail of the whispered words, Cozy had taken all this in, and told himself that he had judged her harshly.

'You like music?' Cozy asked.

'I'm nineteen.'

'There's a band on now,' Cozy said. 'You two should stay.'

'Thanks,' Finn said. 'You two are cool.'

'She is, I'm not,' Cozy said.

Through a wall of thick brown drapes, the restaurant opened into a small venue with an old tiled hose-down bar and burgundy-painted walls covered in fliers: GUSTAFER

YELLOWGOLD'S WIDE WILD WORLD, GRETCHEN WITT, FREE MUSIC FESTIVAL FEATURING 3PM LA, VERNISSAGE SONGWRITERS SERIES, ABI TAPIA, JIM CAMPILONGO ELECTRIC TRIO, THE ANIMATORS, KRISTIN DIABLE, SPOTTISWOODE & HIS ENEMIES, ALL NIGHT CHEMISTS.

Above the bar a collection of old tin trays were stuck flat to the wall like dartboards; SPARKLING ROCK SPRING WATER, SCHLITZ, WILLIAM YOUNGER, BALLANTINE ALE AND BEER, HAMM'S (a canoeist gliding through an impossibly blue canyon river), BLATZ (America's 'great light beer'), PEOPLE'S BEER ('it hits the spot'). Dilly threaded her arm through Cozy's and gazed at the trays. 'Don't you think the graphics are perfect?' she said. Nothing, but nothing, was going to shake her belief that Cozy worked in this field.

'Classic...' Cozy said, going along with her version of the universe.

Siouxsie handed out four beers and a band tuned up. A trickle of people entered the parted drapes. Dilly put her beer down on the bar and slid it away. 'Of all the people in the whole world I wish could be like, it's Nico.'

'She's dead,' Cozy said.

'Don't let that put her off,' Siouxsie said, and wrapped her arms around Cozy's waist and stroked his buttocks.

'Did you do that interview?' Cozy asked her.

'Yes,' she said, 'it was fine.'

'What interview – are you famous?' Dilly asked.

'No. It was just a local art publication, that's all. I make decorative glass. It was just a super-fast thing.'

'What did they ask?'

'Just random stuff. Favourite things.'

'Ask me. What did they ask? Ask me. Interview Dilly.'

Siouxsie looked her dead in the eye. 'When did you first start using glass as a medium?'

Dilly looked confused then grinned. 'Nooooo! That doesn't work. Something about ME!'

Siouxsie drawled a question, to placate her. 'What living person do you most admire?'

'And it's meant to be arty answers?'

'It's meant to be the truth.'

'Frida Kahlo, definitely.'

'You're not a reader of the obituaries...' Siouxsie muttered.

'What?' Dilly said.

'Living...' Cozy reminded her.

'Oh, if she's dead, then Mary Portas.'

'Who?!' the Americans asked.

'Mary Queen of Shops! She's English and she transforms crappy little clothes shops into really great businesses and she's very cool for an older woman sort of thing. I heard her interviewed and thought, yeah, yeah, you know what, I have time for you, lady, I could be you in a hundred years' time.'

Cozy looked blank. Siouxsie turned to Finn and shoved an imaginary microphone beneath his chin.

'Finn....! The living person you most admire?'

Finn pointed at Cozy. 'Him.'

The three of them laughed, lazy, drunken laughs.

'Why is that funny? You don't even know him?' Dilly smiled but looked lost.

'Just is,' Cozy said, and set up four glasses of Jack Daniel's with the barman. People squared up to the stage in readiness. Cozy and Finn chinked glasses covertly, with body language that announced an intent to have a good night and not give a damn. Dilly poured her liquor equally into the other three glasses, handed her empty glass to Finn and shoved her way to the front of the crowd, where she stood motionless and stared without expression at the lead singer.

The set came and went and was the kind of okay that liquor made good. Finn shadow-drank throughout, using the movement of people around him to tip on to the floor more than passed his lips. Siouxsie put her arms around Cozy and Finn and smiled provocatively as Dilly returned to them and Dilly hated her with all the strength she had, which suddenly felt like not enough strength to survive New York City.

'You guys should come back to our apartment and have a little smoke,' Siouxsie said.

Dilly snorted disdainfully. 'Sure, where is your apartment, 1973?'

'Yeah,' Siouxsie drawled, ''cos smoking weed was a real seventies-only thing.'

Crowds would have flocked to see the two of them mud-wrestle.

In the cab, Dilly grew melancholy. They crossed the water to Williamsburg and the wind billowed in through the windows. Finn's delight at not knowing where the hell they were was identical in its force to Dilly's fear of not knowing, and her despair at wanting so much from any given moment that she felt perpetually poor.

Williamsburg was dark and quiet by the shore. The cab pulled up on Kent Avenue and Finn watched the lights of Manhattan shape-shift in the black waters of the East River, which sat like an oil slick covertly powering the island by night. Dilly loitered in the back of the cab and pulled Finn back.

'I'm gonna take this cab on back to the hotel, but you should stay and have fun.'

Instantly, he didn't mind the idea, but he said, 'There's no way I'm leaving you.'

'I don't wanna spoil your fun, but it's not for me.'

'I'll come back with you, no worries.'

'Look, Finny-boy, I don't wanna rain on your parade with your new best buddies,' she said with venom. 'And the thing is, I actually want to go back alone. Tomorrow's another day. I'm giving you my blessing.'

He dropped his shoulders in fake devastation while the sweet buzz of imminent emancipation rose through his glands. The cab took Dilly away and Finn looked across the water at the metropolitan meadow of lights and inside himself he felt a child's laughter at fairy lights, and he suspected that tonight would be good, and he felt he could protect anyone who needed him, and fight anyone who deserved it, and drink without getting drunk. And he wished Jack could see him now.

They sat on plastic deckchairs on the roof of the apartment building in the early hours. Manhattan was ablaze and silent. They got high on a gentle curve, with the fresh river breeze. Neighbours joined them and the conversation rose and there was laughter but Finn was too happy to contribute, and listening felt just fine. A man and a woman pulled up their seats and introduced themselves to Finn and told him about a book they were writing called *Dusty & Co.* The front cover was to be a photograph of an urn and the whole book about the personal health problems, physical flaws, frailties, addictions and the manner of death of the world's great dictators and despots. An epilogue would describe the graves of these people. An appendix would detail the human decomposition process. 'It will be the ultimate bringer of perspective,' they said, and added that they were persuading a very rich old woman on the Upper East Side to fund the buying of couture for a book of photographs of designer clothes and jewellery modelled by terminally ill people. Finn started laughing, a naughty, nervous, childish giggle, fuelled by the couple's earnestness. It made Cozy laugh too and Finn discovered the hysteria that fed on itself and could not be stopped, that spread into every corner of your body like a forest fire. He had never known it before. It made him feel sick and happy. The prospective authors of *Dusty & Co.* were as confused as Finn and Cozy were crippled.

More people arrived, and all had the same watery eyes that oozed tiredness and love. Chairs and upturned crates appeared for them out of nowhere. Siouxsie danced by herself. Later she played a game, taking Polaroids of people's naked feet and seeing who could match the feet to the person.

'You two are like the Clonnie-and-Byde of making people feel good,' Finn told Cozy.

'Do you know how cool you are?' Cozy said.

Finn shook his head in disbelief that life could possibly feel so great. He watched Siouxsie stop her dancing and move across the roof and throw her arms around someone and as they let go of each other Finn saw that it was Amy, the waitress from the Gay Hussar, and he sat up and rubbed his face and ruffled his hair, and he looked again and she looked even smaller and prettier than before. She disappeared into the apartment and returned carrying two bottles of beer. She dragged a chair behind her across the rooftop to Finn and handed him one of the beers. 'Cold one?' she asked.

He thanked her and got up from his seat as she sat in hers and it made his head spin a little and her heart skip a beat.

It struck Finn that life was so fucking beautiful when it was beautiful and you were nineteen and high and three thousand miles from your uncle and you thought you were ready to sleep but then the hit of a cold beer on the back of your throat was like a night's sleep and a cold shower. Amy's arm brushed against his the first time she raised the bottle to her mouth, so delicately that he could feel the tiny hairs on her skin touch the hairs on his forearm. She allowed this to happen each time she drank, the lightest of glances against a body that had taken many blows. She pulled her tiny feet up on to her seat and hugged her knees, and they both looked out and enjoyed the view of the toy city and the enormous future.

When Finn woke, the plastic chair had buckled slightly to cradle the shape of his coiled body. The sun was coming up. Cozy was asleep nearby and Finn had the feeling Cozy had stayed out on the roof to watch over him. He observed the minute-by-minute change in the colour of the skyline where the first cool streaks made a blue lava lamp of the highest part of the sky and the glass surfaces of midtown. The roof was warm in sunshine by the time Amy appeared and stretched and yawned, compact and neat already, and impossibly pretty. She made coffee and she and Finn sat on the edge of the roof with their legs dangling over the side, sixty feet above Kent Avenue. The soles of his feet tingled. She left for her day job and he wanted to ask for her number but felt that he should not (because there was, you know, Dilly of course) and then, before he could decide the right thing to do, she said to him, 'You know where to find me.'

Williamsburg slept like a village. Finn dragged his tired limbs uphill to the L Train. Outside a bar that did not seem long closed was a bench made out of a mooring post from the East River, a massive hunk of beaten wood bolted to two blocks of concrete. He sat on it and took in the view. To the west of Kent Avenue was a flattened concrete wasteland and one huge white warehouse standing surrounded by a great rubble lawn banking down to the East River. In the midst of it stood a man with a sledgehammer and a wheelbarrow, looking as if he had dismantled the waterfront single-handedly. It made Finn smile. The buildings and sidewalk either side of the Gotham Marble Works were caked in light grey dust and Finn watched as a breeze picked the dust up and sent it scuttling across the road. Cement trucks and demolition lorries lined the far side of the avenue further up, and four fat Hispanic site workers walked up 7th Street and passed two miniature Latin women entering the Built by Wendy clothes store. Laughter rang out from somewhere inside the Western Carpet & Linoleum factory and a man sat on a skateboard outside the factory listening to Spanish music in a suntrap.

Finn wandered on. Spray-painted in red, yellow and green on to a brick wall on 4th Street were the words 'Art + Sanity = Anarchy'. On Berry Street, two low factory buildings squatted side by side, one with its shutters open to show a display of high-priced, fine decorative glass bottles and jars. Orange glow and white light drew Finn to the threshold and among the slumping kilns he saw hip young things with sculpted stubble, blowing glass.

On the journey back on to Manhattan, as the L Train kicked on the rails and climbed a slope up off the riverbed, he suspected that Dilly would not be there when he got back. Sure enough, the hotel room was empty, but it took Finn a few moments to recognise that not only Dilly but her belongings were gone. On a sheet of SoHo Grand headed paper, resting on the pillow, she had written: *I am going home to my folks'. Come for the weekend as planned. I love you. I've settled the bill.*

She had written down her parents' address in Long Beach but not their number and he knew immediately that he had no intention of going there. And then he saw, in Dilly's deliberately tiny handwriting at the very bottom of the page, *I have your book. I'll give it back to you at Long Beach x.* He slumped on to the bed and jammed the palms of his hands against his face. It was something he used to do at the detention centre: press hard until spots of colour and light appeared in his eyes, creating an impression of outer space, a limitlessness inside his head he could escape to.

8

Jack could barely drag his body to the phone when Holly called from Atlanta at eleven, same as she did every morning. 'I'm glad you're still off work. You're being sensible about being ill, so thank you for that. Are you eating that food I left you?'

Jack paused. He hated lying. 'Yeah,' he said, as he slugged back another dose of cough mixture.

He lathered up his face but his hands were too shaky to use the razor. He washed off the foam and looked critically at his reflection. He refused to be seen like this. It drove him nuts that Finn didn't have a cell that worked in the US. It meant another text to his girlfriend's number, which Finn could ignore, or writing a note, and he felt ungifted when it came to the written word.

Finn – I am not fighting fit and cannot meet up. Sorry but that's life. Hopefully tomorrow. Please take the enclosed in the meantime. J.

This was the fifth, tortured draft. Despite the cartload of mucus in his head, Jack still had room for doubt as to whether his note should be addressed to Dilly as well, so that Finn didn't feel he was snubbing her. But he was not willing to risk Finn thinking the five hundred bucks in the envelope was in any part for her when it was solely for his brother to enjoy, to live off, to make him feel loved and looked after.

The carpeted hush of his building on a weekday mid-morning was a cosmos unknown to Jack. It blended uneasily with the flu-buzz in his head. He challenged himself to get from the apartment to the elevator without a coughing fit but failed. Life was a series of self-imposed examinations for Jack, all set at a fractionally unattainable level. The wad of notes slid back and forth in the envelope as he walked, with a dragging sound like a man in slippers behind him. A memory glanced against him, of his father wearing slippers around the house at a time of day when a boy wanted his dad to be dressed and wearing shoes.

Jack's least favourite doorman, Eddy, was in the lobby.

'Is Connor on?' Jack asked.

Eddy took skilled offence at this, which Jack exacerbated by hesitating before handing over the envelope, a mistake Finn would pay for later.

'Why don't you ever call me Eddy? You never address me by name, like you do Connor and Julius.'

Because you're a dickhead, Jack did not say.

'My brother is coming by to see me – can you give that to him, please? Make it clear, absolutely clear that I am not well enough to see him and I'll call him tomorrow.'

'You don't wanna see him. Got it.'

'I'm not *well enough* to see him. There's a difference.'

'Sure thing.'

Eddy the doorman had arrived from Vermont twenty years earlier and done all the right things to become a successful comedian. There wasn't a Chevy Chase movie he didn't know scene by scene, a Steve Martin DVD he hadn't studied line by line, a Bill Hicks routine he hadn't been bewildered by and convinced himself wasn't really comedy. Notepad after notepad of *Saturday Night Live*-style Vermont-centric material was filled. Not out-and-out funny, that wasn't what he was aiming for, but observational, you know, universal… the sort of thing that made you smile rather than laugh, more intelligent material than mere laughs. He wasn't asking to be a star – although he would have liked a little more recognition for schlepping the open mics – staff writing would have been enough. But it never happened for him and it took him too long to realise why, and when he pursued Sarah Copeland for a date (Sarah was his first unrequited crush back home and he discovered she'd moved to New York City and was working for an investment bank) and he heard her ask him, over an exquisite pork belly he paid for that night, 'Eddy, do you ever think comedy is maybe not where your talents lie?' he resolved to prove her wrong but also joined an employment agency and it was them who had landed him in this goddam awful doorman's uniform which made his neck itch and – this would have taught her a lesson – he never called Sarah fucking Copeland again, the overconfident, overpaid, opinionated little whore.

If there was one thing that Eddy the doorman hated, it was seeing the light of hope not yet extinguished in the young. Which meant that Finn was fucked the moment he walked into the building.

'He's busy. He can't fit you in.' Eddy handed the envelope over.

Finn had jogged ninety blocks and felt good for it, but had anticipated taking a shower at Jack's place. He read his brother's note and sized up the maths involved in a pile of twenty-dollar bills as thick as this one.

'Is he in?'

'Oh, yeah, he's right upstairs.'

'Buzz him, will you?' Finn said. 'Let him know I'm here.'

'He expressly asked me not to do that.'

Finn felt like a fool and cursed himself for letting the doorman see it. He remembered those kids on the estate who showed their weakness, the ones who hesitated, those who cried. He had studied them so that he would never walk in their shoes, had locked in his mind their sad faces and their names which they had allowed to become a mockery in the short-term mythology of a sink estate. David Callahan and Kevin Plowman. He would never allow himself to be one of those guys, never show the doubt or fear, even when he found himself trapped in the worst possible narratives of the underbelly of a fucked-up seaside town in the depths of winter. And how it had paid off for Finn when it came to his uncle, who for three years had battered at the door to him and never got in. His uncle had merely spilled blood, and gone halfway insane in the process, yet himself wept so readily when Finn rained down the blows on him in one single act of revenge, one comprehensive farewell paid in secret while his girlfriend packed and their plane to New York City was prepared. Davey Cal and Kev the Plough, Finn had those boys to thank for knowing right now not to show another hint of weakness to this doorman on a morning like this when both his girlfriend, the best distraction he'd ever found, better even than the pain of training, and his unfathomable absent brother had left him alone on the streets of what he would call, in honour of his absent abbreviating lover, NYC. He was trained for this moment; he was over-trained. And, if his uncle hadn't already bitten a large piece of it back home, unfunny-Eddy from Vermont might have been in danger right now.

He pulled a twenty-dollar bill out from the wad, enough to see President Jackson's quiff, and toyed briefly with the idea of keeping a few notes. But Jack would notice, and Finn did not want Jack to know that he needed the money and Finn's next thought, that Jack might presume he'd counted the money out wrong, was laughable. Jack didn't make mistakes like that.

He re-sealed the envelope with the five hundred bucks inside. 'Are there letterboxes?'

'If you mean mailboxes, sure.' Eddy said. 'But… I can take it.' Eddy held his hand out.

Finn looked at Eddy. He had no idea if this man could be trusted or what the form was here. He knew only that he felt like an idiot because his own brother's door was closed to him and this man knew it. Finn smiled at Eddy, his charming, vulnerable, beautiful, green-eyed smile, and took the envelope to the mailboxes. The blood rose in him once he was outside, the seething, pathetic, angry wave that made him want to explode into pieces. He kicked a dent in a newspaper box. A man fifteen feet away recoiled and hurried on.

Down Third Avenue, ten blocks' worth of traffic lights spawned a moment's silence on the Upper East Side and deepened Finn's sense of abandonment. He had not imagined Manhattan capable of tranquillity. He studied his *Streetwise* and Glenn's note. His jeans were rolled up, the hems above his ankles. He ran again, with the map tucked into his back pocket, springing from the balls of his feet, jogging to the cross streets and striding out between the avenues, making his way diagonally across town towards Chelsea. When no one was nearby, he ducked and jabbed, and stabbed sharp breaths out of his throat. Between 22nd and 23rd Streets, the deep rust of an abandoned elevated train line disappeared behind a red-brick townhouse like a trick of the mind. It made Finn think of *Belleville Rendez-Vous*, his joint best film of 2005. (He categorised films by the year he saw them, not by the year they were released, a system that led to anomalies such as his top two films of 2002 being *City of God* and *Straw Dogs*.) It was one of those New York mornings when most things Finn saw reminded him of a movie. Glenn's boss at the Chelsea Piers was Luis Guzmán out of *Boogie Nights*, but only facially because south of the mouth there was even more of Glenn's boss than there was of Luis Guzmán. His body filled the doorway at the top of an external metal staircase to the Pier 59 service building. Finn divulged his name and the fact that he wasn't from New York City (which did not seem to astonish Glenn's boss) and explained that he was here to take Glenn's dishwashing job while Glenn was 'away' and that he would need paying in cash as he was not here on a work visa. Also, he'd need time off to go to Long Beach to visit his girlfriend's family.

Fatter Guzmán stared at Finn and flared his nostrils. 'What the hell,' he sighed, 'there's no meat on the bone here,' and walked away.

Finn stuck around. He'd seen enough movies to know this could work out. An hour later, Guzmán nearly tripped over him on the steps. 'Come inside,' the big man said. He sat Finn down and poured him a coffee. 'Drink this,' he said, 'then it's *adiós*. I haven't got a job for you. That situation will not be changing. And I'd be careful how many people you tell you're looking for work without documentation, you know what I'm saying.'

Finn retraced his steps eastwards, looking like a small-town cowboy as he gawped through the expansive windows of converted warehouse buildings, slowly realising that the insides were full of what he guessed people called art. Two water towers on a roof stood out in weatherbeaten brown against the blue sky and made him think of the feed-stores on the Sussex farms back home. In the windows of the Bovenkamp Gallery, a painting caught his eye. Entitled *Route 3A* and attributed to an artist called Dot Yi, the picture was of a row of open doors leading to long corridors, but painted on a relief surface at exaggerated angles so that, when Finn moved from side to side, the painting appeared to move in 3-D.

His mouth fell open. He shut it again pretty quick, but admitted to himself that this thing wasn't bad.

Inside the gallery, the twenty-three-year-old woman who described herself as Richard Bovenkamp's PA but was in fact his trainee receptionist watched Finn sway from side to side on the sidewalk to activate the illusion on the canvas, and sneered at his foolishness. As Finn noticed her, she refined the sneer into a pained smile, a smile that Finn immediately interpreted as a look of attraction. Although it was at odds with his innate modesty, the truth was that, in suddenly being inducted into the ranks of the sexually hyper-active, Finn couldn't help thinking nowadays that many women he saw were looking at him with at least a modest dollop of sexual desire and that they knew that he was having sex on a daily basis, and not always horizontally (a detail he still found prestigious).

He took another glimpse at the receptionist. She was remarkable to look at, like a twenty-year-old Meryl Streep, beautiful in an untouchable way, flawless in what Dilly could have told him was a Stella McCartney hound's-tooth-tweed drop-waist coat. She was elegant, and she was large. Really large. Big-boned. Perfectly proportioned. Finn had never really seen a woman so finely tuned in her appearance as to make a tall, powerful frame seem so refined. A large, young Meryl Streep was what she was. Big-boned Meryl. Beryl. That was who she was: Beryl, spiritual big-boned daughter of Meryl, and that was as great a compliment as Finn could imagine giving, because Meryl Streep was awesome in *Adaptation* and by a distance the most attractive elderly woman he could think of. He stepped away, took the *Streetwise* from his back pocket and tried to locate himself. Behind his back, Beryl laughed at Finn for having looked at her as if he stood a chance.

From across the street, in the window of Emerson Fine Arts, Leo Emerson observed Beryl's disdain and asked himself how he had ever possessed the bravery to have lovers. Leo was fifty-four years old, had slept with thirty-seven women in his lifetime, the last of them nine years ago, and wore a Paul Smith suit picked for him by his PA, inside of which he lived gripped by disbelief that he had somehow gotten so old and alone.

'Mr Emerson?'

This was the voice of the seventh or eighth (Leo had lost count) interviewee he had seen in the past fortnight. The voice came from somewhere behind him and sounded eager (ten per cent less eager than the woman who had sat on the same seat an hour earlier and precisely as eager as the man Leo had interviewed yesterday). Like the others, this interviewee had a degree in art history and an awareness that Leo was not paying attention; but, unlike the others, this one believed that being a trainee PA in any gallery was beneath him and was in no mood to take any shit.

On the opposite side of the street, the FedEx truck-stop and the public parking lot were bathed in sunshine, and the young man outside the Bovenkamp Gallery seemed, as far as Leo could make out, to be stopping people on the sidewalk and showing them the Dot Yi in the window.

The interviewee resolved to ignore his prospective boss's indifference and the high tide of futility creeping up the walls of this West 26th Street space, the sort of space the interviewee craved to own by the age of thirty. He would instead comment on how wonderful the daylight was in the gallery and share his thoughts on the art of show-hanging (except he would call it a craft rather than an art) and his brave ideas on allowing natural light to dissipate into dark corners and to change over the course of the day, and how inspired he was by the Rothko room at Tate Modern in London, which was a perfect opportunity to reveal that he had been to Mr Emerson's country of origin without making a big deal of it.

'Leo…?' This was the voice of Astrid, Leo's PA.

Leo turned and smiled apologetically. 'Thanks so much for coming in. It's been a pleasure. Astrid will be in touch.'

The interviewee shifted irritably in his seat and said, 'You're kidding me.'

'Leo…' Astrid intervened, 'Mr Thwaites hasn't… you haven't interviewed him yet.'

'Uh-huh…' Leo smiled, distantly. 'Oh.' He looked out of the window again.

Mr Thwaites rose to his feet and put on his jacket with jagged movements. 'I don't need this,' he said, and approached Leo with the intention of saying 'fuck you' before something tripped in his head and he punched Leo in the stomach. It was not a powerful hit, but a decent effort for a fine arts grad. Leo watched young Mr Thwaites leave, from the floor, where he had landed, and felt his heart thudding for the first time in God knew how long. Astrid buzzed around him, performing a mime of someone offering assistance without being of any.

'Shall I call your lawyer or something?'

'No. I'm alright. In fact, so far he's my favourite.' He rose to his feet and dusted himself down. He went to the window to gather himself and watched the boy across the street, who now had three young women slanting their bodies back and forth with him, ooh-ing and aah-ing at the 3-D painting.

'What's he dooooing?' Astrid was standing beside him. (She had an ability to appear at Leo's side without him hearing her.)

A thin, faint whine of laughter sneaked out from the roof of Leo's mouth as he watched the boy. 'Being young and enjoying a painting… I guess.'

'He looks ridiculous,' she muttered.

'He has taste. I'm thinking of buying a Dot Yi.'

Astrid looked appalled. 'You never told me.'

'Did I not?'

Finn and the women said their goodbyes and he took a few steps down the street. Behind the twelve-foot fencing of the Suffolk Street parking lot was a tarred shed. It reminded Finn of home, of his dad's shed at the foot of the garden, the tedious shed of a man who never made anything or repaired anything but needed yet another place in which to hide from his family. There came from memory the smell of melting creosote in an English summer. The door to the shed was open and trembling in a breeze from the Hudson. Inside, a newspaper fluttered at the corners and a Thermos of coffee held down a pile of receipts. Beneath a work bench, half-hidden by a blackened Dickies jacket, was a metal cash box with a key standing in the lock on the lid like a ballerina on a music box. Finn took a hard look at the parking lot. He saw no one. In a fractional moment, when the warmth of the sun hit his cheekbones, and the universe consisted of nothing other than the information his eyes had snapped in the last thirty seconds, a decision was made which demanded of Finn only that he did not hesitate or doubt. He moved gracefully across the tarmac and into the shed. He opened the box, grabbed a handful of notes and slipped them into his back pocket. He marched away, looking down at his feet, as if what he couldn't see couldn't catch him. He crossed the street and stood at the window of Leo Emerson's gallery, pretending to look inside. He let out a lungful of air and his breath was corrugated by fear. He felt the sun on his back and that his feet were rooted to the sidewalk and his legs were shaking.

Leo had felt life detaching itself from him in recent years. He lived with the impression that he was watching the world play out in front of him on a screen, out of reach. Now, this sensation had reached its zenith with the boy on the other side of the glass acting out something remarkable and notorious and fictional. The parking lot attendant appeared and the boy responded by walking into Leo's gallery where he pretended to look at the art, while hiding half his face beneath a shock of jet-black hair.

'Feel free to ask me anything you'd like to know about the work,' Astrid called out.

Finn looked at Miguel Santos's *Sleeping With Myself, Context IV* and said to himself, She calls this work?

'Thanks,' he muttered.

Between the paintings, Finn cast glances across to the parking lot where no drama seemed to be unfolding. Leo detected the boy's lack of confidence in what he'd done and saw hope in that.

'English?' Leo asked him.

Finn stopped, as if caught red-handed. 'How d'you know?'

'You sound it.'

'I haven't said anything.'

'You said "thanks" to my assistant.'

Finn glanced and saw that the parking lot attendant was standing on the sidewalk, with his hands on his hips, looking perplexed as he surveyed the street. 'You English too?' Finn said, not taking his eyes off the scene outside.

'Well… yes, once upon a time, but this is home.'

The parking attendant stared in Finn's direction. Whether he could be seen through the glass, Finn wasn't sure, but talking to this old English guy seemed like a good idea, if he could think of anything to say.

'Pretty lucky to live here…' he ventured.

'Maybe lucky, maybe I worked hard.'

'Lots of people work hard and don't get to live in New York City,' Finn said, distracted.

'You make your own luck,' Leo said.

The parking lot attendant stepped out on to the tarmac. Finn watched him closely and muttered, 'If you make it, it's not luck.'

'What are you doing here?' Leo asked him.

'Here in this shop or here in New York?'

'It's a gallery, not a shop. New York City.'

'I know this guy who lives here and he's in prison so he said I could use his place and so…' Finn stopped. That story never came out right. 'Are these paintings for sale?'

'Of course.'

'So how come it isn't a shop?'

Leo fell silent. He felt unsure of himself. He didn't know people who stole and had friends in prison.

'A paintings shop,' Finn said, to be clear.

'Gallery is just what everyone calls them...' Leo faltered, and then saw a grin transform the boy's face, turning him from villain to child.

'I know,' Finn said. 'Ignore me, I'm in a mood.'

Leo looked curiously at Finn and, finding the old man's silence weird, Finn smiled politely and left.

Leo watched the boy step out into the sunshine and head east, half-disappearing in the glare of the sidewalk. A small, barely noticeable gap opened up in Leo's thoughts, prised open by the sun, an opportunity he couldn't make out. But, whatever it was, it was different and, for Leo Emerson, something different was the most covetable of possessions right now, the one thing missing from his collection.

He followed the boy out. 'Young man!'

Finn turned.

'Do you need work?'

Finn nodded.

'Would you like to come and work in my shop?'

Finn eyed Leo with suspicion, took a look across to the parking lot. 'You need someone?'

'I wouldn't be asking if I didn't.'

'For money and everything?'

'More than you can afford to say no to.'

'What if I didn't have a visa?' Finn said.

'You don't have one,' Leo replied. 'One condition.'

Finn took a step back and looked away. 'Here we go...'

Leo walked towards him and said in a firm, hushed voice, 'You do not steal from *me*.'

There was silence. Finn nodded, and looked embarrassed. Pleasantly surprised by the boy's lack of guile, Leo turned to face the sun. He took a deep breath and shut his eyes and felt the warmth on his face and the shock of the new, and doubted those who said there was another cold snap to come before a longed-for spring. 'You like that painting opposite?' he asked.

Finn didn't like the idea that he had been watched. 'Not really into paintings.'

'You're into that one, though.'

Finn shrugged. 'It's alright.'

'My name is Leo.'

Finn nodded.

'Now you tell me your name. That's how it works.'

'Finn.'

Leo strolled back to his gallery. 'Come on,' he called, playfully. He hadn't been playful for years. The boy's suspicion amused him. 'Astrid, this is Finn and he's starting work with us today. You can stand the others down.'

Finn loitered near to the entrance, unable to take seriously the idea of working in a place like this, with people like these two. He put his hand into his back pocket and felt the bills.

'Stand down those others with their history of art degrees?' Astrid asked.

'Yes, them,' Leo said, beckoning Finn to the desk. 'Show him the ropes. I'm going for some tea.'

'Maybe this isn't a great idea,' Finn said.

'I agree,' Astrid said.

'Maybe,' Leo said to Finn, and turned to Astrid. 'Show him,' he said, firmly.

Leo strolled to Ninth Avenue, aware that he was bold enough to hire the boy, but too cowardly to stay while Astrid knocked him into shape. He took his seat in the corner of the Maison Claudine pâtisserie, where he was a regular and where, two years earlier, the stark recognition that the possibility of marriage and family had slipped through his fingers and left him in a weightless bachelorhood had reduced him to trembling wreckage and he had escaped out on to a side street, where Madame Claudine had found him suffering an apparent heart attack. He sat here now with the strong beating heart that his physician had found no fault in and turned his attention to the arrival for her shift of a particular waitress and the movement of her elegant, thick-set body between square wooden tables painted the same matt black as the walls and ceiling. He watched her thighs brush against the tables and felt them send a vibration that only he could detect through gold-rimmed plates imported from Montpellier, tiered silver trays bearing jars of home-made jam (today, *framboise*, *cerise noire* and *abricot*), hand-written menu cards, pale orange napkins with silhouettes of nineteenth-century ladies promenading beside the Seine, pots of white and brown sugar cubes and ceramic dishes of unsalted butter. Each of these objects delivered to Leo the shivering, whispering message that *she* had arrived. Leo watched as she hung her coat on a hook in the narrow corridor that separated the tea room from the kitchens. Her actions were identical every day, yet somehow her routine simmered with potential to the same degree that his lacked any.

The waitress's name was Willow. She had never introduced herself but Leo had overheard Madame Claudine address her. When he daydreamed of being with her it was not an image he saw, not a snapshot of domestic paradise or the erotic charge, but a feeling of worth gained by being good for her and by meaning something to her. She placed the check on his table, smiling inwardly in anticipation of the man's customary generosity. While savouring the last vestiges of her smell, real or imagined, Leo looked at the familiar figure of Bellini's *St Francis in the Desert*, arms outstretched amid rocky outcrops. The poster of the saint was set into a garish, thick, round carved gold frame with silver-sprayed butterflies stuck to the sides, a spotted bow-tie pinned to the top and a fine silk doily dressing the bottom of the frame like a mini-skirt. This manner of decorative embellishment was the signature of the café's owner, Claudine Ardant. From Bellini, Leo's attention drifted to the antique frosted glass door of the café, on which was etched the number 238a, in reverse. Beyond that, in the frosted movement of pedestrians on Ninth Avenue, he found a place to settle distantly into his fantasies of Willow.

An hour later, he returned to work and was met by the sound of belly laughter, a noise not traditionally resident when he and Astrid were alone in the gallery. He found Astrid hiding in the kitchen.

'Is the boy alright?' Leo asked.

'I don't know,' she replied, with unusual meekness.

'What have you done with him?'

'I made him read all the catalogues from the last year's shows, so he knows our artists...'

'And how is he doing? He can read?'

'He keeps laughing.'

Leo peered round the corner into the gallery at the exact moment Finn threw his head back and roared, flapping the catalogue like an oriental fan and dropping it on to the desk.

'Everything alright?' Leo asked.

'Who writes this stuff?'

'Me...' Leo said. 'I do.'

'It's hilarious,' Finn said, turning to his boss.

'Read me a humorous bit,' Leo said, daring to approach.

'Uh-uh.' Finn stood up and rolled his shoulders loose. His arms seemed long and elastic and powerful. 'It's all horse-shit to sell the paintings, right?'

'Exactly right,' Leo said, stoically.

'Okay,' Finn said. 'Got it. But I can't talk like that.'

Astrid's voice came from off-stage. 'You won't be talking to anyone.'

Leo had no idea what to do with the boy. He was still struggling for ideas at four o'clock when he left work early, leaving Astrid to close the gallery and see the boy on his way. The first streaks of pink bled into a pale afternoon sky and Leo found himself rooted to the sidewalk. A familiar thought returned to him: that he could afford to stop. He could close his business and devote the rest of his life to doing good things for charitable causes without having to give up One Lex or a single facet of his lifestyle. He would make no such life change, of course, in the same way that he would never sail in the bay, learn Spanish or read *American Fine Art Magazine* from cover to cover, and in the time it took to unfold his Brompton he realised two things: that his love affair with art and with Chelsea was fading, which did not alarm him; and that he was a coward, which did.

He walked his bicycle to the 303 Gallery and in the back room found himself transfixed, not by Inka Essenhigh's canvasses, which he would have admired greatly had he remembered to look at them, but by a four o'clock April moon ascending into view, framed by the first of two skylights in the roof. He stared at the moon as if it had something to tell him. He was lost. Nearby, a woman was crying on a friend's shoulder. Snivelling and angry behind horn-rimmed glasses and cherry-coloured lipstick, she said, 'If I hear another person say "it's Dr Seuss-y" I'll scream. I mean what's the fucking point?' Leo left, fearing his lack of sympathy would flaunt itself.

Passing Frank's Auto Repair Shop on 21st Street, Leo remembered the elderly Italian man who would sit outside the workshop on a ledge built into a bricked-up arch. Framed by the arch, he would preside in oily overalls and watch all passing events with a wide-legged stance, his palms pressed firmly on his thighs, a rag thrown over his shoulder. Leo and Frank would talk, about whether the man's two sons would ever marry, about the neighbourhood, the possible development of the High Line, why to never trust a remould. The old man disappeared from his ledge one day and Leo would stop and pause long enough for the sons to acknowledge him, which they sometimes did, but without offering any word on their father. People simply disappeared, Leo had to tell himself, and years later, on days like today, they would emerge from a cupboard in the corner of your mind and trouble you, like a mystery you forgot you had charged yourself with solving.

A photograph appeared in his mind's eye, in the style of Eve Arnold's Chinese reportage, which he admired. The photograph was of his apartment, and it was lit by the same soft dusk through which he cycled now. He could see every room from every angle all at once. There was stillness throughout and it had settled so deep that the silence was irreversible. It was a study of what awaited him, an image of the pang of loneliness that would open the door to him this evening as he reached for the handle. Solitude was stripping the structures of his life of peace, and the air that drew tears of moisture from his eyes was the first cool, dry air of the year, liberated at last from the icy grip of the long winter and not yet strangled by the humidity of summer. The glow of the sky was rich in oxygen and Leo felt that, even now, the yearning inside him did not preclude hope.

The cherry blossom on 28th Street formed a guard of honour for an appreciative face. Leo had once read that a disease spreading through a forest would gradually meet a growing resistance to its canker, that the further into the forest the sickness spread, the greater the trees' immunity would become, as if the trees passed word one to the next of the encroaching threat, and cured themselves in an act of instant evolution and fellowship.

He decided not to go straight home, and made a call to his brother-in-law. 'I will be in Home Furnishings in half an hour,' he announced in a G.K. Chesterton tone.

'Marvellous,' William replied, an American who sounded more English than Leo.

Both men hung up, William's face now adorned with a grin at the prospect of seeing his greatest friend. He remained sitting with his stockinged feet upon his desk, heels touching and feet splayed. The slim pea coat suit he wore was redolent of a bygone time. Nobody had asked him to, but he felt that his workplace required an attire that genuflected in the direction of its postwar heyday. He contemplated the last of his four daily cigarettes. The anticipation of rolling a cigarette was more magical to William than the smoke itself. Expectation was a source of sublime pleasure, but had to be married to the certainty of its fulfilment. Doubt was not welcome. He was a religious man not given to soul-searching.

Vaughan Williams' *Lark Ascending* drew to a close, taking an imperceptible step into silence. The apparent perfection of its final moments drew a modest rapture through William's afternoon. He switched off the CD player, as nothing could immediately follow it. He looked again at the photograph that had arrived that morning in the post, a faded grey image of a flood of people at the main entrance to the department store in which he worked. The photograph was undated but William's growing familiarity with such images enabled him to place it in the 1930s. The vast majority of the crowd were women and among them a young girl had turned and seen the camera, and was looking now at William across a distance of seventy years. He switched on the kettle and looked up through a window set high in the room. A plane sliced the blue sky and it came easily to a man like William to picture the eternal Manhattan through the cut.

His office was a garret, tucked into the roof of one of New York's oldest stores. The exterior of Italian-style Tuckahoe marble and its Art Deco additions had once matched for flamboyance any of its rivals in commerce on the Ladies' Mile. Now, it was a sole survivor on Sixth

Avenue, Macy's aside. The original painted sign remained on a west-facing brick and terracotta façade of the building,

A.T. FOUNTAIN'S DEPARTMENTAL EMPORIUM EST. 1902

and to the very particular type of New Yorker who still patronised the place, it was simply 'Fountains'. Those people were few in number, ageing, wealthy and opposed to change.

William was archivist to the Fountains Emporium, a job negotiated for him by Leo, once Leo had convinced Fountains that their archive was worth attention. Joy claimed that her husband had the best job in the world and for any shy, risk-averse, old-fashioned Anglophile, content in his own company and free of ambition, the case could be argued. William surprised himself, having never taken an interest in photography or history before, with his enthusiasm to set about the decades' worth of disordered photographs, prints, and papers stuffed into boxes and shelves in the store's attic and which chronicled Fountains' life so far. He did so with the zeal of an apprentice, and sometimes with wonder, and ten years into the job he still felt a burning gratitude towards the man who was, at this moment, crossing town to join him.

The kettle boiled and William spooned into a teapot the loose-leaf tea from Postcards of Mayfair that Fountains imported. He put on a new CD. There was always music in the attic. He listened to Chopin, Ravel, Mozart, Vaughan Williams and Delius. Bruckner, when he was feeling brave. Maybe a little Elgar, though he quickly tired of it until the next time, and never Bernstein. He could not abide Bernstein. He left the tea to brew and climbed a stepladder to the deep-set sill of an ornate arched window, at which he sat on a tapestry cushion (Soft Furnishings, fifth floor) two hundred feet above 17th Street, eye to eye with the leaded rooftops of the Kingston Academy where the gargoyles and the gulls lived among the slate and leaded canopy and the hushed sound of the streets below. He opened the single hinged pane in the window and smoked his cigarette. He looked at the girl in the photograph and she looked back at him. She had arrived in response to William's efforts to unearth historical photographs of the store and accounts of life in it, some for the store's cumbersome website, but most contributing towards the opening of a permanent archive. He trawled online picture libraries, contacted historical societies and colleges, and wrote to customers whose families had patronised Fountains for many years. The material arrived sporadically, offering William a welcome break from cataloguing the long-abandoned archives around him.

Many of the old photographs and newspaper cuttings he received in the post were unsurprising; the crowds on the sidewalks outside Fountains, the Ladies' Mile in its glory days, the horse-drawn carriages, early motor cars on Broadway, a glimpse of the elevated lines. What he found more compelling were photographs taken inside the store, faces consumed by the novelty of the camera, store assistants standing in line holding linens or items of homeware at an angle for the lens, others standing proudly beside exotic decorative furnishings. These faces existed in a faraway kingdom of magnesium light, and those looking William in the eye seemed to be trying to warn him of something.

He had experienced a recurring dream since becoming an archivist in which he found himself smoking a cigarette on his window ledge, high enough (because it was a dream) to see the five boroughs. Scattered across them were expansive sloping patches of earth. These sepia spaces were the graveyards of New York, the resting places of all those faces in the photographs he received each day and of no one else. Every dead New Yorker that had ever lived had shopped at Fountains. They had the city surrounded.

He slotted the photograph of the girl into the edge of the window pane, from where she could look down on the city that had been her realm when she walked the earth.

Something in how the girl looked at him reminded William of Susan French, of the uncertainty in her eyes. He drew on his cigarette and looked across the room to the mattress on the floor in the corner, on which Susan lay asleep, enjoying a moment of respite during her fraught human tenure.

William searched for absolutes from life, and the peace he gave to this girl (she was a woman but too frail to earn the word) in small, gratefully accepted pieces seemed to be one of them: a good thing, surely a good thing. The sight of her gladdened him and scared him in equal measure; it always had done, since he first took her in. He wrote a note and placed it on the floor beside her bed, telling her not to worry, that he would be back soon.

9

The couch Leo had seated himself on was on a small raised platform dead centre of the Fountains Emporium Home Furnishings department. He slouched and made a good fist of appearing as brazen as a man so bereft of direction could. He wondered if the boy would turn up for work at the gallery tomorrow, and noted on the wood-panelled stairwell a series of Japanese water prints he had acquired for the store in 1997. Leo acted as fine art consultant to the Fountains' board of directors. For two decades he had valued the store's private collection on their behalf, advised them as a buyer of art, antique furniture and decorative objects, and consulted for members of the board on a private basis, hanging on the walls of their uptown apartments and country houses works by the likes of Kandinsky, Arthur Boyd, Maureen Gallace, Rothko, Nash, Lowry, Piper, Wyeth N.C., Wyeth A., Wyeth J., and Patrick Hughes.

Currently, Leo was negotiating a commission from Fountains for one of his artists, Tilhoff, whose realist interiors were brilliant, and as angry as realist interiors could expect to be. The Tilhoff commission was less the will of Fountains president Sidney White and more that of his grandson, George, a recent and unlikely addition to the Fountains senior management who was yet to inform his grandfather, or any other member of his family, that on a recent trip to Istanbul he had met and married a Syrian student eleven years his junior whose name George himself was still mispronouncing. Leo could imagine neither George White nor Tilhoff's interiors working in this place.

William joined him on the couch. In no hurry to say anything, they settled like two pieces of a greater whole, docking into place. They had liked each other from the start, when Joy brought William to meet her brother at One Lex – had found themselves to be perfectly in tune. 'I'm the gooseberry when it's the three of us,' Joy had said on many occasions since.

Leo rarely brought girlfriends to join them as it diluted his time with his William. They spoke every day, they put thoughts and newspaper cuttings aside for each other, laughed at things they were doing that the other would hate (art and religion yielded plentifully in this regard).

Sofia Passarella (Human Resources) watched them bask in each other's company as they surveyed the store's village life. To Sofia, who was making her way back to her office clutching a Fountains pillow to her breast, William and Leo were mischievous boys and handsome older men all rolled into one lovely smoke.

'Hello, you two,' she said.

'How are you, Sofia?' William replied.

'I'm good. What are you guys plotting?'

'A riot in Men's Undergarments,' Leo said.

'Good luck with that.'

'You want me to have him removed?' William said.

'Would you?' Sofia replied, and smiled as she went back to work. Her crush on Leo, 1999–2002, had long since been confined to the vaults, but there would always be a softness in her regard for him that could sometimes feel like bruising. It had taken an extraordinary measure of courage on her behalf to tell Leo Emerson that she believed she had fallen in love with him (from a distance and in the course of three brief encounters in the store) and it had only increased her feelings for him, the pained, tender way in which he had told her that he did not share the attraction. Even now, Leo always looked for the lightest of comments when they met, just to distance them both from anything that could be honest and therefore in any way uneasy for her. He knew that this might be enormously patronising of him, suggesting she had not got over him, but it seemed polite. What a minefield it all was to him, how easy he had once found it, and how erroneous his path in withdrawing from all such encounters these past years for fear of making the wrong decision, for fear of adding to the body count of lovers from whom he had failed to understand what he wanted.

Leo sighed. William looked at him, his eyes asking him if he was alright without creating a ripple on the surface of things unsaid.

'We look like two old poofs,' Leo said.

'You picked the tartan sofa,' William replied.

'Two old poofs planning to re-feather their nest.'

'Found a new assistant yet?'

'Yes.'

'Joy has a theory about it.'

'Oh, good,' Leo said, 'I like my sister's theories.'

'It's not profound. You don't pick a new trainee because you want to pack it all in.'

'Not profound...' Leo agreed.

William smiled. They both put an arm along the back of the sofa, arms that crossed without touching, cradling the space behind each other.

'Did you say you have found someone?'

'Sure did.'

'Can't wait to tell her she's wrong.'

'You won't, though.'

'True.'

Leo had once dreamt that he and William became stuck inside a Beckett drama on one of these sofas. The dream had possessed the cloying airless quality of a mild nightmare but when Leo woke he missed it and tried to descend back into it. This dream had been the offshoot, he had reasonably presumed, of Angela Simpson's attempt to take him to Boston to see a production of Beckett's *Happy Days* in 1997. That casual (and rather lovely) invitation had become mired in complication, as her suggestion that they see the Beckett on the Friday night and then take a drive through some early fall colour over the weekend became choked and strangled by Leo's attempt to shoehorn the experience into twenty-four hours so as to make it back to Manhattan for dinner with William and Joy on the Saturday (without giving Angela any reason to feel invited to join them).

'Let me get this straight,' Angela had said. 'I'm inviting you for a weekend and you're saying yes to half a weekend?'

Leo's answer, in the affirmative, spoken through a voice filtered by self-doubt as he wondered why he was prioritising a run-of-the-mill bite to eat in Joy and William's oh so average local diner over Angela's Boston hay-making weekend (they were crazy good together and would barely see a single turning leaf beyond the hotel window, and he knew it), was met by an altogether more informed and knowing decision on her part, to end their time together (eight months, which was bang on Leo's average bat for the 1990s).

Although Leo had resolved in some uncommitted (naturally) manner to respond to his Beckettian mistake by remaining single for a period and getting a grip, he had not intended that period to last nine years, and had never contemplated the possibility of Angela being his last lover of the millennium, nor of getting six years and four months into the new one without another. It bothered him these days that he had been unable back then to break an informal and habitual dinner date with his sister and brother-in-law. (Angela was by no means the first to play second fiddle.) He was open to change, but not right now. He had presumed back then that, unlike every other man, he was from a mould where age would have no effect on him, and his choices would never narrow. Anything he had chosen not to do, he could always revisit at a later date. There was always tomorrow. But the tomorrows had become days like today, when he arrived at a point like this one, watching some or other Sofia Passarella who could have been his destiny and borne his child.

The difference these days was that it was too late. Truly, actually, utterly, finally too late. One could do many things in life, but one could not do everything, and Leo would never do that. And his need to weep about it, to openly mourn the death of the life he had sleepwalked around, the guttural desire to talk about it to William, the rock of his adult life, was one of those many items on the list he saved for another day.

He fantasised about taking Joy and William on holiday, a Pullman train to New Orleans, or a road trip in a hired Chevy Bel Air east to west (Leo had driven across the States with lovers three times in the eighties and would love to show William and Joy the open road). Or, if he could ply the two of them with enough Ambien, a flight back to the UK and on to Europe. Florence, Naples, Athens. Everywhere. Christ, anywhere! Leo had visited an artist in Oregon once and wanted William to see that place, and South America, the great cities of Rio or Buenos Aires that he loved so much, or Montevideo, which he had not yet seen. He imagined flying William and Joy first class and unlocking the wanderlust in them. Imagining it had become an activity in itself, in the absence of their showing any interest in going anywhere or any appetite to be airborne. His fantasies had detail, like that for his sixtieth birthday in five years' time, when he would take the two of them around the world in first class. Against the backdrop of extraordinary cities and mindblowing landscapes, he would map out for his sister and brother-in-law their retirement (which he had well in hand financially, no fantasy) and at the heart of this retirement the daily breakfasts he and William had once enjoyed would be reinstated.

Oh, what a wonderful time Leo was destined to have, around the next corner. He would take William with him on his annual trip to London, a trip he himself had failed to make these past three years. He loved London, and had adored returning to East Anglia, but these days the connections had worn thin. And something about leaving New York City made him unsure nowadays. The longer you lived here, the more improbable the rest of the world became, and the more unnecessary.

He found William watching him and wondered if he knew exactly what he was thinking. It was possible, and he liked the idea.

'Buy you dinner?' Leo said.

'It's vigil night,' William said. 'I wish we could.'

'You can. Give it a miss.'

'Join us and rid the world of evil.'

'I haven't got my Batman suit with me.'

'We'll bib you. What's your new employee like?'

'He's something of an unknown quantity. Which I like. There's not enough unknown quantities.'

'One is one too many,' William said. 'I'm sorry to say it, but I gotta go.'

Leo squeezed William's shoulder. 'I'm going to stay a while,' he said. 'I'm comfortable.' He did not want to go home. William knew this, and rested his hand on Leo's back for the faintest of precious moments before returning to his room in the roof and shutting the door quietly behind him as Susan French turned in her sleep. Beneath the sheets, her legs were tucked tight to her body. Her arms were thin and pale but her face was no longer hollow these days. She looked free of worry and that pleased William greatly. He watched her fingertips draw shapes on her cheek as she dreamed.

Asleep or awake, Susan possessed the quietness of a woman who dared not disturb the air around her. She lived in a Section 8 apartment in Clinton in which her big brother could stretch out his arms and touch both sides, when he was at liberty to do so. As a fifteen-year-old, she had written a short story about a girl who did not want to take up any space in the world. When her teacher put it in for a Thomasson Foundation writing prize and it won, Susan ran away from school to avoid the prize-giving, and instead of going directly home she loitered at the bus station and by nightfall she had left Nebraska. She'd reached New York City before her family noticed her absence. She was a mouse of an addict who had turned up at the Club one hot July morning last year and, in a voice one needed to put an ear against to hear, apologised for her atheism, politely refused to inform on her dealer, whom she loved, and asked for help to get off drugs. She wore a pale blue sheer blouse that the pastor could see her ribs through. The church registered her with a rehab programme and assigned William and Joy to visit her every week. At the end of the visit, Joy would ask to use the bathroom and Susan would tell her where it was, as if it was the first time, and as she left the bathroom Joy would leave two twenty-dollar bills on the kitchen cupboard beneath a bag of fruit she and William always brought with them. At the outset they brought her bananas and oranges, but one week Joy bought kumquats, for no good reason she could think of, and the sight of them reduced Susan to hysterics and it became a ritual, an affectionate joke, that Joy sought out obscure and exotic fruit under which to leave the money.

When they talked about Susan, which they did a lot, as well as pray for her every day, William and Joy referred to the first time they saw Susan laugh as the Night of the Kumquats. Nowadays she often smiled with them, and would sit forward with her elbows on her knees and her hands cupping her face, listening keenly to the flow of easy, teasing conversation between Mr and Mrs Fairman (as she insisted on calling them), whose tactile affection towards each other was a thing of wonder to her. To Joy's amusement, Susan watched William's every move with adoring puppy eyes. This was in part because he was the man she dreamed of having for a father, but also a consequence of their complicity, for the only secrets in the world that William kept from Joy were his knowledge that Susan was still a heroin user and the sanctuary he offered her at Fountains.

He had visited Susan alone (this Joy knew about; he had a fifty-dollar Fountains gift token from last Fourth of July and rang Joy to suggest he take it to Susan on his way from work). When he had let himself into her apartment, he had feared she was dying, such was the depravity of her fitting and the fear in her eyes. And the desire to put her out of her misery, to give her whatever in the world she wanted, to resurrect that smile of hers from somewhere beneath the wreckage of her features, was so great that he would have done anything for her. When she explained what she needed he went gratefully for her to the address she had given him, where a woman of Susan's age was waiting for him to say the words 'Cooked Cura'. He returned as if holding a bomb in his pocket. His heart thumped and his head reeled with fear and lust at the thought that this mythical substance was in his hand, that he was, finally, on the front line of some small drama, that something other than the beautiful routine he had been blessed with was upon him. His fingers felt the shapes inside the bubble wrap, deciphering them as three syringes. They contained a substance he knew nothing about but which he accepted would help her in the way that prayer could not. He took them to her and it thrilled him. She instructed him to put two of the syringes in the refrigerator and he was astounded by her ability to stem her shivering and becalm herself to inject, and he was in awe of the peace that overwhelmed her and the deep, aching smile that took possession of her face as she stepped back from pain and knowledge for a short while. He had never seen such silent ecstasy on a human being's face. It was exactly how he imagined a good death to be.

Having a secret from Joy amounted to a crisis in William's life and he had told Leo all that he knew, which was this: Susan's job with a cleaning company in the Bronx was part-time, three nights per week, a meagre result of a ragged, now defunct back-to-work scheme for which she had used her brother's address in Mott Haven to qualify. Daytime sleep was a rare commodity in her apartment. The building heaved with people who rarely worked and attracted visitors like flies licking the sticky detritus of indefinable business. Sometimes, Susan was so tired during the day that she went out to sleep in the restrooms of the McDonald's on Pennsylvania Plaza, where she could sit on the toilet seat and rest her head on her knees. William had told Leo how he had bought an inflatable mattress and with a sense of guilt created a corner for Susan in his office, with cheap floral bedsheets, and a small shelf with some paperbacks and space for her spectacles and a glass of water. His fear at what he was doing had subsided with the belief that he was doing good, if not an understanding of why.

Susan came often, needed no persuading, craved the rest it offered her, almost wept the first time she woke and William made her hot tea before she went to work. She would call, and meet him at the goods entrance. She slept in her clothes. William liked the company and felt sure he was doing the right thing.

Leo had asked his brother-in-law if he was in love with her and William had replied with a clear conscience that he was not.

'Then why is this a problem?'

'Because it's a secret and we promised no secrets.'

'When you were both five?'

William had smiled, and laughed a little.

'Everyone has private stuff, Will.'

We are such able advisers when it comes to each other's lives. Both of them had thought it then. And William had admitted to himself that it was the chaos of Susan's life that drew him in. In Susan he could watch the world's disarray writ large, dabble in it, taste the exotica of it. But it was a different thing which he admitted to Leo.

'Occasionally,' he had said, 'on a certain sort of day, it feels like having a child.'

'Why need that be a secret?' Leo had asked, and had seen by the way William's shoulders dropped that it needn't be. Joy would be wonderful about it all. But William wanted this to be his own.

'There's a difference between keeping a secret and telling a lie,' Leo had said, 'and you're not in love with her.'

'I'm not,' William had agreed, 'but once, she woke in the middle of the afternoon and I didn't hear her come to me. I was sitting in the window smoking and she joined me on the ledge and took the cigarette from my fingers and dragged on it, and it almost felt a little as if...'

William had allowed the words to fall off the ledge of his conscience.

'I bet that felt nice,' Leo had said. 'It's impossible to be kind and not keep secrets.'

In that moment, William had considered the true scale of this man's sanctioning of him, which seemed endless.

The garret was dark and quiet, and made Susan's sleep the greatest presence in it. William switched on a light and filled Susan's glass with water and woke her, tenderly. They moved like a whisper to the elevator on the floor below and parted out of sight in the long shadows of the cargo ramp on 17th Street.

'Thank you, Mr Fairman.'

William strode out, and felt God's presence in the warming Hudson breeze and in the rusty hues of the abandoned High Line. Weeds sprouting from the disused elevated railway flashed glimpses of flowering colour and, try as he might, he could not imagine the thing renewed the way people were talking about. He liked it as it was, familiar and obsolete.

Joy was waiting for him outside the Club. He watched her shiver a little at the same breeze that had ushered him gladly through the streets to her. She grinned at him from a distance and wiggled childishly. Her granite-coloured raincoat hung loosely from her shoulders, suggesting a desire to jump into puddles rather than join the weekly vigil of the 'Drugs Deal Death' group.

William and Joy did not read Pastor Edwin's daily blog, nor hang around after Sunday worship for the discussion forum. They did not believe in turning to prayer for banal or material requests, made sure they never caught themselves saying things like 'Jesus loves you' despite being firmly of the opinion that he did, and they maintained an irreverent sense of humour about religion. But they did like those church groups that dealt in black and white and marked out the boundaries of the nation state they called right and wrong. The Drugs Deal Death group and the recently created Campaign Against Victimless Crime were the twin cities of that nation state.

As always, the volunteers were divided into three groups, and William and Joy were in the same group. Once, and once only, Pastor Edwin had separated them, as he thought it would be healthy for them to interact with the other parishioners as individuals. The following morning, Edwin had received a phone call from William making it clear that he was not to indulge in such an experiment again.

Joy and William helped each other on with the standard issue luminous orange Drugs Deal Death bibs and kissed on the lips. William suspected they were the only members of Drugs Deal Death to kiss on the lips in public, and possibly in private too. He offered his arm to Joy as the group walked up Eleventh Avenue. They took up position at the entrance to a seven-storey building on West 44th Street, with a realtor's office at street level and a known drug-dealer on the fifth floor. A pale young man emerged from the building, and sighed at having to navigate the high-visibility posse. 'Must be that time again.'

'Must be...' one of the group replied.

'Have a good night,' the man said, walking away. Someone called after him, 'God bless you, child,' prompting Joy and William to wince and catch each other's eye.

The posse had been William and Joy's idea. William had read about a community group in Fairlawn, Washington DC, whose experience had been that dealers moved on quickly when bugged by regular vigils, not because they felt intimidated (drug-dealers tended not to feel intimidated by the Church of the Disciples of Christ and their like), but due to what Fairlawn called the BPF – the 'butt pain factor'. He and Joy had presented the article to the Club and felt a drop shadow of gravitas added to a life lived in lower case.

He glanced at her now. She looked wonderful to him tonight and he was surprised by a surge of disappointment that, with her in that coat, they were not out with Leo. After three years of standing passively on the sidewalk in prayer, his appetite for the vigil had deserted him without warning, explanation or apology.

Pastor Edwin turned to Bob Kelly, the most physically forbidding man in the group, and asked him if he would like to 'do the honours'?

'I'd like to volunteer tonight,' William said, taking a half-step into the circle. 'Bob or Kevin or any one of the big guys always go inside, and it's unfair that they have to do it because they happen to be six feet tall.'

Joy reached out to tug on William's sleeve, but he was already out of reach. This was news to her. The others nodded their approval, with the exception of Randall Hicks, who at five foot six was the same size as William and didn't like this change to the accepted wisdom. The way Randall Hicks was seeing things right now, thanks to that short-arse do-gooder William Fairman, he'd now feel obliged to volunteer next week or look like a pussy.

'Would you like to rehearse it with me,' the pastor said, 'as it's your first time?'

'Yes. Good idea,' William replied.

William faced the pastor. 'Good evening. Well, I just wanted to wish you a good day and to say that Jesus...' William hesitated, 'Look, I'm not gonna act it out properly, I'll just run through the lines to check I know them, but I can't do it for real until I'm, you know, up there...'

'In the theatre of war,' someone said, irritating and worrying Joy in equal measure.

William cleared his throat. 'Good evening. Jesus Christ our Lord loves you deeply. The caring and attentive ear of Pastor Edwin at the Church of the Disciples of Christ is available to you should you wish to seek spiritual guidance and forgiveness for the lives you are blighting. With love in our hearts, we ask you to remember the children in your life, and to ponder the fact that those to whom you sell cocaine, heroin and ketamine were innocent children once, and are still somebody's daughter, somebody's son. We will return again and again to keep vigil outside your door and pray for you. I wish you peace and happiness and the love of our Lord.'

A modest applause rippled through the group. Joy watched as a couple of the men patted William on the back and he disappeared inside.

William switched the church camcorder on to record as he walked along the fifth-floor corridor, which, like the stairwell, was surprisingly clean. Opening the door to the apartment, the dealer did a slight double-take at William's height, looking initially at the blank space above William's head where Bob's face would normally be. The dealer slouched in the doorframe and sighed, his shirt unbuttoned halfway down his pale, flabby chest. He stared at the camcorder.

''Sthat on again?' He had a stoner voice and a strong lisp.

'Yes, it is.'

'Go 'head then. Do your sthpeech.'

Riding the elevator down, William felt disappointed. He had volunteered somewhat in the hope of some glamour, but he now suspected that the bigger guys had been slightly embellishing the danger factor up there on the front line.

'How d'it go?' someone asked.

'Fine.'

'Was he aggressive?'

The temptation to paint a little drama into his life was great, but he resisted. 'He was non-hostile.'

'Well done you,' Pastor Edwin said, and signalled to the group to bow their heads while he asked the Lord for fortitude to rid the neighbourhood of its vestiges of addiction and gave thanks for the reduction in drug use in Clinton (Joy and William's millennium petition to return the Club to using the name 'Hell's Kitchen' having fallen on stony ground).

Joy linked her arm through William's as they wandered away and whispered in his ear. 'My hero... After dinner I'm gonna take you home to bed.' She said it in a southern drawl. 'So don't eat anything heavy.'

New York City remained gripped by a schizophrenic season of mild spring days and bitter nights, and William and Joy walked among a people uncertain that they had yet seen off winter. They linked arms on Tenth Avenue and he asked her to marry him and she rested her head on his shoulder and consented. Somewhere in their quarter-century together, they had swapped accents. Her Englishness suited his workplace to a T, while the taste for the exotic she had shown traces of possessing before settling in marriage seemed sated by becoming a New Yorker, accent and all.

Outside the Amish supermarket they stopped to take a closer look at the exotic fruit and she touched the sandpaper skin of the sapodilla.

'It's from Mexico. Ripens after it's picked.'

'Perfect.'

They bought two, and headed across to the Italian eatery, where they met Di and Jeff McGuire for dinner every week, after the vigil. They were joined later by Adele, a single mother of an eight-year-old boy, who had been working in the health store with Joy for fourteen years. Adele had become a part of their gathering five years ago when she divorced, but still felt she merited a place there only in tandem with Joy. For this reason, she would always arrive late so as to give Joy, William, Di and Jeff the time without her which she presumed they coveted. (They did not. They loved Adele to bits, and considered her a lousy time-keeper.)

Di and Jeff Maguire said they had news. They shuffled forward on their seats to share it. Di pressed the palms of her hands on the table and straightened up. Jeff looked proudly at his wife, prompting her to speak. William's instinct, in this demi-moment between Di opening her mouth and being interrupted by Adele, was that it had to be cancer or a new apartment, and it didn't feel like cancer.

'I already know...' Adele said.

'It's true, I came into the shop yesterday and spilled the beans to her,' Di said.

Mung beans, William said to himself. He found it extraordinary that anyone bought anything from the shop Joy and Adele worked in.

'Know what?' Joy asked. She hated news.

'We are going...' Jeff said.

'... away...' Di said.

'... for a yeeeeear,' Jeff and Di said, in an elongated fashion. Di stamped her feet excitedly and grinned.

'I already knew,' Adele repeated.

'I don't understand,' Joy said, with a nervous laugh, and looking at William helplessly.

'Where to?' William asked.

'Everywhere,' Jeff said. 'We're going travelling. Europe, the Middle East and Asia.'

'Travelling!' Di reiterated, marvelling at the word, and its application to her life.

'The Middle East?' William was bemused. 'Have you joined the Marine Corps?'

'Very funny,' Jeff said.

'What about our weekly meet-up?' Joy asked. It just came out.

'It's wonderful!' Adele exclaimed. 'It's awesome. Well done, you two.'

Despite his confusion, William made a genuine attempt at taking an interest. It was beyond Joy to do so and, feigning a migraine as the food arrived, she left abruptly. William followed and they walked home in one of the many forms of silence available to the wedded.

By night, the cherry blossom on West 36th Street was a hostage to the shadows above the street-lights and to the rumble of tyres ramping down into the Lincoln Tunnel. William looked out from his living room. The street seemed gloomy. He noticed the blackness of the windows on the South Clinton Community Hall and remembered his fear of empty buildings as a child, of apparitions at dark windows if he looked at them too long. He heard Joy lock the bathroom door and sensed that, contrary to her earlier promise, she was not going to take him to bed and make like a Tennessee hooker. He listened to Mr Coonan's footsteps in

125

the apartment above. The old man had lived there for half a century. He might nod at you but he never said a word, as if the gunshot wound on his neck prevented it. William opened the sash window and leaned out to peek at the partial view of the upper reaches of the Empire State Building, a view that had excited them greatly when they viewed the apartment in the fall of 1980. From the other side of the street a man's whistling came from a warehouse entrance draped in slatted plastic sheets that glowed orange. This was a nightly sound, a part of the inventory of familiar things in which William and his wife had unwittingly invested the graspable truth.

Why would our friends want to leave all this for a whole year? That's a lifetime? Who the hell chooses to go camping in Turkey? How can they claim, in 2006, that a country like Jordan is perfectly safe? William asked himself these questions as the McGuires' itinerary repeated on him like bad meatloaf. There came a short burst of traffic on Ninth and Tenth Avenues, and with it the clatter of loose panels on a semi-trailer, and then the roads cleared simultaneously and the city was silent again, momentarily post-apocalyptic. Into the silence returned the whistling man, brushing the slats aside to emerge on to the sidewalk. The plastic slats were now in darkness. The man rolled down the shutters and locked up and put a cigarette in his mouth. He bowed his head to light his smoke and as he took a drag he tipped his head back and looked at the clear cold night. He saw William at the open window and raised a hand. William waved back and watched the man descend into the deep bowl of swathed tarmac on Dyer Avenue, the sinkhole that fell into the mouth of the Lincoln Tunnel, with west midtown growing into something new above it, something made of glass not brick and in no way unique to William's city.

William tapped on the bathroom door and Joy let him in. Wordless, they rotated around the cramped space, he washing his face at the bathtap while Joy washed hers at the washbasin, he brushing his teeth at the basin as she sat on the toilet seat and peeled the contact lenses from her eyes. She raised herself a few inches, lifted the seat beneath her and threw her lenses into the bowl. They didn't mention Di and Jeff Maguire.

She brushed her hair at the living room window and he filled two glasses with water and walked past her to the bedroom and placed a glass each side of the bed. He folded back the duvet and opened the curtains and turned off the bedside lamps, allowing the pleasant, soft, cool glow of light on Worldwide Plaza to illuminate the room. It was a light they enjoyed making love to. 'Cinematic light for non-cinematic bodies,' she would say, and he would protest on her body's behalf. And he was right to, because in the warm curves of Joy's body he had found pleasure and sanctuary that he once thought impossible, and he yearned for her body these days more strongly even than twenty-seven years ago. He yearned for it tonight, to be held by her, to come in her, to sleep in her arms, where all was safe and known and there were no surprises.

She joined him in the bedroom and placed a vitamin pill beside his glass of water and one beside hers, for the morning. She threw her gown on the chair back and climbed into bed and lay on her back without kissing him. She would find no solace anywhere tonight, not in William, and not in her love of the Lord, which was not immune to the mood swings she worked so hard to hide from the world.

She looked at the ceiling. 'Why did you volunteer to knock on the door?' She said it without accusation and without warmth. She said it to the soft urban glow of the room.

He lay on his side and held her hand. 'I'm not sure.' There was silence. He stroked her arm. 'So, I'm not your hero any more?' he teased.

'Something could have happened to you. What would become of me if something happened to you? What would

I do? Our friends go away and you start doing things impulsively. I'd be dead if something happened to you. We discuss everything. That's the way we've chosen. If you're going to break ranks then maybe I will too.'

She turned her back. The air brakes on Dyer Avenue beckoned William's thoughts out through the window to the city and the many things he loved about the beginning of each new day of his life in this town, and the inevitable rebooting of his and Joy's contentment which the morning could be relied upon to bring. Joy's breathing came interspersed with the occasional heavy sigh, designed to draw attention to her displeasure and the fact that she was not yet asleep and should not be ignored. This continued for ten minutes, and made William smile (a smile that Joy could hear perfectly well), until she rolled over and cuddled up to him. He put his arms around her and squeezed her and she laughed to herself.

'What are you thinking about?' she asked.

'Di and Jeff.'

'And...?'

There was silence.

'Why would they want to do that? Yuk.'

She loved him for saying that.

10

Finn woke in the hovel to the noise of an animal being tortured on a nearby rooftop. He dragged his clothes on, splashed cold water over his face and discovered the heating had packed up. Behind the building, men worked on imprecise projects at the lock-ups and lean-tos of corrugated iron. Radios played and steam gushed from vents out into a day colder than the last. The sound of the wailing animal continued. It struck Finn that, in going to prison, Glenn had taken a step up in the world. He missed Dilly's body.

A man smoked a cigarette and watched his dog, a dark-faced German Shepherd that winced at being called by name. Marvyn. The man, strong and slothful, wore a red satin tracksuit, bare-chested and the pillow of his belly exposed. Marvyn sniffed the broken paving slabs. The man nodded to two passing teenagers and took a call on his cell. He erupted into booming laughter and muttered 'hee hee hee' as if they were three words in their own right. A couple with two young girls crossed the green steel footbridge which spanned the East River Drive. As Finn pressed his face to the window to watch them, the girls pressed their faces to the wire mesh and waved at the fast cars below, and it brought to Finn's mind a narrow road bridge across the A21 and his father's idea to take his wife's ashes to the lake she drowned herself in.

'It's a beautiful spot, boys.'

It's the place, Finn and Jack had each independently thought, of her last and worst anguish and a constant reminder of her suicide. Only their father could have come up with such a flawed idea, and seen it through.

'Like we want to come here to think of her,' Jack had whispered, at the water's edge.

'Like we want to go anywhere,' Finn had said, merely thirteen.

He watched the girls on the bridge wave goodbye to the traffic and follow their parents into the East River Park and he reminded himself that he had not shared with Jack the fact that he had dumped their father's ashes on to the A21 from the bridge at Stocks Green. He was never going to tell Jack that; he didn't want to vex him or hurt him spiritually, only physically. He would put other ashes into the urn or tell Jack he had scattered them somewhere nice, at some pretty lookout spot with a wooden bench to sit on and a nice fucking view where Jack would be free to reinvent the past on his rare visits home.

There were games of softball and soccer in the park. Two fencers duelled on purple concrete. Joggers ran parallel to the highway and the river. An elderly couple meandered with their arms threaded together, on a ritual stroll from their apartment in Peter Cooper Village to the Williamsburg Bridge and back, and Finn wondered if they had children and grandchildren who loved them and saw them; if they had got things right or not. The man in the red tracksuit was on the other side now, legs splayed, hands on hips, belly out, staring at a women's soccer game.

Finn watched the factory buildings and funnels on the far side of the river draw themselves in thick charcoal against a sun-stunned white sky. Shouts rose from a ball game and the turbulent river spat shattered glints of yellow light from close to the shoreline. A ferry was swallowed up by the shadows of the bridge and Finn headed out. At the foot of the stairwell a man shuffled through a pile of junk mail. He was in his early thirties but he already looked abandoned. He wore a heavy woollen suit that had a bad smell. He had no shirt and no shoes or socks. Beneath a beanie, his spectacles were taped together and sat on his face at an angle, distorting his eyes. His voice was faint and nasal.

'Did you hear my fox sound?'

Finn squared up, just a little. 'It woke me up.'

The man sniggered through his blocked sinuses. 'You can't blame me for the hours a fox keeps.'

Finn glanced at how the shoulders of the man's suit slumped lifelessly on an inadequate torso, and at the dark hairs on his pale, bare feet. He wanted out of the building but at the door curiosity stopped him.

'You have a pet fox?'

The man nodded his head triumphantly. 'You had to ask! I never said I had a fox. I said I had a fox sound.' He peered at Finn like a man who needed glasses, not a man wearing them. 'I've got thousands of sounds. Most of them would defeat you.'

Finn smiled politely. He walked out of the long shadows of the tower blocks. East Houston was wide and bright and bleak where the cross-town river breeze collided with the uptown harbour draught. There was no sign of Amy, or of anyone, at the Gay Hussar so he headed west. On the sidewalks of West 25th Street, outside the housing projects, a bitter Friday morning unfurled. People sold household possessions, used clothes and cheap jewellery from sheets laid out on the sidewalk. A man sanded down the legs of a kitchen chair and beside him was a stool with a ripped vinyl seat which was freshly taped up and it was not clear to Finn if the stool was for sale or for the man to sit on. If he'd asked, he would have been told that it was both. The sidewalk was a murmur. All was serene and all was desperate and it seemed improbable to Finn, the wealthy man a few corners away in the big art shop with a paid job for him. But something about the morning and the cold, crisp, sun-filled air hitting the streets advised Finn not to let suspicion darken the day or shut any doors.

Beyond Tenth Avenue, the crockery and old T-shirts were replaced by canvases and installations. He arrived five minutes early and felt more comfortable than he had expected to. It wasn't that he trusted Leo, that was out of the question, but he felt he couldn't be let down by a place like this because he expected nothing from it. Not, he decided, such a bad position to start from.

For his own part, Leo felt insecure. He had long suspected that his sense of humour had deserted him and, now, Finn's presence was sure to expose that fact. As he opened up a box of croissants from Maison Claudine, he asked Finn what he thought of the paintings currently on show. Finn smiled politely and caught the smell of warm, buttery dough and batted away the longing for a home that it stirred in him. He slid his hands into his pockets and his shoulders up to his ears and pulled a face that said he'd rather not answer. It was the non-committal way in which he had learned to survive the adults in his life, and it felt natural to use it here, with a man who was most certainly too good to be true.

'The artist, James Williamson, is from California,' Leo told him. 'I've represented him for fourteen years.'

'I wanna go to California.' That felt like a safe thing to say, and honest.

'Do you like them?'

'Sure.'

Leo's face invited more from him, and kindly.

'They all look the same, you know,' Finn muttered, 'water towers and stuff.'

They fell silent and Finn battled his guardedness with a wish to be polite to this man who had not yet screwed him over.

'Like *The Last Picture Show*,' Finn said, to appear more willing.

'Ah! A wonderful film,' Leo said. 'A classic. You like films?'

'Yes, I do,' Finn replied, more openly. It was good to be asked a question he knew the answer to, and it encouraged his curiosity. 'How much do you get? Eighteen grand for a painting the size of a tea towel. How much do *you* get?'

'Fifty per cent.'

'Seriously, though…'

'I am serious. I get half.'

Finn was incredulous. 'Half?' Spoken like a cold bullet.

Leo nodded.

'Fuck right off!' He laughed the words out of his throat. 'You didn't paint it.'

They fell silent. Leo stood his ground, feeling unexpectedly relaxed. 'Go on,' Leo said. 'Keep going. What's in your head?'

Finn shrugged. 'How much you give to charity,' he muttered.

Leo laughed to himself.

'That's what's in my head. When you're little you think anybody who makes loads of money gives most of it away so that things are even. But that's when you're little.'

'You like things to be even?' Leo asked the boy.

Finn pulled a 'dunno' face and retreated. He was not from a background where discussions unfolded like this. He smiled, in case he had sounded rude. Like many with the ability to wreak physical damage, he was placatory by nature.

To avoid further conversation, as he was tired of the concentration it took not to self-destruct, Finn walked around the gallery. Leo observed him. It was like having an animal on the loose – not a dangerous one necessarily, but an unknown quantity, outside its natural environment.

It was the quietest shop Finn had ever been in. As the morning wore on, his thoughts drifted to ways of delaying his return to the hovel. He tried Dilly's cell from the landline in the store-room. She didn't pick up and he didn't leave a message asking her to post him the Hemingway book, even though that was what he wanted. He felt no need for her until he thought of being in Glenn's place alone, and he suspected that this was not a kind way to need someone. He asked himself, would he have sex with Dilly in Long Beach if it was the only way of getting his book back? He believed fervently he would not, but felt uncomfortable that he could not promise it to himself.

Leo was distant, sometimes looking out across the street towards the Dot Yi in the window of the Bovenkamp Gallery. Chelsea was calm. The gallery was quiet. Astrid filled the void, as she picked at a meagre, lifeless salad.

'I've joined the Kabbalah faith in the last year, young man, and it's a huge part of me now – not that it's changed my outward life so much, but my inner life is a Kabbalah one these days.'

Finn noted that he was addressed as 'young man' only when being sent to prison, sexually dominated, and, it now seemed, at work.

'It's something I'd like to talk about, if you're interested, now that it seems you really are gonna, you know, work here, which is extraordinary.'

Finn smiled and let the hair fall over his face, as his eyes tended to tell the truth. His take on religion and organised spirituality was so negative that he chose not to share it.

'You know what?' Astrid said.

He shook his head. How could he possibly?

'You're the first person I've told I'm Kabbalah who hasn't immediately said, "Is that the Madonna thing?" You should be very proud of that fact, I mean that.'

That, Finn said to himself, would be because I have no

idea what Kabbalah is. In truth, he had very little notion of what Madonna had ever done to get so famous. So he smiled politely at all of it, which only encouraged Astrid.

'What annoys me,' she said, 'is why pick on Madonna? Everything has its famous members, doesn't it? I mean Tom Cruise is in the Scientology one – he's their, you know, big name. Every religion has celebrities attached. Judaism has Woody Allen. Catholicism has the Pope. So why pick out Kabbalah?'

The phone rang and Astrid grabbed it. Finn looked at Leo helplessly. 'I'll give a sign when I know what anybody round here is talking about.'

That made Leo's mind up: the boy was staying. It was worth having him here just to watch him try and make sense of Astrid. First, though, Leo needed to buy himself some time to work out what Finn was going to do. He had no idea of the boy's abilities, and was aware that Astrid knew this and was waiting for it to unravel.

'I won't make a habit of asking you to run errands but I have a little ritual with my sister and my brother-in-law and I thought you could do it for me this morning, if you don't mind?'

Finn shrugged. 'It's your shop. You tell me what to do.'

Leo wrapped the second box of pastries in a carrier bag and handed it to the boy, gave him an address and a set of keys and pointed him in the right direction.

'So – ' Astrid sat back on her chair ' – having given a complete stranger, petty thief and illegal worker the keys to Joy's apartment, you can now try and work out what the heck you can get him to do while I continue to do all the work that a qualified new assistant was going to take off my hands.'

'That's the sum of it,' Leo said. 'Sorry.'

'Remember how you said it'd be good to get fresh input when writing our brochure intros?' she mocked, 'Well, get the little thief to do that.' She plunged her vocal cords into the deepest, most guttural voice she could get out of her famished frame. '*All art looks the same and this is all like todal bullshit man and paintings cost like way too much.* The end.'

She had made Leo smile without at all meaning to.

'Oh, God, no...' she sighed.

'What?' Leo said.

'You're perking up.'

Finn swallowed the streets with his stride. It was a shiver through the length of his body, how good it felt to have a job in this town. The smile on his face turned heads. Nothing on Tenth Avenue escaped his hungry eye: the Ethiopian smartphone repair booth, the low-rent gold-trader, the Korean grocery store... every little detail was perfect for being unrecognisable from home. A florist's spilled on to the sidewalk and Finn stopped a moment with thoughts of Amy but he wasn't sure if she'd want flowers from him, and he felt bad towards Dilly. He walked on, as fast as was possible with the box of pastries balanced in his hand. Outside a second-hand furniture store, a man reclined on a deckchair in the cold sunshine, wearing a pair of shorts and sunglasses, his saggy grey-haired chest arched to the sky. Finn squinted in the sun and laughed to himself and remembered how he and Jack used to walk this same way, fast as they could without running, fidgeting with laughter, once a year when their mother baked a cake for the Barnado's tea party on the estate. The shapeless, inedible once-a-year cake that the boys were charged with delivering to the community centre on Manor Road, and the year they finally became too embarrassed to do it and ditched the cake in the bins outside the Robinson Crusoe pub and tried to keep a straight face the rest of the day, back home. It became an annual ritual, Finn and Jack taking their mum's cake to the pub bins, and often they'd see Steve Bachelor, landlord at the Crusoe, sunbathing on a lounger in the car park with music blaring out and a face that didn't care what anyone thought of him.

Finn let himself into 443 West 36th Street and climbed the stairs with Leo's weekly gift. He placed the bag on the doormat and, as he stepped back to double-check he had the right door number, he had the sensation of a man planting a bomb.

On the other side of the door, William lay awake, listening to the rustling at the front door and the sound of fast-moving feet down the stairs, too fast to be Leo's.

'The new assistant,' he whispered. 'The unknown quantity.'

Joy stirred. William turned on to his side and looked at her. It was an age thing, he knew it was an age thing, the transformation in one's appearance when asleep, the fact that his wife had looked like Sleeping Beauty once upon a time and now, on mornings like these when he woke before her, he glimpsed her death mask. Mouth open, jaw slack, a breathing losing interest in itself. An age thing. His age, all in the eyes of a beholder more preoccupied by growing old than ever before. And he didn't kid himself he was any different, always knew upon waking when he too had corpsed the night away.

He took his first deep, conscious breath of the day, squeezed his eyes open and shut. He rebooted his system with a positive thought, that to grow old without a fear of death was a gift he could thank his faith for. He smiled anew at the sight of his wife, the woman of his dreams.

Today was their late start. They both had one a week and, whatever day Joy's rota gave her, William took the same morning off. Once upon a time he would inform his employers but, truly, it did not matter to the Fountains Emporium what time William Fairman pitched up for work.

The beginning of a new day on this fine earth was a thing beloved by William. Serenaded by NewsTalk 77 on the kitchen windowsill and the rising smell of coffee, the view across the four- and five-highs was cherished by him, held tight to his chest as one of the few things he would not want to live without. On a flat roof behind 35th Street a wiry-looking old dog straightened its front legs and stretched and yawned and, although he couldn't, William fancied that he could hear the languid whimper from its mouth. A bullet-shaped scratch in the sky, reflecting the sun, rose from JFK through the scrawls of other take-offs. The voice on the windowsill told William that service on the elevated 7 was restored following an overnight fire, and that a new website could tell him when the place he lived had suffered an earthquake of any size or description, and that included New York. There were thousands of earthquakes occurring every day beneath our feet without us knowing it or thinking it was anything more than the rumble of traffic. He opened the box of pastries that he had brought in from the doorstep and smiled at the sight of them, placed them beside the wine rack that took up too much space on the worktop. Wedged between the rack and the wall were a bundle of brochures for vacation tours of the Napa Valley and Sonoma region, trips William preferred to read about than to take. Sometimes, in conversation, he and Joy had to remind themselves they hadn't actually been to these places. They talked a good holiday and never left Manhattan.

The marvel of their kitchen was the way the sunrise blinded the window. William loved to start his every day on earth here. He and Joy had made love on the worktop many times. Once, as they did so, he'd looked out across the rooftops and wondered if he was the most highly sexed Christian in the Club.

He poured her coffee and took it to the bedroom. She was sitting up in bed, speed-dialling, barely conscious. He set the mug down on her bedside table.

'You're perfect,' she muttered.

He pointed at himself and made a question mark of his expression.

'Yes, you.' But she looked serious, about the call she was making. He listened in from the living room.

'Di, it's me, I know you're always up at this hour... we'll spread the maps out and have a good look at your trip... use William and me as a contact when you sub-let... please forgive my crabbiness last night, it was awful...'

William drank his coffee at the kitchen window with a smile on his face and the sun flaring the gaps in the west side, gaps that William did not want filled by chrome and glass. He felt proud of Joy for waking with an urgent need to put right the previous evening. She joined him at the window and hugged him. She was responsive now that she had rebalanced a world listing from her lack of generosity (notwithstanding how unappealing in every way the McGuires' travel plans still sounded). She felt tiny to William this morning, in his arms. Sometimes she seemed bigger than him; other times he enveloped her when he held her. He liked both versions. They both liked both. The variation seemed to share itself equally and according to their needs.

She sat quietly in the living room. He watched her from the window, understood her silence. She was still bugged by a lingering self-reproof about her behaviour the previous evening, and he knew that she would not talk about it any further, for, despite her strength of character, and the way she caught the eye, she was shy and didn't want to be deciphered. He had looked on as, purposely or not, she had hit the perfect note across the years in seeming to give everything of herself to all people while revealing nothing. William's understanding of this was more than the backbone to their romance – it was the reason for it. It was, for Joy, love itself.

They walked together to the health food store Joy worked in, Complementary, and parted with a kiss, and William felt his soul gladden at the prospect of the walk to Fountains which he loved so much. His morning walk was the ball of energy in the eastern sky made flesh on the sidewalks of the neighbourhood he adored. People drinking coffee in a window on the avenue, the bins spilling over with trash, a gridlock of umbrellas, the uncertain expression of a tourist strayed too far off-Broadway, it was all God's work to William, wonderful in its steadfast familiarity and for escorting him to the routine of his beautifully solitary job.

He loved to walk. It had begun, probably, on his first Christmas Day in the city, which he'd spent alone, living a newly arrived bachelor life in a rented room in Bloomingdale, having met neither Joy nor Jesus. He had walked the stretch of Fifth Avenue from Washington Square to the Park that Christmas Day, to lend structure to it, and been delighted by snowfall across the late morning, and by shop-window-gazing and greeting strangers on the sidewalk. He gave to the homeless and gazed out with a calm, dewy-eyed thrill from the windows of the coffee shops he stopped in, reminding himself, proudly, that he was a long way from Illinois. He arrived at the Park as evening fell and the street-lights lit a new-dusting blizzard, creating a moment in time exquisite enough to bind him for life to this town. By the time he found one corner of a table to share in a packed Barney Greengrass, he felt hewn from New York granite. The sight of his own parents strolling Fifth Avenue with him and Joy a year later was something that to this day, this glorious spring day, William was able to shut his eyes and relive on demand, and feel ecstatic about. His idea of a heaven was being returned to them. The way he imagined death was a simple, painless turn of the head to find his parents returned to Amsterdam Avenue, taking their suitcases out of a taxi and looking up with incredulous happiness at the sight of their son with his arm around the beautiful Joy Emerson.

William installed himself in his office in the upper vaults of the store and got down to work with two further walks to look forward to. The first was a late-morning stroll on one of the shop floors (he let his mood lead him, but it tended to be Maps & Antiquities) and the second a lunchtime walk of a dozen blocks to Calvani's on 21st Street, where he stood at the bar to sip a double espresso and where the cut of his suit and the mildness of his manner lent him the appearance of a dormouse of a man, either a bachelor, or a man wedded to a tyrant of a wife with an opera singer's bosom.

Today, he returned from Calvani's with a sandwich, which he ate while he worked. Susan French texted at two-thirty and by three o'clock she was coiled tight beneath the bedsheets in the corner of the office. She turned faintly in her cracked, porcelain sleep then did not stir again, not even when the 'Adagio Assai' of Ravel's *Piano Concerto in G* was interrupted by a call from the ground floor.

William squinted at the phone, as if asking it if it meant to ring. It was a rare occurrence.

At the sink in the corner, he slooshed with mouthwash and combed his hair. He took the stairs to the tenth floor and crossed the broad parquet aisles laid with Oriental rugs, passing the vast Whitaker chandeliers and the oldest operational wooden escalator in Manhattan, the worn beauty of which he marvelled at still. In William, familiarity bred not contempt but deeper love, at home and at work, and, with the confidence of a man who felt loved in return by the stately, fading institution that employed him, he took the elevator to the ground floor and in his modest, unhurried style ambled into the offices where a solid, disgruntled man in his sixties stood next to Fountains' new young general manager, George White.

The sullen man greeted William's arrival by folding his arms across his chest. He had a brick imprint of a forehead, tight-knit red hair, and a freckled face pulled taut by overexposure to the sun during a lifetime's sailing off Westhampton. Moisturiser had never been an option.

Only then did William notice an elderly woman seated in the corner. She looked ferocious, familiar with wealth and getting her own way. She had watery eyes and a drinker's nose and a tight perm from the realm of the genderless, and beneath these features, or perhaps because of them, William could see that she was the man's mother. Their name was Bolton and, although there was not much about Fountains that George White truly understood, he was only too aware of the fact that the Boltons were of eye-watering value to the store.

Bolton. The name wormed its way through William's brain until it made a connection. A year back, Mrs Bolton had sent William an envelope of photos of her Martha's Vineyard summer house. These photographs dated from the fifties all the way through to the fledgling years of the twenty-first century. The house had been interior-designed and stocked by Fountains after the war, and many interesting items of practical and decorative furniture had been added from the store over the years. He remembered her letter, stately but illuminating. Her husband had died recently and she was sifting through hundreds of loose photographs stashed away in cardboard boxes and had remembered William Fairman's letter requesting archival material relevant to the store.

The snaps old man Bolton had taken all his life had unwittingly created a twentieth-century portrait, decades' worth of Fountains employees delivering to the Martha's Vineyard home. One of the photos had been on the Fountains Emporium website for over a year, and that was the reason for Hunter Bolton III's visit with Mummy. That photograph, dated 1999 on the website, as per the date written on the back by the late Hunter Bolton II, portrayed a George III giltwood side table in the centre of the garden room and the two Fountains employees who had delivered it. The men stood happily, looking relaxed as they posed for the old man, having done so plenty of times over the years, and pleased, always, to make the trip up to Massachusetts to this beautiful pile where time stood still except when it came to the old man's tipping, which was way ahead of inflation and came gift-wrapped in the same enthusiasm that had helped Hunter II take over Hunter I's shipping firm, turn it into a construction business and add six zeros to its value.

'We've made a mistake, William, an innocent one,' George White said.

William smiled politely in turn at everyone in front of him. He waited to be introduced but instead George beckoned him to a computer screen and pointed at the photograph of the Boltons' garden room on the website.

'That should not be on public display,' Hunter Bolton III said.

'We'll take it off,' George said. He had already stated this a number of times prior to Mr Bolton's insisting that the man responsible for this situation be wheeled out.

William straightened up and produced the curious smile of a man wondering what the problem was. In Mr Bolton he saw a handsome man with an ugly heart who had come here to have the last word, but he castigated himself for being judgemental.

'My mother's sending you these photographs was not an invitation to publish them on your website. It certainly was never that.'

It had been exactly that. Mrs Bolton had been nothing but enthusiastic in her letter. William knew it, and so presumably did the old girl, whom William spared the indignity of a glance.

Very few people visited Fountains' creaky and slowly developing website, but Murphy's law insisted that one who had was the ex-wife of Hunter Bolton III, and she had been particularly interested in the 1999 photograph, featuring as it did, in one corner, the Claude-Joseph Vernet which Hunter had given her as a fiftieth birthday present in the hope of saving their marriage. The painting had disappeared from their Manhattan apartment when she retained the place after their divorce in '97, and Hunter Bolton III had insisted he didn't have it and had not held back when chastising her for allowing such a treasure to go missing.

The old lady broke her silence, with a voicebox that nowadays sounded shrill when attempting to sound dominant. 'That painting is worth two million dollars and my son should never have given it to his wife in the first place.'

Mr Bolton tensed up and immediately transferred to William his anger at being reprimanded publicly by Mother. 'You need to correct your mistake,' he said, addressing the horizon over William's shoulder.

'My mistake?' William asked.

'It's easily done,' George White said, brightly. 'Easily fixed.'

'You got the date wrong,' Bolton said. 'You can be clear about that. '96 not '99. The photo was taken in '96.'

William could picture the old man's handwriting on the back of the photo. He could have the photo in the room for them in under ten minutes, but knew that was the last thing that was wanted.

'We can indeed,' George said. 'Not your fault, William, but we need to rectify this with a letter and make clear the correct date of the photo. And change the website.'

'1996 and no later,' Bolton said, then indulged in a spot of repetition. 'My mother's sending you some of Dad's photos is not an invitation to spray them all over the atmosphere.'

George White nodded eagerly at William. William looked at the wall beyond George for fear of showing his disdain. Hunter Bolton III stopped grinding his teeth and his jaw muscles settled back down to sleep after a decent workout. He had been far from convinced when his mother had persuaded him to take their complaint to the store in person

(Hunter Bolton III went to very few places in person), but now he was pleased that he had. It was good to have a presence, and, since his wife had remarried so happily and so modestly and so very, very quickly after he left her, Hunter had felt a little lonely in the world. It was good to get out and have contact with people like this. He felt satisfied, in as much as he felt anything.

William returned to his office in the heavens, discarded his tie and put into a drawer the note from George White in which was set out the exact wording of the letter he was to write, confirming his mistake in dating the photograph.

He rolled a cigarette and took it to the window. The air that crept in through the small open pane of glass was warm. He was convinced that spring had taken hold and the doom-merchants were mistaken in believing there'd be another cold snap. He looked down on a miniature 17th Street. On days as beautiful as this, he felt he could lay his hands upon the people below and make them as content as he. He could heal these people. He could heal Mr Bolton and his mother who, it occurred to him, could be the girl from the photograph tucked into the window beside him. A girl of, say, twelve years old in, say, 1935, would now be an eighty-three-year-old woman. The thought spooked him and enchanted him too, and he instantly felt a strong belief that it was her, or that, even if it wasn't, the fact that it could be meant something. He admired the old bird for her longevity. What an amazing, wonderful world, he told himself. Too good to spoil with a lie: he would not write the letter, or alter the website.

Susan joined William at the window, moving more quietly than the air. She took the cigarette from William and drew on it. She climbed the stepladder and sat on the deep sill. Her feet were bare. William climbed up too and they shared his cigarette and his cloud. Two hundred feet of steel, brick and human flesh beneath them, Mrs Bolton asked her son to stop a moment while she caught her breath. She had felt a little dizzy when she got up from her seat to leave, born from a quiver of repulsion at her son's tendency towards brutishness in public. Her husband had been such a kind man, despite his success. She missed him terribly. She composed herself and then marched ahead of her son, because she knew how it annoyed him, and pushed through the doors of the main entrance on to Sixth Avenue. She hailed a cab, before her son could, and it took them uptown, to their residence overlooking the Park.

11

Leo gave Finn a hundred dollars. 'Take this for now. At some point I need to sort out what I pay you.'

'And what I'm doing,' Finn said. 'You haven't given me anything to do.'

He set out in search of ways to delay his return to the hovel. He shadow-boxed on a ball court at dusk, in a dark corner of the Piers, out of reach of the overhead lights and a few yards away from Glenn's dishwashing job. Tied to a mesh fence was a poster of a cartoon George Bush, eyeballs popping out of his head, sucking Condoleezza Rice's penis. The breeze moved them back and forth.

He walked and came to the disused elevated rail line he had noticed before. A billboard on the bridge bore the legend: COLLECTORS WANT TO BE DEALERS, DEALERS HOPE TO BE STARS, AND CURATORS DREAM TO BE ARTISTS. Patrick Mimran.

Finn noticed the nodding grass heads above the billboard, which swayed in the glow of streetlights on Tenth Avenue. He followed the rail line north, walking beneath it and alongside it, pursuing the promise of something he might understand, the presence of something rural insinuated by the stalks. He entered a goods yard where the night lay soft above a confluence of rail tracks that reflected the lit orange sky and bled corrosion into the dark ground. Finn knew there had to be people here somewhere but was propelled forward by the same nervous exploration that had taken him down into the quarries and up into the treetops of Sussex as a boy, in a perpetual quest for a corner of the world he could kid himself had not been discovered or that here, in the overbuilt city, might have been forgotten. On the far side of the goods yard, iron stairs rose to the elevated line, and he clambered up on to it, placing his feet on the most solid parts of the condemned steps, ignoring the KEEP OUT signs and the gaps where the metal had disintegrated.

Manhattan offered him new variations on solitude, and this was the best yet. The rooftop water towers gathered like crows on the skyline, and watched the little lost English boy pick his way through the rust meadow, every cell of his body more at home for smelling the weeds and for feeling the drag of long grass. He had walked railways before, played chicken on the main line with lads from the estate, and in this place, abandoned, gone to seed, Finn could imagine remaining.

In a scrapyard beneath him, colossal iron girders lay discarded like pick-up-sticks in a giant's play pen. Around him, sumac had sprouted from the flakes of rotten sleepers in front of a warehouse with pink graffiti on the walls and two small windows that watched Finn. He read the graffiti he passed on a corrugated-sheet wall, spray-painted in silver and sky-blue: 'Moose', 'Kansas', 'Gas', 'Nerds'. He recognised apple buds and the horizontal slashes of cherry tree bark. Brittle, hoary grass framed a view below of the FedEx lot opposite Leo's gallery. Tarnished and bitten by the winter, the grass was yellow and brown and copper and beautiful and cold, flown in from the Midwest in honour of the ghosts of the West Side cowboys who preceded the elevated trains. This wilderness had tended to itself while the city looked elsewhere.

Finn hated himself for thinking it, but it seemed imperative that Dilly, and people like her, should never find this.

He walked south on the lumpy, ragged tracks and the sleepers shone in the urban light against icy grey shingle. Thick, gnarly twigs stuck out at angles beneath the petrified relics of cow parsley, and at a bend above 18th Street he came face to face with a twenty-foot-high, shirtless, muscle-bound Armani male model. From forty feet below the ripped torso, tanned and glistening in the shadowy chill air, came the shrieks of laughter of four girls stumbling home in big heels and small skirts. Finn looked down at them as a giant would.

He slept tucked against the girders, hugging himself to the illusion of shelter and warmth where the ivy was thick like a solid wall. He lay on his back, the huge cast-iron rivets mountainous to his eyes, and he felt happy. He listened to the whisper of the cool air rising off the Hudson and the miniature sleeping lives of a million New Yorkers drumming along the railroad lines and reaching his ear like a distant playground. He was safe. Stars appeared just before he slept and he was not sure if he was dreaming them. He remembered the small cupboard in his grandmother's bedroom on the other side of the estate. He dreamed of the night she died, that he walked past her body and opened the small cupboard door and found rows and rows of shelves all full of toys and games. He walked for hundreds of yards to the end of the shelves and where they ended there was outer space, lit fluorescent by stars and planets.

He turned in his half-sleep, pressing against the dollar bills in his front pocket, the touch of which and the open air afforded him a smile. Gentle vents of air swept along the line, reminding Finn of the silent murmurations of starlings above the Sussex Levels, the way they painted the sky inky grey. The vents came through like a slow train, symmetrical above the tracks, and he allowed one of them to usher him into the same deep, carefree sleep that his big brother was craving in the same moment.

It irritated Jack, the sight of the five hundred dollars sitting in an envelope on his kitchen worktop. Sometimes, Finn made no sense to him. And, when Jack was sleepless, what he didn't understand overwhelmed him.

The list he had compiled of places to show Finn made him feel like an idiot now. Thank Christ he hadn't stuck it to the fridge during his baby brother's oh, so short stay. He had printed it out on company letterhead and it was a niggling embarrassment about that detail that had prevented him from pinning it up where Finn and his girlfriend could see it. He folded it now into his pocket and resolved to get something useful done, even though it was getting late. He slugged a dose of the cough medicine that was failing to make an impression on him and stood over the laundry basket waiting for another dizzy spell to pass. When it had, he was left with the thought of how constructive, how pleasing it would be to get his and Holly's pile of home towels and sports towels washed. It was a sizeable pile, what with both of them being one-time towel users (no exceptions) and keen athletes.

The netherworld of the basement laundry was deserted yet bore the sounds of human existence. The elevator shafts cranked and groaned here. Loose objects left in pockets chimed rhythmically. A door slammed somewhere distant, and the occasional, unfathomable noises that a high-rise building made of its own free will came and went with the same absence of explanation that had confounded many in Jack's place before him. Sounds to shrug off. Through the pulsing green of a tired, failing, out-of-tune striplight, the clock on the wall read near enough ten-thirty. Jack examined each towel as he placed it into the drum of the washer – for what, he had no idea. He mixed the large bath towels with the small hand towels, layering them because he had read that this was the right thing to do. He had once noticed a ring of dirt on Finn's collar as they walked to school and that evening found all Finn's school shirts embedded with grime around the neck. He had washed them, woken even earlier than usual to dry and iron them, and from that point on had made sure to keep up Finn's laundry so that his kid brother never stood out or got picked on.

He wasn't familiar with the night shift down here. Sunday mornings before the gym (Jack), tennis (Holly) and brunch (together) was their usual time in the dry heat of the basement, with the fabric softener smell and the drone of the machines and the scratched linoleum floors and the elderly in search of company, the aggrieved in search of respite from an unreasonable partner and the cute young roomies in hot-pants or pyjamas in search of something just a little bit less straight-looking than Jack, although he often got a second look. The night shift was different, the wall of sound from the unmanned machines louder (although that could have been Jack's head cold), and greater the sense of being down among the intestines of a building buckling beneath the weight of the lives above.

He came up for air during the wash cycle. He was exhausted and sat in a heap outside the building, and watched the lights of the Kinsale Tavern casting pools of orange on to the busy, hurry-home sidewalk, the Celtic signwriting above, the shapes of movement inside through windows heavy with condensation. The avenue was busy but behind him the lobby was quiet. The doorman was out back and no one was around. A man sat at a second-floor window above the tavern looking on to the street, lost in thought or perhaps listening to someone behind him that Jack couldn't see, being told he was no longer wanted, being told how much he was adored, being told there was even more dog shit than usual on 96th Street today, told to wash the dishes, come to bed. Or maybe alone, after all; Jack couldn't tell. The man was still, as still as Jack, and perhaps even more solitary. Jack hoped not. He had the capacity to worry about complete strangers, which in New York City was borderline unmanageable.

A Hispanic man stepped out of the tavern and took a look through the window next door at the state of the pre-cooked Tex Chicken. Jack watched him through the blur of people passing on the sidewalks and the streams of southbound traffic. Everything about everybody was noticeable to Jack because anybody might have been a clue as to how to live here, a pointer he could not afford to miss. In his country of birth, seeing a Hispanic-looking man hitch up his jeans while looking at a fast-food menu would not be noteworthy to him. But, here, still, three years in, he wondered who everybody was, where they went home to, what they worked as, how they survived, what page of the history book they appeared on. Every person Jack saw added to the overwhelming feeling New York City gave him, that there were far too many people here for it all to stick together. He rose to his feet and stepped to the kerb and looked south down the avenue, wondered again how it all could have been built so quickly. He sometimes lost his nerve at the thought of providing food and electricity and love for all these people, as if it were his job to do so.

Topped up to his requisite levels of unbearable burden, he returned to the basement, stopping to read a flier freshly taped to the lobby noticeboard.

www.snuggleup.com

A HIGHLY PROFESSIONAL CUDDLING SERVICE.
SNUGGLING, CUDDLING, CHAT, MOVIE DATES
AND ALL ACCEPTABLE PLATONIC ACTIVITY.

$50 PER HOUR MANHATTAN. $40 PER HOUR BROOKLYN,
QUEENS, THE BRONX AND STATEN ISLAND.

It figured, Jack thought, that even a cuddle cost more on Manhattan.

In the laundry room, a couple in their mid-forties taped Snuggleup fliers to the wall. Jack recognised them from the building. They were his precise image of Big Sur people or San Francisco, the sort of couple you noticed. They gave the impression of having wandered into Manhattan barefoot. They said hi to Jack and he said hi back and the man said, 'Oh, poor you,' as Jack's ill-health could not be missed.

Jack sat across from them, by his drier, feeling a hot prickling across his back and weakness in the legs. Through the noise of the machines he said, 'Is that for real?' and could hear his voice inside the clogged spaces of his own head without being sure he had spoken loudly enough to be heard.

'Oh, sure. Absolutely,' the man said.

Jack pulled a face at the idea. The man smiled warmly and said, 'That's totally cool if you've got people you're close with, but there's a lot of disconnected souls out there.'

'They don't all have fifty bucks an hour.'

'Most people living in this city have fifty,' the woman interjected.

Jack could not believe that was true, but he saw her point. 'I'm sorry,' he said, 'I'm being cynical and I don't mean to be. Hypocritical. You should charge what people are willing to pay, same as we all do. It's just a strange idea to me, paying to be held.'

'We understand totally,' she said, and smiled with her eyes. Jack looked at them – they were green – and tried hard to rally against the idea that just about everything in the universe was to do with sex, but eyes like hers made it hard to argue. 'You'd be amazed how many people need this.'

'Not at all,' Jack said, 'I'm amazed people can admit it.'

There was buzzing in his ears from the legions of mucus encamped in his sinuses. It mixed seamlessly with the noise of the drier, and the more he looked at the couple, the more he wanted to drive through California with a partner who needed no persuading to be there with him. The couple were saying something else to him but the noise in his head was like a stage curtain between them, or the glare of the sun in dreams when it was impossible to open one's eyes fully, so he smiled at them and nodded and turned to watch his drier.

The man tore off one of the strips and handed it to Jack. 'Website's on there, man. You should have one.'

'He should work for us, be a snuggler,' the woman said, tilting her head to one side as she studied Jack.

Jack made to laugh at this but got bent over by coughing instead. When he righted himself they had gone. He sat forward and dragged from his pocket the list of excursions he had made for himself and Finn, and mocked himself as he read it. One: the Circle Line. (Jack thought about it: this was an okay idea, a thoroughly safe start. Touristy but excellent, a complete overview of Manhattan with some staple highlights and a few surprises thrown in.) Two: a walk across the Brooklyn Bridge. (Ditto. Safe. A sure thing, involving a physical activity – walking – to occupy them if conversation was stilted.) Three: the reading room in the public library. (A decidedly dubious idea, but the place meant a lot to Jack and he hoped it would to Finn too. Seemed unlikely, though, now that he saw it in print.) Next: a Knicks game at the Garden. (Another surefire hit, and maybe take him into the public library en route to the Knicks so that he's distracted thinking about going to the game and doesn't realise he's in a library until it's too late.) Five: Inwood Hill Park. (The geological gem, but who was he kidding? Scratch it.) Five: the Met. (Pushing it, but worth a try.) Six: the Lower East Side Tenement Museum. (Really reaching here, but so interesting and important. Or Ellis Island, if the ferry ride sells it to him – a ferry ride, what is he, eight?) Next: the Park, take a ball. (Safe bet.) Next: the Flatiron Building. (He would insist and Finn would get it once he saw it, from the angle on Fifth Avenue and Broadway.)

Jack shook his head at the list. His idea of a good time was possibly no one else's. Surely not Finn's. He scrunched up the paper and threw it across the basement, straight into the bin. It didn't touch the sides. He took pleasure in the perfection of his throwing arm (where were the nubile roomies and the green-eyed hippies when you wanted them to see you at your best?) and it released a playfulness in him which, along with his fuzzy head, prompted him to climb up on to the bench that was there for folding dry clothes on, and lay on his side. He rested his head in the palm of one hand, and fell asleep to the heat and metronomic drone of the drier.

Finn was woken by the cold in the dead of night and lay still and watched the sky and thought of Jack holding his dad as he died on the roadside, and everyone calling Jack a hero for not allowing his father to die alone. He felt dry and sick in the mouth and then a tingle of heaviness coursed through his spine and drew him back down into deep sleep and the next thing he knew he was curled on his side, regaining consciousness in daylight. The sparrows were singing louder than the traffic on Tenth Avenue. He opened his eyes and watched the tip of a grass stalk staggering in the breeze, knocking against the spire of the Empire State Building. He saw the blue of grape hyacinth where his hands lay. He jumped to his feet and rubbed his face and walked to the side of the line. He gripped the railing and looked over at the grey, patchy Chelsea side streets. An optical trick on a somnolent mind made the drop to the street below seem like a mere step away, one moment, and then a mile high. He imagined the torture of being able to see a normal life far beneath you and not return to it, to know for sure that there was no going back, that your life had slipped beyond a tipping point towards death on a day that had started like

155

all the others. Had his dad known for sure, as he stumbled along the roadside, that he was finished? Had he cared? Had he regretted that he would never see Finn again? When Jack arrived, had his dad wished that Finn were there too? It was the first time Finn had thought deeply about it. He had been adamant from day one that he'd not catch himself caring.

He found a staircase near to where a beaten-up grand piano with chainsaw cuts and burns lay strewn among the weeds and he took the steps down to Little West Street and naïvely believed that the disused elevated railway line was his secret and he whispered to his brother, 'I know something you don't know.'

Jack would never spend a night the way he had just done, Finn knew that, and, while it saddened him that his brother would be so alarmed by his doing those things that were as natural as breathing to him and which made so much more sense to him than many of the working parts of the world, it struck him that if he and his brother teamed up they would amount to one rounded, interesting individual. He was going to have to discard a lot of this thinking, or his desire to give Jack a taste of life with Uncle Trevor back home would be beyond rescue.

Leo and Astrid watched Finn mooch into the gallery on time but with the indelible mark of one who had slept rough. They stared, with almond croissants held up to their open mouths. The boy sat at the desk with them, shuddered once from the cold in his bones and picked up the third pastry, taking a large, predatory bite. He looked raw. His hair was rope, and defied gravity. There was grass on his clothes and the imprint of an industrial-sized rivet on his cherry cheek. Astrid sat forward and studied the visual information available to her.

'Where did the little thief sleep last night?' she asked, slyly.

'Up on that disused railway line…' Finn said.

Leo stood up. 'What! Why?'

Finn shrugged. Astrid shook her head. She had long ago perfected the art of not being impressed by anything. She took a second bite of her croissant and pushed it away, out of her own reach.

'You said you had a place to stay,' Leo said. 'The guy in prison. I remember details like that. If you lie to me, this doesn't work.'

'I have. I just liked it up there.'

'It's madness. People sleep in beds!'

Astrid laughed at Leo's distress and told him to calm down. Finn shrugged, confused by the fuss. 'I liked it up there,' he repeated.

'Enjoy it before they feng shui it,' Astrid said. She turned to Leo. 'The eleven art history graduates you turned down would have slept under a roof last night, as well as being legally permitted to work.' She was in one of her clipped, friendly, organised moods and by mid-morning she was deep in conversation with a public art space in Boston and Leo was being screamed at down the phone by the artist called Tilhoff, who was next to show at the gallery. Leo inched the receiver away from his ear. The further the receiver travelled, the clearer Finn could hear a raised voice down the line. By the time the voice stopped, Leo's posture had buckled a little and he looked bored. 'Does it really matter, Tilhoff?' Leo asked. The line went dead. Leo smiled phlegmatically at Finn and put down the phone. 'Never ask an artist if it really matters.'

Finn was sceptical of any man choosing to have only one name. 'What was that about?' he asked.

'A rather magnificent, sad old department store wants to commission Tilhoff to paint six very huge, beautiful paintings of the store's interior and to pay him one hundred and eighty thousand dollars to do so. He insists each painting should be a triptych, three panels side by side making one picture, but Fountains, that's the store, don't want that.'

Finn raised his eyebrows in disbelief. 'I'll paint them a few pictures for a hundred grand,' he said. 'Is your painter guy pissed off?'

'They're all pissed off,' Leo said, and he didn't yet know if he was deflated or liberated by the fact that he no longer cared. He rose to his feet, rubbing his hands together. 'Enough of that, I think it's time you came and looked at lots of art.'

Oh, shit, Finn thought.

It began with Leo taking Finn to a large, open space with concrete floors and banks of ivory daylight at tall frosted windows. 'This is Andrea Rosen's place. This woman has great integrity.'

'She doesn't take fifty per cent?'

Leo shot Finn a dark look and found the boy smiling impishly, a new expression, far removed from Finn's default setting.

'I like her taste,' Leo said.

'I'll like it too, then...' Finn said, in all seriousness.

'You don't have to like it just because I do; that's not the point.'

'No, I'm happy to. Makes no difference to me.'

Leo let it go. He took him on to a Fairfield Porter retrospective at the Betty Cuningham Gallery where a tall, elderly security guard stood with a heavy bible in the palms of both hands and his head at a right angle to his neck as he read it, the exact same angle at which his grandson used his cellphone. The whole place felt dead to Finn. He didn't like it, nor did he like being dragged in front of the photography of Nan Goldin.

'They're just snaps of her mates. I could do that.'

'But you haven't done that.'

'Artists should do stuff I can't do.'

'Good.'

'What's good?'

'Opinion is good.'

Next up was Van de Weghe Fine Art where, in hushed tones, Leo introduced the boy to the work of Jean-Michel Basquiat (surely a nineteen-year-old would relate to this). 'He started out as a spray-painting graffiti artist, he was very cool, and a terribly important artist. He was in a punk band with Vincent Gallo, and he worked with Bowie too.'

Finn nodded in a way Leo couldn't read.

'He was a pretty interesting figure,' Leo said.

'Was or is?'

'Was. Dead at twenty-seven. Overdose. Give me your opinion.'

Finn took a good hard look. 'He didn't overdose on the ability to draw.'

Leo took pleasure in Finn's disdain, in the purity of it, unadulterated by malice or learning. And he took even greater pleasure in telling Finn how much the Basquiats cost.

'For Christ's sake...' Finn muttered, giving up on the human race. But there was something Finn liked in the old man, a looseness in his movements as he looked at the art, an openness in his face, the absence of alcohol in his bloodstream, and Finn embarrassed himself by thinking how good it would be to introduce Leo to his brother, the way other nineteen-year-olds would bring a girlfriend home to impress their parents. *Jack, this is my boss. I work for him and he pays me! You see, bro, I'm doing it all by myself. I don't need anyone. I'm not asking for anything.*

They took a break in Maison Claudine and Finn was surprised at how awkward Leo became with the waitress who served them and at how he watched her go and muttered aimlessly, 'It would be nice to help someone like her, you know...'

'Yeah,' Finn laughed under his breath. 'I think I know...'

They sat in silence until Leo panicked belatedly. 'I didn't mean someone black or someone poor or a woman...' he stuttered.

'I know,' Finn said. 'You meant someone beautiful, who you want to sleep with.'

'There are some people,' Leo replied, directing the conversation away from his crush on Willow, 'who want a painting on their wall because it will speak for them and about them. It says that this man or woman has the wealth to own this work of art, the aesthetical dimension to want it, the taste to choose it. This painting mirrors some part of them that they wish to be seen. Fifty thousand dollars is, for some, a reasonable price to pay for such esteem. And if it proves to be the price of love, if someone loves them for the person they assume them to be because they are the owner of that painting, then it is cheap at the price. I know men and women who have spent millions on art because it buys them dignity, status, which matters a great deal to some people, if such a thing can be bought.'

'Can it?'

'I don't know.'

'How much have you bought for yourself? Art, I mean.'

'Some.' Leo stood. 'Quite a bit. Let's get back to it.'

The entrance to the PaceWildenstein Gallery was the first place to catch Finn's attention without Leo's instigation. He sloped inside and saw thousands of white Styrofoam cups set out in a glacial landscape. 'That's pretty cool,' he muttered.

'It's about waste, I think,' Leo said.

'Is it? Oh…'

'What do you think?'

'Nothing. It just looks good and it's made of plastic cups and…' He laughed to himself.

'And what?' Leo asked.

'And it's just good. *End of*, as my brother would say.'

'Tara Donovan is the artist,' Leo said.

'It looks best from way back,' Finn said, 'like a snowstorm.'

'You've got a brother back home?' Leo asked.

'I've got a brother.' Finn picked up a leaflet describing the work. 'But who buys something like this? You can't put it in your house.'

'You like it, then?' Leo reconfirmed.

'It's okay.'

'Hallelujah! There's nothing you don't like about it? Nothing crap? Nothing ridiculous?'

'No. This one was good. You've saved your reputation, after all the horseshit you've shown me up till now.'

Finn wandered out. Leo followed, his spirits buoyed by the boy's teasing, and something in the Sonnabend Gallery caught his eye. Seeing his boss ready to divert into another gallery, Finn walked on. 'Let's stop now,' he said, 'before you ruin it.'

'I'll catch you up.' Leo went inside. He leaned close to an azalea made of painted bronze, with tiny, golden human hands growing from the tip of each branch. The desire to buy it for Willow suddenly burned a trail through him.

After work, Finn resumed his hunt for inexpensive ways of delaying his return to the hovel. The thought of going back there exposed the dark, angry ridge landscaped into his feelings. A private viewing had spilled out on to the sidewalk on 25th Street. At the entrance was a poster advertising an exhibition of hand-printed original photographs by Arthur Tress. Finn took a bottle of water from the ice tub and made his way through the packed corridors to a cramped gallery. The black and white prints had been taken in the sixties. He saw a highway junction in the Bronx, a man passed out in Central Park, a guy sitting on a telegraph pole floating on the Harlem River. It was hot in the room with all the bodies, among them handsome women who smelled good to Finn. He readied himself for unwanted attention; if anyone were to ask him what he thought of the work, he'd say *It's about waste, I think...* and move confidently on.

He came to a photograph entitled *Cemetery View*. Thousands of tombs covered the contours of a vast cemetery and above it an elegant panorama of Manhattan levitated like a grey ghost in the haze. The gravestones swelled across undulating lawns, a high tide of human history written in slate and stone. Finn remained looking at the photograph for some time, and felt able to climb into it, walk back to Manhattan across the lawns.

He twisted through the mêlée back to the street, scooping up a handful of canapés, which he took to the Piers and ate with a view of the currents in the Hudson. He saw the man from the Tress photograph floating past, his legs straddling the telegraph pole, still drinking, still young, powerful, eternal. The photograph was forty years old. He wondered if the man was still alive. For the first time, he understood that a city had its ghosts, layers upon layers of them. He had thought that ghosts were for the country, for big lonely houses far from the crowd. He thought about Nicole Kidman in *The Others*. He had loved that film, the absence of words. And at fourteen he had loved her and he had believed he'd be perfect for her. The fact that she was a ghost only seemed to strengthen his belief that they were suited. But of course there were ghosts in a city, the ones who built it, pulled it down, rebuilt it. He saw that now. And that this city was good at sweeping up its rubble and allowing its ghosts. Suddenly, violent acts and violent men seemed feeble to him and he thanked New York City for reminding him of that. No wonder his brother who loved history wanted to live here. Maybe Jack buried his head in history because he struggled with today. Maybe his brother had a blind spot there and needed help with that. Maybe beating the crap out of him was not the best way to do that. Maybe it was possible that a kid brother could know things a big brother hadn't yet grasped. For a moment, all these things with his brother seemed possible to Finn. And then, instantly, the possibilities fell away, water through his fingers, and, faced with the improbability of Jack ever listening to him let alone learning from him, he couldn't remember what it was he had thought possible with his big brother a moment ago.

He ate his snacks and saw Nicole Kidman, fleetingly, and she seemed to smile at him. The river was deserted. The picture show in his head fell empty. He left the Piers and returned to 25th Street as the gallery cleared. He went in part to further delay his return to his lodgings and partly to get more food, but also because he felt compelled by the photograph. He went against the tide and found the cemetery view in the emptying room. Left alone, he indulged in the sensation that the photograph had been taken for him, that it existed specifically for him to see. He felt opened up by it. The wide open space, dotted with headstones, mirrored the feeling that his chest and ribs were being prised apart and air forced into spaces he had never been able to breathe. It was too soon to know if he was suffocating or breathing properly for the first time.

Nearby, a man coughed politely and mentioned that the gallery was closing.

'Where's this photo taken?' Finn asked, forcefully.

The man peered at the photo. 'It's very special, isn't it?'

'I'm not buying.'

'I get that.'

The man took off his glasses to take a closer look. 'Somewhere in Queens,' he said, 'from the title, obviously. I mean, its looking at Manhattan directly from the east, isn't it, clearly... so, out there somewhere.'

'How do I get to Queens?'

12

William was surprised by a knock at the garret door. Visitors were rare. He switched off his music as George White stepped in. The grandson of store president Sidney White (and the unashamed beneficiary of nepotism) took a look at the room. 'Christ…' he muttered. Even though the ceiling was a lofty, vaulted space, the fact that it sloped (eighteen feet above his head) prompted George to stoop. 'Full of character up here…'

'Yes, sir.'

George grimaced at being called 'sir' and kept hold of the expression. 'I've had Mr Bolton and his mother back in. You didn't send that letter, did you?'

'It would have been a lie.'

'Why a mattress in your office?'

'For my back. I lie on it for twenty minutes during my allotted lunch hour.'

'Interesting ticking. I've fired you.' This was said casually.

'What!' This was not.

'They wanted blood. And Christ knows they're worth a drop or two. It had to be yours. They've lost a two-million-dollar painting thanks to you.'

William grasped the back of his chair and lowered himself on to it. George spread out his arms in protest. 'What sort of a sixty-year-old man brings his mother with him to make a complaint?!'

William stared, incredulous, at young George White's indifference to what he had done. 'You cannot...' he stuttered '... fire an employee for refusing to lie.'

'What's wrong? You look like you've seen a ghost.'

'This job is... perfect. I have to have this job.'

'Oh, don't be dim, William, we'll give it back to you soon enough. Just had to give the old trout and that hideous fucking man something to make them feel important. Just keep your head down for a bit. No one knows you're here anyway.'

William put his head in his hands. He hated madness, and this felt like madness.

'It seemed the right thing to do,' George said, unperturbed. 'I mean, it worked. Mr Bolton the fifteenth or whatever he calls himself seemed genuinely happy about it. He nearly smiled at one point; it was kind of gross to watch. I've written the letter and thrown in a pound of flesh. I kind of did it on impulse but, at the risk of repeating myself, the Boltons may be repulsive people but they and their buddies are worth a fortune to us.'

William looked at George as if at an exhibit. He needed a description of some kind to read, because he couldn't identify what he was looking at. Every impulse he could get a grip on told him this was a bad idea and that the unconcerned, slick, beautifully turned-out man in front of him, hunched beneath a ceiling more than twenty feet high, was making it up as he went along.

'Are there any other rooms like this up here?' George asked. 'I could have a den.'

There were three further rooms that William knew of, the other corners of the roof space, all identical to this one, but boarded up. He didn't want any neighbours up here, so he shrugged. 'I don't know.'

'I haven't thought all this through, but for now you'd better get a cab into work and come to the goods entrance.'

George went to the mirror above the sink. He smiled at himself, though stopped short of winking, a man on the brink of a chaos he mistook for greatness. 'Gotta go change my suit; there's art to be bought. I'll be seeing your brother later.'

'Brother-in-law,' William corrected him, and immediately regretted doing so, as having Leo for a brother was one of the many wonders of life for an only child from Lincoln, Illinois.

George White stopped at the door. 'Is there a separate elevator, a way of you coming and going without being seen, just for now? I don't imagine the Boltons come in here often but it would be just my luck.'

William sighed and said reluctantly, 'There's an old stairwell to 18th Street.'

'Perfect. Whatever that is, use it.' George paused on his way out. 'I'm sure you're awesome at what it is you do, so keep on doing it but just… don't exist.'

Left alone, William didn't move for some time. He had always resented the term *nervous breakdown* being applied to him (by Joy, and only the once) but it was as good a description as any for the direction he had been headed before Leo got him this job. When the barnstorming twentieth century was running its course, William was in his sixteenth year auditing for a company who pulverised him with red-eye flights up and down the Eastern Seaboard. On one such trip, coming into La Guardia from Charlotte, his plane circled the city for half an hour in a stack and he shifted across to a window seat to watch the lights. As the plane made circles above Long Island an idea began to trouble him and, with the twinkling lights beneath him growing no nearer, the idea dug its tail into his skin and he couldn't pull it out. It was simply that, all of a sudden, flying seemed a little bit too much like messing with God's blueprint – *You guys down there, walking, those feathered guys up there, flapping* – and getting home to Joy felt beyond reach. To land this plane was an outlandish idea. It struck him that to die in his own home, in his own bed, paved a clear and straight path to the Lord and to his parents, whereas death in the air would simply bring oblivion, an ending doused in fear, as far as far could be from what his God had intended. William was not a guy who messed with the Big Guy, so why was he up here six times a week, pushing his luck in mid-air, precisely where his Maker had not wished him to be?

It was instant, his loss of nerve. Even as he travelled back to 36th Street in the comforting bosom of the E Train that night, William had known he couldn't continue. With his peers reaching their fifties with plans of travel and change, William wanted only to get home, wait to see if the millennium was going to be the end of the world and, if it wasn't, to cosy down with Joy in their own small, unattractive nook of the city, and do good things there.

His employers of sixteen years listened to his concerns and proposed that he get over it or quit. Thanks to Leo, Fountains offered him the quiet life at half the income. They also offered him a desk on the accounts floor, to allow him to move between the lonely attic archives and a more sociable environment, but he never used it. He loved to be alone all day and with Joy all night. He knew that his loss of nerve had frightened Joy and on the same occasion she used the term *nervous breakdown* she expressed her admiration for the way Leo remained so undaunted by it, so infinitely supportive of William when it had all felt so perilous to her. They didn't need to talk about the flying. She had always hated it too. And she didn't care about having less money. She loved him. She wanted him unchanged, unshaken, and with William reinstated they were even happier than they had ever been.

George White's aftershave lingered for the rest of the working day, at the end of which William made to the old north staircase. It had been closed to the public since 1964 and the windows bricked in. The beam of William's torchlight caught the engraved gold departmental signs on the swing doors to every floor, each one of them nailed shut and accessible only to ghosts of a golden age: Interior Decorating Department; Menswear; Corsets; Art, Bric-a-Brac and Lamps; Misses and Girls Department; House Gowns and Negligees; The French Display Room; Furs and Fur Garments; Rugs; The Mourning Department. It all felt underwater to William, the wreckage in forgotten depths.

The stairs deposited him on to 18th Street. He cast a disdainful look at the cabs and hated the thought of taking one to work. He rode them like a dog, with the window down. How idiotic this all was, and yet William could see that George White, for all his ignorance, was right on the money in understanding that firing the little man served a big purpose. William was the beacon shining tonight in the life of the Boltons. The fake flames that had engulfed his tidy little form this afternoon blazed the message that their standards, their times, their games, their pursuits, had meaning still. Their epoch was not at a close, they were not dead and buried, and would yet sustain against the barbarian invasions. This faceless, forgettable man, fired for not being up to their own laudably high standards, was the person who saved the Boltons from oblivion. Their dying breed could not be lost to Fountains, for they, and the few Russians and Arabs drawn to the store's timeless tastes, were the modern-day equivalent of the crowds piling through the doors on the Ladies' Mile, and if they were lost then all was lost because the crowds were, most certainly, gone forever. When the girl in the photograph walked through the doors of Fountains a few years before the Second World War began, she entered a store of limitless riches, extravagant window displays, *gratis* lectures on current trends in fashion, complimentary tea and cigarettes, no-obligation interior design visits to upstate homes. Nowadays, the store offered to their valued customers the sacrificial lamb that manifested itself in this particular instance as William. It was enough to make a humble man proud of his place in the grand scheme, and proud William would have been if he weren't so unnerved by having to pretend he didn't exist, an idea that felt a little too close to the bone for comfort.

In an act of monumental defiance by his standards, he ignored the plentiful cabs and walked home. He called Leo and asked him what he thought of the whole thing.

Odd, was what Leo thought. 'That's an odd thing to do, pretend to fire someone. And not necessarily that easy to pull off. You want me to talk to George this evening?'

'No. Thanks. No. I just need to get home.'

'You okay?'

'Yeah. How's the show looking?'

'I've no idea any more,' Leo said, and laughed. 'But Astrid seems confident. You know, she really doesn't need me here, I can come and meet you.'

'She needs you, sure she needs you.' William said. We all need you, he thought.

'Sure you're alright?'

'Yeah. Just want to get home.'

Leo stood with the phone to his ear for a few moments after the call, as if checking William was headed safely in the right direction. The April show was billed as Tilhoff Realist Interiors and, when Leo had visited Tilhoff in his studio two months earlier, giant oil on gesso interiors executed (Leo's choice of word) in photographic detail was what he had seen. But, two days before this evening's private view, Astrid's Tuesday morning had been capsized by the arrival of a pallet-load of portraits from the mononymous artist. By Tuesday lunchtime, she had been more frustrated by Leo's indifference to the five thousand dollars wasted on the brochure than by the artist's intransigence.

Thereafter, the build-up had gone well. Four of the nine large canvases and one of the four small ones had sold to collectors since the show was hung on Wednesday and Astrid was buzzing. Even Finn, though unsure about the outsize limbs (deliberate), bug eyes (deliberate) and three-nostrilled noses (Tilhoff's signature detail), had gushed that Tilhoff's portraits were 'not that bad'.

In the gallery, there was a moment of calm. Astrid had disappeared. Finn was making a cup of his unconventionally strong, sweet tea. It was the way he understood tea to be, the way the guys at work back home liked their tea (he tended to be the one making it for them), but to Astrid and Leo the brew was an abomination, although Leo occasionally accepted a cup and took a sip, fancying that it reacquainted him with memories of a working-class England that he was forgetting he had never experienced in the first place.

Astrid returned with a shirt from Seize sur Vingt for Finn. It was the sort of thing he wouldn't wear for money but consented to for Leo, who, she implied, wanted to smarten him up. Nothing of the sort had crossed Leo's mind, but Astrid was operating on a particular unstoppable inner turbo of hers which kicked in for private views every fourth Thursday. The Astrid-turbo was breathless, excited, passionate and borderline frenzied. At six o'clock, Finn would discover, she changed clothes and changed down a gear and became calm, confident, charming and knowledgeable, and she queened it over the evening, cradling a glass of champagne from which she never sipped (waiting instead for the privacy, later, of her own apartment, where she could down a bottle of pinot inside two hours).

She persuaded Finn to do up the top button of the shirt, which was slim-cut and mauve with subtle yellow stitching and faint pale blue lines. Doing up the top button was, she explained, *the style*. Finn disliked it, but she insisted it looked great on him and even winked at him. (The wink was caused by a turbo malfunction, itself caused by glimpsing Finn's quite extraordinarily beautiful, smooth, lean, muscular torso as he buttoned up.)

The torso had no chores left to do, no more errands to run. Finn's list of tasks for the afternoon was replete with ticks. Astrid ran a tight ship and always had the gallery ready for a private view two hours before the doors opened. Despite this, she watched disapprovingly as Finn took his mug of tea and sat on the steps to the sidewalk, creasing the $175 shirt as he bathed in the lowering April sun and pulled at his collar. He smiled a little at God knew what and emitted a short punchy sigh of metropolitan pleasure. He dared not jinx it by admitting it, but West 26th Street had the potential to feel safe. He drank his tea and strolled lazily, confidently, muscularly across the street to the Bovenkamp Gallery. Dot Yi's painting looked even better with a brew. He moved diagonally, pivoting through his ankles, and at the same time up and down on his haunches, taking perspective to its human limits and getting the most awesome of 3-D shifts from the painting.

Beryl Streep watched Finn with her customary blend of amusement and scorn (ten per cent/ninety per cent), an expression that, once again, she transformed into an alluring smile when Finn glanced at her. He decided the moment had come to step inside now that he understood art and was, according to Astrid, wearing the sort of shirt you wore to a gallery. Inside were seven more of Dot Yi's 3-D paintings, each of them four times bigger than the one in the window. This was 3-D paradise. A Yiorgy.

Finn turned to Beryl. 'I like these paintings.'

'I know,' she said. 'The whole street knows.'

The only other punter, George White, shared a knowing smile with Beryl. 'Aren't they exquisite...' George agreed, wearing his fine art face, the one that resembled the constant detection of a bad smell, even when smiling. On private view nights, George was groomed with such diligence and expense as to appear handsome at a glance, and he accentuated a trace of Ivy League in his vowels, for Beryl's ears. There was no Ivy League on his resumé, but the voice sat well with his position at Fountains and with his ambitions for the evening because tonight George was out to buy art, although the Dot Yi's were not on his list. He admired them, but he didn't want them on the walls of his Meatpacking District loft conversion. The only thing he coveted here was Beryl, which was possibly why he had not brought his Syrian bride along with him.

Finn asked for a price list and a catalogue. Beryl's left hand flinched in the direction of the shelf hidden beneath the counter, but she stopped herself. She was not going to waste a glossy full-page catalogue on this punk.

'All the pieces are thirty thousand dollars,' she said, employing speech as a cold slap across the face.

Finn stood firm, determined not to look shocked by the numbers, but he suspected he was blushing. George strolled over, the sharp tap of his brogues echoing the room. He had donned a William Fioravanti suit for the evening, with his top two shirt buttons undone. He was slight and in lesser cloth would have looked scrawny, but instead he looked rich and fine.

'What's your angle?' George said, affably.

Unlike many, when Finn didn't understand a question he remained silent, until the moment passed or the questioner made themselves clear.

'Yeah…' George White smiled inanely at the mute boy. 'Is it the movement, the comment, its contextual element, or are you looking at it decoratively – which I don't disapprove of, by the way?' This toying with the cowboy was his shot at flirting with Beryl.

Finn shrugged. George returned to the canvases, peering close, looking for clues as to what the hell he should be doing with his trust fund. Beryl watched him and wondered if she could overcome George's lack of sexual appeal to enjoy that which was quantifiably attractive about him.

Finn took a sip of his tea and froze, not wanting to swallow for fear of the crude sound it would make in the uptight silence, and not knowing in what order he was supposed to view the paintings. He used the sound of the man's footsteps between paintings as cover to swallow and crossed to the painting nearest the entrance. Bigger, more intricate, more colourful and, a modest sashay from side to side confirmed, even more mindblowingly three-dimensional than the painting in the window, it was indescribably cool.

'You want to buy one?' Beryl asked.

'No,' Finn said. 'But she's a pretty good painter.'

George White's face lit up and he sniggered. 'He...'

Beryl smiled and nodded to back George up. Finn felt sweaty and his spine tingled.

'The artist is a he, not a she.' George made clear.

'A man called Dot...?' Finn asked, dubiously.

'That's a nice new shirt,' Beryl said, deadpan.

'Thank you...' Finn said, uncertainly.

'I always like that straight-from-the-packet look,' George added, riffing with Beryl, ramping up the foreplay.

'It's a good colour on you...' Beryl added, removing her knickers for George and staring defiantly at Finn, daring him to react.

Finn felt the familiar old nausea of the encroaching bully. 'It's from Sezzy Van,' he ventured.

'Sezzy Van...?' she asked, confused.

'Yeah.' Finn shuffled his feet.

Another silence ensued. Finn wanted to turn back to the paintings but it seemed too huge a movement.

'Do you mean the shirtmaker Seize sur Vingt on Elizabeth Street?' George White asked.

Finn swallowed, crushed by the muteness that tradition-ally served him well. He heard a sound which reminded him of the hiss of steam from the radiators in the hovel. It was Beryl, crying with laughter, trying to stifle it, really trying damned hard. A whine was escaping between the fingers of the hand she had clamped over her mouth. She shrieked as she doubled up, and assumed the exact bent-over shape that Finn's mother used when vomiting in the garden before breakfast.

George White strode behind Finn's back with a flourish and pulled at his collar. 'Let's just check that it's not a – what did you call it? – *Sezzy Van* shirt!'

Finn snapped his arm backwards and cracked his elbow into George White's face. In the same fractional moment, he turned and gripped George's throat, kicked the man's legs from under him and nailed him to the floor with the downward pressure of one rigid, outstretched arm. Suddenly, a paper-thin moment from normality, there were spots of George's blood on the floorboards and the two men found themselves eyeball to eyeball. George White's face turned purple. Beryl remained frozen. (She was in fact marvelling at the way Finn had kept hold of his mug of tea and not spilled a drop throughout this whiplash-quick manoeuvre.) Belatedly she grabbed at the desk phone, knocking it to the floor.

'I'm okay,' George said to her, scraping the words out of the narrow opening in his throat, through which he then called Finn an 'animal'.

'I'm calling the fucking police,' Beryl stuttered, handling the f-word with the conviction of a non-smoker lighting a cigarette. She dropped her cellphone too.

'No,' George White croaked, as he studied Finn and pondered a couple of business ventures he did not want the police to become aware of. 'A mistake... wasn't it, my friend?'

Finn stared lifelessly at George before releasing his neck. He stood over him, his frame pumped up and powerful, watching the dream ebb away. He had been here before, in this exact moment, watching his freedom slip through his fingers. But then, there had been nothing to lose. Now, he found himself thinking of Amy, tiny, amazing, beautiful Amy, and he wanted to undo the day. It could not be right that pricks like this man beneath him got to offer him forgiveness, got to choose whether or not he walked free. Even the thought of being torn away from Jack angered him and he realised that he could never, would never, hit his brother. And although he was determined to hate Jack for deserting him, he felt the emancipation in letting go of the wish to hurt him.

He poured his tea calmly over George White's tailored crotch and walked away.

'Ungrateful bastard,' George White complained, and already both he and Beryl couldn't wait to tell friends their pimped-up version of the incident.

Finn returned to work and kept his head down and tried to fend off the blackness circling his mind. He hid in Leo's office, out of sight of the growing crowd. Leo ushered him into the throng, gently, protectively, and Finn fought to stop himself flinching. The people sounded like birds in a cage to him, shiny, dark-feathered birds pecking at the innards of their own evening and watching him side-eyed. The darkness grew in his head and the light touch of Leo's hand on his shoulder reminded him of his uncle's when he would lead him out of his room and he would see that his aunt was out of the house and that his uncle had him to himself. Finn knew that Leo did not deserve to be associated with this, that he was worthy of Finn's best behaviour, Finn's true self, but he was angry and the scent of the bully was caught in his nose and not to brush Leo away was a mighty task.

As the gallery filled, Astrid buzzed and Leo grew increasingly uneasy watching Finn, and beckoned him to join him and Tilhoff and Tilhoff's elderly uncle, who had taught his nephew to paint during summer vacations on Nantucket, a detail Tilhoff chose to omit from his self-penned impoverished angry young man biog.

'And what do you think of the work you've helped exhibit tonight?' the uncle asked, with the remnant kindness of a man who had nurtured pupils all his life.

Tilhoff placed his hand on Finn's shoulder and said, 'You don't have to answer that.'

Finn shrugged him off, unimpressed by the artist's warmth towards him, given how charmless he had been whenever he spoke to Leo. With a sway of his body and a smile held hostage by tension, Leo invited Finn to leave them. Finn fixed his stare on the uncle.

'It doesn't matter if someone like me likes them, we all know that.'

'Bravo...' Uncle Tilhoff said dreamily, blind to the danger. *'Does an emerald become worse if it isn't praised? – so enquired Aurelius.* I'll think of you as my little British Marcus Aurelius from now on.'

'I'd rather you didn't think of me at all,' Finn said.

'Finn...' Leo said his name, and hoped that the boy recognised the plea in it.

'Sorry...' Finn whispered, through the barbed wire in his throat, as he heard laughter and looked up to see George White strolling in with a Band-Aid across the bridge of his nose, wearing a new suit purchased five minutes earlier in Comme des Garçons on 22nd Street and lifting a glass of champagne from the table.

Finn made a gun of his hand and extended his arm to aim it at George White.

'What are you doing?' Leo whispered.

'New suit?' Finn called out, loud enough to silence the room.

George saw him and smiled cockily. 'Yes. I won't charge you. I don't imagine you could cover it.'

Astrid stepped forward. 'What's going on?' Leo pulled her back, as if the gun were real.

'You've wasted your money,' Finn said. 'You could have walked in here naked, everyone would have told you how good you looked. You wanker.' And he pulled the trigger.

'Get out,' Leo whispered, though he intended to shout.

Astrid stepped forward and hammered her fist against Finn's chest. 'Get out!' she shouted. 'You're fired, you're so fired.' She shoved him and he allowed the momentum of her attack to march him out on to the sidewalk. Leo disappeared into his office. Astrid dusted herself down and stepped back inside. George White finished his drink. Beryl peered through the glass from the opposite side of the street and someone said, 'Is this performance art?'

Beneath the Hermès billboard on 18th Street, where he first allowed himself to stop walking, Finn's mind hurtled towards the image that was permanently wedged into that faultline to which anger invariably lured him: the image of Jack catching his father when he fell. For a few hours the thought of it would eat away at Finn. He had lost sight of which of them he resented, Jack for being there to hold his dad, or his dad for being held. It was simpler, nowadays, to resent them both and allow them to distract him from thoughts of how badly he had let Leo down.

Leo's absence fell over the corners of the private view like a dull aura of malfunction and Astrid summoned him from the corner of his office. But, even as Leo was apologising to Tilhoff and working the room, he was already looking over his shoulder to the window in the hope of a prodigal son.

13

Leo could not sleep. When he felt like this, embarrassed by the need for William and Joy's company, he raked through his address book, the names he had bought art for, spent evenings in the city with, weekends in their upstate houses, men he had found much in common with, women he had slept with, lived with. Finding not one he felt able to call, his mind strayed towards insatiable thirsts, like that for Willow, a craving that laboured under the illusion that the last twenty years had not yet occurred.

He saw it simply as a skill he did not possess, to remain central to people who cared for his company. Tonight his loneliness felt shameful, magnified by the boy's crashing out of his life. Solitude was a self-fulfilling prophecy, a crude oil that had gotten into the blade and phalanx of his wings. Bored by people, he yearned for them. He felt that he could sometimes hear the fibres of senility twisting in his head.

His experience of Manhattan had become one of absence. In the eighties, a girlfriend took him to decrepit warehouse buildings and he swept up the best young artists there. Years later, he met her at Keith Haring's funeral and they resolved to remain friends forever and forgot what they had seen in the idea the instant it was diluted by the beginning of a new day. He had fallen out with no one and kept in touch with the same number. The neighbourhoods and artists he had loved in the early years here had transformed into something polished and no longer served to accommodate his seclusion and glorify it for him. He had always been alone in some unacknowledged way, he realised, but in the eighties and nineties Manhattan was his mirror image, full of bright circuses bearing the illusion of love and kinship. The cleaning-up of the city had left him unmasked.

Lately he had found that if he was interrupted when talking he wanted to weep, and could not find the will to resume speaking. When he did have conversations, they filled him with regret, with the feeling that he had done too much talking, even though he had not. Women who showed interest disappointed him as he felt they could do better. When he tried to talk to her about it, Joy mimed a cigar and Groucho Marx eyebrows and accused him of not wanting to belong to any club that would have him as a member.

The previous Christmas, in the bitter end days of 2005, he had visited Maison Claudine for tea and found himself on the brink of another collapse and it was on this edge that he had seen Willow. He had watched how her face stayed constant but never blank as she listened to other customers, the kindness of her expression, the swaying of her hips when she moved between the tables. The longer he watched her, the better he felt. When she brought him his tea, he looked at her skin, the minuscule dark hairs on her arms, at the strength of her shoulders, the dry skin around her hairline. Fleetingly he saw her big brown eyes, and, as she walked away, he looked in wonder at the way she pressed her hands to her ribs. In the bars and coffee shops of New York City, such moments of indefinable grace anchored the lonely to the hope that they might be better off in love, and filled the air with the sweet, mind-altering drug of possibility. He had imagined that she was still by his side and that she went down on her haunches and asked him if everything was alright, laying her hand very lightly on his leg. In her other hand she held a small, delicate bone china plate with a *tarte au citron* on it and Leo could smell the zest and it seemed to come from her skin. 'You seem lonely,' he had imagined her saying to him as she placed the plate down and leaned forward and took him in her arms. She was large and beautiful and she wrapped him up. They both laughed. His laughter came from deep in his heart where every picture of his parents sat and every memory of their kindness. Willow held him tight and he held her, it seemed for hours. The city fell dark. He cupped his hands around her face and thanked her for not letting go too soon. None of this was strange. She said she had enjoyed it and that he should take care. And, like every other thing Leo imagined happening to him to make him feel whole again, it had happened effortlessly, fearlessly and without risk of rejection.

After dreaming all this, he had stared at his hands until his tea went cold and the café emptied and Madame Claudine sat on a high stool working through her receipts until whatever time the English gentleman wished to leave. The Christmas lights in the windows blinked at Ninth Avenue and Leo had remained in his chair, oblivious, imagining a world in which all this could possibly have happened, a world in which such gestures were commonplace, where people saw in others the need for love and gave it, instinctively, without question, regardless of appearance. They held them, they stroked their arm, they kissed their cheek, they made them smile, they walked on. People stopped on the sidewalk to embrace strangers. No one escaped unloved.

What had passed between Leo and Willow last Christmas was an invention of his imagination but it had sustained him somehow in this long, waning winter. He stood at his apartment window and faced the night, saw in the seams of the dark sky a changing season.

Somewhere, his early life had separated from the one he was living now, so cleanly that his former years seemed to belong to a different man. In meeting Finn he had been offered the chance to reunite with that man, the one who had ideas and galvanised people, affected them, opened doors for them. And now he had thrown the boy out for bringing a mere ripple of disorder into his life and he loathed himself for it.

It was seven in the morning and he was sleepless. He stepped back into the shoes beneath his bed and walked through the drizzle on Irving Place in the clothes he had lain in, combing his hair in the reflection of an antique shop window.

'Morning, Mr Emerson.'

The greeting came from a man wiping down the outside tables of a café. To be familiar here, to be known by name, considered a neighbour, had been an aspiration once.

Inside the café, he saw lying in wait the recollection of a distant Hallowe'en and although he warned himself not to indulge in any more recollections of lost love he could not help himself and fixed his sights on the memory of a woman in a cherry tartan wool coat, her brown hair tinged with bronze and in a fringe, her skin tanned a warm shade of cobnut, Aladdin shoes with laces crisscrossed around her ankles. She was the same age as Leo, which was a former age. Her face was painted, for eighteen Hallowe'ens ago, and the memory of it finally threatened to break Leo's heart today. It had been four in the afternoon and the light was beginning to fade on red and golden leaves on the sidewalk. The café had been full of people. Leo had watched the woman from his table inside as she waited for her order. Others ordered after her and left before her. She waited without seeming to grow impatient. Her feet tapped the floor, pivoting on her heels. She used both hands to neaten her fringe. She turned to look out of the autumn window, noticed many things but did not see Leo. He watched her, wondered why she was waiting so long, wondered who she was and whether he had ever seen someone so pretty. He saw no ring on her wedding finger.

She changed the weight on her feet. In a lull in the café, she was the only person left waiting at the counter.

'Did you order something incredibly complicated?' Leo said. And she laughed. He saw the smile break across her face first, saw his words enter her head, saw her like them, saw it all a moment before it was happening.

'I know!' she said, smiling at him.

Life was like that then. He saw it all in advance, saw the waves parting for him more often than not, and he didn't stop to think.

'I've seen babies born and raised since you ordered.'

She laughed again, more fully this time, with her mouth wide open and her teeth bared. She laughed from her belly. They made love at five in the afternoon and she went to her party late, leaving make-up on his face, a trace of cat's whiskers. She asked him to feed her before she left. She walked around his apartment with his shirt on. It swamped her body and consumed his heart. He cooked her angel hair pasta while she showered and he felt exultant at how life could be, at how well an afternoon on Planet Earth could treat him. He indulged in replaying in his mind the smile that appeared on her face as she stepped into his apartment and whispered *Oh, my Lord...* and the way she had turned to look at him with those eyes that wondered who he was and what he did. They sat opposite each other and she ate ravenously and he imagined marrying her. He pictured waking up to her every day of his life.

'Life's so funny,' she said, and put her tartan coat back on while still chewing the last mouthful of food. At the door she said to him, 'So, I'm guessing let's not do the numbers thing... let's just have this gorgeous few hours on the last day of summertime?' She waited a moment, then kissed him. 'You were lovely,' she whispered, and left.

He had once had the capacity to strike up conversation. It had been effortless to make someone laugh. He had once been a human being acting on instinct, giving and taking in the same breath, not stopping to think. Overthinking was the death of you and was all he did these days. He wanted to hold a funeral for the old version of himself, to hear a eulogy or two, see her again in her tartan coat, somewhere among the mourners in whatever row of seats towards the back that she felt was appropriate. Today, in the spray-like rain on Irving Place, for the very first time, he asked himself why he had not stopped her, why he had not said, *No. Let's.* It might have won her heart. She might have wanted to hear that. Today, eighteen years too late, he finally noticed the moment she had hesitated before leaving.

'No,' he said to the man cleaning the tables, who was asking him if he was alright and did he want to come in out of the rain. 'No,' Leo said, 'let us do the numbers thing. Let us meet again and not allow this to slip out of reach.' And, perhaps, he told himself, it was that moment at the threshold to his apartment, when he did not say to the lover with cat's whiskers, 'Please take me with you,' that was the end of the first life.

The morning was grey and musky, with blocks of humidity trapped in the cross streets, and the tepid drizzle unable to take hold of the day. Umbrellas were up. A young boy caught rainwater in his mouth as it ran off a canopy. His mother yanked him away, but was not harsh with him. Irving Place had a knowingness about it this morning, the bedraggled air of revelries ended and lessons learned. Though barely more than a mist on Leo's face, the rain had fallen all night and created rivulets on the sidewalk. His hair became soaked as he crossed town, and he enjoyed running his fingers through it, the same way his sister liked to walk barefoot through Leo's apartment and on to his balcony. He was outside the pâtisserie before it opened. Claudine Ardant let him in and he sat alone, wondering if he might look less old, more handsome to Willow, with his wet hair swept back. He knew he was looking for the wrong cures in the wrong places.

He enjoyed the silence of the café before opening, and appreciated the place for what it was: his.

Having a secret was good for an ageing man, Leo felt, a resting place for flirtation. Claudine Ardant did not know that the Englishman she had brought in from the rain this morning, called an ambulance for two years ago, and many times observed looking lost and handsome in her café, was her landlord. Leo had bought the building with the opening salvo of the first fortune he'd made on this island, miscalculating by a few streets the Chelsea art boom but nevertheless destined in the long term to make a mint on it. He bought it for his children, for Joy's children, not knowing then that he would come to have more than he could have imagined to leave behind and no one to leave it to.

238a Ninth Avenue was all his, a tall, thin, elegant building constructed in 1899 by the Corlessi Brothers, both of them romantic brutes with a signature fascia of looping interlinked carved figures that few New Yorkers had taken the trouble to look at in the last century but which Leo noticed high above a realtor's board in 1993, on the day that his mother died. (Leo spent big on the occasion of each of his parents' deaths, and on that of the woman he was engaged to in England and whose fatal heart attack at the age of thirty had precipitated his emigration.) The building came with incumbent tenants, Gluckman Trading, an import-export business that inhabited a mundane plateau of modest success, apparently unaffected for better or worse by the peaks and troughs of economics. They inhabited the top four floors of the building and, on witnessing the vast discipline and microscopic imagination of his tenants, Leo had decided that the vacant ground floor would provide a contrast and that he would charge a minimum rent to attract a worthy or creative occupant. He paid Dazelgio & Son five hundred dollars to empty two decades' worth of junk, paperwork, damaged furniture and obsolete word processors until the ground floor of 238a was the empty shell of one light-starved room and a ropey-looking kitchen at the back.

Leo imagined a variety of pleasing scenarios: a second-hand record store or bookshop, a tailor, a vintner's agent, a bootmaker, a small charity. He pictured many different tenants for that nebulous space beneath Gluckman Trading but he could never have imagined Claudine Ardant, who arrived with the snow and offered Leo's agent half the knockdown price, who herself painted every inch of the ground floor matt black, hung lace curtains on the Ninth Avenue windows, charmed the city inspectors and opened 'Maison Claudine', a French pâtisserie where it was always dusk, and where pale orange light escaped the tissue-thin lampshades, and in which were served loose-leaf teas and fine fresh-ground coffee and pastries and cakes (oh, the pastries and cakes!) and in which Leo Emerson rediscovered the sweet tooth of his childhood.

Long before this quiet, damp morning, where the city's reticence made a church of the streets, Leo had realised it was too late to introduce himself to Madame Claudine as her landlord, that it would only seem strange not to have done so sooner. Instead, he enjoyed the secret and had instructed the agent to assure her that she faced no rent increase for as long as she chose to remain.

His sleepless night drew level with him and in his crumpled suit he went to the restroom and threw cold water on his face. When he returned, he saw Willow tying the apron ribbon around her waist as she started her shift and he hurried out of the café without ordering.

The sun had burned its way through the mist on to Ninth Avenue and Leo lamented the passing of that season which permitted him to disappear inside his winter coat and dig his hands in deep. He sent Astrid a text: *Is he there?*

She replied. *Who?*
Finn!
Oh, him.
Is he there?
No.
Call him please.

Leo quickened his stride but didn't seem to walk any faster. He had a physique that was not built to rush. Astrid called him. 'He doesn't have a cell. We don't have an address or anything for him. You kinda took him in without asking any questions, remember?'

'This is ridiculous,' he said. 'We have to know where he is. Why on earth didn't we give him a phone that works over here? He's an employee.'

'Leo, it's 2006 and I only got you to carry a cell with you last year; now you want every petty criminal you take in to be given one?'

Leo ignored this. 'He said his place was down in the East Village, didn't he, or was it the Lower East Side?'

'I honestly don't know, I wasn't taking too much notice. Do we care? I'm not saying we don't, I'm just asking, do we? I'm not even asking why we do – just tell me if we do and I'll set to it. I don't personally care; people come and go.'

'We do care.'

'Then fine, I'll try and find him. Don't hassle me about it, though, I'm selling paintings.'

Within sight of the gallery, Leo turned away, flagged a cab and headed back in the direction he'd come from. He asked for Tompkins Square Park and when they got there he told the driver to work his way up and down the streets.

'I'm looking for someone,' he said, and didn't care how it might sound.

They drove back and forth, east to west, then west to east, first the East Village, then the Lower East Side. Leo gazed at the sidewalks and at the greasy swirls and fingerprints of the taxi window. The meter ran and the sun rose into a fresh sheet of clouds and the light evened itself out across Leo's world and the driver buried a faint shake of the head as they repeated their route, south to north. Leo fell asleep and the driver pulled up and drank coffee from a flask and watched the women on Avenue B. When Leo woke, he told the driver to continue and later when the driver burst into laughter it shook Leo and brought him back into the present, where he could see and hear no obvious cause for the driver's mirth. Maybe something he had seen outside, maybe a thought that crossed his mind or a voice in his ear. Either way, Leo realised he had not been looking for a long time. Finn could be anywhere; he could have just walked past.

'Take me home,' Leo sighed.

'Give me a clue,' the driver said.

From the balcony of his penthouse apartment at One Lex, Leo looked down on to Gramercy Park with the same pleasure that the key-holders of the rectangular garden looked at those not permitted to step inside it. A squirrel stop-started its way across 21st Street. A Tibetan terrier barked at a song sparrow, which took refuge on Edwin Booth's head. Leo watched from his vantage point among the mock orange, jasmine and mandevilla which Joy had planted out on his balcony over the years. He sucked in the view of the new Schrager hotel and apartments going up opposite and the ripples in the canvas banner making water of the words *Showstopping Luxury Residences*. He liked the construction phase, when a building had its belly hanging out, and he regretted that all too soon the site would be reduced to the mere finished article. He switched off his cell, unplugged the phone, put on a winter coat and spent the afternoon on the balcony, drifting in and out of sleep. When he woke, the lights of the Chrysler Building were twinkling in the dusk. On the day he had secured this view as his own, the thirty-five-year-old with a mean gift for discovering canvas genius had said out loud, on this exact spot, to an audience of just himself, *For such a view was I born*. He had seduced twenty women on this balcony with the assistance of that view but could no longer reconcile the swagger of that younger man with himself. He disliked that man and considered him the thief of his present-day happiness. He recalled, too, the offer he had made to provide Joy and William with a bigger home, nearby. They had flinched at his generosity, not knowing how to convince him, on the crest of his wave, that there was nothing they could want less than to live in Gramercy Park.

Leo felt safest here, suspended in mid-air among his plants with a two-thousand-square-foot capsule of beautiful objects behind him. When the chill defeated him, he returned inside and took his local paper into the living room and on his Queen Anne wingback armchair he read about Lucca Passaro, whose apartment in Long Island City had been destroyed by fire the previous day and who had said to a journalist that he felt unburdened by losing everything – his lifelong music collection and all his family photographs and his high-school reports and essays and every object he had accumulated in forty-one years of being alive. Losing them all had given him a sense of freedom, he said, and he felt light and unhindered, and he could see, for the first time in three years, a clear way of getting over his divorce.

The apartment wrapped its dark arms around Leo as he stared at the wall, thinking of Lucca Passaro. Distracted, eventually, by the gloom, he leaned forward and untied his laces, slipped off his shoes and slid them beneath the chair. He reached out and switched on his Art Nouveau bridge-arm floor-lamp with burlap shade, which gave a mushroom of warm light to the room and erased the city from the windows. He rose to his feet and walked softly through the apartment, turning on the nineteenth-century marble and ormolu table lamp in the lobby, Chinese celadon table lamp in the study and Regency bronze table lamp in the drawing room. He drew the curtains and returned to the wingback where he sat in silence again, motionless but for the movement of his head as he scanned everything in front of him, every object he owned, every piece of antique furniture, the spine of every book, every work of art hanging from or propped against his walls.

By two o'clock in the morning, he had emptied the shelves and the walls were bare. Thirty piles of books stood tall in the room, some for the auction house (he would donate the proceeds), one for a friend, some for the charity shops, many for the library off Union Square, a smaller pile that he thought Madame Claudine might like for the walls of the pâtisserie. The paintings were stacked against each other along the walls. He knew the man who would auction them all for him and not cheat him of a dollar. The piles stood like Easter Island figures trespassing on the gloom of a large, lonely Manhattan apartment. He weaved his way through them to a bottle of Lagavulin and lay on the bed in his suit, his head unaccustomed to the clammy exhaustion of fearing for another's wellbeing. Tomorrow would be emptier without Finn. He had enjoyed seeing the world through the boy's eyes, and the stirrings of renewal at having someone other than himself to worry about.

14

Outside the Gay Hussar restaurant, the owner sat on a bench, gazing at a deserted Ludlow Street but seeing nothing of it. Cigarette in one hand, black coffee in the other, she was tired and quiet, with song lyrics writing themselves into her head. She smelled of wine.

The way she studied Finn as he came to an uncertain halt in front of her bore traces of the affection she kept mostly hidden beneath the burden of translating this in-vogue hangout into some sort of a living, into a life good enough to make a song and dance in her heart that might drown out the ticking time-bomb of a rent increase that would surely blow her out of the water one day, same way she was ushered in over the drowning body of the previous, even less profitable tenant. Her soundest business move might have been to place a bet that the spot she was sitting on would become a glass condo within ten years.

'You're kinda early in the day, cowboy,' she said, with screwed-up eyes.

'You too,' Finn said, looking inside for any sign of Amy.

'I wish this was early. This is late. This is what's left of the night before. This might be more than coffee can help me with.'

She reminded Finn of the land girls in the old wartime posters on Jack's bedroom wall, back when they were brothers.

'You know Amy, the waitress who works here?'

The woman laughed to herself and sat upright and drew on her cigarette. 'Yes, I know Amy, the waitress who works here.'

'She due in any time soon?'

''Bout eight hours.'

Finn pulled a face and looked across the street to where Dilly had bummed her cigarette. Every new morning in New York City made ghosts of the nights before. He wondered if the ghost was doing okay, imagined her posting the Hemingway book to him and telling him she was happy and didn't want to meet up. He let out a breath, fearful that he was being unkind. What an uneasy revelation it was for him, to discover he could want so little from an ex-lover and want it now.

'You can leave your cell number.'

'I don't have one.'

She squinted up at him and produced another smile for her own consumption. 'Cute...'

'Would you tell her I came to see her?'

'At eight o'clock in the morning. I will.'

'I was passing.'

'Well, passing stranger, I'll tell her.' She got up and stretched and muttered the words, 'Oh, fuck,' and wandered inside.

Finn took her place on the bench, glanced inside the restaurant at the table he and Dilly had sat at, and took out his map in exactly the manner that would have annoyed the hell out of her. He hesitated, constricted by an uneasy feeling about himself. He presumed it was a misgiving that he had been ungracious to Dilly, but realised it was Leo he was worried about. He rested the map in his lap and thought about it. Dilly was her very own home-made explosive, and she had deserted him. He was not the captain of that ship. But Leo he had let down, which was why he had tried not to think about him this morning. Leo might not turn out to be any better than the rest, but there again he might; the law of averages suggested someone had to, one of these days. The older man had deserved better than the version of Finn that Finn had served up. His heart sank. The seeds of the apology he owed planted themselves. He opened his map, double-checked the route, and allowed himself a few more moments of sunshine on the bench before heading uptown.

Arriving in the ticket hall at Grand Central Station half an hour later was the latest extension to his hard-earned and carefully guarded quixotic other life, the one he had never let his peers see, in which he watched *The Last Picture Show* in a small cinema on All Saints Street in the quaint part of town that his neighbours on the estate called the Gay Quarter and would have taunted him for visiting; the life in which he read *The Catcher in the Rye* by torchlight in the attic of his uncle's house where he could not be reached, thanks to a pull-up ladder; the life in which he lay in bed with Dilly imagining a city so vast and cosmopolitan and modern that none of the cast of his first life could possibly find their way there, except for Jack.

In the netherworld of Grand Central's concessions Finn bought a map of Queens. He rode the elevated 7 beneath Manhattan, out into the daylight and fifty feet above the Borough. At a corner restaurant called Kay's Place he queued to buy water beside sticky-looking tables with bottles of ketchup and Tabasco sauce. A woman in her seventies sat with a blonde, corkscrew-haired boy of eight or nine. The two of them shared a bowl of fries. She allowed herself one to every fistful he took. On a saucer between them, a dollop of ketchup had become an artist's smear. Salt grains were scattered across the table-top. Finn watched the boy and the woman a moment longer than he might have done. If you yearned for something badly enough, everything seemed to pertain to it.

There was an old jukebox in one corner and next to it a bald man with an *Elliott Smith RIP* T-shirt was installing an ATM machine. His buttocks were squished against a window festooned with posters demanding that St Teresa's church be saved. Bicycles leaned against the other side of the glass, on the sidewalk along Queens Boulevard. The saddles looked ready to melt in the sun. A fading banner read YES WE HAVE $2 PABST BLUE RIBBON.

The walk to the New Calvary Cemetery was lead-lined with backyards of junk and the debris of people who did things for themselves, adapted things, fixed things, made things last. Barriers of buckled corrugated iron separated them from the grinding Expressway and it all felt homely to Finn. He watched his trainers hit the sidewalk and could have been anywhere and he forgot about everything beyond his own footsteps until the slope to Greenpoint Avenue offered up to him the mountain range of brick and steel peaks called Manhattan. The sight of it took his breath away and then gave it right back, and his chest filled with the simple wish for a modest quantity of hope in his life, an amount that would go unnoticed and so be granted him without enraging the gods.

He stopped at every intersection to stare at the city in Cinemascope, and entered the gates of the cemetery with a rare and undefined sense of purpose. The slopes beckoned him to progressively better views. The glaring sun above Queens and black storm clouds over Manhattan conspired to paint the city silver. On the pale grey tombstones the sun was blinding and Finn squinted to read the inscriptions. Basilio, Pavone, Cantasano, Guariglia, Stasa, Lucilento, De Salvio, O'Sullivan, Duggan, O'Neal, Callan, Gaffney, O'Donohue, O'Rourke, Kiernan.

He had never been inside a graveyard before, and for a boy of nineteen with four dead grandparents and two dead parents that was some feat. Maybe he should have done, because from the cemetery the city began to make sense to him, and people too. He felt a little more sympathy for them, and a little less betrayed. It wasn't just him; it didn't seem to have quite worked out for anyone.

If this is the deal, he thought, then little wonder no one knows how to handle it all.

Laid out at his feet were the bodies of those who once upon a time were New York City. And above them lay the city they built, which was the city that spawned them. Each presided over the other, the living over the dead, the buried over the standing. Neither could claim victory. He stood in awe of the view. This was church. This was veneration. This was remarkable.

But it was not *the* view. It was not the photograph.

This view skimmed over the graves to the tips of the famous skyline, hinting at death and hinting at life, but not offering a clear picture. This was a thin view beneath a huge sky. The photograph had been taken from somewhere else, where the cemetery was the dipping, swelling, colossal sea of stones, and Manhattan a lofty altar in full view. Why this mattered to him, whether it mattered, he still had no idea.

He was hot and lay on the grass. He looked at the sky and felt the tombs encroaching on the corners of his view. Given the inevitability of a mighty big full stop one day, he felt a snarling disdain for the living dead back home, those who had the opportunity to live but didn't take it; those like his aunt, bystander to a boy's suffering. He resented her more than he hated the bully she had chosen to spend her life indulging. He despised the memory of her daytime-TV voice: 'Of course, Finn here has suffered loss, but it's nothing compared to what his big brother went through. The…'

She would search for the word here, every single time, always the same way, as if it were the first occasion she'd ever thought to use it.

'... trauma...'

Sometimes Finn would mouth the word as she said it.

'... trauma is the only word I can think of to describe it. The trauma of actually being there as his father died, *plus* the loss, is what poor Jack has to live with.'

Finn heard this story whenever his aunt had a visitor. Always identical, the words and the intonation, the pauses and expressions, a repeated, precision performance. Every one of her friends and neighbours who came by to meet the orphan Finn heard the story of Jack's harrowing loss. Finn was not mentioned; he was merely in the room, and he came to recognise that these visitors anticipated a coffee morning with Oliver Twist, and did not expect to be staring into the chest of a six-foot-two teenage athlete, whose muteness both appealed to them and appalled them.

'This young man's brother literally caught their father in his arms as he died.'

And if Finn tried to leave the room his aunt would bar him with an outstretched arm. 'Don't go, Finn, Mrs Prentice has come here especially to meet you. Be polite. The least you can do.'

There was one lady whose face Finn could picture, still. She was the one who said that perhaps Finn didn't want to talk about it, that she didn't need the detail, that she was just very pleased to meet him, and they should talk about something else. She was the one who had noticed Finn mouth the word 'trauma' just before his aunt said it. She was not invited again. She had thin lips and a strong face and her hair was long and already greying, and she was tall and upright and her eyes were kind and Finn couldn't imagine why or how she knew his aunt and uncle, because she seemed intelligent and subtle. She had a diamond ring and an eternity ring on her wedding finger. Her eyes were blue and her skin was pale and she had honey-coloured freckles on the bridge of her nose, which was a little angular. And his heart felt close to bursting out of his chest with the desire to be taken in by her.

But, with Mrs Prentice, and Mrs Hughes from next door, and Mrs Sherman from the Rotary and Cheryl Davison the deacon, and a dozen others, Finn had no choice but to listen to the story of his father's death, as told by his aunt: of how his father drove drunk through a give-way at the crossroads at Castleton's Oak and wiped out a sixteen-year-old boy in the passenger seat of the car he hit. Of how his father left, ignoring the dead boy and the unconscious driver. How he stole himself away from where the glow of the pub lights fell on to the wreckage as people came out on to the lane, their curiosity nudged by the sound they had heard and stalling then in the silence of momentary visual miscomprehension. How 'the father' (she never called him 'my brother') stumbled into the darkness beneath the swaying canopies of the oak trees on the glebe, reeling, emptying of blood, half of it left on the roadside. How he called his eldest son and how the smile that overwhelmed him when he saw his son coming to him seemed to capsize him and he fell and died in Jack's arms.

And it wasn't that Finn's aunt was saying anything untrue. There was no need to embellish: the story had everything. A mother's depression after giving birth to Finn (spoken about openly in this house in front of Finn, used by the uncle against him), her alcoholism, a father who did not drink as he tried to hold the family together, who devoted himself to Jack's education as Jack showed promise and Finn hid his, a drunk mother and desperately lonely father who saw in their elder son's education the possibility of rescue from themselves, and a deft, seamless, extraordinary and nonsensical handing over of the alcoholic baton by the mother to the father in the last year of her life, a baton he took on with some fervour and devotion after his childhood sweetheart took her gin-raddled body out on to the reservoir and then to the bottom of it. Finn's aunt had every right to tell such a story when she had none of her own, but it was just that, whenever Finn heard the legend repeated on these stifling coffee mornings, he appeared to be living with his aunt and uncle now because Jack's parents had died, not his own. Finn sometimes had to remind himself that they were his parents too, even though the die was cast before he could walk or talk, had been cast in the act of his being born, in his being a life too many for his mother to bear. He had to remind himself too that there had been shards of affection towards him, little flickers of maternal warmth among the wreckage of his twelve years with his mother. They tended to come in the twenty minutes' grace when she had had one drink but not two, when she could be funny and outspoken and it remained safe.

'We only had a second child 'cos we were running out of things to do together and we couldn't afford a camper van. Thought a baby could kick-start us,' she said, near to the end of her life, when she seemed to be improving, coming out of a slump.

'How'd that go, Mum?'

'Well, not successful. But we got you, Finny.'

It was the most affectionate thing she had ever said to him and, as if to make up lost ground, she'd followed it with two weeks of cursing him and throwing anything she could reach from her bed at him before doing him a favour and dying in the far reaches of the valley they had flooded the year she was born.

'Do us all a favour, Mum...' They were the last words Finn ever said to her.

He stripped to his waist as a riposte to the sweat running from his armpits and marauded across New Calvary Cemetery, which ran into the Mount Zion Cemetery, searching for the photograph and pursued by a rainstorm sweeping across the New Jersey Marshes and South

Manhattan. It scraped low across Queens and caught up with Finn as he wrestled his shirt back on and took shelter beneath the Expressway. The traffic above him whined and droned and, when the centre of the storm hit, pockets of wind trapped beneath the Expressway howled around him, seeking an escape. When the rain abated to a mere downpour, Finn ran from the underpass, leaving behind those souls trapped beneath it, those who were excluded from the graveyards for reasons he did not care to know about. He ran on the balls of his feet to raise himself above the flash flooding on Greenpoint Avenue, a small act of defiance against the elements that was instinctive but of no practical effect. From the jolting carriages of the elevated 7 he saw the entire silver city disappear behind a veil of rain.

Back in the hovel, Finn draped his wet clothes across the cold radiators and the sight of it was homely despite the chill in the room and the damp in his bones. With the bedsheets wrapped around him he studied his map and it made no sense to him that he had not found the photograph. He toyed with the thought of calling Jack. Jack would like his interest in the photograph. It was a bit like taking an interest in history. But if he were to tell Jack he'd got fired it would sound as though he was asking for help, and if he were to shiver with cold it would sound as though he was asking to move in. Instead, he showered under a dribble of cold water. Later, he felt horny and tried to dispel the memory of Dilly's thighs parting for him. From above him, he heard quivers of laughter and the low rumble of conversation, carried to him by a chance permutation of pipework, vents and ducts in the carved-up, fucked-up building.

In the flickering, sticky aisles of Elsa's Food Market, he found that for $2.99 he could buy a chicken, vegetable and melted cheese pie big enough for four people. With 0.4 per cent broccoli content, 0.8 per cent carrots and an unspecified percentage of sweetcorn, there was clearly no need to waste his cash on further side vegetables. The oven warmed the hovel tenuously. He raided the top of the cupboard into which Glenn had rammed his possessions and duly found a modest but significant bundle of adult films. He settled down to porn and pie.

His arousal proved short-lived. As the bareness of his surroundings reminded him that the DVD was not the same as the real thing with Dilly, and that a pie that pushed the definition of the word 'food' was now a part of his body, his right hand stumbled upon a lump on his right testicle. A hot panic rippled through his body. He cleared away the food and switched off the porn, as if removing them would remove the lump. He sat at the small circular table into which Glenn had carved his initials on the morning of his hearing, and delved into his underwear to check and double-check that he had found what he thought he had found. He sweated, he cried, and, in order to remain faithful to the promise he had made to himself to never be let down again, he didn't call Jack even though he wanted to.

He sat outside on the steps. The gully no longer frightened him now that his death was imminent. He entered the first phase of big calm, sure in the knowledge that if the fox man or any other fucker bothered him tonight he would take them out, without hesitation, without effort, without a sound. But there was no one. He sat there until three in the morning. When he returned inside he reached up to the kitchen cupboard door, in the beading of which he had wedged Leo's card. He sat at the table and dialled the number at One Lex and when Leo answered, thick with sleep, Finn said, 'I ate a pie thirty centimetres wide tonight. I should not live alone.'

Leo's heart shivered a little with happiness. He listened to the boy's breathing and asked him what was wrong, and Finn told him, and when he had told him he said that he was frightened and didn't know what to do.

'What you do,' Leo said, 'is stop worrying. Men get this a lot. I'll call my doctor tomorrow and he'll check you over.'

How good it felt to be spoken to like that. Finn savoured it for a moment.

'Look...' Leo sounded agitated. 'Tomorrow I'm getting you a cellphone – a mobile – because I have to be able to contact you. I need to know you're okay, otherwise this is all too much for me.'

15

Jack still couldn't hold a razor steady but, if a shave was impossible, fresh air was not. Striding out a couple of blocks to restock on cough mixture would be a good move, he decided. Come to think of it (he turned back at the elevators), he should push himself a little and turn this into a spot of exercise, give himself a jump-start. He would march a few blocks with Holly's mini-wrist-weights on, and take things from there.

Unshaven, temporarily gaunt from not eating, fuelled by cough mixture and coffee, he shuffled out on to 94th Street performing arm raises with cerise-pink wrist weights. For a shy, easily embarrassed British man, Jack had his moments.

Women in green overalls were planting shrubs around the red oak trees on the Avenue. Behind them, 94th Street climbed the slope past Precious Nails to brownstones stacked up the hill with rowan trees and firethorn out front by the steps. The neighbourhood felt different during the working day. There were shops Jack had walked past and never noticed. Third Avenue was pale. A mist hung over the Upper East Side and its monochrome triggered Jack's dreams of the Indian trails. Reading in depth about the Lenape Indians and the Wiechquaesgecks had established a world of primordial rains and muted colours in Jack's imagination. He loved the avenues, each one of them a trail still.

His breathing was cleaner for being outdoors, but his body was weak and he rested inside among the echoes and shadows of the Church of Our Lady of Good Counsel, which appealed to Jack's penchant for Manhattan's Grand Gothic. He came here often, when the place was deserted. He knew the service times and how to frequent the place without exposure to Mass or Catholics. Religious or otherwise, Jack found people alarmingly complex, unnecessarily so. He had convinced himself that he was happier on his own, most of the time.

It had not always been so. He had been open and talkative as a child. Relatives and neighbours had commented on it: how freely and happily he talked to adults, the spontaneity with which he'd position himself beside them and talk in flowing colour about what he had just come from doing and what he was off to do next. When Jack entered the grammar school the openness left him, and, when his parents took the boys from the estate they had been raised on, they made it clear they were doing it all for Jack, and his easygoing nature deserted him. He lived then in the choked space between his parents' pride and Finn's bewilderment.

When they lived on the estate it all worked fine and Jack never complained about the string of buses he had to take to the grammar each day. But his parents moved them off the estate to the lesser of all the streets that spread out from the edges of the town like fissures on a drunkard's nose. They moved in pursuit of the expansive life their elder son was bound for, with his good brain and hard work, and lived among people who had nothing to say to them and in time those people included Finn, who every day had to make in reverse the journey to his old school that his parents had considered too onerous for his big brother.

At the pinnacle of what Finn and Jack's parents deluded themselves they could afford was that exhausted cul-de-sac on the edge of the old forest. The straggling pines and the clapboard houses that had been young when George Best was beautiful were hemmed in now by new private developments and bigger houses, by richer people and the vast screening trees they planted. The shadows of these trees had long since made a permanent winter of one half of the cul-de-sac (Jack and Finn's half) and this gloom was the detail first commented on by the very few parents of Jack's schoolfriends who visited, as they drove away. They would sigh with relief, mutter *Never again* and comment on how Jack's mother could put away her drink. The shadow of the pines, the shadow of the drinking, it was all anyone said about them.

They lived beyond their means in no man's land, in a house kissed by moss and the fossilised imprint of creeping ivy. They wrote cheques to purchase the life they had window-shopped in the grammar school car park, but it didn't assemble. On a good day, they felt merely as isolated with these people as they did when they were alone. When they were caught over-reaching, possessions would be sold while Jack and Finn were out at school. Jack had resolved to always have money. It had embarrassed him as much as it confused Finn that their parents clung by their fingertips to the ability to marshal Jack's education while falling apart in every other respect.

Finn was proud of his brother's intelligence but, when his parents expressed their hope that he would follow his big brother to the grammar, he scuttled his own academic chances so as to deny them, took pleasure in it and in returning every day to be educated with his peers from the estate. Jack was not unhappy at school, but his little brother's indifference towards the grammar, and the need to concentrate so bloody hard all the time, made him subdued and serious, and very, very organised. The more organised he was, the better he did, and the better he did the more his parents dished out the sort of praise their first child craved. He watched with envy the liberation Finn won for himself by eliminating any trace of potential about him. His parents' praise became over-reaching and aimless, and lost its allure. His room became his world. It was neatness that made Jack feel good. Order. Being quietly on top of things. Having no frayed edges.

He emerged on to the sidewalk and watched the withered hands of the branches in the trees of the small park opposite wave to him in the same breeze that failed to rouse the Papal Flag or the Stars and Stripes hanging limply outside the church. He passed the fruit stalls on 86th Street and the thin townhouses and bare magnolias. He hid the wrist-weights in his fists and passed through a muted, airless East End Avenue, where the traffic was a soft swish of slow-moving tyres in the misty rain. A tide of tiny Oriental-looking kids in bright yellow raincoats spilled out of a kindergarten as a text came in from an unknown number.

Hi, handsome – looking forward to see you again. xD

He presumed it was a mistake. Suddenly, the children were under his feet and the only sound he was aware of was the creaking of the swings in Carl Schurz Park. He did not want children. Family made him nervous. He didn't understand the dynamic between family members. Any decision he had made concerning his little brother he had felt unsure of. He doubted every word he had said to Finn since their parents died, and was uncertain about everything he had done. With a defeatism he would not allow in his professional life, he was resigned to the sensation that all he could do was take a stab at doing the right thing and try to appear surefooted for his brother's good. To the same degree that Finn made him feel useless, New York City offered Jack a feeling of permanence, of being enveloped by something that made sense to him. He had read its story; he understood its birth, its actions and motivations.

Two dogs went for each other's throats in the dog run. Jack heard them as he reached the wide, strong, steady-moving river that cradled the Upper East Side like a muscular arm. It was a favourite spot for him; it reminded him that he was on an island busting a gut to stimulate him. From the outset, he had had the sensation that there was always something extraordinary going on in Manhattan just beyond his reach, but this did not trouble him – far from it. He wasn't looking to join the party; he was happier living in its reflected glory and maintaining a semblance of order. He could enjoy the periphery to the same degree that he couldn't have dealt with the centre.

Across the river, a lone woman on Roosevelt Island wandered through the damp haze to the lighthouse, stirring in Jack the romantic longings his peers had no reason to suspect him of, and a desire to walk on water. His cough had worsened. A parcel of phlegm caught in the back of his mouth but his throat was sore and he did not want to swallow. He looked for somewhere to spit, considered the East River, but didn't have whatever it took to do so in public. He swallowed instead, and the bitter taste swayed him to treat himself to a coffee and he decided that a wet shave at York's might transform him.

He broke a rule and drank his americano in public, on the 6 Train. (Jack did not like people eating and drinking in public.) A stooped man who had once been elegant, sitting shoulder-to-shoulder with him, took a slim brown paper parcel from his pocket. He slid one finger under the fold to break the tape without tearing the bag. He eased a paperback book out into the world and, carefully, so as not to dig his elbow into Jack's side, folded the paper bag into the shape of a bookmark and placed it inside the back cover and laid the book on his knees. In the brief moment that savours an unopened book, Jack read the cover. *Collected Poems. Robert Hayden.* The man opened the book randomly and pressed the pages apart without hurting the spine. Jack began to read the poem on the right-hand side. *Sundays too my father got up early and put his clothes on in the blueblack cold...* The man shifted in his seat, crossed one leg over the other, and came to rest in a position that stole the poem from Jack's view. Jack was not a consumer of poetry but he felt disappointed. He wondered if the man had shifted in his seat deliberately, then cautioned himself for thinking something so petty.

The area around Hunter College was Jack and Holly's favourite approach to the Park in spring, beneath the blossom of 70th Street. From time to time, maybe three times a year when he'd allow himself to go unshaven through a holiday weekend, Jack liked to have a wet shave at York Barber Shop and she would go into the shoe shop and the bookstore while he was in there. The area gave Holly the sort of warm, safe, sloppy, shoppy feeling that she loved on her days off, and what Jack enjoyed was to see that pleasure in her. He acknowledged to himself that travelling thirty blocks to get the occasional wet shave at York's was probably something of a cliché, and that being known by name in a less polished local joint would carry more credibility, but he liked the place and the signed framed photos in the window of Woody Allen and, intriguingly, Charlotte Rampling, and a bunch of other actors he didn't recognise (and the guys in his office could go hang; he wished he had never mentioned it to them). He stood looking at the photos now as he realised that he could not join them today because it would be selfish to risk passing his cough on to one of the guys in there. Wouldn't it? Yeah, damn, it would. The sinking feeling was one Jack knew well: it came upon him whenever he saw there was a right thing to do that was contrary to what he desired. The dragline of feeling responsible. He had been hooked up to it for as long as he could remember.

He entered the bookstore and gazed aimlessly at the shelves, simply to connect with Holly in her absence. It was an afterthought to enquire of the bookseller if they stocked a poet called Robert Hayden. He bought the book and read the poem at his seat outside the café on Lexington which Holly was fond of. As he read it, he fell so deep into it that he did not acknowledge the waitress placing the coffee and sandwich in front of him, a discourtesy he could not abide in others.

> Sundays too my father got up early
> and put his clothes on in the blueblack cold,
> then with cracked hands that ached
> from labor in the weekday weather made
> banked fires blaze. No one ever thanked him.
>
> I'd wake and hear the cold splintering, breaking.
> When the rooms were warm, he'd call,
> and slowly I would rise and dress,
> fearing the chronic angers of that house,
>
> Speaking indifferently to him,
> who had driven out the cold
> and polished my good shoes as well.
> What did I know, what did I know
> of love's austere and lonely offices?

He read it twice more then drank the coffee and pushed the sandwich away, as if merely ordering and paying for food amounted to sustenance. He slid the book into his jacket pocket, an act so neat and pleasing that he regretted that it was impossible to do so with a history book. Until today he had found poetry flimsy. History was all backbone.

He got another text.

At Long Beach, I mean. You have to join us there.
Bring your girlfriend. Dilly x

He listened in on a powerful elderly woman on the next-door table as she talked into her phone. 'What is your name, honey?... well, that's wonderful... Jean... that's a wonderful name and you know what, Jean? You can do anything, you're incredible, you can get us better seats than that, all four together, four in a line or two behind two I don't care which, I know you can make this happen, Jean, because you are strong and you are your parents' pride and joy, Jean... are they? Well, there's no such thing as dead, not truly dead, Jean... and you can improve on these seats you've sent me, I know you can...'

Jack admired it, this New York City way of knowing what you wanted. He wanted his bed. And he wanted Holly to be in it and to hold him. But he wanted her to be naked, not always wearing one of her fuc... sodding ubiquitous nighties.

He sent Dilly a reply.

Thanks for the kind invite. Please get Finn to call me now as I'm free to talk. Jack.

He waited. The woman got herself better seats. Two birds eyed up Jack's uneaten sandwich. He called Dilly's number and got her answerphone. *If you've got something interesting to say, wait for the beep. If you haven't, don't bother.* He hung up, texted Finn on Dilly's number asking him to call, and headed home, feeling faint again. Dilly soon called.

'Hey, Jack Sprat,' she said.

'Is that Dilly?'

'Who else?'

'Sure. Okay. I hope you are well. Can I talk to Finn?'

'You hope I am well? Is that, like, a question? Are you asking me if I am well or, you know, informing me of your hope that that is the situation, my being well?'

'It means how are you?'

'Good, thank you. How are you, Jack Sprat?'

He couldn't stand her. 'Is Finn there?'

'Not right now. You coming to join us at Long Beach? I'd like to see you.'

'It's kind of you and your parents, but can you just get Finn to call me?'

'Okay, Jack Sprat, be well.' She hung up.

Back on the platform at 68th Street station, he saw a young woman reading a book and a man attempting to get her attention by waving his arm across her line of sight.

'Excuse me… miss?' The man had a soft voice. 'Excuse me, miss?'

The woman looked up from her book.

'You have the face of an angel,' the man said. He smiled an evangelical smile. 'I had to tell you.'

The man was clean-cut but his sincerity unnerved the woman, Jack could see it in her forced smile. It was a smile designed to avoid antagonising the man, to curtail his unwelcome attention, a smile balanced so as not to stir either hostility or encouragement, a smile that tried to convince itself there was nothing to be afraid of. It was a lot of work for one smile.

Jack glared at the man, and wondered what he possibly hoped the woman's response might be.

Thank you, that means so much to me.

Thank you, you wanna grab a coffee?

Thank you, do you want my number?

Thank you, I think I could love you.

Thank you, let me blow you.

'The face of an angel…' the man repeated, stepping closer to the woman.

She pretended not to hear him and stared hard at her book, which was trembling.

Jack stepped towards them. 'How about mine?' he asked the man. 'What does my face look like?'

The young man sized Jack up and the woman took the opportunity to walk away, down the platform.

'She seems uneasy,' Jack said. 'It would be nice to leave her be.'

'I disagree,' said the man. He followed after the young woman.

'Please…' Jack said, his voice cracking a little, under the strain of having to beg a man not to scare a woman, having to beg a strange woman to tell his own brother to call him, beg his girlfriend to be less like him and elevate them on to some more abandoned level of existence that he was incapable of reaching.

The man stopped. He turned and looked at Jack, and his face filled with blood and his shoulders slumped. He walked away, vaulted the turnstile and returned to street level. Jack watched him go and then took the book from his pocket and opened it. He turned the pages to the first poem, then looked along the platform at the woman. She was looking steadfastly the other way, down the track and into the tunnel of darkness from which would come the steel tube to transport her to the next moment of self-doubt or joy. She was pretty, and Jack glanced at her a few more times, in the hope that they might catch each other's eye.

Thank you for helping me, you're a lovely man.
You're welcome.
Are you alone?
Yeah.
Shall I hold you?
I'd love that.
I would love that too.
But she didn't look back at him.

16

The morning was bitter. Cold currents out in the bay nudged a miniature breeze through the pot plants on the balcony of One Lex. The serrated leaves on the birches in Gramercy Park were the only evidence that Leo had not slept through spring, summer and fall.

Swayed by an aberrant nostalgia, he diverted south to the French Roast on Sixth Avenue. This had been Leo and William's breakfast haunt for many years, before Leo had got William his job in the attic with its earlier start to the working day, and before William and Joy's idea of what constituted New York City had shrunk to the twenty blocks either side of West 36th Street. Back then, Leo and William had had breakfast together every single day of the working week. Leo missed that, and it was sentimental of him to take their old window seat. He had presumed that such wistfulness would be saved for old age.

He watched a nearby table where a grandfather with a slow, high-pitched voice and ill-fitting dentures, his son and three grandchildren – two boys and a girl – formed a raucous table of five. The children were not tall enough to sit and get sufficient down-force on their knife and fork to cut their food, not even with their elbows reaching for the ceiling, so they stood and ate that way, pressing their chests against the table and leaning across their food to be as close as possible to the conversation. Leo was older than the father, younger than the grandfather. He was, he imagined, possibly a little of both men (except without the family of course, he reminded himself, as if he was a fool to liken himself in any way to men with children.)

'I need to use your phone, Pop,' the father said.

'Why?' the grandfather asked.

'Why! To shovel snow.'

The kids liked this line. One of the boys sniggered.

'No, you cannot.'

'What am I, twelve? Lemme use your phone, will you?'

'What sort of call is it, personal or business?'

'It's personal, I gotta call their mother.'

'Why are you calling Mummy?' the young girl said, swivelling to look at her dad while harpooning her food.

''Cos I wanna talk to her, sweetie.' The dad stroked her hair and gestured her to concentrate on her food. 'Dad, give me your phone.'

'As long as it's not work – you are not calling work, not all day, that's the whole point of today, Melissa said so.'

It was loving between them and it was robust. They both turned to watch a tall, Edith Sitwell type of woman walk past on Sixth Avenue, with a boxer dog on a lead. The younger boy leapt. 'Look! Look! That's a pitbull, it's so mean-looking, a pitbull, look!'

The brother and sister rebuked him theatrically. 'THAT'S NOT A PITBULL!'

'YESITISSSS!'

'It's a boxer, you fool.'

'It's a pitbull, I saw a movie about them!'

'Still doesn't make it one.'

'What movie?' the father asked. 'What movie did you see about pitbulls?'

The boy shrugged. 'I dunno, just some grisly movie.'

The father looked horrified. The grandfather leaned back in his chair and spread out his arms and announced to his adoring juvenile audience, 'It's a boxerbull, you all got it right. They're from Mongolia. That was a male boxerbull. *Boxerbullis ferocissimus*, from the Latin *Boxerbullissimo*, meaning "he-of-flattish-face".'

The two boys narrowed their eyes at each other and sat up straight, then roared.

'That's not true!' the younger boy called out, uncertainly.

The eldest boy squirmed, as if tickled, and painted a smile across Leo's face without Leo knowing it. The granddaughter stared open-mouthed and silent with a sausage on the prong of her fork at the wondrous creation that was her grandpa, and further down the restaurant a middle-aged woman who was keeping her recent diagnosis a secret so as to save her family the misery of the whole predictable unfolding scenario watched Leo's smile intently and listened to the kids' laughter. The dad placed an arm around his younger son and sat back, letting his belly relax over his belt. The phone call to Mummy seemed forgotten. He whispered to the boy, 'I think you're right, it's got some pitbull in there somewhere.' The boy studied his dad's face adoringly before being noticed. Laughter like that must be fantastic, Leo thought. He laughed with William and Joy but not like this, not belly laughter like this.

On Sixth Avenue, Leo buttoned his coat up tight against a physique less slender than when the coat was new. His eagerness to go to work was as uncharacteristic these days as his return to the French Roast had been fanciful, but he missed seeing William every day and was glad he'd gone back.

He felt the fractional taste of snowfall on his lips and noticed a profound, sudden drop in temperature across the neighbourhood. He looked south down Sixth Avenue where grey snow clouds filled the gap in the skyline. Fast on the heels of the stillness came a single gust of wind, moving northwards up the avenue like an empty wave and flicking the blossom from the trees. Above the heads of the people, blossom danced and swirled and Leo felt like the only man who could see it. The tumbling cloud came off the bay, billowing out across the harbour, full of snow, casting downtown into unnatural shade, and, as the cherry blossom flew horizontally from the trees, thick, feathery snowflakes descended vertically through the petals. Leo watched the white and pink against the dark green paintwork of Sammy's Noodle Shop. He inhaled the smell of melted chocolate from a street vendor. The snow and the blossom tumbled and flew and for the first time in half a decade he dared to hold his gaze down Sixth Avenue, and the snowstorm hurried towards him and he cried at last for the people who had died and the children of his who would never be born and he clenched his fists against the stupidity of how he had allowed time to dance over him. The snow came thicker now and sent the spring-clad populace scurrying for cabs and cover. The wind dropped and the blossom fell with the snow; they danced and dropped together and landed on the sidewalk where the flowers remained and the flakes made a brief impression, then melted away to nothing.

Leo's cellphone trembled against his ribs. He took a call from the clinic. The doctor could see Finn at noon. Leo took a look back through the window of the French Roast to see what the children made of the spring blizzard but he saw only himself reflected against a glare of white. He walked carefully on the slush despite his impatience to arrive. He called Astrid, asked about her weekend plans and commented on the snowstorm, before asking if she had organised a cellphone for Finn yet.

'I have been at work for eight minutes,' she told him. 'One of which has been invested in this conversation with you. No, I have not yet sorted out a cellular phone for the boy.'

'Is he there?'

'Yes, which is curious considering you fired him.'

'You're too literal for your own good,' Leo said. 'Make sure he doesn't leave.' He felt a lightness in his walk, and the memory of the swagger he possessed when growing his business and taking lovers as if the day would never end. There was a time when he felt in control of everything he was interested in, where he chose these streets and they didn't choose him. And in the spirit of that time he commanded a taxi to be his and it took him to Fountains. 'My dear man,' he said, when William answered his call, 'I am heading towards the Fountains Emporium Coffee Shop, no less, upon the fourth of your many floors, if you'll join me.'

William recognised this cocky voice from the past. He had forgotten it. It made him smile, despite his captivity. 'I can't. I'm not allowed out. I can't even invite you up because George White is coming to see me. I've complained about the situation.'

'You complained? Good for you.'

'Well, I didn't complain exactly.' William laughed at himself. 'I didn't complain at all. I just said I needed to talk to him about being confined to my room.'

Leo redirected the cab towards the gallery. 'Will, could we not have our breakfasts again? I miss them. You could get your limo to bring you to the French and wait for you while we eat and chat, then take you to work?'

'I miss the breakfasts too. It's a car not a limo and I hate it. I hate all this, I just want my old routine back. I miss Susan. I don't mean I miss Susan, that's not what I meant to say. I mean, I worry about her not getting enough rest.'

'Of course. What does my sister think about it all?' Leo felt a bit mean for mentioning her.

'That it'll blow over and go back to normal.'

'Sure I can't talk to George for you?'

'I'll do it. But, thanks.'

'Will?'

'Yes?'

'Joy's right. It will blow over. I've got a good feeling today, about everything.'

'She is normally right about things.'

'That's the spirit.'

By the time Leo reached 26th Street, the snow had stopped and the clouds were stretched thin across the sky, torn here and there to reveal the pale blue lagoon above. Leo marched into the gallery. 'Good morning, young man! What's new?'

'Nothing much,' Finn said. 'I'm obsessing about my bollocks.'

'Welcome to the rest of your life,' Leo replied, without breaking stride to his office, where Astrid was laying out a set of slides.

'Good morning, good morning!'

Astrid raised an eyebrow at Leo's vigour.

'What are we up to?' he said.

'You are looking at these, the Croatian painter I told you about, very very young and very very good. I am hung-over and not to be messed with, and your little puppy is fiddling with his snow globes.'

'Indeed...' Leo replied. He turned and watched Finn moping at the periphery, one hand rammed inside his pants. 'You've a doctor's appointment at noon,' he called out, 'so stop worrying.'

They sat down for coffee, around the main desk, upon which Astrid doggedly placed the lightbox that bore the Croatian's work.

'Could you wash your hands, please?' she said to Finn. 'You've been inside your underwear all morning.'

'Is your underwear clean on?' Leo asked, conspiratorially.

'What? Er, yes...' Finn said.

'Then he doesn't need to wash his hands,' Leo said, and passed Astrid the plate of croissants. 'But he can go last.'

Finn looked at Astrid triumphantly. She ignored him, theatrically, but the corners of her mouth raised a little. 'What do you think?' Astrid asked.

'The Croatian?' Leo replied. 'Pretty work, devoid of ideas. Empty. We'd sell them but I don't want to.'

Finn watched Astrid slump and knew that Leo would not have noticed. And his heart sank as Leo pushed the slides across to him.

'Take a look and tell us what they make you think of, in your own time, in your own way,' Leo said.

'Uh-uh.' Finn shook his head. 'I'm not going to say any stuff about anything any more – just gets me in trouble.'

'That wouldn't work,' Astrid said. 'You can't work here and not have opinions.'

'There's a difference between being honest about art, which you are, very, and telling my clients they're wankers,' Leo said with the indulgent smile that Finn provoked in him.

'Yes,' Astrid said. 'Be honest, but choose when not to air your opinions.'

'That's just lying.'

'No, it's not,' she said. 'It's being polite. It's holding back. Having a filter. You have to learn these things. They are skills.'

'You do it all the time already,' Leo said. 'You don't tell everyone you walk past who is fat that they are fat. You do it every day: you filter your thoughts all the time, unless, in your own case I suspect, you're angry or you feel attacked.'

There was a pause, in which Finn suspected he was meant to be stunned by their wisdom. Leo seemed different this morning and Finn saw no point in being dutifully silent when they were telling him to shoot from the hip, and given that he was a dying man with a noon appointment with the reaper's fuckbuddy.

'Okay,' Finn said. 'If we're talking honestly. I think she – ' he pointed his croissant at Astrid ' – doesn't want to be your dogsbody. And she only plays the role of tough person because being your... I dunno... mother is not what she wants so she's not being herself. And if you let her make some decisions on the paintings without making changes to everything she does, then she could be herself and then she'd probably be a bit more of a laugh. I think you want to change that waitress's life because she's black and does a badly paid job and you want to sleep with her. When you're my age you can say, "I really want to fuck that waitress," but because you are seriously old you feel you have to disguise it and say "I really want to help her."'

In the silent aftermath of the emotional carnage rained on them by a quiet young man's unedited opinion, Astrid blushed and came close to taking a bite of her croissant, and Leo supped his coffee and the gallery began to feel new to him again. And he knew that, if the boy didn't remain, he might lose something (he had no idea what) that would never be offered him again. He shut his eyes and saw a single petal of cherry blossom falling, falling, falling, tumbling through the air, head over heels, and landing softly, so beautifully softly on the sidewalk, and he knew that, if he could only believe in gentle landings, then he could allow himself to take pleasure in this city again.

Finn left early, to take a long, slow walk across town to the clinic. But walking simply made him more conscious of his testicles. He took a seat in Stuyvesant Park. His right hand remained tucked inside his underwear, touching the lump inside his ball sack, and guaranteeing him a bench to himself.

The clinic was airless and stifling. The hum of machinery infiltrated Finn's head, intensifying in unnoticeable increments until it was deafening in its own way. The packed waiting room and general inertia of the place told him he was not going to be seen at noon. The first hour he waited gave him ample opportunity to sweat in exactly the region he had most wanted not to, plan his funeral, to fantasise that before the tumour reduced him to rubble he would have the good health – and testicular armoury – to have a sexually athletic love affair with Amy, fly to England to finish off his uncle, escape back to New York and die with Amy and Jack at his bedside. He wrote his eulogy.

Ninety minutes after his appointment time, with the original cast of the waiting room replaced, he asked the receptionist when he would be seen. To do so was a mistake, and he knew it as soon as he'd spoken. The receptionist reminded him that he was a *fit-you-in*, such status being, it appeared, a notch lower than jihadists and mothers that supplied crack to their own children. A further fifty minutes passed. Finn filled it by opening negotiations with the eternal powers that be, so that, in the event of God and heaven existing, he received a room in a different wing of the afterlife from his mum and dad.

Dr Minnis was in equal parts charming and repellent, and mistaken in the belief that Finn would be captivated by his preference for English soccer over American football. Framed photographs of Dr Minnis's two sons were peppered over his desk and shelves, and were of such blandness that Finn wondered if the children had come with the frames. Crate Minnis and Barrel Minnis. Finn filled out a questionnaire about his general health and sexual habits while Minnis spoke of his own sporting achievements at high school and med school before announcing that it was time to take a look at the 'worrisome area'.

'You going to apologise for the two-hour wait first?' Finn asked, remaining resolutely seated.

Dr Minnis was caught between his sitting and standing positions as if unleashing a fart while popping up on to the surf. And behind his thousand-dollar laser-white smile the rest of his face was a cradle of confusion, his eyeballs lava lamps of bewilderment. 'Yes,' he gasped, finally straightening up, 'my boys love their soccer.' The life had been squeezed out of him and he said little else, other than to mutter rudimentary instructions to guide Finn through the process of pulling his trousers and underwear down and lying back. Afterwards, as he washed his hands, he said, 'We need to get that looked at.'

'You just looked.'

'I mean a scan.'

Dr Minnis kept talking but *scan* was pretty much the last word Finn had heard. He went back to the hovel and prepared for death.

Scan.

A cocksucking motherfucking scan.

He cried in bed. All the things he could have cried at in his life and hadn't, but tonight he shook from sobbing and he knew he was going to die. The anger rose in him. Dying was all that anyone did in his fucking family. Sleep didn't offer itself up as an option so he went out and bought booze and cigarettes, to herald the onset of a non-smoker's certain cancer. He placed them on Glenn's circular table, where they remained, unconsumed. He thought of Amy. He wanted to call her. He wanted to hold her. But he guessed that she didn't want a bollockless chemo-raddled boyfriend. There was no one in the world he could trouble with his dying without feeling that he was being the most tremendous pain in the arse, and that was what he had always felt about being his parents' son, that he and his brother had been an annoyance to them, he much more so than Jack.

He tried to sleep but his thoughts dwelt on the prospect of spending eternity avoiding his mum and dad. New realm, same old shit.

17

Jack's health deteriorated in a barefaced refusal to comply
with his recovery schedule. He fell asleep during Holly's
morning call and spent the rest of the day feverish and
looking back on stuff he didn't care to remember. In the
margins of sleep, vivid, accurate pictures of his home town
appeared like a pop-up book fallen out of his blind spot.
Between the two halves of the town, below the terraces of
tall, despairing Victorian houses that lined the West Ridge
and the East Hill, was the scar that could be seen from space,
the alluvial plain that prised open the gorge that split the
town. At the base of the ancient flow of the plain was the
chalk bowl that seemed to have swallowed up houses and
roads that never existed, and banked precariously around its
edge was the sink estate where Jack and Finn were born and
which Jack's brother loved very much and where the grey
blocks of flats and squeezed-thin houses held their breath
above the drop.

Behind the teeth of slate houses on the edge of the
grinning bowl, in a triangle of unclaimed land where the
children gorged on blackberries in late summer and the
adults fly-tipped in winter, stood five enduring beech trees,
corralled by the estate into nothing more than their distant
memories of ancient forest. One tree stood apart from
the rest, in the others' shadow but with views across the
foot of the alluvial plain to the sea and the fishing boats

and amusement arcades and the shingle beach. Young Jack climbed to a bough five feet off the ground, and his parents applauded. He sat there often and pondered his life and tried to make sense of his parents' behaviour.

His parents called the beech tree 'Jack's tree', and Jack loved that for the illusion it offered that his parents might be watching him climb the tree or aware of him sitting in it. When Finn started to walk, Jack's mother told her eldest, 'One day you can teach Finny to climb your tree,' and Jack logged it for the future. His mother was never truly sober after Finn was born. When she drank, Jack climbed the beech tree and sat five feet above the world. When she couldn't cope, she gave the boy to her elder son and if it was dry on the ground Jack lay beneath the tree shoulder-to-shoulder with Finn and they watched the branches sway and the patches of sky between the boughs and the sunlight blind them, and they talked in cathedral whispers.

On a Saturday lunchtime, when Jack and Finn's parents were each in their beds and Jack was resigned to not getting his homework done, the two boys zigzagged their way down the slope of the forests in the scrub, squeezing the resin out of the nodules on the pine trees and inhaling it until their eyes watered. They ate sandwiches beneath Jack's tree, and afterwards, with the taste of the pine transferred from their fingers to their mouths, they spat globs of resin on to the ground from the first bough of the great tree and swung their legs. Their father stepped into the backyard wearing his dressing gown and slippers and smoking a cigarette. He looked half-heartedly beyond the fence for his children and Finn spat out a little more bile and climbed to the next bough.

'Hey,' Jack whispered, 'be careful.'

'I'm okay.'

'I know you're okay,' Jack laughed, 'but you're also only six. That's too high, come down.'

'I wanna see…' Finn said.

'That's way too high,' Jack said.

'Come on,' Finn said and he kept on climbing, without hesitation, as if he did not possess the ability to doubt his footing.

'One of us better stay down here,' Jack said.

After that, Finn used to sit in the crown of the tree watching the temper of the estate and the shapes of the sea and the shadows that lurked beneath the water, and Jack would sit on the low bough, craning his neck upwards to keep watch on his baby brother, burdened with the jitters that seeing Finn up there should have given his parents. Sometimes in summer their mother would look out over the fence and laugh to the rattle of ice cubes and call her little Finny a monkey up there in the sky and wave across the wasteland at her clever, grown-up son and call out to him, 'Isn't he a mad monkey, that little one, eh, Jack?' And Jack would look up to his little brother, at what his body could do.

The next year, when Jack turned thirteen, his parents moved them out of the estate to the beginning of the end, and Jack bid the beech tree good riddance and didn't return for five years until the night the men on the reservoir found his mother, and his father committed himself to the Herculean task of drowning his sorrow. On that night, the boys slipped away from the cul-de-sac with their sleeping bags and returned to their first home and slept beneath the beech trees, watching the planes come in from Europe and a few stars that penetrated the glow of the town and the drift of the clouds, and listening to the throaty rumble of the TV from their old living room and the repeated rhythms of canned laughter. Jack suspected, that night, that he would use his father and his brother as an excuse to keep himself to himself during the university years he was embarking upon. His instinct was right. He turned down Manchester for London and returned home most weekends in his first two years, to shield Finn and to scrape his father up off the floor. His chronic shyness with the women who found him handsome and evasive went unchallenged and unrepaired by his absence from life outside of the lecture theatre, and in his final year he moved back home and commuted. That was Finn's happiest time, and Jack knew it. In the evenings, the boys went running together, silent but for their breathing which was in perfect harmony and which allowed Jack to forget for one more hour that he felt close to breakdown. He had lost a mother and a brother, and gained a drunkard and a son, and it all felt too lonely to sustain.

He remained at home when he got his first job in the City. A girlfriend in the office was put off by the apparent indifference of Jack's refusal to stay over more than once a week or take her home to his raddled father and increasingly feral brother. Then came Holly, who had fallen for Jack's looks, manners and compulsive tidiness, and marched into his office to announce she had a spare ticket for a Rachmaninov concert at the Royal Festival Hall which she would take him to in return for dinner and that he'd be able to get the late train back home to the coast. She spoke of the proposed date as if she already knew it would be an ordeal for him. From the start, she seemed to understand him and made no demands that would challenge his duties. In Holly, Jack saw the chance of escape the moment she voiced her intention to move back to New York City, which was in the interval, that first evening. For Holly, he would create a new, brighter version of himself, in which his humble beginnings were the central myth, one which he cemented by taking her back to the estate the day before they left for America, to show her the house he had started from and the tree he had 'taught Finn to climb'.

Jack had thought a great deal about his baby brother coming to visit him in New York, had imagined that day

he'd take Finn to Inwood Hill Park to see the rocky outcrops, and to Pelham Bay and the Palisades to share his
knowledge of the Inwood marble, the Manhattan schist
and the Fordham gneiss in a way that Finn would find
interesting, though Jack didn't yet know how that would be.
He had pictured the two of them standing together on these
rocks that New York City was built on and he had hoped
that something about it would anchor them there. This
would happen thanks to his own ability to be fascinated by
these things and to understand them, and something would
somehow make Finn finally love this about him. Instead,
Jack was waking up to the idea that if you were nineteen and
pissed off and had a choice between a geology lesson from
your brother (but it was not that, it was much more than a
lesson, and this was what pained Jack: his inability to present
it as what it really was) and a sexual education from an older
woman, then a nineteen-year-old would have an easy choice
to make. Instead of being Finn's rock in New York City,
Jack had no idea where his kid brother was, and he realised,
finally, in the depths of his flu, that he had no right to know.
And that this could be how it was always going to be.

18

William took the few steps with Joy to his new daily pick-up point outside Ladder Company 21, where he had already established a tendency to nod, imperceptibly, at the seven steel plaques on the wall. It was eight-forty-five on the bip. His car would arrive between eight-forty-five and eight-fifty and deposit him in the cargo area beneath Fountains by nine. He was bang on time. This was his new routine, courtesy of George White, almost one week in, and he hated it.

'He might as well put me in an orange boiler suit.'

They were signed up to the Club's on-line petition to close down Guantanamo but had not gotten too involved owing to feeling safer for the place existing. Joy pulled a sad face and teased him: 'Poor you'. He smiled at his own petulance but the smile creased his mouth like nausea. She cuddled him and agreed it wasn't funny.

He loved the old routine. Routine made sense of Manhattan. Without it, how could they know which way to turn in the infinite city? Routine made devotion possible; how else to steer clear of the other people they might have become?

Until the intervention of George White, William had walked hand-in-hand with his wife every morning to the health store where, as often as not, the guys outside the Municipal Taxi Drivers' Association hollered to Joy and she called back as she unlocked the place. During this salvo, William would try to look at ease by staring with forced assurance along 43rd Street at the health club or, at this time of year, the sublime blossom, as if he'd seen something fascinating that left him, oh, hardly aware of the men flirting with his wife and her expertise with them. Or, he'd gaze imperiously southwards down Ninth Avenue at the Port Authority's arsehole.

Joy had worked at Complementary for twenty-five years. Her first job in New York was as a legal secretary but she'd resigned from it on realising she didn't like to be in tall buildings, a noteworthy discovery for someone seeking office work in Manhattan. She had made it up the Empire State Building only twice, with Leo when they first arrived (when the excitement of everything and the supportive arm of her big brother covered her fear), and with William, immediately after he proposed to her in the Red Flame, and the queasiness of that latter occasion had prompted her to rule out ascending to great heights again.

Complementary had little custom in the early years other than a few pale regulars. But that was Hell's Kitchen. In the Clinton-Hell's Kitchen hybrid of 2006, business was good. Stevie Logan, the owner, paid Joy and Adele a little more these days, was apologetic for the change of pace that success had brought and allowed Joy to bail out once or twice a month and take the ferry to Sandy Hook where she walked on the beach with her shoes off. William was unaware of these excursions and used to leave her every morning and stride through Hell's Kitchen to Fountains, feeling as though he owned this part of town, confident in the nirvana of each day being the same as the last. But now, his day began by watching Joy walk away to enjoy their routine without him. She appeared unfaithful and, as she disappeared around the corner on to Tenth Avenue, a sickening realisation hit him: that this temporary set-up was going to run and run. The Boltons weren't, by the look of it, going to die any time soon, and William's working life might confine him to the attic for years. This was a prison sentence. George White had messed up, big time.

He called Leo. 'George White has screwed up!' William announced, to Leo's voicemail, then hit a wall with his plan of action, and hung up.

Hell's Kitchen lay beneath a clean cover of low, blinding cloud. Over New Jersey hung a drape of charcoal grey. The join in the weather hovered over the far bank of the Hudson and the city remained caught between winter and spring. A puddle of oil on the sidewalk reflected the characterless sky and a coil of blackened rope snaked through it. On the mesh fencing a sign in yellow and black advertised a two-day bodyguard-training course. From beneath the soles of William's Cheltenham brogues, through the concrete and steel of the Dyer Avenue underpass, came the growl of engines in the entrance to the Lincoln Tunnel. He loved the noises of New York City by day, and was untroubled by them at night. He was lucky in that respect and thanked God for sound sleep. Beyond the NJ Transit parking lot, the lead patina roofline of the Croatian Catholic church reflected on the underside of the clouds, painting them a faded green. Further down 38th Street, a line of men pushing hot-dog trolleys emerged from a warehouse alley and headed into midtown. He counted them, seventeen, eighteen, nineteen in total, all of them a little beaten-up but sparkling chrome in the April sunshine as the car from Fountains turned the corner and pulled up beside him. Alone on the back seat, it dawned on him that without the walk to and from work, and his strolls around the store and to lunch, he might age rather rapidly. He let out a sudden breath, a combination of fear and disgust, and called Leo again.

'What's up? That message was not very... you,' Leo said. 'You got it?'

'Just this second listened to it. George White is screwing you?'

'Screwing up.'

'Tell me, Will.'

William looked at the back of the driver's head. 'I can't.'

'Right...' Leo said. 'You mean you can't because you can be overheard.'

'Yes, I mean that.'

'Let me speak to George for you.'

'I don't know...' William said, and was on the very edge of accepting the offer when Leo said, 'You know, it's actually the idiot who made the complaint we need to speak to.'

'Is it?'

'George can't change the fact that he's told them you're fired. But, given that you're not fired, if the man who got you fired could be asked to have you reinstated, George doesn't have to do anything, except let you go back to how it was. Think about it, Will.'

William did just that, as he negotiated the abandoned torchlit stairwell. Although he welcomed the exercise, the climb had nearly killed Susan and she had not returned since. For that reason alone he now hated the 18th Street stairwell.

He couldn't get on with his work. His music collection offered up nothing he wanted to hear and he found himself gazing at Susan's mattress and trying to mastermind a way of getting through the store and up through the office levels to his attic without being seen. Among the floral patterns of the bedding the idea came to him of going to see old Mrs Bolton, and not her son. He dismissed it as crazy. But that night he failed to make love to Joy for the first time in his life, and the next morning he felt car-sick on the way to the store. He savoured a cigarette at the small open window and blew smoke up towards the gods. The Promised Land was the place where nothing had changed and his lust for it so strong that he could see none of the reasons not to go see the old lady himself, to get reinstated in the job he had not lost.

He dug out her letter, wrote down the address and, although taking the initiative did not sit comfortably with him, found himself loose on the streets, walking uncertainly from the store to return the universe to its axis, with the intention of stopping off at Complementary to talk it through with Joy.

He stopped beneath the Port Authority bridge and buttoned up his jacket against the howl of trucks around and above him. Through the glass walls of the Project Find Seniors' Day Centre, a woman mouthed into a microphone to elderly folk bowed over their bingo cards in a room of scattered plastic tables lit an epileptic green. It was so important to stay fit, he reminded himself, another good reason to walk the entire way to the old lady's place and, he now decided, not stop to discuss this with Joy, who he suspected would talk him out of it.

He had not thought through what he would say to Mrs Bolton, and his ability to go with the flow and riff this thing out was something he questioned as he tackled the saturnalia of construction in the backside of the Trump Tower. He was not one of life's riffers. A billboard offered him luxury two- to five-bedroom residences starting at three million dollars. The air space was owned by a vast film poster for *The Da Vinci Code*. Nothing looked right to him on Central Park West. People talking on the sidewalk beside him sounded distant. A bus passed in silence. On the walls of the Ethical Society he read an inscription, *Dedicated to the ever-increasing knowledge and practice and love of the right*, and the word *right* seemed to be testing him. He looked south to reassure himself that the lines of midtown remained straight and true. He reminded himself that a mere twenty blocks away was his wife and that all was well. But it was a little harder to breathe in this part of town, he was convinced of it. By his standards, he was at altitude.

In an attempt to gather his thoughts, he took a seat in Le Pain Quotidien and was charmed by the interior as well as by the name, naturally, to an extent he would not have permitted had he known it was a franchise. He asked for an English breakfast tea.

'We don't have it, we have Brussels breakfast, it's identical, in fact it's actually more English if you know what I mean.' His waiter was Eastern European and bookish and likeable.

William smiled gratefully. 'Thank you, that'll be fine.' When it arrived, his tea was in a pot, with a large bowl to drink from and a small bowl for the used teabag. William asked what he was supposed to drink out of and the waiter pointed to the large bowl. Foreseeing only awkwardness, William requested a cup and saucer.

'We don't have them.'

'A mug?'

'Uh-uh.'

'Anything with a handle?'

'No, man, I'm sorry. It's our thing.'

'It's fine. Thank you.'

'You okay?' the waiter asked.

William looked confused. 'Yes.'

'You're shaking.'

'Am I? Well, I just need that tea, I guess.'

A woman wheeled a buggy into the café. She was alone, and talking aloud. 'He and I are simply not ever going to be compatible in that regard but need that be the end of the total world? What do you think? Because I think we have great synergy and there's a great deal of harmony there despite how he sometimes likes to portray me and that's a helluvalot to have together. And the other stuff, I mean, we can work on it or live without it or, you know, other people, whatever, but we are very secure together and have a great place we wouldn't afford alone, and a good time. I don't know what you think...'

The woman leaned forward and repositioned her baby's pacifier, and seemed to be telling the infant that it was '… twelve years since I even considered that sort of thing with a guy… who with? With Sparks of course, you remember, Sparks, the guy who used to winter in Aruba, that was a very free expressive relationship but no, yuk, no way, no urge, no interest, uh-uh. And that's really not where our problems lie, at all, not significantly, anyway, yuk, I was younger and he was hot. I'm not saying Mark isn't hot but, you know…'

William watched the woman, open-mouthed. A younger man at the adjacent table said, 'It's really damn hard to seem like a mad person these days, isn't it? Talking to yourself in public used to be the clincher, but nowadays people presume you're just on your cell. One has to do something more impressive to make it clear you're cracked.' He leaned closer to William. 'She's talking on the phone. It's in her ear, beneath all that crazy hair.'

William wondered just how old his nerves were making him appear. 'I'm aware of that. I'm fifty-five not ninety-five.'

The man took offence so William smiled at him and confided. 'What I'm not aware of is when it became okay to have intimate conversations at the top of one's voice in public.'

'You don't look ancient,' the man said, gathering up his things. 'But you sound old as fuck.'

When the man had gone, William smiled publicly to try to negate his sadness at being on the end of such aggressive language. Drinking hot tea out of a bowl with no handles did not make him look any younger or more dextrous. He gave up, paid up and got out. He had four blocks to go and it took three and a half of them for his mind to belatedly catch sight of the truth that there was no way Mrs Bolton was going to invite a stranger with a grudge into her apartment.

There was a doorman, who let him in, and a concierge behind a desk. Without deciding what he should say, he reminded himself what he shouldn't: I'm not here looking for trouble but I just need to see the defenceless, wealthy old woman who lives in the penthouse.

'Good morning. My name is William Fairman and I'm here to talk to Mrs Bolton. If you could tell her I'm from Fountains Emporium – ' this seemed like a building in which to name-check the store's full title ' – and only want to talk on the phone or intercom or whatever...' His voice trailed off. He should have written to her. He should have come here with a letter and delivered it and maybe he would have bumped into her and she would have seen in his body language that he was not here to cause trouble.

'Take a seat, sir.'

He walked across to a chesterfield, noticed the doorman observing him from the sidewalk, and sat forward. He watched the elevator doors to one side of the lobby. The concierge spoke into a phone in a hushed voice, seemed to William to be miming. A smaller elevator door opened at the far end of the lobby where it had blended invisibly into the walls. Inside, the elevator was velveteen and luxurious. A bald-headed man poked his head out and studied William until the doors slid shut again. A few minutes passed and the concierge took a call. The small, hidden elevator arrived again in the lobby. The doors opened and William watched for the bald man to appear but there was no one inside. The doors closed again.

'That was for you,' the concierge said.

'How was I to know?' William asked.

The concierge nodded to the doorman, who came inside and summoned the elevator back and beckoned William with his white-gloved hand. The elevator was a miniature room, dark, carpeted and scented, with a sumptuously upholstered bench seat and a small table with a Chinese vase holding a delicate posy of freesias. The flowers were haloed by the glow of a single weak, smoky yellow downlight in the elevator ceiling. There were two buttons, L and P. The doorman pressed P and backed out of the elevator as the door shut. Ascending, William nodded at the trembling flowers as if they were both in the same boat.

The elevator opened directly into the drawing room of the penthouse apartment and the crowded opulence meant that it took him a moment to notice the stout, tweed-clad figure of Mrs Bolton amongst it all. The room owned her as much as she owned it. The elevator door closed like a murmur and disappeared seamlessly into the wall. She beckoned William to join her, and through a doorway to another room he saw the bald man from the elevator. He stood in overalls, paintbrush in hand, and watched William closely. He was tall and intimidating, and at least twenty years older than William.

'Now,' Mrs Bolton said, 'you sit down right here.' Her voice became more haughty in her efforts to be amicable. She pointed to a high-backed armchair with side wings and watched William take his seat with great dignity for such a pathetic man.

'Thank you for seeing me, Mrs Bolton. I need you to have me reinstated.'

'My son is working,' she said. 'Or, at least,' she corrected herself, 'he's at work. I will get us some tea. I'll make it myself, Marie's not in until noon.' Her mouth widened and trembled under the strain of what William realised was her attempt at a smile. 'We can *talk turkey*,' she added, deliberately, as if recently taught the phrase. She went into the kitchen. Somewhere out of sight, the bald man cleared his throat.

William's chair was deep. It sank him low into a soft cushion, and raised his feet an inch off the floor. On the opposite side of the room was a grand picture window through which he could see treetops and a big blue sky and beneath which, William presumed, would be a view of the

Park more stunning than any he had seen, from a vantage point he would never have again. A shift upwards of a few inches would have given him the whole vista, but he felt unable to change his position now that he had settled into it. His cell vibrated. He peeked into his inside jacket pocket and saw Joy's name but knew it would be rude to take the call. He could hear the tinkering of chinaware coming from the kitchen. His cell vibrated again and he was still toying with the idea of listening to Joy's message when the formidable lady reappeared, crockery and silverware trembling on the tray in her hands. She walked with a ballerina's turnout and a fishwife's gait.

The apartment was airless. Surrounded by the clearest views and oxygen on Manhattan, it forbade William both. Mrs Bolton put the tray aside as if the notion of their actually drinking tea together was out of the question.

'What was your wage?' she asked, curtly.

Her chair was fractionally behind his and he had to lean forward past the wing of his chair to look back at her. 'I just want my job back, it's terribly important and it will be very easy.'

'That would be completely unfair on Hunter. He took a position, and the one thing he cannot bear to be is undermined.' (This was not entirely true. A more exhaustive list of what Hunter Bolton III could not bear to be would have included: inconvenienced, interrupted, told no, and in the same room as a non-white person.)

His mother continued. 'Now, your wage... the fact of the matter is, I do feel a little guilty, but to compensate you I have to make some sort of calculation based on your earnings.'

William felt the energy drain out of him. 'I just need you to say to my employers that you would like me reinstated and they will do it. I know for a fact they will. It is more simple than you can imagine.'

Despite being firmly seated upon a chair worth more than the annual salary he was being asked to disclose, William felt that he was on the brink of falling off it, and that if he fell off his chair he would fall off the world. They sat in silence for a while and the old lady's breathing altered as her benevolence turned to impatience. She had not been contradicted by anyone since acquiring widowed status and she found it irksome. She went to her bureau and sat at it and took a cheque book and a fountain pen from the drawer.

'No!' William snapped. 'It has to be my job.'

'Did you just raise your voice to me?'

The decorator stepped into the room. 'How are we doing in here?' he growled.

'How are we doing in here?' Mrs Bolton asked William.

William glared at the man, in despair at how simple this all could be if the old lady would just do what was asked of her. A phone call now to George White and he would walk to work tomorrow, be smoking a cigarette with Susan in a matter of hours.

The decorator goaded him with his expression, dared William to get this any more wrong than he already was doing.

William muttered, 'We're doing fine but it absolutely has to be my job. I beg you.'

'I'm going to make it five thousand dollars,' the old lady said.

The decorator came forward. 'Then, I'll see you out.'

William rose from his seat. It seemed to take him forever to do so and he had a premonition of old age. He felt cornered, powerless. He placed his hands behind his back, the way his father used to do. It always made him feel a foot taller, which was sometimes welcome. He saw himself for what he was: the little man without choices. If he hadn't known that before, he knew it now, in this apartment, squeezed between the henchman and an old lady's loose change. He was not going to get what he had come for. But he wanted something out of this godforsaken place. Perhaps a little respect would be nice, and to see the view. He liked the idea of a rich person who owned the view knowing that William Fairman was a good man, a giving man, a man with no material ambition and a generous heart, the better man. The love that was trying to burst out through the walls of his chest every living day, the love that was waiting there inside him in limitless supply should his wife ever unearth a frailty in herself and turn to him for help, or if Susan French should ever ask to be taken in completely, adopted and cared for, the love that made him yearn for Leo to be completely happy, the love inside William that knew satisfaction only in countless small acts of unnoticed kindness – that love cried out right now for a one-off moment of recognition and to turn down a rich woman's money, which might just feel good enough to repair the disappointment of not getting back the job he hadn't lost.

He went across to the window. Indeed, it was a magnificent view. 'Thank you, Mrs Bolton,' he said.

She remained stony and said, 'I'm so pleased…' in the tone of someone who was anything but.

He heard her pen scratch across the surface of the cheque. 'Your full name, please, dear.'

He turned and looked the decorator in the eye and sneered a smile at him that said, *You would not do what I am about to do.* He cleared his throat, holding a clenched hand to his mouth. This was his moment. It was small and harmless and second prize, but he wanted her to know. He wanted everyone to know. He always had, from the moment he saw the light of God. It was not how he was meant to feel, he knew that, but he didn't see the harm in this one woman of substance and her Rottweiler knowing that he was good.

'Please make it payable to the Church of the Disciples of Christ.'

She would mention this moment one day, in this magnificent room, to her friends: the small man who wanted to give away everything.

Mrs Bolton glared at the wall in front of her. 'No,' she said. She put the lid on her pen and crossed her arms.

William slumped. He cursed himself.

She turned to him. 'I know the first name is William. But now I'm confused. Should I be generously writing you a cheque, or calling the police – or perhaps your former employers?'

'Or getting me my job back…' William said, beseechingly. 'Please.'

'We're not discussing that again. And I'm not funding your church.'

William felt a little faint. His heart was thudding. He knew nothing about what to do, only that he shouldn't be in this place. He was furious at himself for being here.

'Alright, payable to me, William Fairman.'

'But you'll just give it away.'

'No, I won't!'

The decorator stepped forward. 'Don't take that tone.'

'Sorry,' William said. 'I promise I'll keep it.'

She picked up the pen. 'F-a-i-r-m-a-n,' she asked, as she wrote his name.

William walked closer and as he watched his name appear on the cheque a panic rose in him and as he caught sight of a new wave of insight into the myriad flaws of his being here. He had arrived with a plan that worked only if she played the part as devised by him for her. But rich people didn't allow themselves to be scripted by others. They were now way off the page, and in her handwriting he saw clearly the name of a man who had come to an old rich lady and extracted compensation for a job he had not lost, and exposed Fountains for their lie. He had never imagined himself capable of having such effect.

'My job, please. As if nothing had ever happened.'

'How ungrateful,' she sighed, finishing off the cheque and ripping it out of the book. She held it up for him to take but didn't look at him. He looked helplessly towards where the elevator was hidden, marched across the apartment and groped the wall for a button. In his anxiety he couldn't locate it. He darted for the first door he could see. It took him into a small lobby where through a glazed door he could see a stairwell.

Down in the lobby, Mrs Bolton and her decorator emerged from the elevator as William reached the ground floor. She held the cheque in her hand and the decorator stared threateningly as William continued out through the swing doors and on to the sidewalk, terrified of the sensation of being pursued. He heard Mrs Bolton's voice ring out: 'STOP!'

They'll think I've mugged her, William thought.

He ran, and in his jagged movements two distinct, liberating truths came to him: that he could stand to do any job as long as he had Joy to go home to, and that he wanted to take care of Susan, properly, openly, with Joy. He saw a cab up ahead, and the Park. The Park across the street seemed a good place to go to, to hide, to gather himself. But a cab seemed right too, the quickest way home. He grabbed for his phone and fumbled it as he ran, juggled the phone two, three times, then caught it and called Joy.

'I have to tell you all about Susan French, and you have to forgive me,' he said.

'Sorry?' she gasped.

His arm was raised as he ran, he realised, to signal for a cab he must have seen or imagined, but he was looking across to the Park and the swaying manes of the spring trees that seemed to be speaking to him, saying something urgent he could not decipher but drowning out the distant sound of Joy's shouting from the phone, 'What the hell do you mean? What does that mean?!' and then a hot, tingling sensation shot through him as he realised he had strayed out of bounds, and as he felt the excess space around him, the absence of buildings, the removal of the sidewalk, he knew he was exposed, as if in mid-air, treading water, being picked up off his feet by the swaying trees, and the feeling that had accompanied him through the day, of being in the wrong place and heading further in the wrong direction, crystallised perfectly as he glimpsed the seven-ton U-Haul truck that hit him and dragged him down to an underworld of grease-caked metal.

Deafness was immediate, but the dark was not. Across the sweep of tarmac that separated his cheekbone and the kerb, he saw Mrs Bolton arrive and stare. She slumped, as if taking a blow to the stomach, and then, in the next instant, she straightened up and the expression on her face withdrew into her skin and left her lifeless, and she turned and walked calmly away, as others lurched into William's field of view and knelt over him. He could see them talking into the silence, and then, he could see nothing. He was alive but there was nothing to prove it. No sound, no light, no shapes. It altered only later when he realised he was being lifted. The faint impression of motion rippled his senses and an image formed in the liquid of his mind's eye, an Ektachrome slide projected on to a distant wall, of the vase of freesias in the small, lavish penthouse elevator, blooms cut and placed where they could only die, after bringing a little colour and perfume to a very few people in a small, enclosed box travelling up and down, up and down, a lightless shaft.

19

Leo stopped outside Richard Bovenkamp's gallery and admired the Dot Yi. He took a call from Astrid, expecting her to test his interest in the painting. Instead, he heard her say, 'You need to get over here.' He turned and saw her standing in the window of the gallery. The sun burned through the clouds and Astrid looked back at him without expression and he understood immediately the nature of what it would be, but was wrong in presuming that it would be Finn's name that came from her lips, not William's.

Leo explained who he was to one of the receptionists at St Luke's Roosevelt but the words sounded strange to him.

'He's my sister's husband.'

He felt he should say more. He is my brother-in-law. He is my closest friend, one half of my entire family, the love of my sister's life, the one man standing at the door to an apartment in this city to greet me with open arms. He is William, 'William' is the only word that describes all the things he is to me.

Initially, he saw only Joy kneeling at the bed. He could not see William until he forced himself to look. What stole Leo's breath was not the visible injury but the lifelessness, the vacuity to William's face that remained even when he opened his eyes, slowly recognised Leo and smiled at him, causing the oxygen mask to rise on his cheeks. Leo raised his right hand in return and wiggled his fingers, a gesture that amused

William. This exchange took place not so much behind Joy's back as above it, her head bowed in silent prayer.

Leo touched his sister's arm. When she turned there was anger in her face, and when Leo held her he had the ludicrous sensation that it was an enormous effort for her to allow him to do so. She was rigid, as if under attack.

'Going to get a coffee,' she said. 'Back in a minute.'

Leo lifted a chair from its position at the back of the room and placed it silently beside the bed. He threaded his hand through the tubes to rest it on William's arm. 'I'm here,' he whispered, and both men enjoyed the sight of each other. A nurse came and Leo moved away to give her room to work. He went to the window. Steam rose from vents on the roofline into a vivid blue sky. The streets below played him a silent movie and on to the screen stepped Joy, leaning backwards as if assaulted by the sunlight and fishing sunglasses out of her bag. She sipped her coffee then bowed her head, and went down on to her haunches. She put her cup down and held her head in her hands. Leo pressed against the window to watch her. He heard the nurse leave, and far below him his sister rose to her feet and commandeered a taxi which stole her from the scene. Her coffee cup remained abandoned on the sidewalk, unnerving Leo with the way it made 58th Street resemble the scene of a disappearance.

From the bedside, Leo grew quickly familiar with the hospital's sober rhythms, the porters and nurses passing left to right and right to left, the sounds from off-stage, the beat of the monitors hooked to William's body and the warm, pacifying simplicity of crisis. Within an hour, he could not imagine life beyond this place.

The nurse returned. 'How's he doing?' she said.

Leo whispered, 'No sign of life at all, apart from his breathing.'

'Breathing is right up there, when it comes to signs of life,' she said.

He left messages on Joy's cell at three and five and seven. At nine o'clock, he called the apartment and told the machine that William was fully awake and the nurses had sat him up in bed.

'I'm here,' she said, urgently, her voice squeezed as she leaned her ribs across the arm of the couch.

'Where have you been?'

'I found myself standing on West 36th Street, no idea how I got there.'

'In a taxi,' Leo said.

'We were meant to be bulletproof. And everything in the apartment feels like make-believe.'

'It isn't,' he assured her.

'When I was outside, looking at our building, I felt sure that my life would not be waiting for me inside. I took a Restoril and some 5-HTP and dreamt the apartment was full of people and I moved through them, asking if they had seen William, but his name meant nothing to them.'

'Maybe the Restoril wasn't such a great idea.'

'It turned into an orgy but everyone wanted Susan not me, and I ended up serving coffee for them all and asking them, "Don't you find her too painfully thin?"'

'Just a stupid dream,' he said. 'Don't worry.'

It was silent for a while between them.

'I love you, sis,' Leo said.

'Thank you very much, Leo,' she said, chilling him with her detachment. 'I bathed and put on a little make-up, put on my raincoat to come back to the hospital and sat on the couch, just for a moment.'

She stopped abruptly, as if something had occurred to her, and Leo heard only her breathing, and then even that seemed to stop. He had watched all day the way the fast-moving clouds sent shadows and sunlight swooping across the hospital walls. Now, in the silence, the walls darkened and the evening closed in on him.

243

'You there?' he whispered.

'And I'm clutching my bag to my lap as if I'm eighty years old and I cannot move, I cannot get up from my seat and I don't know what's wrong with me.'

Leo hesitated, unsure what to offer. 'They're pleased with him. He's talking a little.'

'He should be here with me.'

'No,' he said, as kindly as he could. 'You should be here with him.'

'It's funny. I spent all this time wanting to look after that girl more than we do and now I could kill her if I went near her.'

She hadn't known she was going to say any of this, nor did she mean to hang up as abruptly as she did.

'What are you talking about?' Leo said, to the space she had vacated.

The next morning, she appeared at sunrise, well before visitors were allowed, a show of devotion wasted on William, who was uninterested in everything, even the kisses she dotted across his face and hands as she settled beside him, kisses that prompted Leo to retreat to the chair in which he had spent the night.

William allowed the luxury of detachment, the gift of his vacant, broken state and empty eyes, to permit him to observe his wife unflinchingly. Her face seemed a mix of doubt and accusation. She laid her head down on the bed.

Leo watched William's fingers twisting gently in Joy's hair. The sun moved off the room and left a cool, flat light that was more painterly. Leo beheld the scene from afar and included himself in the family portrait. As if reading his mind, William turned his head, with agonising slowness, and sent a minuscule smile across the room to Leo's appreciative ever-presence. As Joy lifted her head, Leo was amazed to see William close his eyes and feign sleep. He watched his sister unable to be still, nor grasp the value of doing nothing. He observed her as she aimed accusing looks at the nurses who came and went, as if saying to them, *Are none of you going to tell me to go home and get some rest, give me some pep talk about playing the long game, it being a marathon not a sprint?* It was Leo who finally did that for her. He kissed her cheek. 'You look tired. He's asleep anyway. I'll walk you home.'

'If you think so…' she said, and appeared perfectly reluctant to leave.

She scooped the fresh air into her lungs and asked Leo if he minded walking at pace. She needed to get her blood pumping, she said. She looked powerful and tall to him and he struggled to keep up. He saw her look at a woman and a man in the window of a dive bar, breaking from a wet, open kiss to put bottles of beer to their lips. He watched her stop and stare at them until they saw her and stared back.

'I hate being alone here,' she said when they entered the apartment.

Leo made coffee and watched her pour a glass of wine.

'Argentinian…' she said, aloud but to herself. 'Vibrant, muscular. Ar-jen-teena. A handsome people.' She downed the first glass.

'You alright?' Leo asked.

She raised her eyes at him and he acknowledged that it was a stupid question.

She took a bath with the second glass. Leo browsed a volume of *The Earth from the Air* and fell asleep on the couch. He was woken by the sound of Joy talking indiscriminately. 'Everything is random,' he heard her say. Despite the fug of his short, broken sleep, it was clear to him that he was not meant to take up the baton of conversation.

'We never really know anyone, not truly,' she said.

He didn't agree and he didn't say so. Two-thirds of a bottle of malbec was reminding her that that it was pure chance that she was living the life she lived.

'I so nearly turned back at Southampton as we boarded the liner.'

'I remember.' He yawned. 'Thank God you didn't. It's the best thing that ever happened to me.'

He watched her arch herself backwards on the chair towards the living room window and crane her neck to look at midtown. The alcohol made her head movements unsteady, like those of a child constantly buzzed by new thoughts and sights and sounds.

'A thousand windows looking back at me, telling me I could be standing in any other room in the world right now, if I had done one thing differently in my life. It's all so flimsy.'

He fell asleep again as he listened to her go to the bathroom and brush the red dye of Latin grape off her teeth. He felt a blanket settle on his body and heard the door close.

When he woke, he called her and she picked up immediately. 'Wait a second, Leo. I'll take the sirloin. Rare to medium rare.'

Leo listened to the buzz behind her voice. 'Where are you?'

'The Clinton Corner House,' she said.

'I thought you guys boycotted any restaurant with the name "Clinton"?'

She called her waiter back and Leo listened to her ask for a side salad instead of fries, in a separate bowl. 'I do not like bloody salad,' she told the waiter, and, 'It might be time to lose some weight,' she told Leo.

'There again,' Leo said, 'I thought you boycotted every restaurant that isn't the Red Flame.' He put his shoes on and sipped some tepid coffee.

'Have you ever thought it remotely possible that William could be having an affair?' Joy asked.

'With the drug girl?'

She gasped. 'I had prayed you wouldn't have a clue what I was talking about but you know.'

'I know that he isn't. Hasn't. Wouldn't.'

'You don't, actually. You two think you're inside each other's heads but he was starting to tell me something.'

'Not that.'

'I'm so angry. I'm so angry that for the first time I've reason to be furious at him and I'm not allowed to be. It's choking me. You can't be jealous or angry with a husband in ICU and he's made it impossible to love him just when I have to most.'

'You're wrong about this.'

'Leo, you're my brother. Mine, not William's. Tell your own sister you know, one hundred per cent absolutely know for certain, that he isn't in love with her.'

'There's no such thing as absolute certainty so I can't tell you that.' Nor could he tell her that he loved William more than he loved her. 'But he promised me he wasn't and I have complete faith in him.'

He was leaving the building now, wedging his cell under his chin as he put on his coat and looked for a taxi.

'Okay,' she said. 'I'm hungry. See you in a bit.' She hung up.

Already, the corridors leading to William's room felt like home, the only place on earth Leo wanted to be. The scent of disinfectant and the film of gel on Leo's hands were the flames and hearth of crisis, that much-maligned state of being in which life finally offered him the clarity and purpose he craved. It was a long time since he had felt this good. He threw his coat aside and drew the chair to the bed. William was asleep and Leo rested his hand on William's arm. He was here to save him.

20

The quantities of jelly spread over Finn's testicles seemed generous. He was not accustomed to undressing in front of strangers. He watched the monochrome screen, his right testis larger than the left (what was that about?), and nervously voiced his relief at avoiding an erection. The almost friendly sixty-year-old nurse ventured that not many men became sexually aroused when waiting to discover if they'd got cancer of the balls.

'When you put it like that...' Finn agreed.

The fractional trace of a smile made her exactly the sort of woman by whom Finn still, at nineteen years, six feet and eighty-five kilos, wanted to be held. He was regretting his decision, when given the choice of removing his jeans and underwear altogether or pulling them down to his knees, to plump for the latter. It had seemed the more dignified option but how wrong he had been. The nurse handed him an economy-sized roll of heavyweight tissue and told him he was 'through', a word to which he attached a short-lived terminal negativity as he wiped himself dry and hitched up his trousers – short-lived because she soon added, 'You're all clear. Those little guys you can feel are non-cancerous polyps. Very common. And unless they grow large or painful there's no need to do anything about them. You are fine.'

'Not dying?'

'Not even a little bit.'

It struck Finn that this moment was possibly the first time he had felt strongly, in the positive sense, about being alive. With Dilly, he felt free in some ways but he was not himself with her, so the pleasure he experienced with her did not apply, strictly speaking, to him. Even when she had been visiting the most glorious of sexual acts upon him, he could tell that there was a difference between joy and pleasure. Right now, he felt a happiness manifest as optimism and lightness, and that was entirely new.

Finn headed out and the fresh air made his skin cold where the gel had been. He took a call on his new phone from Leo, who launched straight in.

'What did they say?'

'I'm all clear. It's a tulip.'

'A polyp?'

'Yeah.'

'Very good,' Leo said, withdrawing the concern from his voice for fear of sounding ridiculous. He paused, and in the space where he might have mentioned his brother-in-law's accident there was, instead, silence.

'Thank you, Leo,' Finn said.

How good that sounded. 'You're welcome.'

'You okay? You sound sad,' Finn said.

'No, I'm fine.'

'I can tell you're not fine but I won't stick my nose in,' he said. 'I know when adults are lying.'

He walked a block of silence before Leo replied.

'My brother-in-law is in hospital after an accident and I'm concerned.'

'Will he be okay?'

'Yes, he's gonna be fine.'

'Fine like you're fine, or really fine?'

'Really really fine,' Leo said. 'He's doing well.'

'That's great. I'm sorry it's happened.'

'Thank you. You back at the gallery?'

'No. I've got to go somewhere.'

'Okay,' Leo said, cautiously. 'But you are coming back?'

On the opposite side of First Avenue, there was a new building of small, stylish-looking apartments, like pods. In one, Finn saw a middle-aged woman sitting with her back curved over an upright piano keyboard, playing a piece of music one-handed, her left ear listening intently to her own playing, her fingers working a series of notes that only the walls of her apartment could enjoy. And he bet himself that she and Leo would be perfect for each other, living the deeply felt, unexpressed life. He saw his own reflection at street level and the knowledge that no one would consider him capable of such thoughts. Now, although a guardedness about him remained, he told himself that Leo was almost certainly an okay human being.

'Yes, Leo,' Finn said. 'I would like to carry on working for you, please.'

'Oh,' Leo said. 'Very good. Well, then... I'm pleased.' His voice faltered and he hung up.

The Gay Hussar was quiet. Finn leaned forward on the counter to look for signs of life. The owner appeared from the restrooms holding a bucket and a mop. 'Hey,' she said. 'Looking for Amy?'

Finn nodded.

'She's not in today.'

He slumped and she laughed to herself. 'Don't slash your wrists.' She gave him the address of a Japanese restaurant in the East Village. She rolled a cigarette, sitting on the bench on the sidewalk, and texted ahead to Amy as she watched Finn go.

Amy stood alone, out in front of the restaurant. Her hands were clenched and her stance compact and neat as she scanned the street. When she saw Finn, she bowed her head and smiled at her feet. She removed a hair clip from the bun in her hair. It fell almost to her shoulders, like a wave too modest to make a splash. They said 'hello' at the same moment. He was shaking a little. She took both his hands and went up on to the tips of her toes to kiss his cheek, then led him inside to the kitchen at the far end of the restaurant. She introduced him to her aunt and uncle, who were preparing food. They were in their late forties, and attractive. The uncle had a quiff and the looks of a film star. They spoke to Amy in Japanese and her right foot lifted behind her and rested against the calf muscle of her left leg, just as Finn had seen it do on the first evening.

He had never eaten Japanese food. Dilly had at one time implied that she had eaten it on a trip to Osaka, before it became evident she had not yet been to Japan and she'd blamed Finn for getting the wrong end of the stick. The aunt brought food out to them at a table by the window and teased her niece.

'What she say?' Finn asked.

'She's being stupid,' Amy said, unable to look him in the eye.

He told her she looked really nice but the start of his sentence was buried beneath the sound Amy made putting the lids of the miso soup on the table, and she replied, 'It does, doesn't it?' Her aunt called out from the back of the restaurant and Amy shook her head shyly. 'My aunt and uncle are trying to embarrass me,' she said.

'That's nice,' Finn said, and boy, did he mean it.

'They are very nice people,' Amy said.

'Nicer than mine,' Finn said through a grin.

'It doesn't seem fair, does it,' Finn's uncle had once said to him, 'that another sixteen-year-old boy is dead at your father's hands and you have your whole life ahead of you.'

This had liberated Finn, in allowing him to realise just how unintelligent the man was. It made a mockery of the anger and violence. It didn't bring it to an end, but it gave it a certain crucial insignificance. Finn had no longer felt touched by the violence after that, knowing that he would one day be free of this man, while the man would never be free of himself.

Amy and Finn took a walk and Finn was aware that he had not spoken in a long while and the silence began to press against the walls of his head and the more he tried to conjure up a conversation, the further he got from finding one.

'I just found out I don't have a tumour on my gonads.'

Not what he'd planned.

'Gonads?'

'My balls. Testicles.'

'Right.' Not what she'd expected, and she laughed.

'They scanned them,' he said.

'Uh-huh,' she said.

'The woman at work calls them my snow globes. I don't know why I'm not shutting up.'

'The woman at work knows about your... them?'

'She knows everything.'

'Right. She sounds efficient.'

'That's what she is.'

'That's excellent, about your balls.'

'I'm really pleased,' he deadpanned, and she laughed again.

The silence returned, so he broke it. 'About my balls...'

'About your rocks...' she said.

'About my nuts...'

'Hey!' she said, 'awesome news about your plums...'

'Sure is a relief about my old marbles...' he said, 'the family jewels, the gems...'

'Your *kintama*...' she said, with a strong Japanese accent.

He thought a moment. 'Hanging brains...'

She screamed at that one. They came to a halt. Ahead of them, a grey heron stood perfectly motionless on the sidewalk, on one leg, looking into the 6th Street and Avenue B Community Garden. The heron was familiar to Finn, from the dykes and rivers of the Sussex Levels he would disappear to alone in his early years, and the presence here in the East Village of something from home made him feel that he'd been caught fleeing the crime scene that was his upbringing.

A man's denim-clad backside emerged from a van on 6th Street. It belonged to a well-built guy in his sixties with a flamboyant moustache and long, lanky hair. His rolled-up, studded black shirt exposed tattooed, oil-stained forearms. He cradled a lifesize wooden statue of a cormorant which he placed next to the heron. He clambered back into the van and dragged out a large potted tree, scraping the tub across the sidewalk to the entrance of the garden.

'Pin oak...' Finn said, under his breath.

'What?' Amy asked.

'It's a pin oak tree,' Finn told her, shyly.

She studied him as he watched the moustached man lift the carved wooden birds back into his van. The man sized Finn up. 'Could you lend a hand?' he asked.

'Sure,' Finn said, and liked the sound of the word in his mouth, the same way he liked the idea of being a New Yorker.

They carried the tree into the garden along a gravel pathway to the man's twelve-foot-by-six-foot plot. The man straightened up, ran both soil-flecked hands through his hair, then shook Finn's hand.

'Thanks,' he said.

'Sure.' Finn recycled the word. If it ain't broke...

'Good autumn colour, pin oak,' Finn said to Amy, as they walked away, and he smiled the same apology that followed anything he said with authority. In direct contrast to most men she knew, he suggested to the world that he knew less than he did.

They walked the community garden in silence, avoiding obvious platitudes about the place that could add nothing to their happiness. Bamboo stood high against the windowless wall of the first building on 6th Street. Hydrangeas spilled through the mesh fencing on to Avenue B. A tool shed bore the haphazard marks of reparatory bitumen patches and non-matching wood-stain. Around it, small blossoming magnolia and cherry trees were unkempt and expressive, caught in mid-conversation. Blotches of pale lichen had stepped across from them on to the shed. The other trees in the garden were neater. Finn saw plum, pear, mountain ash, willow, maple and elm.

Amy pointed to a large blue flowering tree in the centre of the garden. 'What's that?' she asked.

'Chinese empress tree,' he said. 'The people I work for won't sell them. Call them weeds.'

'Big, pretty weed,' she said, putting her hands on her hips and taking a good look at it.

He shrugged. 'I don't know.'

'What's your job?'

'I drive a truck full of trees.'

She smiled at the minimalism of his chat. He smiled back, curiously, at her expression.

'You deliver them?'

'Yes. And we plant them up.'

'You like that?'

'I did.'

'Don't like it any more?'

'I'm not there any more.'

A noticeboard had a potted history, photographs of the garden when it was an empty, disused lot in 1981, photos that already looked dated of the residents who created the garden, and a history of the Barusch Housing Complex which told them that the buildings stood on what was once the East River, and that the 6th Street Community Garden had been salt marsh. A wooden sculpture, like a huge bonfire stack made of old timber, stood shoulder-to-shoulder with the five-storey building next to it. Tucked in among the timbers were rocking horses (or were they carousel rides?), wooden geese and toy cars.

They stood over goldfish in a pond and Finn could see Amy's toes wiggle through the canvas of her shoes. They passed the man planting his pin oak tree and the man said, 'Thanks again,' to Finn and Finn hesitated and said, 'Can I...? That's not right.'

'How so?' the man said.

'You're telling it life's going to be easy, with all that compost. Just a little compost mixed into the soil, that way the roots get a leg-up, but not too much and they know soon as possible what they're in for.'

'Massively cool,' the big guy said, and Amy decided she would kiss Finn this day.

On the street corner, Finn turned to her and explained that he had to go away for the weekend. He asked if he could see her when he got back. She said that, yes, he could. They wandered on and she told him they could walk to Tompkins Square Park together and then she'd have to go to work and he felt her hook her little finger around his little finger but when he looked down he saw that it was her index finger. He had never seen hands so small.

They agreed to meet at Leo's gallery the following Monday, at one o'clock, when Finn was back from Long Beach. They held hands and, momentarily, her lips touched his lips, then she left. From a distance of thirty yards, she shouted out across the elm trees and the people,

'Your gonads!'

'My man tonsils!' he called.

She backed away, shouting louder every time. 'Your *pelotas*!'

'My knackers!'

'Your nuggets!'
'My love spuds!'
'Your golden pillows.'
And she danced away.

21

From what William could work out, his body was a hard shell. Beneath its surface, his organs functioned, more or less, and his mind turned. He looked out through glassy morphine eyes at Sidney White and the other elders of the Fountains board as words tumbled out of their mouths, unfathomable to him, while they explained to Leo why the store could no longer employ William, as if Leo would translate it into whatever language this stupefied version of William Fairman could understand.

William peered out from his body as if a vast space lay between him and the elders, pipe-cleaner figures at the foot of his bed, in suits half a century old, on plastic chairs that bent to the curves of their spines. He didn't know what time or day it was. His world was a blur of ungraspable monochrome and a fluid, humming sound that cruised around his head with no edges. Joy was not in the room and William sensed a shift in the world that left him neither shocked nor bereft by her absence. Something had lifted itself out of him and taken flight the previous day as the hours passed without her and he felt himself begin to die in tiny increments. All he wanted now was the peace to acclimatise to the emptiness.

He slept. When he woke the elders were gone. Leo crinkled his eyes affectionately. William raised his head an inch off the pillows, a Herculean task, looked at that part of the mattress he would once have expected Joy to be seated on, then closed his eyes again. Inside the newly fortified castle of his mind, William had a visitor: a vivid picture of the street in Lincoln, Illinois, where he grew up, and of the lakes outside of town and the soft, grassy sea of fields stretching out to the state park. He hadn't thought about the place for many years. He saw the house on South Hamilton Street. At first he could not see his parents but if he looked past the house, across the plains, his mother and father appeared on the front porch, in his peripheral vision. For as long as he didn't look directly at them, they remained there.

Feeling no deficit of love, nor any frustration with his parents, William had left them nevertheless, first for Chicago and then for New York City. He'd returned home often, with no appetite for Illinois, but a yearning for the man and woman who had raised him. He remembered his childhood in Lincoln with affection, grew to like Chicago, and quickly loved his life in New York City and fell under its spell. He took with him to that great metropolis his parents' unspoken belief in the futility of going abroad when America offered more than one lifetime could accommodate. The more he met them, the more unnerved William was by people who travelled, and he could not believe his luck when the wanderlust in Joy began to drain out of her through the open wound of her vertigo and her dislike of flying, to a degree he could not have dreamed of when he first encountered the tornado of self-belief and physical exuberance that came packaged with Joy Emerson's fiery eyes and mane of walnut hair.

She appeared to him now, in colour. Only this image of her, walking towards him on Ninth Avenue, could maintain its crisp, defined edges and stand out against the dense, pinhole-camera world into which he had been deposited by a bucketload of morphine and the underside of a seven-ton truck. He saw her in high definition, at the anti-drugs forum when they first met. Her passion for the cause had swept them out of the Wednesday night meetings and into bed, where he had discovered that lust could be shared with the same woman he prayed with, did charitable acts with. Until then, he had seen a future in which prior to a dull marriage he paid good money for the experience of a certain sort of practical sexual education and momentary hedonism that a man like him (by which he meant a man not abundantly fascinating to women) would not find in the fabric of his everyday life.

Joy interrupted his memories of her by arriving, with Pastor Edwin in her wake. Leo welcomed them and he and the priest watched on as Joy took hold of William's hands, and they interlaced their fingers. Leo rolled up his copy of the *New Yorker* into a tight cylinder and drummed it against his thigh as he went to the door. The priest drew a chair away to the furthest corner of the room and placed it against the wall, where he sat with his hands in prayer, head bowed, oblivious to the way Leo's body language had beckoned him out of the room so as to allow some privacy. William and Joy sat before each other, the formula for their equilibrium mislaid. William broke the silence, with his ashen voice.

'What can we do with our life? What are we good at?'

'We're good at being together.' Her voice was clipped. 'I've worked in the same store for twenty-five years and you index old stuff in an attic. We are not world-changers and you wouldn't be sure to survive without me. Let's just get back on track.'

'I feel different.'

'Of course.'

'About what we believe.'

'Please don't say that. I don't think I'm up for that as well as all this.' She said it softly.

She tightened the grip on his hand. He smiled. She leaned forward and kissed his lips and then she rested her cheek against his. They held each other tight and after she had sat back on her chair they sat in silence and her eyes settled distantly on the bedding and she tried to keep her thoughts in the room and hoped that he would not ask what she knew he was going to ask. But he asked it.

'Did you talk to them about it being a local anaesthetic?'

She looked helpless. 'It has to be a general, Will. You're beaten up and need repairing.'

He placed the palms of his hands over his face, dragging the tubes and wires up off the sheets.

'And, William, there are going to be one or two more generals after today, more than likely. It's a rebuilding process.'

'Jesus!'

'William!'

'Sorry.'

A little time passed and he felt his voice wouldn't reach her but he gave it a try. 'I'm scared of not waking up.'

'I know that, honey. I understand.' She was weary, and in the silence she had enjoyed the excessive heat in the room and the way her head was balanced perfectly, weightlessly, on her neck, allowing her something very close to sleep. 'You will wake up, of course you will.'

'But what if I don't?'

'Well, of course you will, what does that even mean?'

'It means not wake up.'

'It's impossible not to wake up, you can't sleep forever.'

'Die. Obviously, I mean die.'

'Well, you know…' she stuttered '… we have our faith.'

'I have my fear…' he said.

'Let's not change everything,' she said, irritably. He was off script with all this.

'Be nice,' he whispered.

'I'm trying.'

'You shouldn't need to try.'

'I need a coffee to be nice.' She turned around, as if expecting to see a decent coffee stop in the corridor. Pastor Edwin was gazing at her. His smile was like a blanket waiting to catch her and it irritated the sweat out of her. 'I don't think you're allowed coffee yet, but I might go get one. Let's not argue, it's silly. It's not my fault you need surgery and it's not your fault you got run over.'

'It is, actually.'

'And remember, if something happens to you under anaesthetic it's me that'd be left here with no one and nothing; you'd be in heaven. Unless you've not been good.'

'Exactly! *If something happens to you under anaesthetic.*'

'Nothing bad is going to happen. But have you been good, William? Is there anything you want to tell me?'

I don't believe any of it any more, was what he wanted to tell her. But he didn't want to hurt or anger her, so he smiled and shook his head.

She went to get coffee. William shut his eyes. He heard his own breathing and it seemed to come from elsewhere in the room. He contemplated the truth, the one which his yet again absent wife and the priest pressed against the far wall would not want to hear, of how improbable it had seemed, as he felt himself swallowed up by the truck, that beneath this vehicle lay paradise. An ending had seemed more likely, and more deserving of his faith. And he was left with a feeling similar to dreams of being stranded on a cliff-edge or a rooftop where the fear of falling abated only when he gave up hope and jumped. It was the hope of survival that caused him terror.

If that weren't enough for his battered mind to contemplate, there was also the prospect of finding something meaningful to do with the time between now and the second truck, a task that now felt as complicated as life had once

261

been simple. His head turned slowly, painfully on the pillow, until he was looking at Pastor Edwin. 'I know something you don't know,' he whispered.

'What was that, William?' Edwin asked, brightly. He dragged his chair to the side of the bed.

'Faith...' William said.

'Yes, William, faith...'

'You need a licence to sell guns, but faith...'

Edwin smiled helplessly and averted his eyes (always good practice for the day one went under one's truck). He bowed his head in renewed prayer. Joy returned and kissed William on the lips. She tasted of coffee.

'Better?' he asked.

She nodded and sat on the side of the bed and crossed her legs, leaving her bare knees close to Pastor Edwin's face as she took the lid off her coffee and laid it on the bedside table. She took a sip and smiled at William.

'The beauty,' William whispered, 'is you'll never really know there's nothing. So, that's kind of okay.'

'Not as okay as the eternal paradise thing I thought we had agreed on,' Joy said.

'What's happening here with you, William?' Edwin said, softly. He looked up and was met by a vision of the intersection of Joy Fairman's thighs that he would need time and effort to shake off.

'I was run over by a truck,' William replied, his voice weak and slow.

'I mean, what else?' Edwin said.

'It's not enough? Ever been run over by a truck?'

'Use the toolbox of faith that the Church has given you,' the priest said, as he noticed on the bridge of Joy's nose a dab of coffee foam which required licking off. He swallowed. 'I should be going,' he said. He put his coat on (Pastor Edwin lived by two seasons, the ten months of the year he wore his coat, and the two, July and August, when he carried it) and suggested to Joy that he and she have a quiet word in the corridor.

'Now she's here, you're not taking her,' William muttered, returning his wife's backside to the spot she had already started to vacate. The priest left. William shut his eyes and spoke faintly. 'Some of the things that man expects us to believe are clearly ridiculous. What do we think about that?'

'We've always kept a sense of humour about it.'

'It all seems less funny now, more hilarious.'

'And don't personalise it. It's not him, it's all of us. You're stressed.'

'Yes. I don't want to be put under.'

'Gee, thanks, by the way, for reducing our entire life to rubble. I can look forward to no afterlife now, thanks to you.'

William laughed under his breath. 'It's really not my fault. The mustard-coloured paint in the bathroom was my fault, but I'm not to blame if there's no afterlife.'

'Everything's your fault,' she said, and laughed petulantly, after which her face settled into her handsome smile and they held hands. She sensed that the moment to ask about Susan French had just escaped her and she was appalled at herself for wanting to have it out with him before his surgery, with him so terrified. She squeezed his hand. 'I love you,' she said.

'We could have done all the good things we do just for the sake of goodness,' he replied.

'Stop talking in the past tense,' she said curtly, but soon, as the fear in him rose, she lay with him and stroked his forehead and whispered how she loved him and that she would not allow any harm to come to him and that he needn't be afraid. She soothed him until the time came and in the sunset glow, as the hospital fell quiet, the nurse brought the pre-med, rattling like dice in a cup, and Joy fed the tablets into his mouth and handed him the water to wash them down, and she shook with fear as they wheeled him away, by which time William was altogether unaware of his lifelong phobia of anaesthetic and enchanted, rather, by the strip-lights on the corridor ceilings.

22

The mist rising off the East River was the lazy sigh of a city hauling itself to its feet. The vibration of the traffic from Delancey Street was the slow drag on a cigarette by the grocery porter sitting on the tailgate of his truck at the intersection of East Broadway and Grand. The porter wore a brown lab coat and pointed to something on the sidewalk with his cigarette hand, making two men outside Ryan's Grocery Store laugh. The men arched their bodies backwards to counterbalance their pot bellies and one removed his cap and scratched his head as his laughter subsided into a whimper.

The mist snaked between the buildings of the Lower East Side, whispering resentful tales of its stolen waters and depositing a fine, cold, damp dust on Finn's face as he headed out in the collared shirt and clean pair of jeans that he had held back for meeting Dilly's parents. The shirt smelled of Dilly's cinnamon oil and the plan was to leave with the book in his hand.

He lengthened his stride so that the walk to Penn felt like exercise. He liked early morning training, had often run from his aunt and uncle's house before breakfast, pumping his visible breath angrily into the cold air, dispersing it with a flurry of quick miniature punches, running at speed across the common and indulging in detailed fantasies of violence against his uncle and then his brother.

Jack was on his knees at the open fridge, looking at food he didn't have the will to eat. He had eaten three meals in the previous ten days, and none at all in the last three. When he stood up he moved too fast and he had to grip the counter to avoid fainting. He took a slow, deep breath and was rocked by the realisation that if he did not take up Dilly's invitation to Long Beach, which she had repeated this morning, he could not guarantee he would ever see Finn again.

He shuffled into the bathroom and looked at his reflection. This flu was as organised as Jack was and had outmanoeuvred him. Despite efforts to tidy himself up, Jack did not look tidy. The trim, orderly assimilator of the derivatives market that habitually greeted him in this mirror was out of town. He took a razor and soap from the impeccably clean glass shelves inside the mirror cabinet. Two days earlier, shaking with weakness and deprived of sleep by his cough, Jack had carried out the twice-weekly clean of the bathroom and kitchen while listening to Mahler's 4th and by the end of it had been surprised that the faint trace of depression he was feeling but would barely admit to was soothed by imagining not Holly's return to the pristine apartment but Finn's. He guided the razor through the shaving foam on his neck until it reached his chin. He stood a while then let the razor slip from his hand into the sink, disarming himself before further damage was done. He held his right hand up in front of him and watched it vibrate to the rhythms of his perennial battle against all forms of weakness. In front of him now was the reflection of a man bearded by white lather, with a single, clear track of smooth skin through the soap and, from it, a trickle of blood. He washed the soap off his face and plugged the cut.

He took it easy going to the elevator, walking slow, with his head down to avoid head-rush, and arrived in the lobby as Eddy started his shift.

'You look excellent,' the doorman said.

Jack thanked him with a burst of his hacking cough that made even a self-obsessed failed comic wince with sympathy. 'That cough's getting worse, fella, not better.'

'I'm outta stuff,' Jack said, weakly.

'They do Phenovo Linctus at the pharm on 98th Street. It's like nuclear cough mix, pal. Whatever you're using isn't doing it for you. Phenovo leaves like a film of honey on your throat. I love it, cough or no cough.'

Hesitant though he was at taking Caustic Eddy's recommendation on anything, Jack felt convinced by the fact that the new cough medicine was twice the price of his own. He bought two bottles and told the shop assistant not to bag it, immediately measuring out a 20ml capful and slugging it back.

'You look rough, dude,' the shop assistant said. 'I see you a million times in here getting personal items for your girlfriend and you don't look like this.'

Jack let pass the man's inappropriateness and his scandalous misuse of the present tense. 'Right...' he said, putting the medicine into his Barbour weekend bag, a present from Holly last Christmas, which he had not taken to using until she'd convinced him it was not a handbag. (She'd enlisted her mother in Seattle to back her up by phone.)

'What is the deal with your neck?' The assistant pointed his finger at the single track of smooth pink skin running through Jack's beard. Jack walked out. On his way to the downtown 6, he sat against a dented newspaper box and waited for another threat of fainting to pass. In the Penn ticket hall he stopped again and came close to double vision. The hall sang a breathless tune around him, a distant jungle noise distilled from a multitude of voices reverberating around a place where he could see nobody talking to each other. He bought a return ticket to Long Beach and checked the departure board against Dilly's text instructing him when to turn up and where to go. It pissed him off that his oversexed little brother hadn't pried himself away to give him a call or send a text in all this time.

He drifted in and out of sleep as the train dragged him out of the city. In a backyard on the outskirts of Lynbrook, on a patch of grass between a leaf-strewn trampoline and a pile of shattered fence panels, a boy and a girl were playing. They had straw-coloured hair and the shapes of their mouths and the set of their eyes were identical. The girl, leggy and lank, was a study of concentration, assessing the top of the boy's head as she took up position beside him. The boy was standing to attention, his arms straight by his sides, his face convulsed with nervous laughter, his body shaking as his sister swung a straight leg up and over his head. She smiled triumphantly and the boy collapsed into a fit of giggles. The last Jack could see, they were taking their places to do it again.

'We used to play that game,' Finn whispered, to his breath-cloud on the window. He was one train behind Jack, watching the same game twenty minutes later, as the lanky girl tired. Other kids would queue behind Finn to have Jack kick his leg over their head and when Jack clouted Bill Barnes in the ear a fight ensued, but Bill Barnes could neither fight nor Jack defend himself for their hysterical laughter, and Finn remembered the pile of children jumping on top of each other, a human haystack of bellyaching laughter and the realisation that he and his mates were getting too grown-up, too tall, to play the game with Jack any more.

It hadn't occurred to Finn until now, that he might remember the young Jack better than Jack could remember himself, and it struck Finn that he should maybe cut his big brother a bit of slack next time he saw him.

The train crossed the estuary and smoothed an arc into Long Beach. From the bend in the tracks, Finn spied a miniature Manhattan floating above the lagoon. Long Beach station was a different style of movie set from Manhattan. *Back to the Future*, *Groundhog Day*, a certain size of American town Finn felt familiar with. On a red-painted bench against the far wall of the ticket hall he saw his brother, lying asleep beneath a week's beard, his head resting on what looked like a woman's handbag, and his hands clutching a small bottle of medicine to his chest.

'What the hell…?' Finn said. He immediately wondered if it meant bad news, until he remembered that they had already emptied the tank.

Jack stirred, discovered he'd fallen asleep and forced himself awake. 'Hey,' he said, in a daze.

Finn was still incredulous at the sight of him. 'What do you mean, "Hey"? What are you doing here?'

'What do you mean, what am I doing here? I'm exactly on time.'

'For what?'

'Our weekend in Long Beach?' Jack asked.

'I have no idea what you're talking about.'

'I've been getting texts from your girlfriend every day to come join you guys out here and I've asked her to get you to call me every day.'

'Her name is Dilly and she's not my girlfriend any more. She left me and I haven't seen her for over two weeks.'

They fell silent. The mere act of conversation had exhausted Jack, who put his head in his hands and groaned. Finn began to work on a new approach to the day, given that running away from Dilly and her family very soon after arriving might take some explaining to Jack, and the book was not something he could explain to Jack.

'So why are you here?' Jack asked, trying to think straight.

'Oh, you know,' said Finn, 'just to get a couple of things she has and, you know, as friends. But you don't need to stay.'

'Thanks.'

'I just mean, you don't seem well.'

'Frankly I could do with the sea air. This is crazy – can you please let me get you a cellphone?'

'Can you please let me shave the rest of your face? You look like a pimp. You look like… someone else.'

'Well, I'm not, so hard luck.'

'I've got a phone.'

'You've got a cell?'

Finn stuttered. 'Yeah, but only since, like, yesterday.' He changed the subject. 'You do look like utter shit.'

'I don't feel too bad.'

'What's your current definition of *too bad*? 'Cos that track of shaved skin through your beard looks kind of mental.'

They shared a hot chocolate and Finn ate a banana and a muffin and would not relent until Jack agreed to eat some of the muffin.

'I really am not hungry,' Jack protested, and laughed in annoyance as Finn pushed a piece of muffin between his lips.

'When was the last time you ate?'

'Four days, or three, I can't remember.'

'For fuck's sake, Jack.'

Jack measured out another 20ml of cough medicine and pulled a face as he swallowed. Watching him, Finn wondered if perhaps the sickie Jack had tried to cover with the five hundred bucks had in fact just been a genuine sickie, and a generous gift. He cursed himself, over the money.

He took his phone out of his pocket. 'Here, I'll give you my number.'

'How d'you get a cellphone?'

'I stole it.'

'Funny.'

'My boss gave it to me.'

'When you say your *boss*, have you got an actual job?'

Finn shifted on his seat and smiled valiantly at nothing. 'No, I'm imagining it, Jack. You're the only person in the whole world with an actual job.'

The two brothers slipped into their unconnected silence, in the back streets of which Finn wondered why Jack said things like that, and Jack wondered why Finn had gone quiet on him again. Jack shut his eyes. Through the glazed roof, the sunlight fell in pools on to Jack's cheekbones, curing his face of its pallor. Finn watched as Jack slouched down on the bench and instantly slept again. *I hate you*, he mouthed, and watched his brother's chest rise and fall, heard the rattle of his breathing, looked at the dishevelled exterior for a glimpse of Jack somewhere inside.

'What's new?' Jack croaked.

'Thought you were sleeping,' Finn said.

'I was sort of asleep and thinking at the same time.'

'Very efficient. Very you. What about?'

'All sorts... All the holes underneath Manhattan. Holly's tennis skirt. My tree. The real colour of blood. Work, of course.'

'You're talking weird.'

'I feel a little weird, to be honest,' Jack muttered.

'Is that why you have a handbag?'

'Fuck off.' Jack puffed out his cheeks at the effort of sitting up. He held out his hand and Finn lifted him to his feet.

In the restrooms, the brothers stood side by side. Jack threw water over his face repeatedly. He examined the red rivers in his bloodshot eyes and watched on in amazement as his baby brother rearranged his mop of hair with no more than three strokes of his wetted fingers and appeared, instantly, utterly conventional.

23

The enchanted smile on William's face placed him somewhere in his late teens; the goofy, small-town Illinois years. His smile had that same open, amused, what-just-happened quality to it and this was some achievement on the smile's part, given that everything else about him (his broken body, his parched skin, his pyjamas) suggested a man who had never been youthful.

He sat propped up against an expanse of pillows, in the beatific afterglow of the anaesthetic. He was already looking back on the experience as a time of magic, a sleep which had been deep as the ocean, yet momentary, and in the depths of which he had been united with a truer version of himself than waking life had ever revealed. Before the sublime descent into sleep, the man in white had laced warm honey into his blood. Even the memory of it was rapture.

He turned his head and found Joy and Leo on chairs in the corner of the room, slumped against each other in sleep. His head was light, not with a clarity of thought but the removal of it, a serene awareness that something, he didn't know what, had gone from him. This disappearance did not alarm him. Nothing would ever alarm him again. On the contrary, he felt reconciled to his arrival at this juncture, where he sat in a hospital bed with the singular task to breathe and then to breathe again. The prospect of recovering his health to the extent that more than this was expected of him was not appealing. The only thing that appealed was more of the honey.

In the absence of a second helping of his flavour-*du-jour* Fentanyl/BZD cocktail, he shifted between two states of consciousness, the first an acute awareness of his own body, the second, a vivid sense of a universe without him in it. Although he was not aware of his light-footed dance between these two perspectives (if he had been aware, he could not have experienced the second) it began to dawn on him that a man's search for his self was flawed from the get-go, in that the thing being searched for was doing the searching. Hmm. When he peered out through the cracks in his opioid shell at a world in which William Fairman did not exist other than as a passive pair of eyes looking out on the world, this seemed not only reasonable but satisfactory. He suspected that, for the first time in his life, he was high. It was not the time for making decisions.

He slept, and when he woke he felt constricted. Less honey, more blood. Joy was sitting by his side, reading a folder of notes for a Campaign Against Victimless Crime meeting.

'See? You woke up, isn't that great, Will?'

'Possibly.'

She laughed nervously. 'Make up your mind.'

His hand patted the sheet in an invitation to climb aboard. She lay carefully beside him, and, as she showed no sign of wanting to talk, William indulged in holding her and recalling the moments after the anaesthetic was administered to him. He thought about it the same way he used to daydream about entering Joy's body, ecstatically, vividly. He recalled the gelatinous descent into oblivion. The memory of it was the only thing clear to him, and he feared losing it the same way the bereaved feared losing a dead man's voice.

'What happens next?' Joy asked.

He could feel the rise and fall of her breathing, and he felt unaffected by everything, untouchable, as if nothing mattered at all. He presumed that he reeked of the absence of physical desire. The dead air of the room was drying their lips and he had the sensation that his mouth was closing over. The memory of a picture came to him, a painting he had once seen, of a man and a woman kissing, their faces and mouths covered by cloth. He had seen it on his one visit to MoMA but could not remember the artist, although he was certainly well known. He tended not to remember the names of famous artists and had enjoyed how this had made Leo despair in the old days, when Leo was passionate.

Leo slept on, exhausted by vigil, until a nurse came and instructed Joy to leave and take Leo with her, so that William could rest undisturbed. Joy kissed William's lips and Leo stood over the bed saying a silent, smiled goodbye.

The bus took Joy south and at the first red light Leo drew alongside on his bike. He watched her reading some paperwork and pulled a face at her when she looked up. She laughed and they were thirteen and eleven again. She stuck out her tongue as he pulled away quicker than the bus. He cycled hard, wanting to get back to the gallery, concerned that he had been neglecting Astrid. (He needn't have been; she was enjoying having the run of it.)

He was back at work when he saw his sister appear outside the gallery, posting her papers into a trash can on the sidewalk. He came out to her.

'I thought you were going to a meeting?'

'I was – the Campaign Against Victimless Crime.' She pointed to the papers in the bin. 'Which I realised comes with a cast-iron guarantee of a total absence of *joie de vivre*. I counted the word *sin* thirty-four times in the notes and it's given me a strong desire to beat the crap out of something.'

They walked together and she found herself gripped by the beginnings of the sort of hysterical laughter that annoyed Leo so as a teenager. 'I feel kinda hysterical,' she said, and giggled. 'I want to ask him if the two of them eat our exotic fruit when they're having sex.'

He took a hold of her. 'I can accept that you are unsure but I know William has never done that to you. So promise me, wait until he is out of hospital and strong enough to talk about this.'

She pulled a face that reluctantly agreed, and which was then disfigured by contempt for an installation she spied through a window. 'Let's go in,' she said.

'You hate this kind of thing,' Leo said.

'Exactly.'

He watched her stride in, spoiling for a fight, and join the small crowd in a mute disjointed procession around the Piece. He listened to the whispers in the room and the rustle of clothing and watched as Joy brushed against the back of another man and whispered her apology as he turned and she moved away. Leo was surprised by her deftness. She viewed the same man from afar. She looked at others, men and women, setting herself before a certain detail of the artwork she found incomprehensible and shifting her glance to study whoever pleased or drew her eye, staring at them freely until she needed to glance back to the crap assembled in the middle of the space. She circled people, followed them, touched them. She allowed herself to be watched and followed. She projected versions of herself across the hushed floors. Then, as abruptly as she had entered, she left.

Leo followed her out on to the sidewalk where a taxi was already pulling up to her. She turned to her brother. 'I totally get it,' she said. 'I finally understood why people bother to look at rubbish like that. It's all about sex. It's the dance. There's no other explanation.'

She climbed in and told the driver to take them to St Luke's Hospital. She looked at Leo with an innocent smile. 'Come on,' she said. 'He needs us.'

24

Being a short man, Stefano Parker filled the doorway to his house instead with his barrel chest, which stretched the buttoned breast pockets of his gun check shirt out into the day. He was a strong man, with a taut, swollen belly but no fat on him. His wife, Ann, stood backstage of him and the two of them peered from behind the porch screen at the two English boys, wondering where their daughter was. Ann tipped her body to one side to see if she was hidden behind the boys. In turn, Finn looked into Mr and Mrs Parker's house for a glimpse of Dilly, and all three of them looked confused.

Jack, on the other hand, looked tired and ill and dangerous, and was oblivious to the effect. Stefano peered fractionally to examine the single track of smooth skin through Jack's beard and his expression did not convey admiration.

'I'm Finn,' Finn said, in the absence of a greeting from his hosts. 'This is my brother, Jack.'

Jack stood to attention on hearing his name. 'Yes,' he said, and offered his hand. This gesture forced Stefano to open the screen door to them and as he did so Mrs Parker emerged from behind her husband's shoulder. 'I'm Ann. No "e".'

Stefano Parker did not offer his name, which Finn knew anyway, and ushered the boys into the house that he no longer owed a cent on. (There was no one in Stefano's circle unaware of this fact.) Inside, the four of them squared up in a ragged way.

'Is Dilly here?' Finn asked.

'She's with you,' Stefano insisted, despite evidence to the contrary.

'White house,' Jack remarked.

'Thank you,' Ann said. 'We're very happy here.'

'No, I said white, not nice,' Jack said. Finn looked at his brother curiously as Jack pointed at an olde worlde needlepoint above the door which read *Home Is Where The Heart Is*. 'Will you look at that monstrosity?' he said.

'What?' Stefano said.

Finn raised his eyes to the white ceiling in disbelief.

Jack then gestured to what he imagined might be the bathroom door. 'Need to brush my teeth, mouth feels furry. May I?'

Ann Parker pointed to a different door. Jack fished out his toilet bag, and took it to the bathroom.

Life in New York was a learning curve, of that Finn had been aware since landing. Right now, the lessons in front of him were that Jack was not being himself and that height was a big issue for some men and Stefano Parker was one of them. Finn took his own height for granted, although not his strength and speed, as that had been cultivated for protection. Now, a man stood before him who clearly wanted to pin him to the floor and beat the crap out of him until he got some answers. But the chance reality that Finn was ten inches taller meant that this solidly built Italian-American man with crooner looks and an affable menace had to take another route, a less direct one, for no man could take a pin-you-to-the-wall approach to matters if that man needed a box to stand on.

'What the hell?' Stefano hissed.

'You promised us he works in finance,' Ann said.

'We've never spoken!' Finn said.

'Dilys told us he works at AIG,' Stefano barked, 'a respectable company, big salary – a bit boring, Dilys said, not a rock star.'

'He is a bit boring and I miss that right now,' Finn said, trying to defuse the situation. 'I don't even know who he works for.'

'Is it right to know your own brother so little?' Ann said, pointedly.

'I could justify it pretty easy. And by the way, your daughter hates being called Dilys.'

'Who the fuck are you to tell us that, two minutes in my house, you little shit?'

'Who are you to call my brother a little shit?' This came from Jack, propped against the bathroom door, a foamy electric toothbrush whirring in his mouth. 'He can be a little shit sometimes,' Jack foamed, 'but no one calls him that in front of me.'

'What the hell!' Stefano Parker was ready to bust an artery. 'You're in my house!'

Finn made to calm things down. 'No one meant to be rude, Stefano.' (You don't want to tell me your name, I'm going to use the hell out of it.) 'But I thought Dilly would be here.'

'We thought she was with you,' Ann said. She and Stefano looked at each other uncertainly. The sound of Jack's toothbrush receded to the bathroom.

'Well, I'm sure she'll turn up,' Ann said, vaguely, for the benefit of her husband, who she didn't want further upset. 'Why don't I make some coffee?'

'Thank you,' Finn said. He wanted tea, but the atmosphere did not lend itself to special requests.

Stefano retreated across the open-plan to his TV chair. He sat forward at first, looking out across the garden, as he gathered his thoughts and ground his molars. Then, he reclined, electronically, to forty-five degrees and lay his hands across the pinnacle of his belly and switched on the sports. Finn took a seat on the nearby sofa, uninvited. In the window, he saw the reflection of his big brother marching from the bathroom to the kitchen area and tensed up at the thought of him unaccompanied with Mrs Parker.

At the kitchen sink, Jack measured out his cough mixture and knocked it back. The care with which he rinsed the measuring cap under the tap and placed it upside down on the drainboard to dry suggested to Ann that this man did know civilised behaviour, despite the smooth track of skin that cut a path through the carnage of his hollow, unshaven appearance. She led Jack back into the living area and set the coffee tray down. Stefano upped the volume on the sports so as to make conversation less probable. Finn declined the coffee on Jack's behalf. Jack shot Finn a what-the-hell face, which Finn ignored. They argued in whispers beneath the volume of the TV.

'I could do with some coffee!'

'No, you couldn't. You're wired.'

'And I'm hungry, is there gonna be food?'

'It's the middle of the morning, Jack, they don't know you haven't eaten for a year. What's wrong with you? Just be yourself. Couldn't you have shaved while you were in there brushing your frickin' teeth? You look like a werewolf, man.'

'Hands are shaky. I think I might be a bit unwell.'

'You think?'

'Jesus! You sound like Mum.'

'Why, am I slurring?'

'Funny.'

'I'M CALLING DILLY,' Stefano boomed, then waited patiently for the recliner to return to ninety degrees and, for Finn and Jack's entertainment, tip the man of the house slowly out of his seat and on to the rug in a knees-bent standing posture, from which he straightened up and sauntered out of the room.

Jack was open-mouthed. 'Shoot me, the day I buy one of those chairs.'

Ann offered Jack the remote, at arm's length, and retreated to the kitchen. Stefano returned, complained that Dilly wasn't answering her phone, snatched the remote out of Jack's hand (which caused Jack to giggle and Stefano to double take at him) and returned to his chair.

'Watch this...' Jack whispered, with a cupped hand at Finn's ear like a three-year-old. The two of them watched as Stefano slowly re-reclined.

Two hours passed. Jack fell asleep from hunger, his head flung back, neck arched, mouth open. Finn sent Dilly a text, asking when she was going to show.

She replied instantly. *Oh, look who's got himself a cell! Haven't heard from you for a while.*

Not since you walked out, he texted.

That's your version.

He ignored that and asked her again when she'd show up. She didn't reply.

Stefano turned in his seat and attempted to crowbar some information out of his one conscious guest. 'What do you do for work?'

Finn weighed Stefano up. 'My profession?' he asked.

'What do you do?' Stefano replied, impatiently.

'Well, my parents were alcoholics,' he said, brightly, deciding to have some fun, 'and I have a conviction for arson. Nowadays I'm in the art world.'

This was something Stefano retired to the garden to dwell on, taking Ann with him. Finn watched them feign an inspection of the bird feeders as they discussed the threat level orange in their living room.

It was mid-afternoon, when Finn and Jack had seen all traditional definitions of lunchtime come and go without food being served or mentioned, that Dilly's sister called from college in San Diego. Stefano and Ann held a handset each and the three Parkers cooed and chatted and laughed together. Expressions of adoration washed across Stefano and Ann's faces, and Finn confided to Jack that he hadn't known Dilly had a sister.

The Parkers relaxed after the call, enough to sit in the same room as their guests and re-enact the phone call, confirming for each other's benefit what a sunny success of a human being their other daughter was. Not once, Finn noted, had they asked San Diego if she had heard from Dilly.

'Finn didn't even know Dilly had a sister,' Jack announced. 'Weird…'

'I did know.'

Jack looked confused. 'You said you had no idea.'

Finn smiled, with menace. 'You talk too much.'

'You do. And you smell,' Jack replied.

Stefano Parker smiled as though he was all at sea, and talked his way out of confusion. 'You would certainly remember her if you'd met her, no doubt about that, she's a high achiever. Phoebe – we named her after Phoebe Cates – is quite a girl.'

'A woman now,' Ann corrected him.

'A woman indeed,' Stefano mused, causing Finn to wince. The words didn't sound good the way he said them.

'You named your daughter after the virtually irrelevant actress Phoebe Cates?' Jack asked, incredulous.

'I love her,' Ann complained.

'We tried and tried and tried for another child after Dilys Annalese,' Stefano said, sitting forward and addressing Finn, making a big, brooding thing out of ignoring Jack's directness. 'We were determined not to settle for one. It took five years of trying.'

Ann raised an eyebrow at the memory, activating Jack's internal hysterics. He vibrated against Finn with the effort not to laugh.

'When she finally came she was a miracle and, good God, she's so bright and talented. And beautiful.'

The pink glow on Stefano's face faded as a long silence took a grip of the room. The lull reminded him that neither his first- nor his precious second-born were here to dilute the presence of these two strangers. Jack looked as though it was his turn to give birth, his face purple, his head buried in his crossed arms, still consumed by the image of Ann Parker's exasperated face as Stefano humped her halfway to death for five years in an attempt to improve on his first child.

'Is he okay?' Stefano said, aggressively.

'He's just hungry,' Finn said.

'Dilys will be here any minute,' Stefano kidded himself.

Finn suspected she might not be, and felt he understood a little better why Stefano's second-favourite daughter might not want to be here, and he felt that maybe he had failed her. It made him feel sick.

He put an arm behind Jack and opened the window a few inches. He could smell a trace of salt in the air, lifting from seaweed drying in the sun on the beach he had not yet seen. He looked at Dilly's parents, tried to imagine what it was like when they and Dilly were together in the same room, and felt both curious and fearful at the possibility of finding out. As he watched these people defy every gravitational pull of convention by remaining silent for vast lengths of time in front of guests, the breeze nudged a branch on to his hand and brushed a leaf against his little finger and he thought of Amy.

'Shall we go for a walk?' he said.

The silence stiffened. The Parkers looked appalled, as if he had suggested a spot of tag-teaming.

'Just an idea, no sweat,' Finn said.

'Oh, yes,' Ann said, 'a walk along the boardwalk can be quite a tonic. It can be a super thing to do, on the right sort of day.'

As she continued to talk about the benefits of walking, it became clear to Finn that this was a hypothetical speech. No such walk was going to take place. Presumably, this warm, cloudless day was not the right sort of day.

'I'm going to do that thing in the kitchen,' Stefano said, staring meaningfully at his wife as he left the room.

'He wants you to follow him out so you can talk about us,' Jack told Ann. Ann rose to her feet unsurely. Jack nodded reassuringly to her, to signal she should go. She obeyed.

'I reckon they think we've killed her,' Jack said.

Finn laughed dismissively. 'I wouldn't reckon our chances.'

A few minutes later, the Parkers re-emerged and took their seats, with rehearsed smiles. 'Look,' Stefano said to Finn, on a long out-breath, 'if you two have had an awful fight over something or there's something you know, just tell us. We're her parents, for Christ's sake.'

'We were joking about killing her,' Jack said.

Finn buried his head in his hands.

'Oh, my sweet Lord Jesus!' Ann whimpered, folding her hands in white-knuckled prayer. Stefano's chest filled and his face reddened. His hands became twitchy.

Finn slouched back on the sofa. 'We have not murdered your daughter,' he said, wearily.

'You have wanted to, though, at times, admit it,' Jack said.

We've all wanted to, Ann thought to herself.

Finn looked at Jack in disbelief. 'SHUT. UP.'

'But the sex kept you in it, I'd imagine,' Jack reasoned, rising to his feet and ambling into the kitchen for his cough medicine. Stefano watched him, wide-eyed, the way he'd watch a talking squirrel.

Jack yelled out, 'YOU SAID THE SEX WAS UNBELIEV-ABLE, LIKE BEING BACK IN FULL-TIME EDUCATION.'

He emerged and sat on an upholstered chair against the wall of the no man's land between the dining area and the living area. It was the only chair in the house there was no good reason to sit on. 'I don't want to be rude,' he continued, pouring his medicine into the measuring cap and slugging it back, 'but if I don't eat a meal soon I'm going to collapse.'

'There's places in town,' Stefano grumbled.

'We'll eat when Dilys gets here,' Ann said, gentle and unyielding.

'Right,' Jack said, 'fair dos. Am I detecting an atmosphere?'

'Jacko?'

'Finny?'

'Any chance you might stop talking and return to your normal self?'

'It's probably because you've kind of gone and talked about the elephant in the room there, Finny-boy. This atmosphere. Murder, harm. That's the elephant in the room in this particular context, in her own parents' house. In a work context I teach people not to do that. We don't use the word "risk", we don't verbalise that in dialogue terms because everyone thinks that's what we're trying to minimise.'

'What do you say instead of risk?' Stefano asked. This was an opportunity to test the guy's credentials.

'Exposure.'

Stefano laughed dismissively. 'Bullshit, f-ing bullshit.'

'That's a powerful retort, Mr Parker; allow me to mull on all the points you've raised.' Jack threw his head back and began to breathe deeply, loudly, into his chest. He looked insane. Finn and the Parkers watched, horrified. Finn turned his attention to the garden, and latched on to the first vaguely intelligent distraction he saw.

'That's a sugar maple.'

'That's right, I think,' Ann smiled, trying to ignore Jack's heavy breathing.

'JACK!' Finn snapped.

Jack froze. 'What?'

'You're breathing really loudly, man!'

'Sorry. Man!'

Jack sat obediently, quiet, on his chair. Finn stared yet again in disbelief at the behaviour of his brother. He stood up. 'Would you show me your garden?'

Stefano stood up too, looked Finn in the chest and immediately regretted leaving his chair. 'Sure,' he said, cautiously, glancing at Jack and wondering if he was walking into a trap. 'If he steals anything, I'll know it. I know what I've got. We earned it all ourselves. We were born with nothing.'

Finn shrugged. 'I don't think he would. He's doing pretty well for himself, believe it or not. I'd really like to see your garden.'

'You show him the garden,' Stefano told Ann, 'I'll stay here with this one.'

'Fun...' Jack murmured.

All was calm in the garden. Life was on the cusp of breaking through.

'I don't know so much about gardening,' Ann said. 'We have someone in. It's not my area of expertise.'

'What is your area of expertise?'

'Radiologist.'

'Very cool,' he said.

'And yours?' Ann asked.

'Trees. But I'm going to run a boxing gym for kids.' He hadn't known it until he said it, but he knew it was perfect as soon as he heard himself.

She smiled. 'What sort of kids?'

'My sort.'

'That sounds like a vocation,' she said.

He shrugged.

He identified the maple trees she complained were growing too fast as sugar maple, the single oak tree as red oak, and they admired a walnut tree and the silver birch and occasionally she would sigh, 'Yes, that's right, I remember our sellers saying that name.' She stopped in front of an American beech in the corner of the garden. 'This one I know,' she said, definitely. 'This is beech and I know the sellers planted it when they got married and moved in and I know that for a fact because when they decided to move upstate they waited six months to sell so that they saw out their twenty-fifth wedding anniversary here and had their photo taken by the tree.' She turned to him and smiled proudly, laughed under her breath, and he saw a different version of her. 'So – ' she jabbed a finger emphatically at the tree ' – this one I do actually know! And I know that it means it's twenty-seven and a half years old because we've been here two and a half years.'

Finn took a look at the tree. Suddenly, he became distant, deep in thought. In this intense way, he looked at the row of sugar maple which, Ann was right, were getting too big for the garden.

'Trees grow...' he muttered.

'Say again?'

'Trees grow.'

'Even I know that.'

'It's forty years since he took that photograph. And trees grow. It is the right cemetery. It's probably the exact spot.'

Ann glanced back at the house and saw her husband watching, his nose flat against the window.

'I just wanted to know I was in the right place,' Finn whispered.

'Finn, I'm going to be honest. You make me nervous at the best of times, and you talking in riddles about cemeteries just makes me scared.'

'I'm sorry,' he said. 'I'm so sorry. You've no reason to be scared of me, or my brother. I bet you I'm more scared of your daughter than you are of me.'

She smiled knowingly, then darkened. 'But she is okay, isn't she?'

'Of course she is,' he said, and she knew it was true. 'I wanted to be sure that a photograph I saw – of a cemetery – was not a lie. It's just a photograph but it made a lot of sense of things for me. I felt pretty excited that I had worked out where it was taken, felt all grown-up like I belonged in New York City, but then I couldn't find the place. But trees grow and landscapes change. I think I did find the right place. I'm not the idiot people think I am.'

'You're clearly not an idiot. Your brother I'm not so sure about.' It was rare for her to say something frivolous, and, when she did, she felt the urge to hide.

'He's not himself today, but he's no idiot, he's a success.'

Not much of what the boy had said made sense to Ann, but his demeanour made sense, his tone of voice made sense. He appeared misunderstood and a little bit lost, and that all made perfect sense to her.

The distant, subdued sound of a phone ringing fell lightly between them. Ann looked inside and saw Stefano lunge for the receiver, then the grin on his face, and that thing he did when he became animate, rubbing the curve of his belly while leaning back and smiling. He had a great smile, she still enjoyed his smile. She ran inside.

Finn stayed in the garden a while and by the time he went in, the others were in the kitchen and there was Andy Williams on the CD player and Ann sliding two huge dishes, a lasagne and a cannelloni, into the oven. Jack, who was standing behind her slugging back a dose of cough medicine, looked at Finn and at the food and gave his brother a big thumbs-up with deliberately crazed eyes. Stefano bent over a silver tray of garish flutes, pouring a drop of brandy into the base of them, and then champagne.

Dilly had called to say that she was assisting a fashion photographer on location in Harlem and would be with them by eight o'clock. Finn felt deflated, partly by the absolute knowledge that she was not assisting a fashion photographer in Harlem, but mainly by the desire to retrieve his book and get away sooner than that.

Stefano handed out the flutes and the four of them chinked glasses.

'Good health,' Stefano said. 'Here's to eight o'clock.'

'Cheers,' Finn said.

'A Parker family tradition.' Ann smiled. 'We like a champagne cocktail with guests.'

'Especially,' Jack said, raising his glass, 'when you've just discovered your guests haven't left your daughter's body parts in a suitcase somewhere in New Jersey.'

'JESUS H. CHRIST!' Stefano shouted.

'What?' Jack was oblivious. 'Are you from New Jersey?'

Ann Parker slugged back her cocktail and ran to the kitchen.

'Was that meant to be funny?' Stefano asked Jack.

'We eat *now*, yeah? Not at eight,' Jack replied.

Stefano stormed out.

Finn turned on his brother. 'What's in the little bottle, cough mixture or truth serum? All the things people think are funny but would never say out loud, you're saying them today.'

'You've noticed too?' Jack said. 'The weird thing is, I never even thought these things before, and now I'm thinking them *and* saying them.'

'Well, stop.'

'Thinking or talking?'

'Talking.'

'Agreed, but first, how long does lasagne take to cook? I can't last much longer.'

'Jack, do this for me: sit down there and hardly say a word for the rest of today. Be mute, eat a lot, you've got a bad flu or something. And don't drink that cocktail, it's lethal and these glasses are huge.'

'Okay, I will, except the bit about the champagne. It's yummy.' Jack took his glass to the couch, and sat quietly, adjusting to the flavour of being bossed by his little bro. It was a new dish. He sipped his cocktail, felt it slip into his body like a slow, dangerous river of heat, and waited obediently, quietly, for dinner to be served. When that time came, he hauled himself up from the couch and aimed for the dining table far away on the other side of the open plan, a vast distance of plush carpet and useless ornaments and whiteness away. His legs threatened to buckle under him and the room span a little. His body felt too weak to reach the table and the two huge dishes of steaming hot pasta bake upon it, but he made it, and slumped into his chair. He declined the red wine which Stefano was pouring and nodded when asked if he wanted vegetarian cannelloni or meat lasagne. 'Both, please.'

'Are you vegetarian, Mrs Parker?' Finn enquired, politely.

'Ann, please.'

'No "e",' Jack muttered.

'No. But Dilys is, of course, and, well, you know, I thought she'd be here.'

'She will be,' Stefano said. 'That'll reheat just fine.' He had a spring in his step.

Finn took a moment to recall, in the privacy of his own thoughts, the many slabs of red meat he had witnessed Dilly devour in the four months he had known her.

Opposite him, in the privacy of his own sweaty, disorientated, malnourished body, Jack wrestled with his first experience of tunnel vision. He stared at his baby brother until he caught his eye, and mouthed the words, *Help me*, then collapsed face-down, clipping the side of his plate as he head-butted the table and flipping the bake on to his head. Finn, Stefano and Ann froze, staring at the sight of Jack's crumpled body, pinned to the table by his forehead, wearing a wig of pasta.

'That's not good,' Stefano said, and leapt out of his chair. He eased Jack's head up and looked into his eyes.

'Sorry,' Jack mumbled.

Stefano moved confidently and manfully, sweeping the food away from Jack's head and wedging his arms beneath Jack's armpits, instructing Finn to take Jack's feet. They carried him to the spare room, where Stefano laid the bedcover across him and wiped the food from his face and hair.

'Thank you,' Finn said.

Stefano examined Jack's pupils. 'How do you feel, Jack?' he asked, firmly.

'I'm just exhausted, that's all…' Jack whispered. All he could feel was the heat from the food burning his head and the descent into a thick, cloying sleep.

When he woke, the room was pitch-black and he could not be sure his eyes were open. The house was quiet and the universe seemed still. His back felt hot and his body rested. It was some minutes, as his eyes adjusted to the dark, before he realised that Finn was sitting on the side of the bed, and that it had been the sound of the bedroom door brushing over the deep carpet that had woken him.

'Hello.' Although Jack's voice was comically weak, he sounded like Jack again, not the intruder who had occupied his body for most of the day.

Finn lent in close and whispered, 'I've spent the last five hours listening to them and their neighbours debating your drug problem over a game of Canasta. I told them it wasn't the case but they ignored me. I think they decided it was heroin, in the end, after lots of different ideas.'

'Did you play Canasta?' Jack asked, weakly.

'Yes, for a bit, while explaining that what they kept saying, MBNA, is a bank and that what you are not on is MDMA, but my knowing what MDMA is convinced them you must be on it, and me supplying you. Then, I made name cards for Ann-no-E, for all the trees in their garden.

She's going to laminate them and have them on pegs in the ground so she knows what's what.'

'Charmer,' Jack said.

Finn handed Jack a mug of hot tea and wrapped his brother's fingers around the handle. 'They're terrified of you,' he said.

Jack drank the tea. He was in a daze. Finn started giggling.

'What?' Jack asked.

'You fell into a lasagne.'

Finn clamped his hand over his mouth to quell his laughter. Jack rushed to put his mug down.

'Mr Tidy fell into his supper,' Finn squealed.

They squirmed and wriggled on the mattress and occasionally, despite their better efforts, a shriek escaped them.

The Parkers and their friends, the Johnsons, studiously avoided any mention of the high-pitched, hysterical whining coming from the English quarter. They carried their glasses from the card game on the dining table to the other end of the living area to watch college football and bitch a little about their town.

'Also,' Finn continued, 'Dilly called again and now she's not coming until tomorrow lunchtime.'

'Are they pissed off?'

'They're too pissed to be pissed off.'

'I think there might be béchamel sauce in my ear,' Jack said. 'I feel kind of weird and spacey.'

The darkness had removed the jagged edges between them.

'I'm turning in,' Finn said. 'It's been interesting.'

Jack watched Finn's silhouette reach the doorway and disappear into the next room. He remained sitting upright in the darkness and rotated his ankles and stretched his arms above his head and tried to get a feel for how conscious he was. He felt that he ought to be sociable, to put in an appearance given the nature of his earlier exit, and ambled into the living area, forgetting that he was wearing only socks, underpants, a suit shirt and electrocuted hair. He took a seat on the couch next to Ann, worrying her considerably. Stefano and the Johnsons averted their eyes from Jack's state of undress and stared steadfastly at the college football.

'You should eat. You must eat,' Ann said, booking herself an exit to the kitchen as she noticed the attractive muscularity of Jack's legs.

Jack looked across to the other couch and beamed a smile.

'I'm Jack,' he said.

The Johnsons pulled that face that was the smile of fear. Stefano ignored his guest. Jack waited obediently, smiling at various soft furnishings and lifeless family photos which revealed a ratio of, ballpark figure, four photographs of Phoebe to every one of Dilly.

Ann Parker returned with a blanket, and a tray upon which was a plate, upon which was a gargantuan mound of reheated pasta. She placed the blanket across Jack's naked legs and laid the tray on Jack's lap and sat at the far end of the couch from him, pressed tight against the armrest.

'Thank you, Ann,' Jack said, before his first mouthful.

'You're welcome.'

During the ad break in the college football, Stefano reached for his wand and, fatefully, hopped channels. HBO was showing *Last Tango In Paris* and Jack pointed his laden fork at the screen. 'That's a classic. You guys seen it?'

The Johnsons peered at the screen and shook their heads. Stefano ignored him and went back to the football.

'But you've heard of it, right?'

'I don't believe so,' said Mrs Johnson.

'I've definitely heard of it being quite... alternative... but I never did catch it,' Ann said.

'Well, you're just about the only people who haven't,' Jack said. 'You have to see that movie. It's a classic, like I said. Very controversial.'

'Some other time...' Stefano murmured.

Ann cleared her throat at her husband. Stefano raised an eyebrow in private before turning to his wife. She glared at him. He shrugged her a 'what?!'.

'We'll watch Jack's movie,' she said, nodding her head to make it perfectly clear that her decision was final. 'He's our guest and he's feeling a little... unusual.'

Stefano frowned at her. She frowned back stronger. Jack loaded his fork with gooey cannelloni. The Johnsons took a look at the time.

'HBO,' Ann said, flatly. '*Last Tango*.'

'My wife loves to dance,' said Mr Johnson.

Jack strained forward to suck a petrified waterfall of melted cheese up towards his mouth, oblivious to the TV debate and to having recommended the film. Stefano looked at him murderously, and complied with his wife, switching the channel. Jack smiled at Ann as he chewed, and winked as he thanked her again for the meal. When he had finished eating he placed his knife and fork together, and let out a sigh of satisfaction and settled down to watch the film that his hosts had on. The movie was a bewildering living hell for Stefano Parker until he drew the line at Marlon Brando applying cooking butter to Maria Schneider's backside and switched back to sports.

'Basketball...' Jack said. 'Awesome.' He smiled at the Johnsons.

Ann went to the kitchen. She took cream from the fridge, hesitating as she came eye to eye with a Land of Lakes half-stick. She returned with a bowl of chocolate fudge cake with hot chocolate sauce and cream over it. Jack thanked her and tasted it and mmmed at her with a grin.

'You make this?'

She shook her head, coyly, and tucked her legs beneath her bottom on the end of the couch.

'Well, it's wonderful anyway, thank you.'

'You're welcome,' she said, delighted. Treat him like a normal person and he'll try to behave like one, she told herself.

'It's all wonderful; you're both so kind, everything we never had,' Jack added. He returned immediately to his food, oblivious to the disarming effect of his words on Dilly's mum, who could not help but feel an ocean of compassion.

Stefano shook with anger and stared at the game, unable to get the movie out of his head. They all sat in silence, save for the scraping of Jack's spoon around the sides of an empty bowl. When there was not a trace of cake left, Jack got to his feet, thanked his hosts for a wonderful meal, and strolled off to bed, stroking his belly.

Stefano couldn't look his neighbours in the eye.

'An educational evening,' Harry Johnson said.

Stefano saw them out and bolted the front door, despite the presence inside his house of exactly the sort of person he was trying to keep out. Ann cleared away Jack's tray, mulling on how young men were grateful for being fed to a greater degree than her daughters ever were. Stefano joined her in the kitchen. 'Jesus H. Christ,' he muttered furiously.

'Let's turn in,' Ann sighed.

'Uh-uh,' Stefano said, returning to his chair. 'Uh-uh-uh.'

Ann followed him into the living area and waited patiently for him to elaborate. He shifted in his seat, staring at the screen, annoyed that she wasn't taking the bait by asking him what he meant by 'uh-uh'.

'No way...' he added, to prompt her.

Still she didn't bite.

'If you think I'm going to sleep while those two are in my house, you can think again.' He pointed his wand at the

TV and started channel-hopping furiously. 'I'll find myself something decent to watch, not that other filth.'

He kept pressing the button, station after station, settled for the NBC sports round-up, and folded his hands over the wand as though it were a gun, the man who sleeps with one eye open, on the television screen, a Long Beach John Wayne for the noughties. 'I'm protecting my wife and my house,' he hissed, finally looking at her.

She smiled gratefully and went to bed.

25

They brought him oxycontin at four in the afternoon and the pain melted, and again at midnight. At one in the morning, William slipped away in his dressing gown and sneakers, holding the saline drip above his head until his arm grew tired, then pushing it into his pocket. Even as he gulped at the fresh air, the sensation of having departed from his own body remained and he carried himself down the West Side like a balloon on a string.

The opioid veneered his broken body and he felt light and in contact with nothing, and he watched himself come to a standstill in the old yard at the far reaches of the theatre district, where the long-ago-abandoned Stephenson Theatre stood in ruins at the head of the narrow, rectangular enclave which had the air of Miss Havisham's banquet. A Stieglitz mist hung over the edges of Manhattan, stirred by a cool night on the Hudson, and lending the quiet, neglected buildings of the yard the feeling of an impenetrable forest. On a bench on the wide sidewalk, beneath a silver birch tree illuminated ghostly white by a street lamp, he saw Josef Potter, his old boss. William took a seat beside the elderly man and felt immediately at ease with him again, even though Josef had died six years ago, on the first day of the millennium.

'Why leave a good job with real skills and real challenges? You were still young and you chose a job doing nothing.'

'I get a lot done. Life's never seemed busier.' William rested his hand on Josef's arm, only for the old man to draw back from him.

'But you're not doing anything.'

'Not to worry any more.' William smiled. 'I feel okay about everything.'

William continued to speak to the newly married young man beside him, who had stopped on the bench to sober up before going home and had watched as a man wearing a dressing gown in the night had sat beside him and struck up conversation. The young man followed the route of the tube leading from William's arm to his pocket.

'That a lifeline?' the man asked.

'No, it's just a tube. There is no lifeline, Josef. But you must know that by now.'

'I'm Richard.'

'Don't be angry about me leaving. I was never going to be one of life's warriors,' William said.

The man got up and rubbed his eyes. 'Warriors or worriers?' he asked.

'Josef, is it all an impossible dream?'

'Tonight,' the man said, 'I would say that yes, it is. Are you gonna be okay?'

'I believe I am,' William said.

'You should get back to bed.' The man walked away.

William watched Josef cross the street in front of him. A train drew up in the middle of 44th Street and Josef boarded it. The train headed out to the slopes surrounding Manhattan, where it stopped and Josef disembarked to join other men on monochrome hills. The men were in black and white and the fields were toneless also, bedecked by beautiful long grey meadow grass, thick and musty like horse hair. Josef Potter mowed the grass with a hand-pushed lawn mower, then stopped to converse with another man. They looked easy and content together, and familiar. Men on deckchairs were scattered across the hills, looking down on the city with their legs stretched out in front of them and their hands clasped behind their head. The wild grass brushed against their ankles and the tips of the grass looked beautiful in the light which was moonlight and sunlight, and all the men were dead.

William watched them from the bench on the sidewalk and could not understand where between Hoboken and Union City these rolling hills above Manhattan could be, and why had he never noticed them before in all the years. Then came the pain again, in ripples that moved vertically through him, and the wild sweating of his scalp and face that melted him to his knees on the sidewalk. He felt a sadness deep and desperate and in supplication he asked one last favour of his God, to take away the pain.

He shuffled away through the embryonic drone of midtown at five in the morning. The low slate clouds smouldered with light poisoning. He took a bottle of Poland Spring from a garbage can and dregged it. He knew where he was going.

A pocket of wind was trapped in the empty lot alongside Susan French's building. William picked his way through the trash and sat at the foot of an old cedar tree in a patch of yard behind the four-storey building where a bowl of exotic fruit sat in the kitchen window of the uppermost apartment, while the woman who had placed the fruit there lay her head and her mane of walnut hair on to William's hospital pillow and sobbed and screamed out for her sweetheart.

26

Jack sat bolt upright in bed. The room was still black. He couldn't see himself but he felt wide awake. Slowly, the trace of a dark garden appeared through the window. He raised his hand up in front of him and against the grey outlines of the window he could make out the movement of his fingers and he was more aware of himself existing than he had ever been, and less critical of it. He felt good. He felt great. In fact, he felt horny.

He lay back and watched the darkness, and recalled the finest sex he and Holly had had in their four years together. At least, he considered it their best sex, but he was, as in all matters, ready to hear the other side's point of view. Indeed, a conversation with Holly about sex would be welcome. They had sex often enough – just about, at a push – but they never spoke about it. And who was he kidding? It was not often enough.

Their superlative union had, in his opinion, been that which occurred on the night he introduced her to curry. She had never eaten in an Indian restaurant and Jack had put great thought into taking her, for he loved curry and did not want this potential shared pleasure to be stillborn in any old curry house on 6th Street. He took her to Dawat, Madhur Jaffrey's establishment, and when they got home she told him she had been pleasantly surprised by the food and would be pleasantly surprised if he were to join her in the shower. They hadn't had a drink, so exactly which constituent ingredient of her *sarson ka sag* and *murgh jahangiri* triggered Holly's abandon was not clear, but Jack lived in the hope that they would stumble upon it again.

He patted his clothes until he found his phone. It was five in the morning, too early to text Holly. He felt fantastic but he needed fresh air. He needed to walk. He dressed and found Stefano Parker asleep on the recliner, his hands folded across the remote control. Jack tiptoed past him and took a bunch of bananas out into the morning with him. He was ravenous again. The previous evening's late-night movie feast was a hazy memory, as was the day that had preceded it.

The tastefully soft, community-endorsed street-lights of Long Beach glowed gentle green on the street, making the residents feel safe without disturbing their sleep. Jack ate the first banana and tossed the skin aside. It was the first piece of litter West Olive Street had seen in a long while, the first time Jack had littered in a long while, and the first time Ann Parker had seen such a thing from her bedroom window on the many mornings she had woken prematurely and kept vigil for anything of note outside. She watched Jack head down the street, and kept watching, without focus, even after he had gone. She washed her face even though it was too early and she went downstairs. She woke her husband and packed him off to bed, thanked him for protecting her. She had the place to herself. It would seem crazy to Stefano if he knew, but she liked these pre-dawn hours when she could walk around the open-plan alone without bumping into him.

The curved sky above the silent ocean bore a hint of colour, a dread deep blue that was enough to silhouette a ramp slanting from the boardwalk to the beach and the glide of a lone cormorant. Jack felt the oxygen break through his constricted breathing for the first time in weeks and, out of nowhere, the sight of the bird pushed him close to tears. He removed his shoes and walked on to the sand, which was cold beneath his feet. He glimpsed white where the waves were breaking and for a moment he was fishing beside his father and the world was theirs alone. He remembered a cormorant floating effortlessly across the water in the good times he and his father had spent at the reservoir before Finn's birth transformed his mother and she descended from them. Miraculously, his memories of his parents were good ones. He had not forgotten the rest, of course he hadn't, but he had wired himself to remember the good things – always the cormorant above the water, never the body found beneath it.

He sat on the sand and waited for the day to catch him up. If Finn hadn't come to New York he'd not have the sand between his toes. If Finn weren't alive, he'd be alone with Holly, and that would be alone indeed. If he let Finn slip away from him now, what would become of him? He heard a faint rumble and saw the shape of a man jogging with a three-wheeled pram. Jack walked on, his shoes hanging from one hand, the bananas from the other. Benches lined the boardwalk, hundreds of them, shoulder to shoulder. He sat on one and watched the sun come up. The bench was strewn with green and sky-blue ribbons, with origami rabbits and Easter eggs. A brass plaque read;

IRWIN MIAMI SHANE
I can see clearly now that lucky old son!
So whistle up a happy tune, fan our worries away
And watch over the monkey boys
831 forever, Susie
Tennis anyone?

Container ships appeared in silhouette on the horizon and the yawning ocean sky was redolent of the Sussex Levels back home. But Jack's home was a sensation, not a place, something that had passed and left nothing to hold on to except for his brother, and that was like holding on to smoke. He watched the hue of the ocean change. He felt vivid, close to joy, close to tears. He shut his eyes, to prevent the waves breaking over him. He ate. In time, a warmth laced itself into a delicate, indecisive breeze which nudged him towards sleep but left him short of it, in the rare extravagance of a temporarily quiescent mind. There was no clock ticking, no thoughts or ideas. Just a dormant brain and a feeling of effervescence through his body and his blood and the vividness of daybreak and the hunger for food and a hunger he couldn't name that teetered on the edge of happiness and lament.

When Jack opened his eyes he saw a woman lying flat on the sand, washed up overnight by a bone-dry sea. Her feet were bare and her sleeves rolled up, a cautious prelude to summer. She smoked a cigarette. Two rangy adolescent boys stood in wetsuits talking to each other as they studied the shore break. They swam out on their boards and went through the motions on miniature, slow-peeling waves and dreamed of Mavericks and of older girls. Later, a family of Hasidic Jews stepped tentatively on to the sand as if it were the surface of the moon. The father beckoned his children and his wife to follow him. He played frisbee with his son while the mother sat with her four daughters. One of the girls stared with a look of enchantment at a woman in a striped sweater kneeling on the sand with her back pressed against the boardwalk wall, learning lines from a script. She gesticulated as she read. Then she ate fruit for breakfast and poured a drink from a flask, and Jack licked his lips at the thought of tea. Planes flew low and vast across the water and glinted silver in the sunlight as they turned to JFK. Jack walked down to the ocean edge and threw water over his head and face. The taste of salt quickened his thirst and he yearned for tea the way it tasted in the kitchen first thing on a schoolday morning, when he would be the only one up and would make a pot of strong brew for himself and his parents before he woke his brother and got him ready.

He walked back to West Olive Street, where Dilly's mum was up, watching the street from the kitchen sink in her dressing gown. She offered him coffee and he asked for strong tea with a modesty and politeness that reinvented him in her eyes. She put two tea bags into the mug and studiously tried to fathom why any man would want to take a walk so early. Jack washed his face again over the sink and she handed him a towel. She took the plastic measuring cap from the draining board and measured out a 5ml dose of cough medicine.

'Thank you,' Jack said, 'but it should be 20ml.'

'Five,' she said. 'Look.' She showed him the bottle. He read the label. This was strong stuff. Nuclear, as Eddy the doorman had said.

'5ml every four hours,' Ann repeated. 'You really do not want to be overdoing this stuff.'

'Would you call 20ml every hour overdoing it?'

She was too busy joining yesterday's dots to reply. Jack watched the little expressions play across her face. 'And on an empty stomach,' he added.

'No wonder you seemed a little...' Her voice trailed off. She looked at him, apologetically, but was met by Jack's smile and his kind, sane, gentle eyes looking at her. He laughed under his breath.

'Crazy,' she allowed herself to say, to her amazement.

He handed the cap back to her. 'I think I'll give it a miss.'

He took his tea to the couch and sat there. It tasted strong and good. She had sweetened it without asking. He looked out of the window at the trees in the garden. Everything still appeared vivid and unusually clear and the house seemed like a glass cube. His body was tingling and he felt light. The view seemed three-dimensional, the markings of the tree bark animal. Ann sat beside him on the couch. They watched the garden together. She looked down at her own legs, and at his legs, at the aubergine velour of the couch beneath them. She and Stefano had bought the couch from Kohl's in Jefferson City eighteen years ago. She had wanted it instantly because it was deep and swallowed them up, and they had bounced up and down next to each other in front of an easily embarrassed salesman. She had pictured herself and Stefano sharing the couch into their old age but as they left the store Stefano saw his huge, fully reclining TV chair and fell in love with it. He bought it there and then. Now that she thought about it, she couldn't be sure that they had ever sat on the couch together.

She looked at Jack, and found him looking at the glimpse of her breasts in the fold of her dressing gown. They moved towards each other in unison, kissed and groped and began to undress each other. They froze on hearing movement in the house, pulled their clothing back into place and sat motionless, side by side, in stunned silence. Finn ambled in, shuffling his feet across the carpet in that sleepy way Finn had always had and Jack had heard so many times.

'Good morning,' Finn said, and smiled, and scratched the back of his neck.

Breakfast on West Olive Street was a muted occasion that particular morning, with Stefano still asleep in bed and Ann hidden beneath trousers, a polo neck and a sleeveless puffa jacket. Her English guests ate grapefruit halves with serrated spoons. Stefano's halved fruit sat at the head of the table beneath a glass dome fit for a holy relic. The phone rang and Ann hot-footed it across the open-plan to grab the receiver.

Finn leaned across to his brother. 'You okay? There's a funny atmosphere.'

Jack shrugged, which was suspicious. A shrug meant *who cares* or *I dunno*, and Jack never meant either of those things.

Stefano shuffled in and joined his wife at the phone. He patted down his hair and re-belted his dressing gown and looked at Ann with the who-is-it expression. She ended the call, ignored her husband and returned to the breakfast table. Through pursed lips she squeezed out the news that Dilly was not going to be coming at all this weekend. This did not shock Finn. Ann ate her grapefruit as though it were a lemon, then took her bowl to the kitchen.

Jack smiled politely over Finn's shoulder at Stefano, who had his bare feet planted firmly in the thick carpet and stood scowling in the general direction of the dining table.

'Morning, sir...' Jack said, weakly.

Finn turned. 'Good morning.'

Stefano grunted. He looked both confused and hacked off. Ann carried the coffee jug to the table and the house settled into that particular strained atmosphere which resulted from an Italian-American man in a foul mood breathing nasally at a nervous wife who had recently been interrupted while experiencing the first competent caressing of her breasts for more than a decade.

'So,' Stefano summarised, 'your girlfriend's not coming for the weekend.' He leaned back and placed his hands on his hips. It was a gesture that suggested they fuck off out of his house. Jack needed no second invitation, Ann's presence was freaking him out. Finn looked inside his grapefruit husk for the strength to accept that he would not retrieve the Hemingway book this weekend. He tried to tell himself it didn't matter. Was there anything in it he couldn't admit to?

Fuck it. He didn't care. He was not ashamed of the book, and it was time to get out of here.

'And who the hell is Naomi Wolf?' Stefano asked.

'No idea,' said Finn.

'A political writer,' said Jack.

'Why?' said Ann.

Stefano clasped his temples. 'Your daughter sent me an incomprehensible text message just now, it woke me up... said she was quoting Naomi Wolf. Were they at school? Was she that girl with the moustache?'

Jack patted the napkin against his lips and whined, 'I'm gonna wet myself.'

Finn used his napkin too. 'Let's split.'

Jack pointed to the bedrooms. 'We're going now. Just grab our stuff.'

Ann could barely contain her whimpering gratitude. Finn grinned at her and then at Stefano, and followed Jack out of the room. The boys returned instantly, bags slung over their shoulders. 'Thank you so much,' they said, in unrehearsed unison, and walked out.

Stefano stared at the door and at the porch, long after the English men had gone, perplexed and thrilled by the abruptness of their exit.

'No...' Ann said.

'No, what?' Stefano asked.

'What, dear?'

'No? No what?'

She shrugged. 'No... nothing.'

'Sorry, what?' Stefano scratched his balls. One of the pleasures of a guest-free house.

'You're tired,' she said.

They drank coffee, at first in silence, and then with a soft, restful conversation in which they blamed Dilly for it all. It soothed them. They knew where they were when they were blaming her. Stefano returned to bed and Ann sat at the table, and remained there, staring at the bottle of cough medicine on the sink.

At the far end of West Olive Street, Finn and Jack stopped to take a look at their options. From a vantage point two blocks north of them on West Park Avenue, a seventy-three-year-old woman pausing for breath saw them silhouett against the glistening ocean, their bodies defocused and fluid against the silver-black swells of water, their limbs made loose and lithe like a paper cut-out of young boys playing on a beach, somewhere in the past. And it reminded her of a time by Kachess Lake with people she could no longer remember clearly, before she came east to find fame.

The boys looked northwards to the main strip, where the Manhattan train beckoned and the spring heat rose from the tracks and an elderly woman leant against her shopping trolley looking at them.

'We in a hurry?' Finn asked. 'I haven't seen the sea.'

'No hurry.'

On West Penn Street, the red-brick tile-roofed houses and the crown of thorns ornamental trees and the lush lawns and spring bulbs and the country-style porches with swing-chairs and shutters and the white-haired couple playing with their grandchildren made the morning seem a little unreal to Finn, and it struck him that Dilly's parents had moved here twenty years prematurely. A girl cycled no-handed down the middle of National Boulevard, leaning back and slapping her palms against her thighs, and reminding Jack of the bike he owned as a child, of shouting *Look, no hands!* and of his mother applying sticking plaster one-handed, holding her glass in the other hand. The fire hydrants of Long Beach were painted the same pale blue as her nails. Against one there was a placard: LONG BEACH TEACHERS DESERVE A FAIR CONTRACT. The same slogan was tied to the railings on the seafront. Bikes and rollerblades were discarded at angles and in layers on the edge of the boardwalk. On the beach, volleyball nets were being erected. An elderly man trudged across the sand with a bright smile that didn't belong to his gait. Screams of pleasure rose like buffeted balloons into the air. A woman kite-buggied across the firmest stretch of beach and four thick-set Italian men in Lacoste discussed her technique.

On the dunes beneath the boardwalk there was no litter where there might have been, no rolled-up sleeping bags or soiled blankets, only the dots and slivers of sunlight breaking through the decking above on to pristine sand. This, Finn suspected, was not a town that tolerated waifs or strays. He watched his big brother wander down to the surf and stare at the sea. Above him, the planes were slow and heavy and low in the mute blue sky.

27

William sensed that it was morning and that he was outside. The cold that went deep in the bones and offered the illusion of wellbeing came upon him. He found himself coiled on the ground. Above him, a breeze stuttered through the flat, open-handed cedar branches. Pain awaited him, he knew, but for now the oddness of awakening in the Manhattan open and the raised roots of the tree seemed able to hold it at bay.

He had always so loved the rhythmic pleasure of daily life and the belief in something great, but now, in light of the void, the rituals felt all dried up. It seemed of no significance how much longer he remained or what he did with the years he had left. He had no desire to die, no idea how to live. His only craving was to float again downriver to the top of that silky, slow-falling honey cascade and slip over the edge to where there was no pain.

He sat up and held his knees and took some deliberate breaths. The hurt in his body awoke too, like a sheet inside him unfolding, deep and not yet jagged. Above him, he saw the bowl of fruit in the window and imagined he could hear Susan singing to herself somewhere in the apartment, although this was not possible.

The door to the building was held open by a bag of cement. There was dust across the tiled lobby floor and boot-prints leading to a ground-floor apartment. Jay-Z sang from a paint-splattered radio and the throb of it took William's breathing by the hand as he climbed the stairs. He took a moment to straighten up before he knocked on Susan French's door.

She said nothing about his appearance but smiled with everything she had; her eyes, her mouth, the whole delicate intricacy of her fragile relationship to the world, it all poured into the smile which met him.

They sat a while on the cat-smell couch, and she watched him patiently, did not want to ask questions about why he was in a dressing gown and bruised in the face and walking like a shattered man. He wasn't saying, so maybe she shouldn't ask.

'Do you have any painkillers?' he asked.

She laughed at the idea that she wouldn't and leapt up to get him whatever he needed. She returned with the pills and sat cross-legged on the floor at his feet.

'I was hit by a truck,' he told her.

'Shit!'

'I'm okay. I needed some air and I thought I would take a walk over to see you, my dear girl.'

She smiled and adored him. 'I'll do anything for you,' she said.

'I'd like you to go and get Joy for me. I need her.' He hesitated, as he realised he couldn't remember his own address, and instead he tried to describe how to find it.

She made them coffee, putting on socks and sneakers as it brewed, watching the pot from the comfort of an ex-boyfriend's sheepskin coat and extracting a tiny, infinite delight at seeing a second mug beside hers. Before she left she repeated William's hopeless description of where he and Joy lived. When she had gone, he noticed the emptiness the way a child would hear every creak and groan in an unfamiliar house. He took a look at Susan's bed and the clothes rail that stood in the small gap between the bed and the walls.

She was wearing half of what she owned. They could have done more for her.

In the bathroom, he bowed down to the pain and washed his face, brushed his teeth with toothpaste on his little finger. He put the tube of paste back in the cabinet above the sink, between a flat yellow packet labelled Naloxone and a jar of Tiger Balm. In the fridge he found a Jiffy bag with a small block print of a grinning Apache Indian. He took the syringe and needle from the bag and went to the bedroom. He got into the bed and pulled the duvet up to his neck and sipped his coffee. After another sip, he lay on his side and hugged the bedding around him and stared at the needle a few inches away on the bedside table. His body became musty and warm in its own sweat and he found it easy to close his eyes and imagine Joy lying behind him, her flesh pressed against him. He slipped a little towards a halfway house between unconsciousness and the room, and he recalled the sensations of making love to Joy, the refuge of her body, swimming in the warmth of belonging to her, and the amazement, every time, that he could evoke such pleasure in her. To lie naked with her had always been to William an act of escape from some broken place he had not yet reached, and it was escape from his pain that he wanted now, while the girl searched for a home and a wife that he could not remember how to describe. He took the syringe and carefully, naïvely, yet without hesitation, inserted it into the cannula and injected, with the expectation that when he woke Joy would be beside him and Susan nearby too, somewhere in the apartment, like a family. This was a hope, not a belief. He plunged towards insensibility, like the moment of landing in water stretched out in time, dragging him deep. His body weight shimmered through him from the soles of his feet up to the crown of his head and he felt the pleasure of letting go of it all, of hope and expectation and faith, and, after he had wet himself and the warmth trickled down his leg, there came to him enough joy in a second to last an eternity.

Susan headed home mid-morning, having walked the streets of Clinton for two hours with no idea what she was looking for and no desire to find it. She stole croissants from a chic café that was too busy for its own good and ate one of them as she walked through the door of her apartment. It was warm from the oven and tasted rich and buttery and made her happy about life. She found William in her bed and the detritus of his actions beside it. He looked peaceful and old. She understood immediately. She had seen this sort of coma before. She held his head and plumped up the pillow beneath him. She tucked his arms to his chest and neatened the duvet around him so his feet weren't sticking out. She stroked his forehead and finished her croissant, sitting on the side of the bed. She put the chain on the front door and took off her coat and put a big pot of coffee on the stove even though she knew William could not have any, and she washed the two mugs and placed them beside each other on the counter. She felt his presence in the apartment, even as his breathing slowed and became impossible to detect. She drank coffee and held his hand. She lay behind him on the bed and buried her face in the bedding against his back and she felt the mass of his body and thought of him choosing to come here to her and, hidden from view, tucked into the folds of this, her least lonely morning for many years, she smiled.

She put music on for them both. She took frozen burgers from the icebox and fried them with beans. She cleaned the living room as she ate, returning to her plate on the low table between the small, angular movements with which she used the dustpan and brush. She sat on the end of the bed to finish her food and stroked William's forehead and talked to him about many things she would like to do, and later she dialled for an ambulance.

28

Leo looked down at his reflection in the surface of an oil-slicked puddle and caught a rare sighting of himself outside Manhattan. His reflection rippled in time with the judder of trains on the Manhattan Bridge overhead. Sand-slipped glass in the dusty windows of a tobacco warehouse made ghouls of the reflections of the neighbourhood and he wasn't sure why he was here, why he was keeping an eye open for realtors' boards on warehouse buildings. This lack of direction aside, the day reminded him of early forays into Chelsea when he first grew tired of SoHo, and into SoHo when he first arrived.

These streets had once been the dead-ends that lay in the shadows beneath towering overpasses of rail and road, the streets from which a romantic's view of a great, rotting metropolis are made. A man sped by on a red Lambretta, shouting into his cellphone. On a noticeboard outside the deli there were rooms for rent, a bike for sale, yoga classes, Lawrence Mino's Carpentry and Architectural Design service, mannequins at twenty dollars apiece, window-cleaning, office and apartment cleaning, high-res scanning services and Ulysses Nagato, tantric masseur, offering two- and four-handed massage. Presumably, Leo surmised, Ulysses had a massage partner.

He caught his reflection again, in the window. These were, of course, not mean streets any longer. They had not yet had the guttural texture refined out of them completely, but all the telltale detail that Leo's world imported to any neighbourhood was already pitching tent here. Despite this, and the unaccountable sense of unease Leo felt this fine spring day, these streets felt good to him.

He ate in a restaurant with the Manhattan Bridge and the East River spread out before him. It had the piercing acoustics of a school dining hall in riot and was packed: feeding time at the *Jerry Springer Show*. An uncomplicated pleasure at being alive glanced against him, hard enough to remind him he was a coward who had stopped looking at the world. His table was green Formica, bubbled, splintered and torn. On the adjoining table, two women pushed the unidentifiable carcasses on their plates away from them and groaned, leaning back as far as the laws of obesity permitted. In a playground beneath the Manhattan Bridge, two boys swung on a truck tyre screaming and laughing as a brawny, slope-shouldered man spun the tyre in fast circles. Nearby in the park, a large group were having a picnic, singing 'Happy Birthday'. Leo couldn't hear them but it was clear from the cake held aloft what they were singing, and that some were embarrassed to sing aloud and others were not.

A large, cumbersome boy stepped across Leo's line of sight, blocking from Leo's view the picnic and most of Lower Manhattan.

''Scuse me...' the boy said.

He sat down opposite Leo, clattering a white cane against the seat and knocking the table. The boy was in his late teens. His eye sockets sat deep and redundant in his skull, his eyeballs half-turned inwards to the walls of the sockets. Patches of fluffy, pubic-like hair held biscuit crumbs to his face.

'What are you eating?' he asked Leo, loudly.

'Chicken salad.'

'Why?'

'I like it, I like chicken.'

'Where's the chicken from?'

Leo laughed, then checked himself. 'I don't know.'

'Why?' The boy spoke over the last breath of whatever Leo said.

'We don't know where every chicken comes from, I don't think. But I like to eat it.'

'Why?'

'What are you going to eat?' Leo asked.

'Where do chickens come from?' the boy said, speaking relentlessly, without placing emphasis on any single vowel or word.

Leo replied softly. 'Where do you think?'

'The farm.'

'Guess so,' Leo agreed.

The boy took a sliced-bread bag from his backpack, then a broken polystyrene cup and a flask. He took some cheese sandwiches from the bread bag and began to eat, chewing with his front two teeth, bullets of food flying out of his mouth as he spoke.

'What are you doing here?' the boy asked.

Leo leaned back a little, to avoid the flying food. 'I'm taking a look around.'

'Why?'

'Because it's such a lovely day.'

'Where do you live?'

'Manhattan.'

'Where?'

'Gramercy Park, do you know it?'

'Do you live in a park?'

'The area's called Gramercy Park.'

'Do you live up a tree?'

Leo smiled, allowed himself to laugh a little. 'Where do you live?'

'Staten Island.' The boy continued in deadly monotone, 'Do you know the S56 bus?'

'No.'

'Why don't you?'

'I don't use buses so much.'

'How much is a hairband?'

'Er... I don't know, I don't use them either. How much do you think they are?'

'Does your wife use them?'

'I don't have a wife.'

'Why?'

'I don't know.'

'Why don't you have a wife?'

'I don't know.'

'Because you could cut her hair.'

'I suppose I could, if I was married.'

'Have you got a daddy?'

'Not any more,' Leo said.

'Have you got a mummy?'

'No.'

'Why?'

'They're dead.'

'Have you got a son?'

The shape of the boy's skull was uneven, long and angled, a rhombus, as if he had been pulled too hard, too mercilessly out of his mother's body. One ear was higher than the other.

'Yes,' Leo heard himself say. 'Yes, I have.' He had the false impression that the restaurant had fallen silent and that everybody had listened to his lie. The clouds cast fast, pretty shadows against the steel stanchions of the Manhattan Bridge.

'Does he live in the park with you?'

'Yes, he does.'

'What's his name?'

'His name is Finn.'

'Do you have a doggy?'

'No.'

'Why?'

'We're not allowed them in the building.'

'You and Finn?'

'That's right. Have you got a dog?'

'Can you stay and talk to me?'

'What do you prefer, cats or dogs?'

'Can you stay and talk to me?' The boy remained inexorable and without emotion.

'I can stay a while,' Leo said. He wanted to take a flannel to the boy's face. Or he wanted someone else to.

'This cup doesn't feel too good.'

Leo looked at the polystyrene cup. It was falling apart and, every time the boy took hold of it, it broke a little more. Despite this, the boy began to unscrew the top of his flask.

'The cup is broken,' Leo said.

'What is?'

'Don't use it.'

'What is?'

'The cup, your cup.'

The boy began to tilt the flask.

'Don't use it, it's fucked,' Leo said, to get his attention.

The boy stopped and smiled, and muttered a dirty laugh, revealing a slab of cheese stuck to the roof of his mouth. Then, he let out a series of loud, piercing screeches that froze the diners and cast the restaurant into silence.

'Was that a good monkey sound?' the boy asked.

'It was very good,' Leo said. 'Shall I get you a better cup?'

'Don't go.'

'I'll come back.'

'You won't.' The boy raised his head and called out, 'Can I have a cup please, 'scuse me!'

One of the women on the adjoining table leaned over and slid a cup in front of the boy, who picked it up.

'Is that a clean cup?' the boy asked Leo, knowingly.

'No,' Leo said, with regret. 'It is not.'

The boy smiled, fatefully, and shrugged. He crushed the cup in his hand. Leo called a waitress over and asked for a clean cup, then lowered his voice and offered to pay a cover charge for the boy because he didn't want her to kick him out. The waitress told him there was no need, that the boy always brought his own food and drink in. Leo offered to pour the boy's coffee for him and as he did so he smelled the relief of the other diners who hadn't had the insane blind boy sit at their table.

'What would Finn say if you gave him dog food and creamed corn for dinner tonight?'

Again, Leo laughed beneath his breath. 'I wouldn't do that.'

'Not to Finn?'

'Not to Finn.'

'Why?'

'Dog food is for dogs; it's not nice for people. I wouldn't do that to him.'

'To Finn?'

'Yes.'

'How old is Finn?' the boy said, continuing to clip the end of Leo's answers.

Leo hesitated. He glanced at a couple nearby who he knew were listening. He blushed, and muttered to himself, 'How old?'

'How old is Finn?' the boy repeated, robotically, his voice insistent yet without emphasis.

'Nineteen.'

'Is he full of singing?'

Leo smiled. 'I don't know what that means, but it sounds nice.'

'Is he naughty?'

'Sometimes.'

'Why?'

Leo shrugged, distracted by as-yet-unfocused thoughts about Finn and the empty warehouse spaces of Brooklyn.

'Is Finn naughty?'

'He stole some money.'

'Finn?'

'Yes.'

'Did they arrest him, did the cops come to your tree and arrest him?'

'No.'

'Why?'

'He promised me he wouldn't do it again.'

'Do I smell like a panther?'

Leo laughed aloud. So did the boy, with a deep, filthy, hysterical burst. Then the boy screamed again, one piercing, high-pitched scream.

'I don't think it will feel too good,' the boy went on, 'if the cops come and take you away and don't let you sleep in your bed and they make you stay in their house and they ask you if you've been bad. I don't think that would feel too good, do you think it would feel good?'

'I think it wouldn't feel nice.'

'It doesn't feel too nice at all. They take your mom away. Is Finn a tree?'

'No, he's a boy.'

'I'm nineteen.'

'Same as Finn.'

'Is Finn nice?'

Leo stared at the boy. The boy's mouth hung open, waiting for the reply. There was food in his mouth, and spittle. His buck teeth bit on his lower lip (when he paused from eating or talking). The bags beneath and within his eye sockets were profoundly grey. Leo felt a surge of love move through him. It felt hot in his spine. He felt love.

'He's very nice. Just like you. He's a nice boy.'

'Finn is nice,' the boy muttered, reflectively.

There was silence. The boy smiled to himself, at whatever it was he was thinking. 'Is it time for the coffee spoons?' he asked. 'Is it time for the spoons to make lots of noise? Are they dancing? Is it noisy?'

Leo looked around at the other diners, many of whom were watching.

'Where is Finn?' the boy said.

'Finn has gone away for the weekend,' Leo said.

'Is he looking for his mummy?'

Leo smiled at the idea. 'No.'

'Does Finn miss you this weekend?'

'I shouldn't think so,' Leo said.

'Is your plate empty?' The boy peered at the table.

'Yes,' Leo said.

''Scuse me. Don't you want to stay and talk with me?'

'I would like to, but I have to go.'

''Scuse me, are you going to go soon?'

'Soon, yes.'

'Why?'

'I have to get on with my day.'

''Scuse me, is this your day?'

'I guess so.'

'Why are you going?'

'I've lots to do.'

'Why?'

'I'm busy, I guess.'

The boy leapt to his feet and marched away. Leo watched as he stopped at each table and used his white stick to count the number of diners at the table. When he found another lone diner, the boy sat down opposite her and began to talk.

From over Leo's shoulder came a woman's voice. 'You're an angel.' Leo turned to the woman. She smiled at him and momentarily placed a hand on his shoulder. She was his age and, like himself, more stylish than most of the other diners.

She had swept back hair, greying elegantly. 'The way you talked to that young man.'

'I don't have a son,' Leo said, and turned away, back to the din of the room. He needed some air. He had a bad feeling.

At the base of the vast stone platforms supporting the Manhattan Bridge the water seemed to boil in the currents. At the water's edge a man in shorts, the first pair Leo had seen this spring, spoke into a cellphone while walking a corgi with a wide pink fake diamond-studded collar and a pink lead. If he had known how to use the camera on his cell, he would have taken a picture. On Jack Street, Leo watched a film crew loading gear into a warehouse building. A plume of black smoke rose from the roof of the building into the blue. A young guy with a goatee beard in a Belstaff coat held a walkie-talkie to his lips, muttered, 'Oh, shit, you serious? I hope we're insured,' and broke into nervous laughter. Fire crews arrived as Leo moved on. In Fulton Park, people lay flat out on the boardwalk in the sun and a Chinese bride and groom posed for photographs.

Leo noted his lack of fitness as he walked the incline between the waterfront and the Brooklyn Bridge. One of the benefits of being irretrievably single, he felt, was dispensing with any resolutions to get fit. In Cadman Plaza, he was drawn to the drumming of a woodpecker. He crossed the lawn to the periphery of a crowd looking up into the treetops. Leo watched the children, their bodies arched backwards at the will of their supple necks, their mouths hanging open. It was easy to tell the ones who could see the bird from the ones who couldn't, and the ones pretending they could when they couldn't. He would never be a father. This most obvious and least new of facts barged in on his day and hit him like a slow-moving vehicle, and, somehow, left him shocked all over again.

He had last walked across the Brooklyn Bridge in 1995, when he broke up with Rachel Stuart. He had walked across it in order to break up with her. 'You don't accept that anyone like me would choose you out of everyone in New York City,' Rachel Stuart had shouted, across the bridge. 'And that's why you're fucked!' He looked now through the cables to the Housing Corp where, he was pretty sure, Finn lived. He saw a flash of silver on the bridge from the N Train loaded with every woman he had slept with and studiously avoided making pregnant, and he saw the magnificent city stacked up behind the Housing Corp and he imagined Finn on the streets below and pictured the calm perfection of Gramercy Park and wondered if he had devoted his adult life to the art of missing a trick.

The *Queen Mary 2* was docked in Red Hook and reminded Leo of his and Joy's arrival. The thought of his sister became the thought of William, alone in a hospital bed. His stomach turned. He took hold of the cables and closed his eyes and the bridge drifted downriver. He heard his breathing above the city, and the wisps of river air cupping his face, and he envisaged a day when Finn ran a gallery for him through his young, naïve eyes. Leo would attach one sole condition: that Finn only take on artists who knew how to draw and how to paint, people who knew what they were doing and who had ideas, for there was one thing Leo could not abide, and that was the so-called subversion of artistic craft by those who had none. But all that was for the future, on the unlikely chance that Finn would want to remain with Leo. But, if he didn't, there were other Finns out there, and it was Leo's job to find them and inspire them to do something, any little interesting thing with their life. He could do all this and remain a coward, a coward in residence at One Lex, a coward with lots of lovely art, and many books, a man who helped himself and helped others. And he would call Finn's gallery 'The Little Thief' and he would only take twenty-five per cent. Or, maybe thirty-five. To be decided.

He opened his eyes. He took the small vibrating object from his pocket and from it came the calm of his sister's voice, telling him that William was dead.

29

Jack seemed to have returned to his former self. This was less entertaining for Finn, but something of a relief. They stood on the sun-flooded platform at Jamaica, waiting for a connection. Nearby, an old man – he seemed impossibly old to both of them – leaned heavily against his walker. Finn watched the man, how his every breath seemed to threaten his balance, and decided that, if Huggy Bear had lived to be a hundred, this was him. Jack watched the old man too, saw him as a character who had slipped out of the pages of a James Baldwin book, into the outside world where he could not die and his face and body were forever ageing into a collapsed, wrinkled newborn heap. Jack stared, and the certainty and inconceivability of growing old commenced battle inside his head and left him unable to react when the old man rocked on his heels and lost hold of the walker. Finn moved fluidly, instinctively, beautifully across the ground, and as the old man fell backwards Finn ghosted beneath him and cradled the fall of his hard, dead, skeletal weight. Jack saw it all in slow motion, frozen, as if every setting in him prevented him moving towards drama. He watched his baby brother, seeing but not quite comprehending the certainty of Finn's strength and compassion.

The stale smell of the old man's blazer rose to Finn's nose as the man's wrinkled, cadmium-black neck arched backwards and his mouth fell open. In the strange, suspended silence, Finn asked himself if this was death, then heard a slow, raking breath in the old man's throat. The old man's eyes opened and then a smile, and somewhere beneath it the distant echo of his deep, husky laughter, and he shaped his swollen, desperate lips into an O and puffed out a long breath.

'You take it easy,' Finn soothed. He lay his large, muscular, high-veined hand on the old man's cheekbone and pressed his thumb into the gentle dip where the man's nose rose to his forehead, and all the while Jack watched in awe. The man's smile was moist and helpless. He looked up at Finn with a baby's trust.

'What's your name?' Finn asked, as people closed in on the scene.

'Amiri.'

'Amiri?'

'You got it,' the old man whispered.

'You want to get back on your feet, Amiri, or just die on us here?'

'I'll stick around.'

'Anyone we can call?'

'Twenty-six grandchildren.'

'That's a start.'

'You holding me or hugging me?' Amiri said.

'Oh… hugging you,' Finn replied.

There were eleven of them. Jack counted them later. Eleven of them in the photograph he took with his phone. Eleven grinning faces, gathered on a platform bench. At the centre of them, Amiri, an extraordinarily timeworn man leaning forward with a smile that could swallow the hardest heart, aimed straight between Jack's eyes. Next to Amiri, Jack's baby brother. Finn and the old man holding hands. Finn's mouth open in speech, his face blurred slightly in motion as he called out to Jack to get on with it. Around them, the group of men and women who had descended on the scene of the old man's fall, slower than Finn, quicker than Jack. All smiles and laughing, in Jack's direction, the ones laughing at how precise Jack was being, those who laughed when Finn said he was Prince Harry and the ones who believed him, all of them waiting for Amiri Morrison's granddaughter to arrive. Jack stared at the photo most of the way home.

His stretch of East 94th Street was bathed in warm, spring afternoon hues, the beauty of the light in his south- and west-facing apartment a lucky accident that was lost on him. He could have lived in a basement.

He had never gone to bed this early in New York City, not for illness or lust. Finn placed a tray on Jack's lap and seemed eager to leave. There was chicken and rice and stir-fried vegetables in a bowl and buttered bread.

'Eat, then sleep,' Finn said.

'It didn't occur to me you could cook.' Jack's voice was weak.

'Of course it didn't.'

'It looks bloody good.'

'See you later.'

'Where you going?'

'Out. Take a look at something.'

'But you're coming back here for the night. You're staying here.' The words fell perfectly between instruction and invitation.

Finn went to the apartment door. 'Hey, Jack?' he called out.

'Yes.'

'Do you think I'm a little shit?'

'No. Why?'

Finn reappeared in the bedroom doorway. 'You said to Dilly's dad that I could be a little shit.'

There was a little silence.

'You have been; you aren't any more.'

'How have I been a shit?'

'Oh... you know...'

'No, I don't.'

There was silence.

'So... so... quiet. So... cold to Mum and Dad when they let us down. Totally unforgiving of them. They were just weak people. Your silences... that lasted for weeks and engulfed us all and made them so sad. The unspoken way you made clear you could live without them. Your rejection of all my help.'

'What help? You fucked off and just sent me money.'

'I'm a guy in my twenties, Finn. I don't know what to do. I have no clue what to do for you. I'm an orphan too. I just want a brother.' He had wanted to say that aloud for three years. Longer. For more than a decade. But he had not envisaged saying it to Finn. 'I have a little money, nothing else to give.'

'Plenty else,' Finn said. 'I don't care about money. Just be there.'

'Okay, but don't punish me with silence the moment I fuck up.'

'Okay,' Finn said, making it sound so simple.

'Do you think I'm boring?'

'What?'

'You told Dilly's parents I was boring, while I was brushing my teeth.'

'You can remember that?'

'Do you?'

'No.'

They stood in silence for some moments.

'Yeah. You're boring,' Finn said. 'This weekend you impersonated a crack addict, forced a God-fearing couple to watch Marlon Brando slam butter up a woman's arse, and fell into a lasagne. Dullasfuck.' He pointed at Jack's food, 'Eat it, I'm off.'

'I'm going to ask Holly to marry me.'

Finn hesitated before returning to the bed and stabbing Jack's fork upright into the food. 'Eat,' he said. 'And don't ask your girlfriend to marry you just because you're freaked out about copping off with Mrs Parker.'

Jack went to deny it but stopped himself. He stared at the wall in front of him, the bare wall. He slumped. 'You're right,' he said. 'It's not a brilliant idea.'

'Eat. Sleep. Don't propose to anyone.' Finn left.

It was only Finn's second ride on the 7 Train out of Manhattan but it already felt familiar. He sat twisted in his seat waiting for the train to take the subterranean slope and strike daylight. When the view of Manhattan's elegant outstretched body arrived, it stirred Finn's sense of quest and he pressed his face to the smeared window of the carriage.

He decided against going into Kay's Place café to use the restroom and regretted it by the time he reached the cemetery. He picked his way towards the western slope where the underbellies of planes descending towards La Guardia grated against the cemetery sky and he sought out a suitable spot to relieve himself. The ground was harder than he had allowed for and he watched as the contours of dry earth directed his piss in rivulets downhill to a family tomb that bore the name Corleone. He darted forward, overtook himself and kicked dry earth and twigs in the path of the stream, diverting it towards the Irish dead, of whom he had no movie-fuelled fear.

He went again to the highest point, and this time saw what he had been blind to on his first visit: that, allowing for the passing of forty years, in which the trees had doubled in size, he had possibly found the spot. The 1970 of the photograph was long gone. This was the view in 2006. This was his view. And for some reason it mattered. He didn't have the mind to decipher why, only the instincts and bloody-mindedness to have found the place, a sea of souls laid out on the edge of the city which they had fashioned. The living and the dead. He had simply needed to see them together, and to find it for himself, to not be told.

This evening, New York City was the lyrics of a song written especially for him. They had deeper meaning for him than for anyone else; he was in communion with them as no other person could be. He took from his pocket the throwaway underwater camera Dilly loathed so deeply and took aim.

30

William's diary was a plain brown notebook given by Fountains to all their employees each Christmas. Austere in design, the diary was redolent of the costume drama ironmonger shops springing up across lower Manhattan. Leo dismissed these shops on account of being able to remember when ironmongers just looked like this naturally. Now, basic goods like brooms, kitchen scissors, dishcloths and, yes, slim, plain notebooks, were sold for small fortunes in showrooms designed with a blend of prohibition era asceticism and what Dilly might have called a 'Nordic-y, *Wallpaper**-magaziney sorta feel'. The copywriters, creative directors, architects and designers who made Leo wealthy kept these shops in business.

Leo leafed through the feint-lined pages. The first four months of William's 2006, the last of his life, had the same three weekly entries in his impeccable, miniature handwriting: the anti-drugs vigil, Susan French, the Victimless Crime meeting. The one exception to the routine was a quote from Voltaire: *To doubt is uncomfortable, but certainty is absurd*, scribbled in a weak, hospitalised scrawl, two days before he died.

Momentarily, Leo could not remember if he was in his apartment or at the gallery or in Madame Claudine's café, but hints of vanilla told him. He raised his eyes and saw Willow gliding between the tables, saw guided missiles hugging the contours of the landscapes they were sent to destroy, and after that the nauseating sadness of William returned.

Finn arrived and followed Leo's waning gaze. 'Have you spoken to her yet?'

Leo glanced across the café at Willow and pulled an unconvincing expression of indifference. He slipped William's diary into his pocket and lavished attention on his cup and saucer. 'No, I haven't, and correct me if I'm wrong, but I don't think that – '

'You're wrong.'

'I haven't said anything yet.'

'You're always wrong when you talk about her.' Finn smiled, and Leo laughed under his breath and shook his head. 'Talk to her,' Finn said. 'It's simple.'

Nothing, Leo reflected, as he and Finn walked to work, was simple. But, the boy was finding the mating game easy right now so why spoil it for him? Leo too had found it easy once.

The winter had finally given up on Manhattan. The streets had turned the tables and were emanating heat. Leo remembered how he had relished the way Manhattan sweated in summer when he first experienced it. It reminded him of plentiful lovemaking with interesting, creative women. The only thing he could not recall was what the hell they had seen in him.

Astrid greeted Leo with a pained compassion which Finn noticed but did not understand. 'You okay?' she grimaced.

Finn studied Leo's reply for clues.

'I'm fine, thank you, Astrid, thank you,' the older man said, ushering her concern away. He went to his office and beckoned Finn to follow. Inside, he sat the boy down and told him that his brother-in-law had died. He told him that he had decided to buy one of Dot Yi's 3-D paintings from the Bovenkamp Gallery opposite, as a way of a marking the moment, an extravagance to cheer himself up.

Finn listened carefully and told Leo he was very sorry. But death was a eunuch that had lost its power to shock Finn. The big news was Leo's ability to buy a thirty-thousand-dollar painting with loose change. Astrid joined them, leaning heavily against the doorframe to monitor the degree of confidence passing between her boss and her junior colleague.

'You're going to spend thirty thousand dollars on a painting, just like that?' Finn said.

Leo smiled apologetically. 'He'll take twenty-four thousand from me.'

Finn began to speak but stopped himself. 'Could...'

'What?' Leo asked.

'Nothing,' Finn said.

'Maybe,' Astrid said, 'Finn wants to offer some sympathy for your loss, instead of talking about money? Yes, Finn, that's right, paintings are expensive, a nurse's wage for a year, we know, you've said that before. We get it. The price of art is disgusting. Get over it! You think it's all crap but you're being paid from the proceeds.'

Astrid walked away. Finn and Leo shared a wry smile.

'You *want* sympathy?' Finn asked.

'Not really. It's irritating.'

'I agree. Which one are you going to buy?'

'Number eight. What d'you reckon?'

Finn shrugged. 'I like 'em all. They all look pretty much the same to me, but eight's a good number.'

'No sympathy,' Leo reflected, 'but I would like someone to understand, the hole it's going to leave in my life.'

'Okay,' Finn said. 'I'll understand.'

And Leo did not doubt it, that Finn would understand and remain a man who did what he said he would do. *I'll understand you. I'll work for you. I'll be there on time. I'll beat the crap out of you. I'll burn down your shed. I'll never talk to you again. I'll never understand this art stuff. I'll never let you down. I'll die for you.*

Astrid paid her respects that morning by continuing with her job silently, in slow motion and barefoot. She parked her Lanvin ballet flats neatly beneath her desk, and tiptoed around the gallery like a teenager coming home after curfew from a park bench tryst with an unsuitable boy. She evaded Leo deftly, performed somersaults to avoid catching his eye. Disturbed as she was by her own mortality, she was more unnerved by grieving in another.

Finn seemed on the verge of saying something all morning. Astrid knew it and it was driving her crazy. If Leo had left the gallery for five minutes she'd have beaten it out of the boy. At eleven, Finn headed out into the sunshine on the coffee run. Astrid chased after him and changed the order. She didn't want Leo having the rich double macchiato blend he had asked for. 'Get a kind of relaxing, herbal, lift-the-spirits tea for him,' she said, with her caring voice.

'Like a cure-for-bereavement-type thing?'

'Yeah.'

'I wasn't serious.'

'I'm worried about him; it's eleven o'clock and he's still very quiet. I don't want him to... you know... fester.'

'Give him till noon to get over the death of his best friend.'

Finn wandered away, looking all grown-up to Astrid today. She called out to him, 'Get him some resurrect-the-dead tea or something!' and immediately had the sensation of standing in the glaring sunshine of West 26th Street in her underwear, and the feeling that Finn could crush her if he wanted to. She wanted to be invisible.

'Eh?' Finn said. He was squinting at her.

She patted her skirt to check it was still there. 'I was trying your sort of humour. I was reaching out. It didn't go well. I'm dying here. I feel weird.'

Finn smiled. He had turned into a man and she had regressed to the teenager she denied so emphatically having ever been. She returned to the office, bawled out a couple of late payers over the phone and felt better for it. Leo was quiet and methodical, reading letters and looking at artists' slides on the computer screen and the lightbox. He left a couple of messages for Joy and told Astrid to put his sister through if she called.

'Of course,' Astrid said, offended by the idea that she might not have done.

Finn returned and handed Leo his double macchiato and finally came out with it. 'What about me? Would they take twenty-four thousand dollars from me?'

Leo and Astrid froze while they caught up with Finn's train of thought. Leo laughed. 'Only in cash.'

Finn looked at Leo. Leo laughed again, nervously.

'Please let me go over there and do the deal in cash. And you can't ring them in advance to tell them. I just wanna walk in there.'

Leo had flinched once and knew he couldn't do so again. To take his time answering would be to miss the point. Finn had clearly been giving this some thought. Whether it was a matter of proving himself to Leo or something else, Leo didn't know. He knew only that he was being asked to trust a boy he was employing illegally with twenty-four thousand dollars in cash. If the little thief, as Astrid liked to call him, had been doing a sting on Leo from the start, this moment was the endgame. Leo had to act quickly and without caveat.

As if sensing a need to buy him time, Astrid intervened. 'I'm totally sure I had a date with a gay man last night. You want to hear about it?'

'Sure...' Leo said, marvelling at her.

'Not really...' Finn grimaced.

'This guy met me at Reuben's 'cos its right outside where I live but obviously I didn't let him know exactly where I live because I don't know him, he's a cousin of a friend of a friend.'

'So, an internet date,' Finn said.

Astrid was appalled. 'How did you know that?'

'Yes, how did you?' Leo was amazed.

Finn shrugged. 'Because it's fucking obvious?' he muttered, through a Cheshire cat grin.

I absolutely love it when he swears in that accent, Astrid thought.

Please stay and work here forever, Leo thought.

'Please don't tell anyone I'm internet dating, please,' Astrid said.

'Of course we won't,' Leo said. On condition you show me how to try it out, he thought.

'It's a very cool thing to be doing,' Finn said.

'Really?' Astrid said, and suddenly she looked like a girl showing her homework to her parents and collapsing with happiness at their approval. 'You think?'

Finn turned to Leo. 'You should do it.'

Leo shrugged as if the thought had never occurred to him. 'You think?'

'Yeah. It's gutsy and kind of essential. Look, the deal with an English person would be this. We totally back you, hope it goes well, that you meet someone great, we take interest, listen if you wanna talk about it, but we also constantly, mercilessly rip the piss out of the fact you are internet dating.'

'"Rip the piss"?' Astrid asked.

'Make fun of you. Big-time. That's how it would work back home.'

'It's not a Kabbalah dating thing, is it?' Leo asked, suddenly concerned.

'No.'

'Good. I think it's good that it's not.'

Astrid remembered that she had only started talking about her date to distract the little thief from the idea of taking twenty-four thousand dollars in cash out of the building. It was working, for sure, but she needed to finish the job.

'So, he's impeccably groomed, you know, like very thoroughly groomed...'

'Who is?' Leo asked.

'My date.'

'Her cousin's friend of a friend,' Finn said, deadpan.

'Like, seriously well groomed,' Astrid continued, 'and I like men who keep themselves clean but there is a line beyond which it's just a little bit un-male if you know what I mean and this guy was dangerously close to the line in terms of awareness of his own, you know, sprucing. Anyway, when I see this guy I immediately feel totally underdressed and so I say that I wanna go back to my apartment to change into something a little smarter and he says there's no need but, of course, me being me, I insist. Now, I could have just crossed the street and gone into my building but then he'd know what building I live in because we have a window seat at Reuben's. So, I have to walk all the way round the block and wait till he is looking away before going into my building. I change into a Helmut Lang Lyra Twist top I got in the sale for seventy bucks which I love and kind of live in most of my social life and go back and he says he's going to walk me to a bar he likes and I say "what's wrong with this one?" and he's like "no, come on" but we just keep walking and walking and it's a hell of a long way and we walk past three hundred bars and then it turns out we're walking back to his apartment before we go to his favourite bar because now he wants to wear something a little bit smarter because he feels underdressed next to me and, get this, he has a suit that will colour-complement – his phrase – my clothes. My clothes are black. Black. So, of course he as a man doesn't mind me coming to his apartment but I as a woman don't feel safe to go up so he installs me in a bar nearby and returns THIRTY MINUTES LATER wearing this fucking suit and I swear he had

336

taken a shower, I swear. I mean, are there any real men left in this city? No offence, both of you, – of my age, I mean.'

The men stared at her. Finn shook his head as if to reboot to where they had been before.

'Let me buy the painting,' he said to Leo. 'I can't explain why, but it would just be so perfect.'

Leo looked at the floor. He wore the smile that Astrid's convoluted intervention had painted on to him but all he could see was William's face in the patterns of the floorboards and the impossible idea of never being with him again. Ever. It was unthinkable. It stabbed him in the heart.

'Call the bank,' Leo said, winking at William.

Amy was waiting for Finn outside the gallery at lunchtime. In the deepest reaches of his twenty-hour incarceration inside Ann and Stefano Parker's house, it had felt impossible to Finn that he would ever see Amy ever again and he had returned to the city convinced she wouldn't show up. He pressed his forehead against the glass frontage of the gallery and looked at her. She smiled on the other side and he watched the rise of her cheeks and her brown eyes. He heard Leo call his name and turned to see his boss stood at the threshold to his office, holding a large white envelope.

At one in the afternoon, the orphan child of a sink estate in a worn out English seaside town stepped on to a Chelsea sidewalk with twenty-four thousand dollars in his pocket. He held the hand of a petite, beautiful waitress from a restaurant on the Lower East Side of Manhattan, New York City, USA, and the pulse in her wrist beat like the heart of a small, rare bird in his hand and he couldn't believe his luck.

'Is my boss watching me?' Finn asked her.

She glanced back. 'No.'

'The woman?'

She looked again. 'No one's watching you. Why?'

He shrugged and smiled to himself, and stood aside for her as they entered the Bovenkamp Gallery. Beryl Streep watched with contempt as Finn and Amy criss-crossed the floor to activate the paintings' 3-D, like children in a hall of mirrors.

'How much is this one?' Finn called out.

Knowing that her boss was within earshot in his mezzanine office, Beryl scraped out a polite reply.

'Thirty thousand dollars.'

Finn took Amy's hand and walked the line, studying each painting as if on the verge of choosing one. 'And this one?'

'Also thirty thousand dollars.'

'And this one?'

'They are all thirty thousand dollars.'

'This one here, is this one thirty thousand dollars?'

She hated him. 'They all are.'

'Mmm, I can't choose.'

He leaned towards Amy, grinning, and kissed her lightly on the lips. She kissed him too. The grin on his face collapsed. He drew away from her.

'What's wrong?' she asked.

He felt ashamed as he smiled at her. 'Nothing.' He squeezed her hand.

'Is my breath off?'

'No! No...'

She smiled, nervously. He squared up to the painting and stared at it. He thought it all through, lived it once in his mind's eye, the perfect scenario that had fallen into his lap in which he turned and asked Beryl to fetch Mr Bovenkamp, as he was interested in a purchase. Initially, she refused outright, through gritted teeth and a low whisper. Eventually, she agreed, in the expectation that her revered boss would throw him out. Richard Bovenkamp appeared and Finn asked about the artist and allowed the man to woo him, before negotiating a cash price of twenty-four thousand dollars. No, Finn bartered Bovenkamp down to twenty thou and returned with four thousand dollars for Leo, of which

Finn was given a thou by his proud, trusting boss. Finn drew the money out of his pocket and Beryl went into a small, ultimately harmless, seizure. It was a perfect moment. A totally perfect moment.

Amy had wandered across to the far side of the gallery and stood at a floor-to-ceiling window looking out on to West 26th Street. She was on tiptoes, to see above a metal girder that braced the front of the building. Her calves were taut and long, and she was just as she had been the first time Finn saw her, leaning against the bar of the Gay Hussar, standing on one leg. Was he really going to make the first significant act he performed in front of this woman a demeaning one, a petty revenge? Was he really going to use Leo's money to do this when Leo was grieving for someone he loved? He felt the danger in it, of behaving like a fool, and of then needing to devote the next era of his life to distancing himself from what he had been today. Of one act of meanness being irreversible, always present in him in some small way. However good and true he might be with Amy hereafter, she would nevertheless have seen this in him.

'Let's get out of here,' Finn said. His voice was thin. He was blushing.

Beryl's spine lengthened and her poise returned. 'Knew it...' she said, and snorted as they left.

'You okay?' Amy asked, taking his hand as they crossed the street.

He squeezed her fingers. 'Yeah. I was being really stupid. You look really nice.'

'Thank you.' She rested her head against his arm.

'Come and meet my boss,' Finn said.

Leo was enchanted by her, by the hint of a curtsey she gave when she shook his hand, by the way her smile and her skin and her minuteness cast a spell on Astrid, who was warm and soft with her, as if under hypnosis. Leo adored her for not knowing about William, for bringing into the room the world of Amy in which it was not the case that a man named William Fairman had died.

'Can I talk to you?' Finn asked Leo.

They went out back to the office and Finn returned the envelope of Leo's money to him. 'I'm really sorry about your brother-in-law,' he said.

They stood, heads bowed.

'Thank you,' Leo whispered.

Finn heard himself exhale. He wanted to leave the room but felt stuck to the spot. He stared at his feet. 'Me and Amy are going for a sandwich,' he said. 'I'll be back in an hour.'

Leo looked at the floorboards. 'Okay.'

They remained as they were for a few moments and then Finn turned on his heel and left the office. Leo followed him out and noticed Finn place his boxer's hand softly into the small of Amy's back. It pleased Leo to see their happiness.

'I want you guys to take the afternoon off. Get outta here,' Leo said to them. He turned to Astrid. 'Go do something nice, all of you. It's a beautiful day. We'll start again tomorrow.'

Leo watched Finn and Amy from the window. They stopped in the sunshine on the opposite side of the street, for Amy to remove grit from her shoe. She leaned against Finn and removed her plimsoll, shook it and put it back on. Finn stood framed by the high mesh fence of the parking lot he had stolen from the first time Leo set eyes on him. He reminded himself that the untamed boy who had run from that parking lot into his gallery was the young man in front of him now, with a job and a girl and a new set of clothes. He smiled to himself, on a day when it had seemed impossible to do so.

He withdrew to his office and sat at his desk and drew out from his wallet a photograph of himself and William that Joy had taken on Leo's fiftieth birthday. He sobbed until he was exhausted. He sat then, motionless, for an hour, as the tears dried on him and left their mark. Later, he became aware of Astrid sitting by his side, holding his hand. Through the teary mucus filling his sinuses he felt a stab of burning behind his eyes and fought against a new wave of tears.

'I'm okay,' he whimpered.

Her left hand moved to his arm, which she squeezed and stroked. 'That isn't true. Tell me.'

He shrugged. 'Feel sad,' he said.

She leaned across and kissed his cheek. She smelled of cucumber. He heard her lips move and knew she was smiling. 'Tell me,' she said, her voice quieter than her breathing.

'My brother,' he said. 'He was like my brother. We had planned to grow old together. I'm not whole any more.'

She held him now and he wrapped his arms around her and she kissed his cheek again and afterwards she pressed her cheek against his. They held on to each other and from time to time they squeezed each other tight.

'Thank you,' he whispered, 'thank you, thank you.'

'Thank you,' she replied.

She parted from him and looked at him and she placed one hand against his cheek. She smiled into his eyes. 'I'm going to go have that afternoon off,' she said.

'Good,' he said. 'I'm glad you are.'

'And tomorrow, I'll be here and it'll all be as usual, except I'm going to hug you tight when I see you.'

'Sounds good,' he laughed, through the snot and tears. 'Now, get out of here. And go have some fun.'

'Well,' she said, ruefully, 'I'll give it a go.'

'Perhaps you should be having more fun than you do. You've so much going for you.'

She laughed. 'I have some issues.'

He became serious. 'Okay, then. We have to address them. I want you to be well.'

'It's not about me, it's you who's hurting.'

'Every day is about all of us. There's room for everything.'

'You've lost your best friend.'

'Astrid, talk to me. I want you to feel good about yourself.'

'I don't.'

'Then you have to look at that. I'll give you whatever you need, as your boss, as your friend.'

'I need a hug sometimes when I come into work. I need to...' She trailed away into the place she inhabited alone, the world she was evicted to every evening beyond the beautiful, safe, tasteful walls of Leo's gallery, where she would remain permanently if she could.

'You need to what?'

She began to cry. 'I hate myself for talking about me now, when you're going through all this.'

He leaned away from her and looked at her anew, pale and thin before him, and to his own surprise he understood completely, and he felt elated at his ability to do so. He embraced her and he tucked her head beneath his chin the way her father had done and would still do if she ever, ever left this city and went home to see him and the woman he married.

'Don't let go,' she said.

He soothed her and called her *my dear, dear girl* and, when it was safe to expose her once again to the world beyond his arms, he held her face and looked into her eyes.

'You're going to get better,' he told her. 'You're beautiful and talented and if you were my daughter I would be the proudest man on earth. We are going to make you well and everything is going to be okay again.'

31

Joy called Leo at seven in the morning. Her voice was girlish and evangelical. 'Leo, I have realised something. He is blameless. He died when he went under that truck. That is when he left us. What happened after that was not William and I will not have any reference made to it.' She asked him to go with her to the Club after work that evening. 'I know it's so not your thing, but – '

But of course he said he'd go with her.

They walked hand in hand, silently. Leo curled his free hand into a loose grip. At a certain biting point, where the muscles in his hand contracted as far as they could without registering there was nothing there, the tension in his palm and fingers created the illusion of the weight of William's hand in his, if you chose to believe it.

The Club was empty. Joy had chosen her moment carefully. They sat at the back, in ornate pews veneered a sickly orange that did not do justice to the timber, and angled to encourage their bodies to slide off the seat on to their knees. She bowed her head in prayer and Leo raised his to the roof beams. A chandelier of energy-efficient bulbs illuminated nothing but themselves, and the barest sheen of light coated the empty pews. Dust danced in the beams of early evening sun that licked the soundless altar. Leo studied the stained glass. He was no expert, but this place struck him as post-William Jay Bolton, probably the work of one of a WJB's great admirers, recreating his style under his living nose. Leo had no issue with the followers, those who were inspired by the greats to be versions of them. It was a wonderful thing, to have the dedication and the craft to follow, the modesty to be a version. Not everyone could be the genius, the creator of something new. The followers deserved admiration and thanks, the originators awe and the lion's share of the money, although Leo knew it often didn't work that way.

Leo was doing his best to appear comfortable and it amused his sister. She asked him where they should put the ashes. 'I mean, I think you'll go there more than me so it must be somewhere you love.'

He shrugged, lost for ideas.

'I never gave it any thought,' she said. 'I presumed we'd die together.'

She didn't pray for long. Memories, anger, the splintered glass of disbelief at being a widow, made it impossible. The reality of William's departure was a repeating blow to the stomach, immune to her grit. She squeezed Leo's hand as he studied the corners of the church where the light dissipated to nothingness and gave a saturated intensity to the colours of the banners and to the texture of the side altar. Leo thought of John Piper's Romney Marsh churches, even of Kuniyoshi's women and, in the gloomiest parts of the place, of Tisnikar. Colour without light. He was seeing paintings in everything, once more.

Joy watched her brother's face and saw something at work in him again, a glimpse of the keen mind that had consumed and deciphered and admired the visual information it was fed. She had never been in the Club out of hours before and was grateful for the nearest thing to silence life could offer her nowadays. They were both discovering that loss stuck to every part of a person and could only be ignored for so many moments at a time, for as long as a couple of stiff drinks and a few hours' sleep afforded, for the length of one of Finn and Astrid's same-room different-planet conversations, for the few seconds upon waking before they each remembered it all anew and his disappearance flooded back into them. William.

The best way they had both stumbled upon to forget the undertow of grief pulling at their ankles was to torment themselves with the chance of it all, to imagine someone saying to the driver of that truck, 'Let's say Wednesday instead of Thursday,' or, 'Take 68th Street, not 72nd.' Torture was preferable to acceptance. It kept William close and their minds busy enough with the fact of his death to make them disengage from the truth of it. In this way, Leo and Joy were, without consulting or knowing it, swimming again in the same DNA.

The clear view of nothingness that William had spied beneath that truck played on Joy's mind but she discovered she could talk herself out of it. She knew he was possibly right about what he had seen, and she respected his greater experience in the matter now that he was gone, having not respected it at all when he was alive, such was the beatification afforded the dead. She doubted it made any difference.

They left the Club and she said that she doubted she'd return.

Leo was surprised.

'I mean, I'll go somewhere else. Where I'm anonymous. Maybe somewhere more traditional. Maybe nowhere.'

They walked back to the apartment arm in arm. She told him that the idea of a oneness that lasted forever remained a good idea, a clever one, a fine escort through life. She wasn't prepared to abandon it merely on the grounds of its being fictitious. To die in hope was possibly good enough – hadn't William said so himself, when he was high as a kite?

To Leo's ear, all her doubt and compromise sounded very healthy indeed.

'I need a drink,' she said, and found her own high, a lovely, strange, out-of-focus buzz, walking along a busy Tenth Avenue on this spring day with her thoughts a blur. 'I feel very safe,' she added.

'You are,' he said.

'I think of this as Clinton now. Hell's Kitchen was where my beautiful William lived. It no longer exists.'

As was the pattern in these early days, she drank a little, fell asleep quickly and woke an hour later, close to midnight. She had thought about other men when William was in hospital but did so no longer, now that her late husband was restored to perfection in death. She walked lightly around the apartment so as not to wake Leo on the couch. At five past midnight, with the living room window open and offering up to her the final fresh breezes the city would allow for some months, she no longer wanted to live here and wondered if she might have Leo's spare room at One Lex to come back to if she went on some trips. She leaned out to get a glimpse of the Empire State Building, remembered the first time she and William had seen this view, shoulder to shoulder at this window. From that moment, they had been committed to another – this one, when he or she would look at the view alone – and she recognised the expertise people possessed to treat death as something pertaining to everyone but themselves. Even now, she realised, even bereft of William, she was relieved not to be the dead one.

When Leo woke, it was because Joy was tapping his arm. 'Leo, Leo...' She was kneeling on the floor, staring at him, a Tupperware food box on her lap. She looked like a little sister with a big idea. 'Come with me,' she whispered.

He hauled himself off the couch, dressed and watched her place the food box carefully in a backpack. He knew what was inside. 'That can't be all of him,' he said.

'No, just a little bit. Over time we'll put him everywhere.'

346

He followed her, walking in her slipstream through the empty first hour, to the city's most famous attraction.

'You don't do heights,' he said.

She replied, 'You don't do cliché, yet here we are, about to throw William off the Empire State Building.'

She ascended to a height for the first time in a quarter of a century, her vertigo disarmed by the greater force of grief, her hand gripping Leo's. She stepped out into the chill, thin air but kept close to the side of the building. She removed the backpack and handed Leo the container.

'You go do it. I can't go to the edge.'

He looked out at the night sky to feel the direction of the breeze. 'I need to go round to the next side,' he said.

She smiled and nodded.

'You want to come?'

She shook her head. 'You do it for me. I don't need to watch.'

He walked purposefully away, concentrated on doing the job right and keeping an eye out for the staff, whose reaction he could not predict and wished to avoid. He found an empty section of the lookout and took the lid off and in one smooth, confident action held the box out over the drop and tipped it. The ashes caught the breeze perfectly, swooped then flew gracefully away. He spoke William's name under his breath then heard the shuffle of Joy's feet as she appeared round the corner, staying away from the edge. He smiled at her, with tears in his eyes.

'I want to go now,' he said, softly. 'It's too sad.'

'Wait for me on the street,' she said. 'I'm going to go once round. I wanna do it.'

He made an expression to ask if she was sure. She was. He went inside to the elevators, hugging the food box tight to his stomach.

She looked out across the top of the city towards the dark domed sky and the twinkling distant lights that felt like a childhood, and that illusion of seeing the curvature of the planet. It stirred a thrill in her and she was elated to discover that not all life's treasures would be blunted from now on. Already, she could imagine William's ashes draped softly across the city. She edged around the next corner, where two young lovers stared into each other's eyes and adored each other and the young man said, '*King Kong*,' and the woman with him laughed. And then the tall young man, brutally pretty, glanced at Joy and their eyes met and it threw her into confusion because she felt she knew this boy but could not place him and, suddenly, the hinges seemed to be coming off her world. She could not possibly know him but it haunted her, until she saw that what she recognised was not the boy but the unsmiling truth that it would all end so quickly and how recent it was that she and William had been young lovers. She allowed the devastation of that realisation to do its worst to her, and turned to the setting to inspire her, to guide her at least, to an understanding that she had to embark on a new life now, and not on a lifelong memorial to William Fairman. She took a breath and walked to the edge and gripped the side and looked down at the streets beneath her and she saw that she feared nothing any more, not even oblivion, and that her love affair with New York City had come to an end.

32

Many things had rendered Finn speechless in his life but none had undone him with their beauty. The delicate, eggshell sinews of Amy's hand in his were a miracle that did not diminish a second or third time. It was a whole world in itself. They said little as they walked, other than to share the occasional observation, all of which amounted to nothing more than another way of saying *I like you*. He pointed out to her the café where Leo's crush worked as a waitress.

'We all know a waitress is the ultimate kind of woman,' she said. She liked the way his mouth made the tiniest move to smile when he liked what he heard.

She gazed up at the ornate stonework of Maison Claudine and the offices above it and the two of them looked at the tops of buildings all the way across town to the Gay Hussar and as Finn craned his neck to the sky he felt like he got it. He *got it*, that if someone hadn't taken a photograph of Calvary Cemetery and hung it on a wall then already his life would be poorer. And he *got it*, all these unfathomable people who put their eye to a camera, made up a tune, brushed paint on to canvas, carved detail into stone that no one would ever see. It wasn't what he wanted from life for himself – too flimsy, too contingent on other people's opinions – but thank Christ some people were up for going through all that shit. Movies were a part of all that and he'd never felt embarrassed admitting he loved them. He cried at the end of *The Truman Show* and felt hope for himself. He watched an old film called *Birdy* and wanted to climb into the screen. And sometimes, because of what these people did, the thing they made for you to look at, because of a photo hanging on a wall forty years after it was taken, you found yourself watching a grandmother and her grandson dipping chips into ketchup and seeing that old lady spending time with that young boy became the blueprint for your future, for what you wanted to matter in your life, for where your priorities were going to lie. Because of five minutes in a worn-out diner on the way to Calvary Cemetery, you knew that you were going to spend your life encouraging kids, teaching them to be fit, to be strong, to be safe, to know how to fight so that they didn't need to fight, teaching them to watch great films and take a look at some art and treat old people well and treat their girlfriends and boyfriends well. All this, from a photograph.

Amy installed Finn at a small corner table in the window and she went to work. The owner of the Gay Hussar greeted him with eyes that seemed to know something he did not, and from time to time, she put in front of him a small bone china plate with a savoury treat to eat, and each time she told him something new about the Lower East Side: that Trotsky had lived here (Finn didn't enquire who he might be); that there wasn't a single building on the Lower East Side that had not hosted a reported murder; that there was once an orchard where Finn now sat; that at the start of the twentieth century it had been the most densely populated place on earth. If Finn hadn't thought she would eat Jack alive, he'd have introduced the two of them.

Amy brought him tea and rested her forehead against his arm again as if trying to shift some of the thoughts inside her head on to him. He thought he heard her say that he was beautiful, as she walked away. He was somewhere uncharted with her, had never heard such tenderness. Finn took a book from the shelf of second-hand paperbacks and arched his broad, muscular back over the table as he opened it and read the first line: *In Haddam, summer floats over tree-softened streets like a sweet lotion balm from a careless, languorous god, and the world falls in tune with its own mysterious anthems.*

He stopped, and had to reach for his next breath. He watched the steam rise up off the tea. How could such beauty be created from words? How could a line of words he didn't necessarily understand have a taste? A sweet, exotic, beautiful taste that made the world open up in front of him? Everything around him fell perfectly silent, as in the aftermath of a collision, that unexpected quietness immediately after carnage. But this was the violence of beauty crashing into him, breaching his world and leaving him altered, floating on his back in the calm floodwaters of that languorous god, not yet aware that not only would he read this book to the end but because of this book, because of this writer, he would read for the rest of his life.

At six o'clock, the owner served him a cocktail but Finn didn't touch it. He read for three chapters then put music on the jukebox. Amy replaced his untouched cocktail with a bottle of beer, which lasted him all night. He tried not to watch her too much as she worked but he found it difficult. The restaurant filled up and they sat Finn on a stool at one end of the bar and he read the book and each next page was, suddenly, the priority in his life. Cozy and Siouxsie turned up late and they swapped numbers with Finn and didn't stay long and Cozy slapped Finn on the back and looked him in the eye as if to fortify him and Finn didn't know why. Amy took Finn back to her apartment, a small, neatly configured nest in Mapleton. They lay on the bed in their clothes. They looked at each other and he scanned the miraculous detail of her eyes. They both were still and silent, save for the moments when their fingers curled together or they whispered some safe tender thing. Finn undid the topmost button of her grey, cashmere cardigan, and she whispered, 'The thing is…' but said no more. But it was enough to stop him. His index finger traced a repeated circuit around the edge of the next button.

'What's the thing?' he asked.

She looked at him as though she'd prefer for the world to end than to tell him. She forced herself to smile. 'Nothing,' she said, and she kissed him and she put both hands on the buckle of his belt to undo it, and he was so much bigger than her that she disappeared in his arms and it was exactly where she wanted to be and he felt capable of good things. Later, he watched her as she lay tucked against her chest with her eyes closed, and he couldn't tell if she was asleep or not until she whispered, 'You're so lovely.'

He watched the rise and fall of her back, the arrowhead of tiny hairs at the top of her vertebrae, the pale skin of her back and buttocks, and he said, 'No, I am not.'

'Don't say that,' she whispered. 'Why say that?'

After some while, when she squeezed his finger to beckon him on, he told her. 'I came to New York City to beat up my brother, to hurt him… really hurt him.'

'Why?'

'I wanted him to know what it felt like.'

She squeezed again but to no effect. So she asked him, 'And how do *you* know what it feels like?'

'From my uncle. My brother sent me to live with him.'

'How hurt?'

'Big hurt.'

She thought for some time before she asked, 'Did your brother know?'

He did not answer that question. She slid up the bed and wrapped her arms around him and pressed his forehead into her body and they lay there for a long time. She threaded a strand of his hair behind his ear again and again until they slept and occasionally the noises of the street nudged them awake or the voices of her roommates through the walls. The sounds were redolent of a future that had already begun, lived far from Finn's memories. That was why Finn loved the noises of New York City, because they were so very definitely not the noises of home.

Amy moved and rested her head on Finn's chest. She positioned her left leg between his thighs and her negligible weight on one half of his body. She could feel the contours of his ribs and chest muscles supporting her. She rose and fell on his breathing. She stroked his tummy and the pubic hair that ran up to it.

'He didn't know,' she said.

'He was my brother. I wanted to go with him.'

'Did you tell him that?'

She watched his lips part and believed she could see the last of some dead old air squeezed out between them by the words that followed.

'No, he didn't know.'

'Does he know now that you were hurt?'

'No. He doesn't know a thing.'

The silence returned and they were both comfortable in it but soon, anyway, she stirred.

'I wanna make you some tea,' she said.

'I wanna go up the Empire State Building with you,' he said.

'Come on, then,' she said.

'Now? At midnight?'

She shrugged. 'Sure.'

He didn't move. She sat up and reached for her clothes. She smiled at him. 'Come on,' she repeated.

As he watched the night's subterranean laggards framed against yellow-lit walls on the subway platforms they hurtled through, she was unsure of the small distance between her swaying body and Finn's, and of how far away he seemed.

What, Finn asked himself, was the word his brother had used? Atrophy? The atrophy of the imagination. The failure to imagine being the other person. Was that all Jack was guilty of: an inability to conjure up those remedies Finn had never even asked for?

'You okay?' she asked him.

'I was thinking about what you said to me.'

She waited for him to tell her more but he didn't seem to see the need, and she found that attractive. She found everything about him attractive and, as they rode the elevator to the observation deck of the Empire State Building, she told him she wanted to be in bed with him again and he said that he did too, very much, and they kissed and rose into the sky.

She took his hand and led him out to the northward view and she looked into the deep dark knot of the Park at night.

'The thing is…' she said.

'What is the thing?' he asked, softly. And because she looked sad and nervous he wished to reassure her, so he said, 'Whatever it is, it's alright.'

And the trees in the Park were hidden in the blackness that was their own selves, and they swayed the sighing noise of the invisible urban breeze and the thing was that Amy was moving to San Francisco.

And when she finished telling him, and now he knew that San Francisco was the thing, he hugged her to him, and something inside him departed, some tumorous thing that was good to be rid of, and he felt the buoyancy that hung between joy and sadness. He cried a little when she did but it was alright. It was all okay. It was life. She was going, but they had met, and this was the next thing his life was turning out to be. It was still wonderful. She had wanted him enough to not tell him earlier, and that was what he chose to see. He smiled at her, and held her tighter to him so that he could look out across the city without being watched by her, without her scrutinising his every unclear expression for clues to how he felt. An orphan grows tired of being interpreted. He did not feel let down. He would not add her to the list of bruises. She was one of life's joys, yet not one that could seduce him to leave this city.

He watched the tail-lights and the headlamps in the veins beneath him, the flow of the city's arteries, reduced at night to a resting beat. And he saw that in all this tangled mass there was another human being out there with the same blood flowing through his veins as his own, one person left on the planet made of the same cells. And one day, as Leo had experienced, one of them, Jack or Finn, would cease, the blood would stop flowing, the life would leave them and they would leave life, and Finn knew now that he wanted to know this man who was his brother for his entire life and that if he did so he'd find an end to the longing that had threatened to extinguish him every day of his life so far. And, if he was to die first, he wanted his brother by him. And if not... Finn had a premonition of the excruciating pain of one morning waking up to a world without Jack in it. Hopefully dear God, hopefully, that was many years distant, but he welcomed that pain too, the feeling that a part of himself had been cut out of him and stolen, welcomed it as the scar bequeathed by love; he would bear whatever pain that loss would serve up for him one day in return for a lifetime with his brother, and he would beg the stars every night for that desperate day when two brothers were prised from each other to be as far away from tonight as possible, so that they had as much time together as there could possibly be and as little time apart.

And when Amy asked him if he was okay he said, 'Yes,' and when she asked him again what he was thinking about he said, '*King Kong*,' and she laughed with moonlight eyes because she knew it wasn't true. And as he held her, turning his head to one side as she nestled against his chest, he glimpsed a woman staring at him and he stared back at her because she was the precise image of the woman he had always dreamed his mother could have become.

They ate pizza on 28th Street and they made love again and stayed awake, kissing with the very tips of their tongues. She held him tight before they parted on the street corner against the glints of sunlight on tarmac wet from a shower at sunrise. Their heads ached with the need for sleep. She went to work and Finn rode the 6 uptown to Carnegie Hill and walked right past Eddy the doorman, who told him to wait until he'd buzzed up. Finn turned his back and waited for the elevator, with the ease of a man made love to.

Jack made tea, which they drank in easy silence. Finn fell asleep on the couch and Jack moved around the apartment the way you would move around a sleeping child. The building felt solid and firm beneath his careful steps. He went to his room to get a duvet to lay over Finn and found his cellphone vibrating to alert him to the sight of twenty-one text messages received from Dilly in the space of an hour.

Call me it's urgent.

Call me please.

Please help me.

Help me.

Help.

He switched his phone off, felt guilty about it and turned it on again. As he took himself out of the apartment to the hushed corridors to call her, the buzzer rang. He grabbed it before Finn stirred.

'Young lady here to see you,' Eddy the doorman announced, brimming with aggression. 'She's been trying to call you all day. I'm sending her up.'

Jack was quick and firm. 'No. I'm coming down. You do not send people up without my say-so. I'm coming down.'

He hung up and walked softly to place the bedding over his brother, who remained deep in sleep.

In the lobby it was immediately clear to Jack that a doe-eyed Eddy had swallowed Dilly's version of the world without chewing and found in it brand new reasons to dislike the English boys.

'Hey,' Jack said, smiling politely at Dilly.

'Hey,' Dilly said. She was calm and bright and kissed Jack on the lips.

'Let's talk outside,' Jack said.

'Let's talk up in the apartment,' she said. 'Is Finn there?'

'No.' He ushered her towards the entrance.

'Is he not?' Eddy asked. 'I thought he was.'

Dilly turned back to Eddy. 'Thanks for what you said and for the offer, but I'm not interested in dating anyone right now.'

Eddy flushed up nice and pink, nice and quick. 'Of course, of course...' he agreed, swatting the subject away. 'Absolutely. I wasn't suggesting a date, just coffee really, nothing.'

'Oh.' Dilly sounded confused. 'I thought you said dinner, tonight?'

'No,' Eddy insisted, laughing nervously.

'It confounds me that you're still single,' Jack said to Eddy, and walked Dilly outside.

He bathed his face in sunshine, hoping that when he opened his eyes whatever reason Dilly had for being here would have disappeared. He was aware that he would be a hostage to his conscience as soon as she fleshed out her request for help but, confident that he had the skills to keep her out of Finn's life, he engaged.

'What's up?'

'Need you to take me to the Madhouse.'

'What?'

'I have to go to the Cross Centre – it's a clinic for anxiety and stress stuff, like, disorders, make of the title what you will.'

'Why are you asking me?'

She felt stung by his directness. 'It's forty blocks south and I'm in a fresh-air phase of my life. I thought you and Finn could walk me.'

'I'll walk you,' he said, determined to lead her away from the building in which his brother lay sleeping.

The sun had nothing getting in the way of it and the city. People were bringing their lunches outside for the first time in the year.

'Doesn't it drive you crazy that your beautiful, amazing brother never answers his cellphone?'

Jack shrugged.

'Why are you walking so fast?' she said.

'I don't know,' Jack said, 'just want to get you to this place, I suppose.'

'Relax, soldier, I'm still going to be a loon, whenever we get there.'

Jack adjusted down to a walk that was just a little bit unnaturally slow, and Dilly now had trouble not walking ahead of him. They loped out of step with each other for half an hour to the safe haven of Turtle Bay and a hushed estate of low, sterile modern buildings.

'Home again, home again, jiggety jig,' she muttered.

The look of the place was not entirely new to her. She had spent time in its sister clinic in Seattle when she'd had a period of not being able to cope. She had panic attacks sometimes. When they got bad, she came to a place like this.

Jack waited in a domed reception area filled with light while Dilly went off to see a woman called Frances. People of all ages sat around Jack in high-backed armchairs reading magazines and sleeping at uncomfortable angles. Jack called

Finn and apologised for being out so long and heard his brother's dribbly voice whisper, 'S'ok bro, no sweat,' and yawn, and a woman stood over him and smiled a short, clipped, functional smile, before saying, 'No phones allowed in here.'

'Sorry. Just calling my brother.'

'Not in here. Your brother could be your dealer.'

'No, I'm not a... you know...'

'You're not a what?'

'A... patient. I'm with a friend. I'm normal.'

She smiled forcefully and with no warmth. 'I'm happy for you, being normal, but no phones.'

'Got it. I didn't mean...'

The woman departed, prowling forward to the next part of her morning and stopping at the front entrance where she transformed and burst into warm, expressive laughter and threw her arms around another woman. 'Look at you, all dressed up for the outside world!' The women squeezed each other tight and howled with laughter and whooped up their day. Watching them made Jack feel light, as if his veins were filling with love, and he didn't know if it was the thought of his brother sounding so at home in his apartment or the warmth of the sun through the high glass ceiling or something about those two women hugging farewell or how little time he'd spent in the office recently. He took a look at the people around him and he knew the option was there if he chose it, to think back on his parents and all the drinking and the shouting and the terrible waste, but it was a subject of exhaustive boredom to Jack, and he was more curious about the deep pool of compassion inside him that had revealed itself in this stifling, sun-filled room in Turtle Bay. How had it taken him twenty-five years and a million people passing through his line of sight to realise that everybody was like him and he was like everybody else – to be liberated at last from the idea that he was meant to have answers for everyone? He saw the vanity of it, the arrogance of it, this impression that he was gliding above the surface of human life trying to fix things but unable to get a foothold on the ground and look people in the eye. How tiring it had been to be Jack all this time, and how lonesome.

He felt closer to his parents in here, saw how easily they could have been different if his mother had been offered this sort of help, and accepted it, and saw that he himself might, like her, become unrecognisable to his true self, if luck was not a lady.

Near to the entrance was an office and a reception desk. On a table to one side were pamphlets about the clinic. He was aware of the danger of impetuous acts, ill-founded resolutions, but he also knew his own mind and his own strength, and he clearly saw his relationship to this place, now and stretching into the future. He filled out the volunteer form and provisionally said that he could do two sessions per week. It would be his secret, for now at least. It was the first decision he had ever made with confidence. Filling in the form had the same clandestine quality as kissing Mrs Parker on the couch in Long Beach. The memory of that kiss and her hands on his pants was all the more pleasurable for its illicitness. It was not just her smell, the fleshy kiss, the nakedness that had felt great, but the insanity of it, the stupidity, the absence of common sense.

Dilly appeared. She had been crying. She marched outside. Jack followed at his own pace and joined her on a small bank of grass where Dilly hugged her knees and screwed her eyes up against the sun.

'Such a nice day...' she said. 'Thanks for coming. I'm going back in for a session later on so I'll just hang here. I don't know how you're fixed but it's great having an intelligent, mature, good-looking man beside me if you can stick around.'

'No, I want to get back. You gonna be okay?'

She had expected him to want to stay. 'Of course I'll be okay. I've had to be, all my life. I've always been alone and had nothing.'

Jack pictured her parents' house on West Olive Street. 'You've a roof over your head whenever you need it. You've got family. You had an education, got nice clothes. That's not nothing.'

She sat in silence for some time, trying to remind herself who Jack was and how he fitted into the tangle of histories and tall stories that made up the windblown branches of her mind.

'They neglected me. They abused me. Made me extremely ill. I've always been alone.'

'They abused you?' he asked.

'You said it.'

'No,' Jack said, 'I didn't say it, you said it.'

She didn't reply. He was gentle. 'That's not true, is it, what you said? Is that a lie?'

'Well, it depends on semiotics, I guess. But yes, it's a lie.'

They sat in silence. She shut her eyes and felt the breeze and the warmth. He watched her face, watched it hold itself at the perfect intersection of a smile and a grimace.

'Dilly...' he began.

'Yes, Jack,' she said, like a child who knew she was about to be lectured. She turned to look at him with a face that threatened to burst out laughing.

'You... are not my problem or Finn's. He and I both deserve a shot at happiness and you would get in the way of that, I feel. You have to turn for help to those who care about you. I don't want that to be me and I won't allow it to be Finn. I'm sorry if that's unkind.'

She looked away and chewed on an imaginary piece of gum.

'Yeahhhh...' she said. She got up and returned inside. Jack watched her go. He phoned Ann Parker and told her where her daughter was, and Ann, who did not seem surprised, thanked him and said that she and Stefano would come immediately. He made his way back to Second Avenue and stood there a moment, with slippers on his feet and not a cent in his pockets, and set about finding his way back to Finn.

33

On the warmest day of September, the day of the picnic, Finn's copy of Hemingway short stories arrived, complete with a birthday card. It sat in Jack's mailbox with the words 'totally private' written in red above Finn's name. Dilly had, eventually, been as good as her word. Finn was not to know (and would never find out) that before posting the book to him she had photocopied every page of it, in the office of the visiting professor of fine art at the Institute of Arts and Sciences in Zagreb, with whom she was having an affair while she studied for her Foundation. With the photocopied pages, she had created a sixteen-by-eight-foot mixed media collage out of Finn's scrawled handwriting and Hemingway's prose and a splattering of her own Pollockesque paint. The piece was entitled *Loverboy* and gained her another distinction and a romantic weekend on the Adriatic.

Finn had considered a variety of options for the book's disposal (throwing it overboard from the Staten Island ferry, or one page into each garbage bin he passed on a day's walking through the Boroughs, burying it in Carl Schurz Park) but he didn't want to delay, nor get arrested in the mayor's backyard, and there was nothing to equal seeing it burn in front of his eyes. He used Astrid's metal shredding bin, in the small yard out the back of the gallery. Leo and Astrid watched covertly, and she kissed goodbye to her bin, but they had learned over the course of the summer to not always ask Finn what he was up to or why.

They drank coffee at breakfast, although Leo had offered champagne, and toasted Finn's birthday as the book's ashes got whipped up by the breeze. Mid-morning, Leo took Finn to Madame Claudine's and put his hand on his shoulder as he told the proprietor it was the young man's twentieth birthday. She kissed Finn on both cheeks and held his hand for a moment, as she asked him, 'What will you do?'

'Today,' he asked, 'or with my life?'

'On your birthday.'

'We're going for a picnic,' Finn said.

'He wants to show us something,' Leo added, and basked in the fleeting thought that Madame Claudine might mistake Finn for his son.

They sat in easy silence together, the two men. There was plenty Leo had thought of trying to say to Finn, but none of it had yet won a rightful place. There was time ahead for that. He handed Finn an envelope. 'I know that money can seem cold, but only you know what you want.'

Finn looked Leo in the eye, and expressed his thanks this silent way. Then he ripped open the envelope childishly, to make Leo smile. He was caught out by what was inside.

'That is... incredible. Thank you. It's so much.'

'You're welcome, Finn.'

Finn stared at the bills. 'It's so much...' he whispered again. He watched Leo stand at the counter and buy cakes for the picnic with a jauntiness to him that made Finn want to tease. He watched him for as long as he could go unnoticed.

They closed the gallery at lunchtime and walked in the warm late summer sun through Chelsea to the uptown C. 'I would like us to go for walks together, the three of us, from time to time,' Leo said. 'This is the first time we have all been out together like this, in the open air, with things to look at and sounds to hear. We are going to do this regularly, at least once a week, just walk and talk for a while.'

'Sure thing, Forrest Gump...' Finn said.

'Not between November and March we're not,' Astrid said.

'It will make me supremely happy,' Leo said, ignoring them. 'I can show you both off.'

And he meant it. And they both knew it, and glanced at each other.

They took the 7 out to Queens and Finn left his seat to stand at the doors and look out as the train climbed clear of the East River and curled over Hunters Point with a dramatic look back over its shoulder at Manhattan, and then on to Sunnyside.

'Said it once, saying it again,' Astrid confided to Leo, 'this is a very weird venue for a picnic.'

'His birthday, he gets to choose,' Leo muttered. 'It'll do us good.'

'How?'

Leo shrugged. 'I've no idea.'

'I think I preferred the old days, when you were miserable and didn't engage,' she said.

Finn led them from 40th Street station to Kay's Place where a handsome, wide-eyed, rough young man was waiting for them. He had on a shirt and tie, beach shorts and flip-flops. A scar ran from the corner of his eye to his temple.

'This is Glenn; he just got out of prison yesterday,' Finn said.

Glenn and Finn stood shoulder to shoulder, equally upright and powerful, but Glenn looked more hard and more vulnerable.

Leo shook Glenn's hand. 'Welcome back, if that's the right way to put it.'

'Works fine for me,' Glenn said.

He shook Astrid's hand and kissed her on both cheeks, as if he'd been released from finishing school. She had never felt hands so rough.

Glenn held a large flat box of cheap milk chocolates with a ribbon on, which he handed immediately to Finn. 'Happy birthday,' he said.

'Thanks, man.'

They all took a seat, save for Leo, who went to the counter and ordered their drinks from a resilient-looking woman who looked as if she owned the place and who said of Glenn, 'That man drinks a lot of coffee, even for these parts.'

Finn took a text from Jack, apologising that he was running late from work. He opened the lid of the chocolates and offered one to Astrid.

'At two in the afternoon?' she asked.

Finn shrugged.

'It's half-empty,' Astrid said.

Finn looked in the box. It was more than half-empty.

'I was starving,' Glenn said. 'Sorry.'

'You're fine,' Finn said, containing a grin. He hardly knew him, but Glenn made him laugh.

'Why would you want to celebrate your birthday in a cemetery?' the newly liberated man said.

'Good question,' Astrid said.

Finn shrugged. 'I just like it.' His phone rang. 'Hey, Jack!' he said to it. 'You're where?' Finn leaned towards the window and peered out. 'I can see you... it's not a problem... we're just chilling... don't worry about it...'

Jack was still on the phone, apologising for being late, when he entered the café. Both men hung up and Jack marched towards his brother with a velocity that seemed to make an embrace inevitable, but he stiffened up at the last and touched his brother's elbow as he said, 'Sorry I'm late and happy birthday again, bro.'

'Thanks, Jacky.'

The five of them walked along Greenpoint Avenue to Calvary. Finn guided them through the cemetery to the slope at the far end and from the top of it they stood and took in the view before them, the sea of tombs and the long, elegant, floating city. A silence came over them, awe-inspired.

Finally, Astrid said, 'It's incredible.'

Finn delved into his pocket and took from it a crumpled photocopy of Arthur Tress's photo of the cemetery. Leo loved to see this, the way the photo was folded so messily in Finn's pocket when he loved it so much.

'This is the spot,' Finn said.

'What is that?' Glenn asked.

'It's the best photo ever taken.' Finn handed it to him. 'And the man that took it stood right here to take it.'

They all peered at the photo and agreed that it was a good-'un. Like Leo, Astrid could see that Arthur Tress had taken the photograph from a higher vantage point than the one where they stood. She looked around. Maybe he'd hired a cherry-picker or even scrambled up on to the Expressway. She kept these thoughts to herself because Finn was happy where he was, and because he was exactly the sort of person who would, given half a reason, climb up on to the Expressway, and she did not want her little thief getting himself hurt or arrested.

There were elm trees on the brow of the slope. They laid out a rug in the shade, alongside a bench. Leo had his cakes from the café, Finn a carrier bag with crisps, nuts, bananas and an extraordinarily large bag of onion rings. Astrid produced salads, raw carrots and a pot of bulgur wheat. Glenn's sausage rolls had, like the chocolates, been started by him on his journey out from the hovel. Jack had brought sandwiches with the crusts cut off, for which he was teased, plus a coolbag with beer and champagne.

Jack took off his suit jacket and his tie. He swigged a beer and it went to his head in the afternoon sun. Glenn placed a mini sausage roll and an onion ring in his mouth simultaneously, and sat back against a grave. He patted the top of the headstone. 'It's what he would have wanted,' he said, with a full mouth. He held up another sausage roll towards Finn, as if toasting him. 'Awesome party venue, this, Finny. Nothing weird about this, nothing at all.'

Jack held his beer aloft. 'Happy birthday, Finn.' The others raised their plastic cups to him. They lazed in the sun and Jack spoke to the blue skies. 'I read that this cemetery was created by St Patrick's Cathedral in 1848 and there were fifty burials a day, half of them Irish children under seven years of age. There's three million people here now.'

'They filmed *The Godfather* here,' Finn said. 'Don Corleone's funeral.'

'One guy I bunked with in prison was in for trying to kill his neighbour's cat,' Glenn said.

'That's disgusting,' Astrid said.

'He got so fed up with this cat disturbing him that he tried to hang it,' Glenn said. 'And I always thought, like, how hard can it be to kill a cat?'

'It's disgraceful,' Astrid reiterated.

'I know, but what I wanted to ask him, except he was kinda untalkative, was how can you *attempt* to kill a cat? You know what I'm saying? How can you *fail* to kill a cat? When you're a hundred-kilo human being, how hard is it to kill a cat?'

'It's an interesting angle,' Jack said, lying back again and smiling at the sky over his head, and aware that Finn was laughing to himself. Glenn sank his teeth into a pastry from Maison Claudine. It mixed with the salty taste of onion rings. 'Christ almighty,' he said, 'this tastes holy.'

Something brought William to the surface of Leo's thoughts. He was never far from them. Something as simple, perhaps, as Leo's wish for William to be here, or a make-believe that William could see him now, so off-piste (by

Leo's standards) and so interested. In the five months since William's death, Leo had received postcards from Joy in Niagara Falls, Vancouver, San Francisco, Yosemite, New Orleans, Hilton Head, Brandy Wine, Boston and Maine. When in Manhattan, she saw a few friends and made her plans with a certain anger inside her that Leo felt he had no right to question when he was incapable of feeling any such thing. He admired her for it, and there was something in seeing her a widow that finally made him see his sister as an adult. Her postcards were full of talk of William, what he would like, what he would find interesting, what he would laugh at. She saw the country for both of them and Leo didn't doubt that at night she talked William through it, in the hope that their current separation was temporary. She did not acknowledge the loneliness which Leo presumed she felt.

He sometimes these days imagined a future as a grandpa to Finn's kids. Today, on this summit, he admitted that it was something he hoped for. Today, he told himself, looking at the view and seeing his name on every tomb, today the dead are born. It took standing in a graveyard for him to find a guttural hunger for life. And it took a lot on Astrid's part to let go of the gallery for one afternoon and the possible things that could be neglected, and to recline on the fresh grass and not worry about green stains on her dress, and to sigh when her work phone rang, because she was feeling so light and happy in the moment before it did.

She handed the phone to Leo. 'It's George White at Fountains,' she said.

Leo took the call and wandered a few paces away from the picnic. As he listened to George, he watched Glenn, whose eyes were shut against the sun and who looked at peace in this setting, just another slab of granite protruding from the lawns. And, when George and Leo had concluded their business, Leo asked if the vacancy created by William's passing had yet been filled.

369

Jack and Finn wandered away together, along the brow of the slope, to the very pinnacle of the cemetery. There, Jack gave Finn his birthday present, an envelope with a card and, written in it, the words *October 1st to October 22nd 2006*.

'What about it?' Finn asked.

'On October 1st you and me are flying to California, and we are going to drive from LA to San Francisco, drive Big Sur. We're going to go wherever you like, Yosemite, Vegas, Northern California, or down to San Diego. We've both got the time off work, it's sorted. That's your present. Three weeks with me.'

Finn laughed. 'Shit. What have I done wrong?' He slid the card into his back pocket and sucked in the air and smiled at the city. 'That's fantastic,' he muttered. 'Thank you.'

Leo took a seat beside Glenn. Astrid joined him, and sat by her boss's side. 'What do you do, Glenn?' Leo asked.

'All sorts.'

'I know a company looking for someone. It's almost the best job in the world. They might need some young blood, if you scrub up well.'

'I scrub up fine. What is it?'

'Archivist. You sort out thousands of photos and articles about the past and the beauty of it is you can be all alone if you like, music on, no interference. You can spend all day in your own thoughts.'

'That's not a good idea,' Glenn said, his voice laced with derision. 'That literally sounds like the worst job in the world for me. It's a fucking terrible idea.' He glanced at Astrid. 'No offence.'

Leo watched as a rim of sunlight kicked against the upper reaches of the Chrysler Building. He looked at the shadows adorning the northeast faces of the city, imagined the streets in shade beneath them, the teeming sidewalks. The people. The lives. The risks. The victories. The relationships. 'You're right,' he muttered, 'it's a terrible job, living in the past.' He looked at Glenn, who was unmoved and disinterested. 'How can I get things so wrong at my age?'

'You mean men don't grow old and wise? That's a shocker,' Glenn said.

Astrid laughed.

'Sausage roll?' Glenn said, offering the packet.

'No, thanks,' she said, turning to him. 'Macrobiotic seaweed and pine kernel salad?'

'No, thanks. Boyfriend?'

'No, thanks. I've decided not to have one for at least a year.'

'That's the life,' Glenn muttered.

She laughed to herself. At herself. They both lay back, on either side of the picnic, and let the warmth lie upon them as the sunlight moved free of the elm trees and threw yellow patterns into their eyelids. Leo retreated to the bench and sat behind the two of them. Finn watched him, from the granite ridge above the cemetery where he sat with Jack, not quite touching, enjoying the silence. Finn picked out individual tombs in the valley and pictured the funeral parties at them on the days of interment. He formed a series of movie scenes in his imagination, one set in the fifties, then another in the seventies. The mourners departing from this field of tombs and returning to New York City, fanning out, dispersing across the streets and buildings. Where were they all today? What had they done with the intervening years and with those resolutions people made at funerals? How quickly did the time go, really? Not as fast as older people said, surely? But why would they all say it if it weren't true? One day he would miss his parents and one day, with the memory of them faded, he would start to love them simply for being his parents (and simply because he would be more forgiving). He would apologise to them for his coolness, for not loving unconditionally, even though he felt no guilt for it and knew he would not have survived them any other way.

371

And for what he had done to his uncle the morning he left with Dilly for New York, he would have to pay. And, although it would preclude Finn from entering the United States again for some years, New York City had already bestowed its gift upon him, in the form of a belief that anything was possible. And it had done so without Finn staying long enough for the love affair to wane. Jack would stand by him, would return to England with Finn and two years later, in 2008, be not unhappy at having left AIG, and be training in medicine. The brothers would move together into a flat in North London and inform no one from their wider family that they were there. House rules would be set, most important of which were that Jack got to have sex in the flat first as he was paying the mortgage ('Alright,' Finn would say, 'but I'm not waiting forever...') and that once a week, without fail, the two boys would sit down to a roast dinner together. Finn would arrive home one evening with a 'Home Is Where the Heart Is' doormat that Ann and Stefano Parker would have been proud of and it would make the boys roar. Occasionally, Finn would grow a beard and shave one smooth track through it.

A breeze picked up, brushed over the graves and settled again, like a bird. Jack stared at the city above the graves and it was as if he had just arrived. From this vantage point, he had the sensation that he had not yet stepped inside New York City, that he was still finding his way. It seemed as if it was Finn who was bringing him here, leading him by the hand, Finn showing him this place they would live together for a short while but long enough to create memories that would never leave them. It all began here in Calvary Cemetery and Jack couldn't explain why. He looked at his brother. Finn was safe and well. Jack had kept the promise he had made to their father. He had been true to what his father had asked of him on the cold surface of the road at Castleton's Oak, with the final breath of his sad, tormented life.

Jack's head dropped. It occurred to him now how clearly he loved the name 'Finn', how much that word meant to him, that word which was the last to ever escape his father's lips. He put his arm around his brother's shoulder and allowed his body to press against the ballast of Finn's physique and he let go of his weight and released his neck from the burden of carrying his thoughts and his family and he began to sob. He allowed Finn to take him in his arms. And he experienced the weightless joy of succour for the first time in his life.

Acknowledgements

My thanks to Tim Craig: friend, confidant and conduit to fine music and words.

My thanks to Oliver Corell for the Coastguards Cottage where much of this book was written, and to Susie Lowe at the Landing, Treacle in Hove, Toad Hall on Grand, the Morning Star on Second Avenue and the Rose Main Reading Room. Above all, my love and thanks to Imelda Liddiard for being a constant and generous host in Manhattan and for sharing her lifelong knowledge of New York City with me over many years.

My deepest thanks to Jenny Hewson and Rochelle Stevens, and to Rosie Price, Matt Turner and Peter Strauss. And to Nick Perry and Jennie Shellard. And to the great Arthur Tress.

Profound thanks to my editor, Vicky Blunden.

Deborah Rogers

I was working on Deborah's notes on this book when she died. I was privileged to be represented by her for my first five years as a novelist. The day she called me into the unique room that was her office to say she wanted to represent me is one of the happiest memories of my life. Thank you, Deborah.

The writing of this book was supported using public funding by the National Lottery through Arts Council England.

Read on for an extract from Tom Connolly's critically
acclaimed novel *The Spider Truces*.

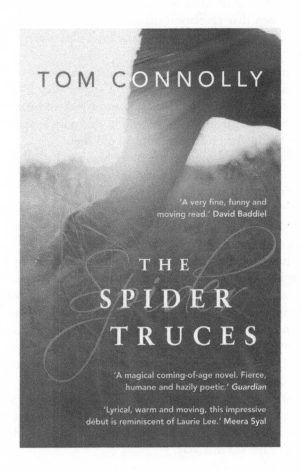

TOM CONNOLLY

'A very fine, funny and
moving read.' David Baddiel

THE
SPIDER
TRUCES

'A magical coming-of-age novel. Fierce,
humane and hazily poetic.' *Guardian*

'Lyrical, warm and moving, this impressive
début is reminiscent of Laurie Lee.' Meera Syal

It was Great-aunt Mafi who told him that spider blood is blue. When that revelation made him feel queasy, she said that spider blood is blue the way the sea is blue when the sun shines. He liked that.

'That's nice,' Ellis said. 'That doesn't give me the willies.'

And Mafi told him that when a spider dies its blood flows out of its body into the seas and rivers and lakes and that's how the earth gets its water, but this only happens if a spider is allowed to die naturally, of old age.

Ellis's dad told him he was more likely to be killed by a champagne cork than by a poisonous spider, but this didn't have the desired effect.

'That's no good! That's just another thing for me to worry about! Champagne corks as well as spiders! You have to tell me something nicer, not something badder!'

His sister helped out too, reading from the encyclopaedia that spiders don't get caught in their own webs because they have oil on their legs, so Ellis took to rubbing oil over his body in secret, every morning. At primary school he was known as Mr Sheen, due to the shiny appearance of his arms and face, and at home the diminishing stocks of cooking oil in the larder baffled Ellis's dad as much as the discovery that soap could no longer form a lather on Ellis's skin.

But of all the many discoveries Ellis O'Rourke made during the truces, his favourite was the first, that spiders give us the seas and rivers and lakes as their dying gift. He still thinks of the sea that way.

And it was Great-aunt Mafi who said to him, 'Any day you see the sea is a good day.' This she said on the day she told him how his mum had died.

He sees the sea every day now. And he waits with a patience a young man should not yet possess.

Even here where it can be so bleak, the sea is often blood-blue, the sort of blue Ellis can fall into. From his rented house, he looks at the water. He loses focus and the water floods in; the image of blue fills his head and for a time that could be moments or hours he is nowhere. Free of thought. He barely exists. It is bliss. Like the mid-air moment of diving in.

The beach is a shingle peninsula. It heads to a point on the south-east corner. Ellis's house faces due south across the Channel. It is the last building before the lighthouse and after that there's the Point. Three hundred yards out to sea, on a sandbank, is the wreck of the *Bessie Swan*, a trawler that ran aground in June 1940, returning from Dunkirk with fifty men who waded to shore through waist-high water. You can't wade out to the *Bessie Swan* nowadays. The Channel currents have gouged out ravines in the silt that are deep and treacherous.

On his first night on the beach, in the pub close by the lifeboat station, the old men had looked on without mercy as the young seasonal fishermen challenged Ellis to swim to the *Bessie Swan* and back. They marched him across the shingle, led by a callous and bloated-looking man in a black woolly hat, called Towzer Temple.

'You swim towards the steeple on the Marsh. The currents take you to the *Bessie Swan*.'

'If you swim straight for her, you'll be in France tomorrow.'

'In a body bag...'

'Do it now and by closing time you'll be back in the pub, a legend.'

'We've all done it,' said Towzer.

'It's tradition.'

At the water's edge, Ellis stared into the blackness and somewhere amongst the fishermen's drunken voices, in which there was humour that Ellis was deaf to, he heard himself say, 'But I'm only renting here ...'

These limp words returned the men indoors, where the evening seemed impoverished and Ellis felt out of place. He began to wonder if they had been telling the truth, that they had all swum the ravines at one time or another, and they really did know best when they said he would be the greater for doing it.

The unfamiliar ceiling above his unfamiliar bed spun a little that first night and every single sound on the beach was new. As he waited patiently for sleep, Ellis noticed the glow of a cigarette at the open window and behind it the face of Towzer Temple, reddened by a map of fissured blood vessels. The fisherman leant easily against the sill, his elbows annexing a portion of the cabin-like bedroom, and as a wide grin disfigured his looks still further, he said, 'It'll bug you. You didn't do it because you're scared. And it's going to bug you and bug you. Goodnight, Mr Only Renting. Sweet dreams.'

Money spiders populate the shingle and leave their egg sacs on the shore. Fishing boats line the beach and there's a lifeboat station beyond them. Ellis likes to go shrimping north of the lifeboat, in shallow tides which scuttle in and out across the wide mud flats of the bay. He made a frame up last year, four foot by two. He wades out against the incoming tide, sweeping his net, and the frame makes a noise like distant music on a small box radio as it cuts through the water. He catches plenty, but could probably catch more if he knew more about it and didn't get distracted by the far-away music.

Near the lifeboat station, the strip lights of the workers' café pulse cold blue through the windows. Ellis usually goes there three or four times a week. People greet him but still don't know his name.

At dusk, when the sky is angry, he heads out along the beach to the army ranges, then inland across the Backs where the shingle is carpeted with moss, and gorse surrounds the scattered lakes. A line of wooden posts betrays the route of a disused railway and beneath his feet he hears the thud of a sleeper encrusted in the ground like a dead bird. He imagines that he's in Montana or the Australian outback or some other place he's never been. He walks until his leg muscles burn. When darkness comes, a line of silver remains on the horizon and silhouettes the container ships, which turn to black. The winds rise up off the waves and tear across the peninsula and Ellis digs his feet into the shingle and allows the furious, thrilling gusts to pound against him like the souls of every man lost at sea. Furious souls or ecstatic souls, he is not sure which. Sometimes, he waits for hours. Patient. Devoted.

There is a line from a song his father once whispered to him and it plays in Ellis's head as he returns across the flatlands to his unlit home. *We must not go astray in this loneliness.*

He moved here on Good Friday, 1989. A mist settled over the Point for a fortnight and the fog signal on the lighthouse boomed across the bay. He opened every door and window in the house and gave the spiders a few hours to move on without being harmed. The rooms gave up their mustiness to the salt air and Ellis felt the same excitement he had felt when he was a child.

So this is where that feeling has been hiding, he thought to himself.

At first he kept up his job, assisting a photographer called Milek, driving two hours to London. Then he worked a little less. Then he asked for a couple of months off.

'To clear my head, Milek.'

And that was a nearly a year ago.

This is another of those slow-motion mornings, Ellis tells himself. He wonders what time it is. He doesn't wear a watch. Any that have been given to him over the years are gathering dust and he couldn't tell you where. He thinks it through. He went out shrimping first thing and then he came back and the metal box was here on the dining table and then he's been daydreaming. So it is probably late morning. He's not idle and he's not simple. It's just a blissfully slow start to the day and he doesn't use a watch. But, yes, he was shrimping first thing, he remembers clearly.

He can always tell if his sister has visited, and even though they are no longer good friends he likes the sensation of knowing she has been in. It means that Chrissie either saw her brother out on the flats and decided to leave him be or forgot to look for his silhouette in the silver bay. Either way, he likes the thought of her leaving him be or forgetting to look.

It is Chrissie who has left the metal box on the dining table. The box was once black but the paintwork is faded now and speckled by a slow rust. Ellis leans closer and looks down on the rust until it looks to him like a landscape photographed from a plane.

He's in no hurry to open the box. He knows the contents exactly – he watched it being filled – and there's nothing there of great significance. But for Ellis, having the box is almost like having his father back in the room and to feel his father nearby is the reason he moved here. Chrissie's world doesn't work that way. Dead means dead, and the inconsequential objects inside the metal box are the sorts of things that cannot combine to mean much to her. She wishes they could and that's why it's taken her a year to give Ellis the box. That's why she has occasionally intimated that she might have lost it, an idea that gives Ellis butterflies because, although there is nothing particular in the box, all the pieces of nothing in particular belonged to Denny O'Rourke, and Denny O'Rourke was his dad.

If you rest your head against the metal box as if it is a pillow, and you close your eyes, and if your name is Ellis O'Rourke, then the crunching of shingle underfoot on the beach outside could be the sound of a spider perched on your shoulder eating a packet of crisps.

He opens his eyes and sees a woman walking. She puts down her bag, unfolds a stool and begins to sketch. A sparrowhawk hovers above the bushes where starlings and rabbits hide. Ellis listens to the wind piping around the lighthouse and watches as the woman with the sketch pad takes off her jacket. She is older than Ellis. Maybe twenty years older. He wants her to get into conversation with him, accept a cup of tea and sleep with him. He wants her to leave later that afternoon and there to be no talking. Only mute understanding. He would never tell anyone about her and would be able to get on with his life without the need for intimacy cropping up again for some weeks. He knows this is all wrong, but such thoughts are risk-free and a habit he's fallen into.

The phone rings, startling Ellis. It's Jed, his best friend.

'I have to tell you what I dreamt last night,' Ellis says immediately.

'I'm fine, thanks for asking,' Jed replies.

'Bear in mind,' Ellis says, 'that I was two years old when man landed on the moon.'

'What?'

'And that I am not a particularly complicated person.'

'You are joking.'

'So how is it that last night I dreamt I was in the living room of the house in Orpington where I was born and my dad is there and my mum, but I can't see her face, and we're all gathered round the TV even though I'm pretty sure they didn't have one, and my sister is just a pair of legs standing on the window sill holding the aerial up into the sky – '

'Wait! You're getting detailed and weird. Let me get comfortable.'

Ellis waits as Jed lights a cigarette.

'I recognise some of the people in the room. There's a few of the guys you and me knew on the building sites, and my Great-aunt Mafi is there pouring gin for everyone. Neat gin. The only historical inaccuracy is that it's not Buzz Aldrin on the lunar surface with Neil Armstrong but Simon Le Bon. And the whole dream is in black and white, not just the TV screen. I look and see that to the left of me on the sofa is a young, unshaven, dark-haired man sitting with his girlfriend. And I realise as I look at this bloke that it's that actor guy from *Man About the House* and *Robin's Nest* – '

'Richard O'Sullivan.'

'Thank you. And I watch him in his studenty donkey jacket, smoking his cigarette and turning excitedly to his girlfriend, and I realise, My God! He doesn't know he's about to become the star of *Man About the House* and to be associated for ever with the greatest thing that ever ever happened on telly when we were kids, namely *George and Mildred*. He will be a part of that, and I know it and he doesn't. Look at him! He's just an aspiring actor watching the 1969 moon landing with his girlfriend and I know what's going to happen to him in life and he doesn't! I know he'll never do Shakespeare or really crack that big screen role and that he will in fact be a sort of good-looking, understated Sid James. And do you know what it made me think?'

'I pride myself on not knowing what or how you think.'

'What else is there to dream? Being with my mum until I was four years old? How my dad was when she had gone?

All the things that are somewhere in my head because I was actually there even though I was far too young to know it? It could crucify you! All this stuff locked away inside your head ready to appear in your sleep, it could bring your life to a standstill.'

There's a long silence until Jed drags on his cigarette and says, 'Your life is at a standstill.'

They go quiet. Jed is the one person who isn't freaked out by Ellis going silent on the phone for minutes at a time. In fact, he considers such pauses a respite. Ellis lies back on the floor and wedges the telephone against his ear.

'You know why it's at a standstill?'

'I've one or two ideas. What's your version?'

'When I'm alone I dream of being with someone and when I'm with someone I wish I was anywhere else.'

'Ah, well, I'm glad you've brought that up because I have some answers for you,' Jed says kindly. 'It's because you are what we, in the outside world, technically term 'an arsehole'. Private. Evasive. You're a daydreamer and you keep all your best thoughts to yourself. People like me and the women you occasionally sleep with get the fag ends of your thoughts. If you didn't make me feel so good about myself just by being you, there'd be nothing in this friendship for me. I am also willing to bet good money that when you are busy fucking the wrong people and wishing you were somewhere else, that somewhere else is wherever Tammy might be these days.'

'Out of bounds.'

'Why? What do you care if we talk about her?'

'I just don't want to… except to say I was more committed to her than she was to me, before you slag me off.'

'Oh yeah, that's right. I remember the evening you went away to America without telling her you were going. I remember that night thinking how "committed" to her you were. Yeah, I reckon your decision not to even call her and say goodbye before fucking off to Iowa could easily have been misinterpreted as a proposal of marriage.'

This is why Jed is Ellis's best friend.

'Fuck off.'

'Up yours.'

They each place the receiver down, gently.

Jed is right. When Ellis lies awake at night – in bed, or on the grass, or on the beach – he imagines that Tammy is lying beside him. He whispers sounds to her which are not quite words but are perfect for an imaginary love affair. He didn't call her before he went away because it might have mattered to her that he was going but it might not and he didn't want to risk finding out. And now two years have passed and he has left it too long.

He can't understand why he feels so lost today. Or why he feels as if time is short when he has the whole of his adult life before him. He opens the metal box and it releases the smell of cherrywood fires in the cottage he grew up in. He sifts through a pile of photographs taken in the fifties and sixties of elderly relations he never knew, moves to one side a prayer card from his mum's funeral in 1971, and picks up a passport-sized document which he remembers his dad showing him years ago. Denny's name is written in ink on the faded cover and beneath it are the words: *Continuous Certificate of Discharge – Ministry of War Transport / Merchant Navy*. Inside are five entries which map Denny O'Rourke's career in the merchant navy, beginning in 1943, age sixteen, aboard the SS *Papanui* and ending in 1946 when his eyesight fell below acceptable standards for service. There's a loose page inside, a temporary shore pass for Colombo Port, dated 15 November 1946.

My dad was twenty then, Ellis thinks. Two years younger than me.

He half closes his eyes and imagines being propelled across the sea, hugging the curvature of the earth, and arriving at Colombo Port. He sits there a while, in the heat, his image of the place indistinct and blinded by the sun. A wave breaks and he finds himself back home, listening to the shingle being dragged by its fingertips into the sea. It is a sound softened by its journey across the beach to Ellis's house and it reminds him of the breeze that swept through the walnut trees on the morning his dad died. Joseph Reardon the farmer, who had been praying for Denny O'Rourke, told Ellis that the back door of the church flew open and a wind swept in at the exact time of Denny's passing. Ellis doesn't know what he thinks about that sort of thing but he does know that in the days and weeks that followed he and Chrissie received many letters and they sat shoulder to shoulder, knee to knee, silently passing them back and forth until their bodies came to rest against each other and he felt a surge of love for his sister which found no expression and would inevitably dissolve as the day wore on. Jed, whom Ellis had never seen hold a pen, wrote a letter; *Ellis, your dad was one of life's good blokes. Not all of us can say that. Be happy. Jed.* Ellis showed Jed's letter to Chrissie and she handed an envelope to him in return.

'Make sense of this,' she said. 'Got it yesterday.'

It was a card from Dino, a Maltese guy Chrissie slept with on and off for six months when she was doing a journalism course in London. Dino had written: *Dearest Spaghetti and Ellis, my condolences at your sad loss. Love Dino.* And try as they might, Ellis and Chrissie could not begin to recall what cryptic, spaghetti-related episode or in-joke had occurred between them back then that Dino had clearly never forgotten.

'Did you ever tell him about the pasta spider webs?' Ellis asked.

'No. We just fucked.'

'You must have done. There's no other possible explanation.'

'I didn't. I tend not to chat about you and your weirdness when I'm having sex. Maybe he was just writing a shopping list at the same time as the card and got confused.'

'Write back to him,' Ellis said, 'and tell him we were touched by his writing to us after dad had pasta-way.'

They laughed until their stomachs hurt. Then they sat awhile in silence and thought their own thoughts and felt the taste of grief on their tongues and discovered that in the space of only a few days the taste had grown familiar and now it felt second-hand. Ellis shut his eyes and watched his father emerge from the bike shed at the cottage, carrying a bucket full of water. Denny swung the bucket round in wide circles above his head but none of the water fell out.

'I thought he was a magician when he did that,' Ellis said. 'Did you know how he did it or did you think he was a magician too?'

'You're doing that thing again,' Chrissie said.

'What thing?'

'That thing of having a conversation in your head and then bringing me in on it late. You've always done it. You're so useless, Ellis. If you were the last man left on earth, you wouldn't notice it for weeks.'

She kissed him and left him to the freefall of random memories in his head.

Another wave breaks. Ellis drops the Colombo Port shore pass back into the box and notices the dark scratched wood of a once familiar picture frame, in which is held a photograph of a lighthouse and a fishing boat run aground. He carries it outside and looks across the water to that same lighthouse and wreck. He watches the fishermen arrive at the huts in their battered trucks. Towzer Temple leans heavily against his boat and coughs himself awake. He takes a banana from his coat pocket and eats it. He delves into the same pocket and pulls out an old crisp packet, which he seems surprised to have found. He makes a chute out of the packet and pours the crisps into his mouth, pulling a sour face as he tastes them. Lazily, he kicks the side of his boat, betraying their stale marriage, and pulls a bottle from the other coat pocket, and starts to drink.

A few hundred yards away, the tide snakes around the wreck of the *Bessie Swan*. Ellis watches it curiously, as if he's arranged to meet someone there but can't remember who.

Perhaps, he tells himself, if I swam out there...

But he knows he will not do it.

If I walked out of the house and across the beach without stopping and dived in and swam there and back and ran straight home and dried myself in front of the fire, I'd have done something extraordinary. I'd have pushed myself. Kick-started my system. If I did it once, I could do it again the next day, and again, and I'd do it every day, it would become second nature and I'd be a different person, the sort of person who did that every day. My life would have changed.

But he's not able to change it. He's too busy. Too busy playing tunes on his shrimping net, watching his neighbour's washing loop the loop in the wind, seeking out pebbles with perfect holes, lying beneath the lighthouse and watching it sway. Too busy photographing clouds when the colour of crimson bleeds into them at dusk. Too busy waiting. Too busy keeping watch.

He takes from the metal box something unfamiliar. It looks like a blue plastic cigarette, and when he picks it up the plastic unravels and Ellis sees that it is the long, thin wrapper of a packet of dried spaghetti, the sort Denny used to buy when Ellis was a child and pasta was as long as your arm. As long as your dad's arm.

MORE FROM MYRIAD

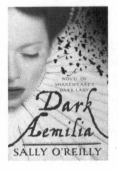

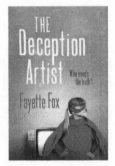

MORE FROM MYRIAD

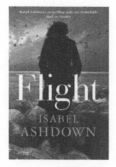

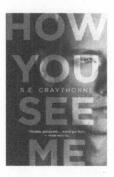

MORE FROM MYRIAD

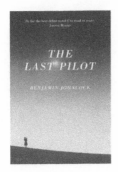

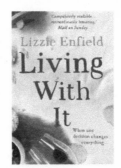

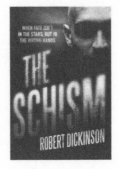

Sign up to our mailing list at
www.myriadeditions.com
Follow us on Facebook and Twitter

Tom Connolly is a writer and filmmaker. He has directed award-winning short films for the cinema and for Channel 4 and the BBC. His short stories and radio plays have been broadcast on Radio 4. His first novel, *The Spider Truces* (a *Financial Times* Book of the Year), was shortlisted for the Waverton Good Read Award and the Writers' Guild of Great Britain Award, and longlisted for the Desmond Elliott Prize. He lives and windsurfs in Sussex.